The Curious Magics Saga

PART ONE

THE SECRETS OF THE ARCANE INTELLIGENCE AGENCY

R. B. FRASER

authorHOUSE

AuthorHouse™ UK
1663 Liberty Drive
Bloomington, IN 47403 USA
www.authorhouse.co.uk
Phone: UK TFN: 0800 0148641 (Toll Free inside the UK)
UK Local: 02036 956322 (+44 20 3695 6322 from outside the UK)

© 2021 R. B. Fraser. All rights reserved.

No part of this book may be reproduced, stored in a retrieval system, or transmitted by any means without the written permission of the author.

Published by AuthorHouse 06/15/2021

ISBN: 978-1-6655-9048-8 (sc)
ISBN: 978-1-6655-9049-5 (hc)
ISBN: 978-1-6655-9047-1 (e)

Library of Congress Control Number: 2021911854

Print information available on the last page.

Any people depicted in stock imagery provided by Getty Images are models, and such images are being used for illustrative purposes only.
Certain stock imagery © Getty Images.

This book is printed on acid-free paper.

Because of the dynamic nature of the Internet, any web addresses or links contained in this book may have changed since publication and may no longer be valid. The views expressed in this work are solely those of the author and do not necessarily reflect the views of the publisher, and the publisher hereby disclaims any responsibility for them.

Chapter One

THE FIRST CHAPTER

This story begins as most stories do, at the beginning. However, contrary to what you might be expecting; this tale does not start with our protagonists. It starts with the beginning of all things, the original Big Bang. The thing that might be confusing to some readers out there, when I say *'the original Big Bang'* I do not mean *'the Big Bang'* which we are taught about in schools across the land. As shocking, or insulting, as it may be to learn, the Big Bang that had birthed all life in our existence was rather inconsequential and mostly insignificant in the grander scheme of things. In fact, by the time our universe had exploded into existence, it had been the two hundred and twenty-third time that a universe had sprung to life in such a manner. *Apparently, everyone else at the time called it a Tuesday.*

For what it's worth, I am sorry to be the one to tell you that our universe of tax credits, pay cheques, and reality television ranks rather low in comparison to the other fantastical universes which are available.

(Before continuing, it's also worth mentioning that there are also much worse planes of existence, but much like this universe, they warrant very little in the way of conversation or effort to detail!)

Our story focuses on the thirteenth universe. A universe of magical creatures and magical, well, everything. Over the years their earth had morphed into a modern-day utopia, filled to the brim with enough fantastical species, creatures, and races that could make even the most hardened fantasy writer blush, cry or hyperventilate at the thought of.

However, the actual magical practices on this world were not as widespread as one might initially like to imagine. Upon a closer examination of any normal family, in any normal household, on any normal street would lead any neutral bystander or voyeur to the assumption that this thirteenth universe was not in any great way vastly different to this universe of our own. Of course, this statement only really rings true upon the proviso that this voyeur ignored the occasional bout of green skin, pointy ears, or the odd set of wings a family might have on show.

Specific scientific discoveries (*such as televisions, phones, cars, and computers*) had given way to many such discoveries and home comforts that we would expect to see in our own day-to-day lives here in our universe.

And herein lies our first conundrum; what exactly does it mean to be normal? It is a universally accepted truth that the Oxford English Dictionary defines '*being normal*' as being '*absolutely and thoroughly, wholly and completely downright boring, forgettable and without consequence within every fibre, atom and cell of this normal thing's existence.*' Before anyone decides to cross-reference with their closest dictionary, this is of course not even slightly true. Being normal is fine. It is ordinary and occasionally, it's expected. It's also frequently thought upon as something to be feared. This fear was stemming from it's close (*and somewhat misunderstood*) relationship with being viewed as '*lacklustre*' or '*insipid.*' From the mightiest king, sat upon his throne of gold, to the last born child of a peasant family, no one wants to be forgotten. To be replaced; to play second fiddle to someone else's greatness. To stand in the all-encompassing shadow cast by the light of another person's greatness.

No man, woman or child wants to feel wholly forgettable and without consequence. To have every fibre, atom and cell of their existence overlooked. No one wants to be second place.

It matters not how interesting your environment or your world is. But rather on the traits of the individual. To this end, you can have an ordinary, run of the mill astronaut, much like the same way that you could have an ordinary run of the mill librarian. You could be a boring lion tamer or the world's most interesting stamp collector. To this end, this thirteenth Earth on this thirteenth universe, despite being home to such creatures that would describe themselves as being '*amazing*' or '*breathtaking*' by our understanding, routinely found its inhabitants caught up in the habitual routines that would define our lives; should our lives ever warrant the need to be read about by any other inhabitant of the multiverse.

In this way, Kiko is no different to you and me.

And for anyone curious as to who Kiko might be, *she is our protagonist.*

As some readers may have experienced within their own lives, being an ordinary person in an exceptional family is tough. It's hard. Rather, failing to live up to the standards that the people closest to you seem to expect from you, is hard. *It's tough.*

On this thirteenth world, Kiko's family were held in high regards. In fact, the Attetson family name carried such weight, that it was somewhat amazing anyone had the physical strength to hold it in high regard at all. With two legendary parents and an internationally acclaimed brother, the heavy, heavyweight seemed to bare down, almost entirely, upon Kiko's skinny, all too human shoulders.

Depending on your outlook in life, Kiko was either an underwhelming, bookish shut-in. Lacking any real tricks up her sleeve to be deserving of her familial recognition. Or she's the last humane beacon of hope in an otherwise godly madhouse of dangerously disconnected, dissociative pariahs, so lost to day-to-day humane normalcy that their complacency for the amazing has left them detached to normality.

She was commonly regarded as both.

To those who know her, she is often referred to as compassionate, warm and kind. If not just a bit eccentric. To Vincent, her brother, she was commonly referred to as '*there*' and '*in the way.*'

Like, seriously in the way, I'm not joking…

"No seriously, Kiko, get out of my way." Vincent's shoulder awkwardly clipped around the side of Kiko's head, sending her red hair into a kerfuffle and her black-rimmed glasses askew upon the tip of her nose.

Apparently being the worlds foremost attuned magic-user didn't stop you from being the world's foremost attuned magic user who's also running extremely late, Kiko mused to herself as she watched her brother hastily speeding through the family home.

The Attetsons were in no way, or by any understanding of the expression, hard done by. Their house was sizeable, spanning three floors plus an attic and a basement. If any of the public had been aware of just exactly how well off they actually were, they might possibly perceive just how hard Cassandra, their mother, had worked to make her family appear humble, or as close to modest as their puissance or power would allow them to appear. To those unaware of their station, this house could still stand as a four-walled testament to the kind of pretentious bourgeois privilege that would make an anarchist's head explode, or a capitalist swoon. A physical manifestation of grandeur for all to see. *Yet, this spacious house, somehow, still couldn't fit both Vincent and his sister on a day like today.*

Vincent could have gotten around his sister in a multitude of ways that could have demonstrated the merest flex of his magical capabilities. He could have teleported past her, phased through the wall or even turned into smoke and evaporated around her, *you know,* like a normal person. But stress has the ability to confound even the most amazing of minds – amazing being one of the most common words to describe Vincent; *'Your brother is amazing!'* or *'your brother is perfect!'* with the occasional *'your brother is so cool!'* thrown in for good measure.

With his perfectly white teeth, his pristinely combed, not too short and not too long black hair, combed effortlessly back to show his clear complexion and his clearer, instantly endearing smile, Vincent was almost perfectly perfect in every way a perfect person would want to perfect. Behind his endearing smile of perfectly white teeth lived his ideally balanced voice, not too loud nor too quiet, too overbearing, or too submissive. He spoke with a honeydewed eloquence that was not at all lowbrow or common but also lacked all hints of pretentious aristocracy. He also never seemed to age, as if one day during his mid-twenties life just decided, 'You know what, you look perfect the way you are' and froze him, forever, like a moment in a photograph for the whole world to see, for all of time and space to appreciate.

Kiko, on the other hand, seemed to have been short-changed by the universe, or rather the multiverse. With her long red mop of usually tangled hair, her poor vision, and her keen skill of being not at all great at speaking to people in the concise and articulate manner or style in which a person should desire normally, ideally, and wholeheartedly to communicate in.

This is to say, she was prone to social ineptitude and awkward rambling. If ever the moment arose to 'put her foot in her mouth,' she would. Of course, not in a literal sense. That would be absurd. But whenever she was given the chance to skirt effortlessly by a moment in a conversation that would not make her trip over her words, or to be consumed by the desire for the whole world to just end so a social interaction would cease, Kiko would bumble her way awkwardly through the confines of the English language. Like the linguistic equivalent of a newborn calf trying to find a steady footing. Not unlike a car crash in slow motion, only both drivers aren't really in any sort of pain. But still, no one willingly chooses to be in a car crash. Except of course for crash test dummies. But do they really get to choose?

This ineptitude with her peers drove Kiko towards a deepened proclivity with her books. The written word being her last bastion of hope. An endless collection of printed words, anecdotes and theses. A universe of clearly printed and defined rules, regulations and requirements. This penchant for paper-based publications had aided Kiko during her schooling years to no end. As it turns out, a studious appetite feeds academic success and this had resulted in Kiko being at the top of her class for all subjects… well, the ones that mattered!

Despite being thoroughly likeable and sincere in her own right, with a usually sunny disposition to life, a willingness to help those lesser off and a razor-sharp intellect (*even when combined with the Attetson family name*) Kiko was rather lacking when it came to friends. Kiko was never actually short on people who considered her a friend, and she was ever truly unpopular. But Kiko was somewhat particular and evanescent when it came to the list of people she actually viewed as being her friends. She was picky.

Kara was one such friend.

Kara had been living with the Attetsons for a few months at this point. The reason for this was rather quite simple. Anyone who is part of a family knows a family is supposed to come together, like the parts of a well-formed machine. However, anyone who is a part of a family also knows that this is not always the case; and sometimes, through no one's particular fault, tensions rise and families fall apart. *This was the case with Kara De'Carusso.*

There was no grandiose incident that had led to this blonde twenty-one year old to be stood in the Attetson kitchen, in nothing but pyjama bottoms and a faded t-shirt adorned with the logo of some long since relevant rock and roll band, immortalised by a member's tragic drug-induced death at a young age. *Yet here she was in all of her abrasive majesty.* Hair messily swept to one side, yesterday's make-up still adorning her face, with a small trail of toothpaste escaping from the corner of her mouth where her toothbrush protruded. Kara had, what many called, a '*rough and ready*' demeanour. A girl not famous for acts of patience or composure. A brash '*just do it*' attitude was her mantra. An approach to life that rewarded little in the way of long term friends outside of Kiko and a handful of others. But despite this, she couldn't quite shake the ingrained affluence of her family's past. Regardless of how hard she rebelled against it. She was always well-poised and well-spoken, despite not always saying the nicest of things. The only people anyone had really ever heard her say anything nice about was Kiko's family. This was probably because they took her in when she had nowhere else to go; after all, altruism has a tendency to invoke indentured civility. It was both unwise to look a gift horse in the mouth or to bite the hand that feeds. *Not if you wanted to keep being fed by the gift horse, that is.*

But Kiko and Kara had been friends for so long now that neither felt any particular need to stand on ceremony. No one else would be privileged enough to see this messy, not-long-arisen Kara in all of her unkempt splendour. However, Kara had also been the only one privileged enough to have seen Kiko devolve into an overly apologetic, drunken, vomit soaked mess on multiple occasions.

Oh, and before I forget, Kara was also a Half-Elf.

Yes, Elves exist in this universe. *Please don't feel the need to freak out about it.* It's really not a big deal. Our universe is one of the few universes without elves walking down the street. (*Well, we used to have them too, but that's not my story to tell!*)

If there is any confusion as to what a Half-Elf is, I'm not going to go into too much detail as to what happens when an Elf likes a Human. Figure it out for yourselves. All I will say on it is that Elves are famously elitist as a society. They shun anything that they deemed as an impurity to the bloodline or in any way improper. Anything dirtying the proud Elven heritage isn't commonly welcomed with open arms. But Kara's family, the De'Carussos, were always welcomed by the old Elven houses at all of the old Elven gatherings. Publicly accepted, at any rate; and that should act as a clear indication as to how rich the De'carussos were. That these Elves would welcome, with open arms (*and hands!*) a family they would otherwise kick to the dirt.

It's also worth mentioning that if the existence of Elves freaked you out, Dwarves, Halflings and Orcs are also a fairly commonplace and daily occurrence on this thirteenth Earth. I understand if you need a minute to process this shocking news.

This shocking, breaking news.

The echo of a nearby television echoed through to the kitchen where Kara and the Attetson siblings were gathered.

"Breaking news. Coming to you live from downtown Liverpool! Where what appears to be a Succubus has arisen, attacking people at random. Events seem unclear right now, Tom, as to where she has come from or what she's doing here. We urge people to stay in their homes! Hopefully, we'll understand more as things unfold, Tom. But there is one question on everybody's lips here today; and that is, where is Vincent Attetson?"

"Some of us have a job to do!" And with that there was a loud boom as Vincent bounded off into another drab proceeding that would again most likely underutilise the true extent of his seemingly endless capabilities.

It matters not if you live here with us on the two-hundred-and-twenty-third universe, or with Kiko and co. on the thirteenth universe, or if you are called Barry, living on planet Barry in the universe where everything since the dawn of time, for some unknown reason, has been named after someone called Barry. But all sentient life seemingly adheres to the same '*building block*' set of rules, despite the universe it found itself in.

These included: no one in any universe likes it when you steal from them, no one in any universe likes it when you randomly threaten them, and no one likes it when people have something that they don't have.

Put it this way, no one deserves to win the lottery. Even if you have never paid to partake in one in your entire life. Naturally whoever wins (*so long as this person is not you!*) does not deserve to win. They never have and never will. They would obviously only waste all that money on stupid stuff. It's not fair and it always should have been you who won. *You deserved it because you are you!*

In this way, a job is a lot like a lottery win, or at least it was in Kara's mind. Despite never really trying to find a job of her own, mostly due to the apparent fact that every job within her vicinity was either '*beneath her*' or '*not worth it,*' Vincent's retort about '*having a job to do*' had rubbed her up the wrong way. As such it had resulted in her giving just about the best sarcastic snort of derision that she could muster the second he had disappeared out of sight. This sarcastic snort was followed shortly by her spitting her toothpaste into the kitchen sink, dirtying the pristinely cleaned metal under its minty freshness.

For the record, anyone confused as to what a Succubus is, or rather what Succubi are; a Succubus is quite essentially a very powerful Demon with the appearance of an extremely beautiful woman. The reason for this appearance is quite simple. Men, on the whole, have a weakness. It's in every fibre of their bones. They can neither run from it, hide from it or deny its existence. *They are beguiled by beauty.* Any well-composed man runs the risk of becoming either a slack-jawed buffoon or entering a childish, competitive like mindset to win the favour of this irresistible enchantress. Originally spawning from the Demon mother, Lilith, Succubi quickly learned it was easier to ensnare the minds of men if you ensnared their hearts first. A Succubus is so used to getting her way that she will quickly fly into a rage if she doesn't get what she wants, or if any man is immune to her charms. It's also worth mentioning to all the female readers out there; *no you're not immune.* There are also thousands of records of women falling for the wily ways of the Succubi. Nice try, you're not getting out of this that easily. *Succubi are like taxes, no one is safe.*

Demons weren't the only creatures on Earth that knew how to turn the heads of men. Cassandra Attetson also knew a thing or two herself. Despite probably being past her prime, being somewhere between her forties and fifties, you would almost be unable to gauge this by her physical appearance. Being both well kept and well dressed at all times. Even when she was being informal with her attire, these outfits were chosen with an almost pinpoint precise accuracy. No colour was too bright as to wash out her appearance and no outfit was too loose or too tight as to ruin the aesthetic. *She knew how to dress and she dressed well.* Everything Vincent learned of etiquette and appropriate mannerisms he had learned from his mother. Like her son, people paid attention when she spoke. She was always cheery enough to be likeable whilst also being clear and direct. She did this whilst also managing to maintain enough of an allure as to not appear as being too cheery, loud, abrasive or overbearing or too welcoming. People always knew where they stood with Cassandra, and seldomly overstepped the mark of over-familiarity. Not too dissimilarly to her eldest son, she always seemed to have the perfect hairstyle for every occasion. Although her hair was a brilliant blonde, opposed to black. Her days were spent working at the AIA, an agency we will get into later, and her nights were spent either with her family, friends or at functions when the need arose. To see her stood next to the scruffily dressed Kara served only to call attention to how unkempt the blonde Half-Elf was currently dressed, as Cassandra made her way past her to the kitchen sink and poured herself a glass of water.

"Good morning, girls." She gave a small smile before drinking her fresh glass. Both girls used this time to reply agreeably to her. "Before I forget, Kara, I need you to go to the AIA. Collin's looking for you."

Cassandra had now moved on to examining herself in a compact mirror, making sure her make-up was presentable to the world before leaving. *It was of course fine.* It always was. Kara, who was not expecting to be spoken to, had little in the way of a reply for being addressed so directly this early in the morning. She gave the least awkwardly dumbfounded response she could muster on short notice.

"Oh, right. Okay. Yeah. Right. Sure." She awkwardly and dumbfoundedly replied, before continuing with. "Um… why is your husband looking for me? Is, is everything alright?" Her panic riddled eyes locked onto Kiko, who merely shrugged. Being lost for words was supposed to be Kiko's area of expertise, Kara wasn't to fond of the '*old switcheroo*' of their roles.

"Oh don't… worry, everything's… fine!" Cassandra replied as she closely examined the reflection of her mascara. Which was obviously also fine, by the way! "Everything is peachy, there's no need to get yourself into a flap, deary." Her gaze drifted towards Kara as a brisk smile broke upon her face before her eyes snapped straight back to her reflection. This time, however, she was checking her teeth. Everything was still, as it had always been, fine. "Right, I really must be off." The compact mirror snapped shut with a '*click.*' "I don't want to be late for this meeting!" She gave a sarcastic smile. "Oh, Kiko, please turn off the television if you're done with it. Oh, and Kara, as much as I appreciate you not spitting toothpaste on the floor like a beast, please rinse the sink when you're done." Cassandra rushed for the door as her bag and coat magically floated down the stairs to meet her.

"Oh and Kara, maybe dress up a little." She pulled her fancy coat over her shoulders. "Ciao, my darlings. Be good!" And with that, she was gone.

"How does she know?" Kara enquired to the back of Kiko's head. "How does she always know?"

"Well stop spitting toothpaste in our kitchen sink then!" Kiko sarcastically replied without even looking at her Half-Elven friend.

Some twenty minutes later both the squirrelly redhead and the stoical blonde were ready for their day. Kiko always chose a somewhat unique attire. Excluding her black-rimmed glasses, today's attire consisted of a plain shirt, small tie and matching waistcoat. Comfy, yet practical brown boots, and her signature dark blue cotton, big collared, double-breasted winter's coat that hung just south of back of the knee. This coat offered a great number of pockets, which Kiko had adapted to having micro-dimensions sewn into them. 'Literal pocket dimensions,' as was the joke she kept telling herself and others. (*She was the only one who would laugh at the joke.*) These pocket dimensions, however, never seemed to stop her from repeatedly donning a brown leather shoulder bag. Even if it was just a normal bag.

Kara on the other hand, perhaps unsurprisingly, was wearing all black. A black leather jacket hid the same rock and roll t-shirt she had on from earlier. She had chosen black jeans and black leather boots too. In her defence, she was wearing a white belt, and to be fair to her white is the brightest colour. So at least she tried, I guess. And to be fair to her again, she did actually spend a fair amount of time applying the perfectly edgy, but not too garish, smokey-eyed make-up routine. It was also somewhat vexing to her that as hard as she tried to look disinterested and a little bit scruffy, the whole outfit was, in its own way, completely on point. Despite how hard she had tried, she still looked completely presentable. Obviously, this was everyone else's fault for not knowing how to dress correctly.

For what felt like the two hundredth time that morning, Kiko found herself giving the same reply.

"No, Kara. I honestly have no idea what my dad wants with you."

"You're sure?"

"Well yes! If I knew, of course, I'd tell you." Kiko said, closing the big oaken front door behind her with a slam.

"I just... it's strange. Why would he want to talk to me? Why at his work?" Kara continued, as they made their way down the street. "Do you think Muhren will be there?"

Now would be a good time to tell you where this street, and therein the Attetson household, actually was. This thirteenth Earth had a Scotland. Perchance you might have heard of the land of the Celts? A place of rain, wind and battered chocolate bars. Like our Scotland, this one shared an island with England. A place famous for grey cities, bad teeth and also more rain. There was also Wales, a principality that was famous for (*unfortunately*) having to share such a small island with both the Scottish and the English; which was a pretty annoying and stressful thing for the Welsh to have to contend with. Also, their flag has a dragon on it, which was a much more memorable design than the flags of either Saint George or Saint Andrews. It was commonly accepted that the Welsh flag designer was by far the most interesting and smartest of the United Kingdom's flag designers, even if the English were too headstrong to admit it. This penchant for unusual, but also much better and more interesting decision making, was later adopted by the Scottish. When the countries of the world were asked later on to choose their national animals. England for some reason chose a lion. A lion has never actually lived in England of its own free will. England is too cold and famous for rain! *(But England did have a tendency to appropriate stuff that wasn't theirs and the world had a tendency to, for some reason, accept it as normal behaviour!)* When Wales was asked what their animal was to be, they again defaulted to the dragon. Scotland, upon realising that rules were 'a load o'shite' decided they wanted their animal to be a unicorn. Because if you're going to go for an animal that doesn't live in your country, like England did, why not go full hog and pick an animal that had never existed in your country but also had a great big horn sticking out of the top of its head!

The quiet town, buried on the northwest coast of Scotland that Kiko lived in was called Liarath. A quaint, sleepy fishing village of an approximate ten thousand people. If Liarath existed on our Earth, it would have been found just northwest of Inverness. Any would-be explorers on our world wanting to find the exact location would have a bad time of it, for the exact coordinates for Liarath would either result in you being hit by a car on an extremely busy series of main roads or staring at an empty field of sheep. Liarath thrived as a fishing village. The smell of the sea stung the air. But it was never actually cold. Despite being Scottish, the weather was usually fairly good. This was of course thanks to magic.

As Kiko and Kara made their way to the AIA, the magical agency for which Collin Attetson worked, Kiko was still being bombarded with questions. For a person who didn't care what people thought, Kara sure had a lot of questions about the opinions of others. Kiko half-heartedly conversed in the musings as to why her father would want to speak to her friend. But as this conversation revolved around one of her parents, the desire to be interested was waning. It was only partially fake at best in the first place. Kiko was distracted, both by what the working day may bring her, but also by a secret concern for Vincent's well being when fighting a child of hell. By all rights and expectations, he would be fine. But when you cared for someone, you worried about them when they fought hell-spawn. It was like a long forgotten, hushed by-law of what it meant to love someone or something. *Right?*

The two girls stopped abruptly next to what looked like an old black rectangular pillar. This pillar would probably look indiscernible from any day to day bollard if it wasn't for the words *'Arcane Intelligence Agency'* and *'press here for access'* which were engraved on the side. Kiko and Kara looked at one another for a moment, before both pressing the button and disappearing from both sight and site.

Chapter Two

THE ARCANE INTELLIGENCE AGENCY

Time travel was a tricky business. Both as a physical act and as an occurrence to regulate. This was in no small part because if given the ability to do so, almost any person on any planet would gladly alter a negative incident or event that occurred to them. Undoing the loss of a loved one, or some elaborate scheme for personal gain being the most commonly sought after aspirations of the would-be traveller of the fourth dimension. As a whole, far more thought was given to the fanciful and rhetorical question of *'what would I do if I could?'* rather than the much more important and practical question of *'what would happen if I did?'* This lack of forethought to the existence of actions having real and tangible reactions had resulted in a fair number of surprising restrictions for any would-be traveller traversing the temporal dimensions of time. The most shocking of these being a bizarre piece of arcane based pub trivia; *who do you think would be the most well-guarded figure throughout all of time?* The answer, as surprising as it may seem, was a certain individual born in a sleepy Elven town secluded on the side of a mountain range in Austria in 1889. This was an Elven baby male, whose parents were unassuming as to what had been birthed. Probably because the name Adolf Hitler didn't mean anything at this point on this crisp morning on the twentieth of April. Some people and events are, unfortunately, eternal. Alas, this included Hitler. With him existing in many forms across the multiverse. Here on the thirteenth world, he was an Elf. On others he was a woman, on some he was a literal animal. - *Some said he acted like an animal on every universe!* - And unfortunately, all but six universes in the whole multiverse had a Second World War. The six that managed to evade it, as lucky as they may initially sound on paper, were not all too better off. *As all six were still fighting the Great War and hadn't actually stopped killing one another long enough to bother naming a second one, or even realising it was time for round two.*

On each of these Earths, the Second World War was entirely inevitable. A blood-soaked destiny no man, woman or child could escape. As horrible as it sounds, bad things happen. So do awful and terrible things that curdle the blood and taint the soul. Changing the world and the air around it for all eternity. *You cannot, under any circumstance go back and alter a timeline you are part of.*

You are literally a part of it. Undoing the reason you are going back negates the reason to go back in the first place. To try to do so is paradoxical. Anyone well versed in the lingo of travelling the fourth dimension is already well aware of what a paradox is. For anyone who isn't, I'll give two examples of them right now.

A *'self depleting paradox'* is a chronological event that cancels itself out from existence. Let's say you are one of all those charming, new baby faced and idealistic time travellers who think *'let's go back and kill Hitler when he was a baby. That will be a fun and swell thing to do.'* Ignoring the obvious, *'you've just killed a baby called Adolf and are now the most infamous baby killer in Austrian history,'* what happens to the seventy-five million people you just saved from death? What does the world become with seventy-five million new variables multiplying away throughout time? *Where does World War Two go?* It was a palpable thing that changed the world forever. If the world snaps back and it never happened, what happens to you? You now never needed to go back to fix the largest war of all time. Because you're named after a famous baby killer from Austria. *Also, there was obviously no war to undo now.* So you never need to go back. If you never go back to kill him, then Adolf lives. Seventy-five million people die again; you discover time travel and decide to go back and kill Hitler. *You're a famous baby killer again.* Well done, you're now stuck in a temporal loop.

Congratulations. *You've now broken time.*

Time will revolve in this loop over and over and over and over and over again. Until there is a tear in the temporal fabric of time itself and a resulting chronomatic black hole emerges as time collapses in on itself.

Like any ordinary black hole, this chronomatic black hole will eat and eat and eat. Until there is no more time or Earth or universe left to consume. Without time, this thirteenth Earth will somehow manage to both freeze in a single moment forever, whilst also for-never, as there will be no one around to look at it and go *'Oh look at that, that famous Austrian baby killer broke time'.*

If you happen to be a well-versed wanderer of the fourth dimension and you are either well skilled or super lucky, you might just pull off the opposite of this. The extremely rare, and impossibly dangerous 'self sustaining paradox.' This being a name given to a paradox that does not delete itself from existence, but instead sustains or even creates itself. An example of this is actually a way in which you could cheat the universe out of the death of a loved one.

For this you will need: one loved one, one ability to time travel and either one clone or robotic duplicate of the aforementioned loved one.

For this example, let's say this loved one is a puppy. *Everyone loves a puppy, right?* So you see this puppy die. You're distraught, but you remember *'Oh yeah, I have a time machine.'* Going back in time and jumping in front of the bullet, car or the MacGuffin that killed the puppy will create a self depleting paradox. This is bad, I'm not explaining why again. Going back further in time, however, and creating a clone or identical robotic duplicate of the puppy and simply swapping it for the original on the big day should suffice. A puppy would die that day, just a clone or a duplicate. *The cosmic scales should remain balanced.* Allowing the original puppy to live. As you just tricked yourself into seeing a clone/duplicate of your puppy die, and you went through all that hassle of making a clone when your original puppy was safe all along. *It's like merging a prank with a god complex.*

All of the ethics surrounding you creating a life form and allowing it to die as part of some temporal game of chess is a conversation to be had in its own right. If the puppy wasn't a puppy in this scenario, but instead a sentient person, they may have several doubts or questions about your character or mental state from now on. But don't worry, I'm sure your local abattoir will have plenty of materials to read promoting any arguments you may have defending the idea of creating life just to kill it. It's also worth considering, if the couples counselling for your newfound god complex doesn't end in the way you wanted, you can always attempt a new self sustaining paradox to fix that fiasco too. *After all, you saved their life, the least they can do is show you a bit of gratitude, right?*

These would be Hitler killers and other paradox creating wanderers led to the creation of the Temporal Bureau of Investigations, where Kiko worked. This bureau was a small part of the larger Arcane Intelligence Agency. An agency founded to monitor all magical related crimes, disasters and mishaps. The AIA for short. Spanning from rather mundane events where a person has only used magic to commit low tier crimes, such as robbery, assault or murder, to the more advanced. Certain spell types were illegal, one such school of witchcraft and wizardry was necromancy. It was both gross and unethical. It was commonly agreed things were better off staying dead, mainly from a moralistic perspective. Again, a huge issue with necromancy as an art stemmed from World War Two, where the Nazi party often partook in rituals to raise the dead to turn the tide of war. This was such a common occurrence during the war, that it gave rise to a common occurrence of the art of necromancy being given the slang name of '*the necronazi arts.*' And as such, a part of the Arcane Intelligence Agency focussed purely on making sure the dead stayed dead.

Other sections of the agency focussed on more grandiose magical occurrences, especially anything that would result in an apocalypse, a mass genocide, or a mass transmutation of the populace into something unnatural. Like the time all of New York got turned into frogs. *Yes, even the buildings were turned into frogs.* As part of their observations of Earth, they also monitored paranormal activity and Demonic outbreaks. Again, for anyone wanting to ace a pub quiz about this thirteenth world's World War Two, there was a special kind of spirit, or ghost, that occupied this Earth.

As previously stated, seventy-five million people died in World War Two. This was the biggest increase in death ever recorded at this time. *(Good luck in the future!)* Before this, if you died, your own personal reaper would give you a choice. If you had something super important to do, you could choose to never actually pass on to the afterlife that had been chosen for you. You could choose to stay, wandering Earth for an eternity as a barely tangible phantasm spooking your way through your chosen house, workplace or special little haunting ground. Few people ever chose this option, but it was still a choice you had. Until one day it wasn't. *Well, it was longer than a day, truth be told.* One day, during the bloodshed of this war, the number of dead people quite simply escalated too high and could no longer be ignored. The archaic spiritual and eternal processes that operated the doors of both Heaven and Hell's enrolment policies kind of stopped working... *The backlog of dead people was simply too high.* As such, for thirty-seven days and thirty-seven nights, it all just stopped. The doors of Heaven and Hell were closed. *Sealed. Caput.* Out of order.

No one was allowed in. And anyone who died during this time was basically ignored. Their choice was taken from them. Heaven and hell weren't taking orders right now. They had too much work (*aka, dead people*) to catch up on. *The backlog of the damned was too damn high.* So anyone who died during this time had nowhere to go. Their options were removed from them. So here they had to remain on Earth for all of eternity. These ghosts were referred to as *'non consenting spirits'* as they had literally no say in this lifestyle choice. (*Or whatever term is more appropriate than a 'lifestyle choice' when discussing how a ghost spends its day.*)

The Arcane Intelligence Agency had also made it their responsibility to re-home these wayward spirits. Non consenting spirits were usually treated with more care and regard than their normal ghostly counterparts. Originally, a member of the institute had proposed banishing these spirits to the Halls of the Howling Horde, back when the non consenting spirits had first emerged. (*The Halls of the Howling Horde was a ghastly pocket dimension, much larger and vastly more dangerous than the tiny ones Kiko had in her coat.*) It was an unfitting place for fallen war heroes. This idea was decided tyo be like school in July, it had lacked class. The member who proposed this idea was called Brian Stanley. Brian's supervisors did not like this idea. Brian's supervisors promptly decided Brian was unfit for service and he quickly found himself looking for work elsewhere. As a species, we can barely cope with going to visit an old folk's home. *We find that hard enough.* So despite this world not dealing with these spirits well, they could have done worse than what they chose to do. Non consenting spirits were usually left to dwell within their own micro-societies. Living in abandoned undergrounds, sewers and any other places people seldomly traversed. Normally being left to dwell in their sorrow, mostly because they were really depressing to be around for long periods of time and posed little in the way of a threat. They made people feel bad, just by looking at them. *So they stopped looking at them.*

All teams at the Arcane Intelligence Agency that dealt with cases relating to the undead, either involving the act of necromancy spell casting or any teams required to deal with the occasional ghost, zombie or arisen fiend, fell under the same task force. Officially named the Bureau of Necrological Investigation. But given their line of work were commonly dubbed '*The Death Squad.*' This might have also been because it was easier and less time consuming to say than the Bureau of Necrological Investigation. And with a nickname like the one they ended up with, it was hardly surprising that this bureau was where Kara had desired to work with for the longest time.

They were also the only people allowed to raise the dead, but only for three-minute intervals and only if it was absolutely necessary and all the correct paperwork was filled out correctly. Got to love bureaucracy! This was also the department where Collin Attetson worked. He is also the final Attetson we will be meeting, for now. We will get to the ever-illusive second son (*Kiko's other brother*) later.

Collin was a kind man, famous for big smiles and open arms. He had a mop of curly black hair and a trimmed goatee. He was usually dressed in dark velvets and silks. The fact he was one of this world's most famous wizards should not have been surprising, given the way he chose to dress. He was a cool man, with a cool job; at least that was Kara's opinion of him. He had a fairly important job as a regulator of the Bureau of Necrological Investigations. Both monitoring the world for the events that may require his teams, as well as bailing them out if extreme situations arose.

Now would also be a good time to mention, the Arcane Intelligence Agency's main headquarters were not on Earth. *The place where it was, was a mystery.* Whoever had known for sure was long since dead and this secret had died with them. All anyone knew was that this place existed and they knew how to get here. This seemed to be good enough. Portals were readily available on almost every street, in almost every town, city, village, and hamlet across the world by now. Being that this was basically the magic police of Earth, meant that this place was always open and it was always busy.

If you had to go there, these portals took you to one of several reception areas. These varied, but were usually stone or metal constructs. These rooms always seemed to know how big they had needed to be and how big they actually could get before becoming impractical. Strange, green goblin-like creatures manned the reception desks. The number of them being somewhere in the tens of thousands to hundreds of thousands. Kiko had found their appearance strange as a child. To her they resembled something human-like in shape, verging on an anorexic appearance. With little meat on the bone, and a dull vacant, gaunt expression. They were creepy and they smelled funny too, despite the fact no one ever really mentioned it. *Again no one seemed to know where they had come from.* These strange green creatures came and went as they were required to do so. It was such an easy task to monitor these goblins that only a small team of twenty people were required to do so. Despite each person having to monitor approximately five thousand goblins each, this was still considered (*by most of the other workers*) to be an extremely easy job. These creatures never got sick, they never got tired or even complained. They just turned up, clocked in and worked. When the shift was over they went, well, somewhere unknown. Monitoring them was little more than a cursory, obligated ticking of a box on some form. Some corporate middle management's attempt of monitorization in case of any issues that may arise in the future.

The AIA receptionists had green, and ever so slightly wet scales, not too dissimilar to those of a fish. Their height varied between five and six foot. They also spoke all the languages of the Earth despite never having been spotted there. They were as much a part of the Arcane Intelligence Agency as the Arcane Intelligence Agency was a part of them. Neither had existed without the other throughout all of recorded history. And when you consider that the Temporal Bureau of Investigations monitored almost all of time and space and had multiple agents travelling throughout time and any given moment, *this meant history was pretty well covered.*

All Officers of the Arcane Intelligence Agency had special access when entering the portals from Earth, like Kiko and Kara had just done. These officers were almost always sent to exactly where they needed to be. The lower floors housed the reception rooms. This led to the Basic Crimes unit for several floors. The offices for the Temporal Bureau of Investigations were next, with five floors. Proceeded by the Bureau of Necrological Investigations, which only had three. Further up were offices that tracked apocalypses and general world-ending phenomena. People here also consulted with many of the more ancient races, like the angels, aliens or any other race that was slightly outside of our grasp. These offices took up another five stories.

There was a crack of light as Kiko and Kara appeared within the main waiting area of the Bureau of Necrological Investigations. The white marble floor clicked and clacked under the heels of all the busy commuters. Posters donned the stone walls, warning of the dangers of approaching ghouls, ghosts and other monsters. Lights flickered from the ornate overhead chandeliers which hung down from the second floor. AIA receptionists helped guide the uninitiated to where they needed to be. Quick footed Death Squads busied themselves, darting off to untold adventures of fighting crimes and misdeeds.

Despite how busy this room was, it was not actually chaotic. Things were intense for sure. But they were under control. Like a well-oiled machine. This civility was never anything short of a miracle. As a collective array of species, the inhabitants of Earth (*regardless of the universe it dwelled in*) were prone to acts of panic, stress and paranoia. These three things when combined with both stupidity and a high enough percentage of a populace led to disaster every time. Two stupid people would assume they were absolutely and definitively right, based purely upon the fact that they agreed upon something. As if being wrong about something was somehow undone by the simple unfortunate fact that you both shared a limited understanding of all the available facts. Would-be time travel conspirators had their own example of this inability to accept the world as it was, this being the '*Mandela Effect.*'

Despite the fact he was officially recorded as dying on the fifth of December in 2013, there was a surprisingly high percentage of people who believed Nelson Mandela had died either long before, or after, this date. Using this shared misconception as proof of alternative timelines and universes. The fact that they were correct about parallel Earths on this occasion notwithstanding, the reason for them believing so was invalid, as even a broken clock can be right twice a day. That doesn't mean these clocks should be used as timekeeping devices. Other proofs for the Mandela Effect in action were almost entirely consisting of people's inability to read or hear things correctly. Brand logos being spelt differently, cartoon characters and logos having altered appearances and misheard film quotes being the best examples. All of these had actually simply been the end result of a high enough number of people getting together and being unable to accept that they were wrong when provided with indisputable facts. *Deciding to create an entire parallel universe should never be used so lightly as to attempt to cover up you're inability to recall facts or dates effectively.* Being a child and thinking a cartoon looked differently from how you remembered is called '*proof that you were a child.*' For some of us, that was a long time ago. No one would blame you for forgetting the correct colour of some puppet that taught you your ABCs when you still had problems chewing solid food.

I promise I am not just being mean towards people who believe in the Mandela Effect for no reason.

Unfortunately, parallel universes don't just bleed into one another. *Life was not created by some great cosmic entity that did not know how to colour within the lines.* A universe was one set timeline. If tampered with it would simply delete itself or it would be the new timeline. The person who changed the timeline would retain the knowledge that they had done so. Like a dirty secret, something only they would remember. But they would be the only ones. The universe would not present this change as a typo on a cereal box. No differently as to how Jesus wouldn't just pop down to Mexico to say '*hi*' because somebody over toasted their bread. The universe is kinda busy right now; so is Jesus. If one universe posed a threat to another they would simply collide. In this scenario, the two universes would play the parts of both the unsinkable Titanic and the iceberg simultaneously. *Both destroying each other in the process.* Imagine if you will two flat kitchen counters. Both kitchen countertops are infested with ants. *Unfortunately in this scenario, we're the ants.* If you were to pick up one of the countertops, hold it upside down and lower it perfectly on top of the adjacent countertop. All ants would be trapped inside and squished. This, hopefully, should act as a simple enough example as to what happens if two universes should '*bleed into one another.*' Again, Nelson Mandela only died once. Anyone going back to save him, or alter the events of how he died would have created a self depleting paradox. He died when he died as no chronomatic black hole had consumed all of existence.

This rant had been somewhat of a similar thought process to the one Kiko was currently having, as she had overheard some poor AIA receptionist having to contend with some crackpot demanding that because some window cleaning spray had changed its logo, this new shade of red was now proof of the Mandela Effect in action and that this was somehow a local non consenting spirit's fault. '*Because, of course if this ghostly veteran was going to change time he would reinvent the advertisement for bleach and not make it so he could pass on to his or her afterlife,*' Kiko mused to herself.

Kara, on the other hand currently had a much simpler thought process to contend with, this being: *'Why am I here? Why am I here? Why am I here? Why am I here?'* And so on so forth.

Being such good friends they could both tell that the other one was agitated, but neither one was about to be willing enough as to say why. Kiko's agitation was presentable by her poorly disguised disdain and derision at some random passer-by's inept understanding of the laws of time travel. *Thus evident by her furrowed brow.* Perhaps caused by her line of work, she had a vast understanding of what was and was not possible when it came to time travel. Her time at the Temporal Bureau of Investigations had taught her well.

And much like how the Federal Bureau of Investigation referred to itself more commonly as the FBI, so too shall I occasionally refer to the Temporal Bureau of Investigations as the TBI; as my wrist is starting to hurt and I'm worried I'll run out of space to write. Likewise, the Bureau of Necrological Investigations was also commonly abbreviated to the BNI. *Mainly because, unlike the TBI, they didn't have all the time in the world to waste saying the full name that was the Bureau of Necrological Investigations upwards of a thousand times a day!*

What time they did have in a day (*which was twenty-four hours for anyone unsure on how long a day is.*) was well managed. Again, these three floors ran like a well-oiled machine. This being because they had to deal with dangerous creatures around the clock. Collin Attetson and the other BNI regulators knew that the best way to minimise casualties was by being prepared and well trained. The TBI were not always around, or allowed, to step in. Unless, of course some preordained paradox existed which meant they had to. It was unclear (*and agents were unsure whether or not*) if there was a TBI agent somewhere who knew where and when everyone would die. If there existed some uncaring, omniscient being allowing these agents to open the doors to their own deaths, without trying to say *'oops, maybe you shouldn't pick that door. Here, pick this one instead.'* If some cosmic spinster was watching the threads of life unwind on a spindle, like Clotho, Lachesis and Atropos from ancient Greek legend and lore. No one liked to think about it, instead just choosing to decide this person didn't exist.

Despite being a versatile powerhouse, all workers of the Arcane Intelligence Agency worked well together. *Few families demonstrated this better than the Attetsons.* Cassandra rarely had issues with her husband, despite her work being more bureaucratic and behind the scenes with her work here, on the aforementioned higher floors. Collin helped run the BNI, and Kiko had begun to impress her superiors within the TBI. Vincent had found himself being the poster boy for the entire agency. A fame derived from how well he usually single-handedly thwarted and overcame any obstacles or evildoers in his wake.

Vincent being a literal poster boy, in this case, led to one such poster of him donning an ink-based set of glasses, a moustache and some stink lines. Doodling was a common vent for childhood boredom, this young child was about to ruin Vincent's grandiose white smile with an inky black tooth, before realising he had been noticed by an auburn-haired girl with glasses and a big blue coat. Kiko raised a finger and winked as she shushed the child, assuring him that this was their secret forever as she walked on by. *Besides, it was about time Vincent had to contend with glasses of his own like Kiko had to!*

"Girls!" A voice broke out above the crowd. Literally in this case, as both Kiko and Kara looked upwards from the crowds to see Collin stood smiling vibrantly as he leant on the balcony that overlooked the ebony hanging chandeliers. He stood upright and ushered for them to follow him to his office.

In the distance, one could hear the commotion of a child being clipped around the ear for the defacing of one Vincent Attetson poster. Obviously, his mother didn't think this hero suited glasses. Or maybe it was the moustache, black tooth or stink lines. The important thing was he was now in trouble, it didn't much matter the extent as to why. Maybe Kara was also in trouble with Collin? Maybe that's why she was summoned here!

Perhaps she had done some terrible, awful deed. Maybe she was about to be carried away to some dingy cell in a dank prison. Even worse, maybe this was a trap set by her parents.

Goosebumps broke out across her entire body. Maybe the prison, regardless of how dank or dingy, wasn't that bad of an alternative when compared to her parents.

Any readers out there that are as curious as Kara was right now, as to why she was here, need only turn the page to find out the answers. Any readers not interested as to why she was here could skip the next chapter, but please don't. I spent a long time writing it and future events won't make any sense. *If you do skip to chapter four, you'll probably have to go back to chapter three anyway.*

Chapter Three

THANKS FOR READING!

Thank you for not skipping ahead to chapter four. For those who did you'll have to read on for a further breakdown of the spoilers, you gave yourselves. This was your fault and you spoiled this chapter for yourself. Death should never be something a person rushes towards or chooses.

For anyone who needs to hears it, you are loved and you and wanted. If not by that unworthy person you *'wanted'* to be loved by, then to hell with them. Because someone else out there loves you. If no one comes to mind, then you're just blind to it. *If you have the time to plan to die then at least spend some time first finding those that care for you.* Find a hobby and make new friends, or ask for help. Asking for help was what Kara had done three months ago when she had asked Kiko for assistance. This act did not in any way make her weak. Neither did Kara's shock at Kiko's willingness to help. Friends tended to help if they were aware of the situation. Kara could feel the walls of her darkness closing in around her. *This darkness fed the voices.*

For once, her just do it mantra was not the best call of action; ignoring the voices was the right thing to do. She had never once needed to question her friendship or sisterly love for Kiko. This pseudo-familial bond was greater than any bond she had with her real family. We choose our friends, but we also have agency when it comes to deciding how we are treated. For some, this was life's best-kept secret. Therapists know of Gestalt's theory. This being that a *'thing'* is not just one thing. Like an engine, some things are sometimes an equation of the sum of the whole of its parts. If a car engine breaks down you don't always rush out and buy a new car. *That would be costly if the need to do so repeatedly arose.* Likewise, Kara being suicidal was not the issue. This sentence serves not to trivialise such a thing, but rather explain that this desire to end all things was an end result. The cause for this was her environment. So by removing herself from this environment, she lessened the effects of her situational depression. As all people (including Half-Elves!) knew how they wanted to be treated. They knew what they deserved. And much like how we know gone off milk is bad, we subconsciously know when we are being treated worse than we deserve. We can taste it. We can smell it. It makes us feel bad.

Kara's relationship with her parents was broken. And much like a broken bone that hadn't healed correctly, had caused an infection to spread through her stately home. Removing herself from Titan Point, her former home, and living with Kiko in Liarath (*even if just temporarily*) had pushed back the darkness. Well, it lit up her psyche. This is to say that if Kara was not mindful, the lights could go out again. And she feared the return to darkness with all of her heart. As well as the return to the tight choking grasp that was the De'Carussos.

But for now, removing herself like an ill-fitted cog from an engine seemed to do the trick. This may have constituted a win for whoever penned Gestalt's Theory. His name wasn't Gestalt by the way, as this was a pre-existing German word. Anyone who speaks German may already know of it, they may also believe that I've butchered its meaning. Likewise, I may have run the risk of angering every therapist and counsellor out there. If everyone could drop in on their local counsellor or therapist and check up on them for me, I would appreciate it! Even though they might appear scary at first, with their big couches and flappy notepads, it never hurt to drop by and check up with one on occasion.

These counsellors are not to be confused with political counsellors. It always helped to keep an eye on the political ones. Two eyes, as often as you could spare them. The English language was a little bit broken and for some reason, two words, whilst identical on paper, meant completely different things when said out loud. But regardless always seemed to crop up.

> *'The context of what you read changes depending on how your brain thinks it was supposed to be read. You could hit a bat with a bat and desert it in the desert if you just thought it was a fair and just thing to do. You could project your opinions about bats onto everyone you met along the way to the local fair as if you were providing a presentation*

on a project that a school had asked you to present. Upon your way to this fair, you could decide to make a grand entrance through the entrance and regale people with your opinions about bats. But you'd best decide upon an entrance quickly, you were running out of time and the future was quickly becoming the present. In the future, when you recall how you planned all this in the past you may have walked past the entire entrance itself.

You could refuse to accept the existence of these accidental duplications and overlook for a second what I'm trying to say. However, in the future, you may find yourself trapped in second place. Receiving a judgmental look from any spelling-bee judge, who chose to overlook the competition. Second place may be all you get, as you refused to accept the refuse, trash and shortcomings of the English language that I'm warning you about now. Don't worry, no one will fine you for not winning. It's fine. You neither need to consult with your local counsellor or to book a therapy session with your counsellor. You could discount my words and object to my opinions. But you still know I'm still going to mention that a discount is an object that belongs in a mathematics book. I'm also done, I won't wind you up anymore, in case you do or say something that knocks the wind out of my sails. It would be a bad idea to start a row. Because if I was secretly a boat you could literally knock the wind out of my sails and I'd make you row back to shore.

For the record, I'm also not a boat.'

This whole dissection of the English language as a structure we use to communicate with was lifted word for word from a presentation Kiko herself had made when she was at school. She graded highly with her teacher. Less so with the pupils.

Kara's pupils (*the ones in her eyes!*) darted nervously over the contents of Collin's office. This office consisted of a back wall filled with bookcases. These bookcases were in turn filled with books. Obviously. A robust red leather and slightly worn out chair hugged the underside of a grand table. This table was cluttered by a series of half-read books and artefacts to be examined. And also one lamp. The light was always useful at illuminating the dark. This lamp however was having a hard time of it. Collin had chosen to sit on his desk and not on his chair. '*God forbid anyone uses something for the purpose for what it was designed for,*' is what the lamp would have shouted if it was in any way sentient. *It was not.* It lacked the ability to think and to speak. *Don't be ridiculous!* This wasn't an animated kid's movie, furniture didn't randomly burst into song or spoken word. If they did this lamp would have had a lot to say about a certain elbow, belonging to a certain Collin, occupying the space a certain desk lamp always occupied. Being unimpressed about this new jaunty angle it found itself in. If this had been the beginning of an animated movie, this lamp would probably long since have leapt across the table and straight into Collin's face and jumped several times on his eye until it was squished flat. Maybe then this animated movie would be allowed to begin.

"So I bet you're wondering why I've asked you here today, Kara?" Collin gave an inquisitive smile as he looked over his half-moon glasses. "We just need to wait on Mrs McDowley, then we can begin." He watched as Kara shuffled awkwardly in her chair. "Don't worry child, it's good news." His smile brimmed again.

The tension was almost palpable. Kiko now watched from the second of her father's armchairs over towards an uncomfortable looking Kara. I mean don't get me wrong, Kara looked fine on the surface. But true friends end up knowing us better than we know ourselves. We can never hide what we really feel from them. Kiko could see as clear as day that Kara had been made nervous by all the secrecy. But Kiko, even if she had no idea why they were here, knew her parents. She knew how fond they had become of Kara during her time living with them and they had begun to view her as a second daughter. Or like a piece of furniture that had always been kicking around the family home.

Kiko did not have long to reflect on her friend. At this precise moment, a slug-like woman entered. This description was unfair to slugs. For anyone confused, Mrs McDowley also wasn't actually a slug. *They didn't want to be associated with her.* This old crow (*again, sorry crows!*) had the appearance of someone over two hundred years old, despite only being in her late sixties. Her grey curly hair was pulled back and thick black-rimmed glasses framed her eyes. Bundles of bloated skin protruded around her ankles and weighed down her legs. An archaically dated pinstriped two-piece dress suit worked overtime; being pulled in all manner of directions as it tried to hold itself together. Some people said that this cantankerous old gas bag was a waste of skin. I'd say she was a testament to the strength or the elasticity of skin. That a human being could bloat so much, yet maintain human form. She was a haunting to look at, a purple-faced monster of broken skin. She still had technically enough life left in her to not warrant being called a zombie, but she was also too dead inside to be ever truly be called alive. Two beady eyes settled on the blonde Half-Elf. Somehow these eyes were both lost to bloated depths of her bloated facial features, yet also magnified to gargantuan proportions by her glasses.

There was a sudden painful jolting *'crack'* as she struck Kara in the knee with one of those small, little hammers doctors use. Kara's knee jerked itself to attention, kicking through the air as she looked at Collin with a panicky demeanour. *Why was she being attacked?* He gave a faked concerned smile back that seemed to indicate either a notion of *'you'll be fine'* or *'good luck.'*

Mrs McDowley was famous for her shortness, both as a defining characteristic and as a description of her appearance. Her medical examinations were viewed as a right of passage. A sort of ceremonial *'well, you survived her. What else could these Demons ever really throw at you?'*

An otoscope was jammed deep into Kara's ear. Mrs McDowley had been with the company for almost as long as anyone could remember. And no one remembered ever having anything nice to say about her. *Also, the otoscope felt really uncomfortable, thanks for asking.* A bright torch was shone in her eyes. Examinations like this were why people feared going to the doctors. People like this was why Kara hated people. Kiko watched on, remembering her first examination from the old bloated slug. She rubbed her knee with the distinct memory of the bruise that had once called it home. Truth be told, Kiko was actually still scared of Mrs McDowley and always did her best to stay out of her way.

"Mouth." Mrs McDowley snapped. These being the first words she had uttered thus far.

"I'm sorry, wha-" A small board pinned Kara's tongue down as this slug-like crow peered at her tonsils. "Say Ah."

Aaaaaaaaaand with as much grace as to which she had entered with, Mrs McDowley had now retreated; the smell of stale lavender and petrulli oil wafting behind her as she went.

"Oh, OK?" Collin watched as she left without a word. "I... I guess that means we're good to begin...? Excellent!" Collin bolted upright allowing one angry lamp to return where it rightfully belonged. Victory had been won this day!

"Sorry about her. I'm told she grows on you over time... apparently." Collin paused for a second as if to evaluate whether or not he actually believed himself. "Anyway Kara, now she's done, I have a job offer for you!" As he spoke he had walked around his desk, when he lowered himself into his chair he spoke the words Kara had waited a lifetime to hear.

"How would you feel about joining us at the Bureau of Necrological Investigations?"

There was a surprisingly long pause. Kiko glanced cautiously over as Kara was sat with her mouth wide open. Not a very gracious moment for Kara... But it was funny though.

'Thank you so, so, so very much. Of course. I'd love to. I won't let you down. Are you sure? I will not disappoint you. When can I start? YES! I can't wait. Are you being serious?' Were just some of the things Kara's brain was telling her mouth to say. But the shock had knocked some bolts and screws loose.

Her brain realised exactly how long had passed unspoken.

'Say something! Say anything!'

"Uh-huh!" That was what her racing brain decided to go with.

'Say something better!'

Her brain hated her right now.

'How embarrassing.'

"I think you'd fit in perfectly here, Kara. And we've recently had an opening." Collin said after a long pause. Kiko noticed her father look down as he tried to cover a case folder with the words *'DECEASED'* stamped on the front in red ink. "I've seen first hand what you're capable of and heard even more from Kiko." He looked lovingly at his only daughter. "If you two could follow me please."

Every time a creature from Earth achieved some form of a life goal for itself, there was always at some point or time a stabbing sensation of self-doubt that followed. This normally stemmed from a sense of self inadequacy, or a fear of failure. There was also a fear of what it would mean to succeed. It's true that these pangs of inadequacy were short-lived and were usually succeed or preceded by a wild celebration of their success.

The thoughts that were currently afloat in Kara's mind were similar to the panic of a driver with a new car. None of the new buttons and levers made sense yet and she didn't want to touch anything. She was struck by a fear of going eighty miles an hour and being unable to find the handbrake.

That new job smell. Workplace friendships were their own mini micro climate she'd have to overcome. An endless parade of interpersonal relationships that were a reflection of authority, aptitude, prowess and a shared history. All workplaces existed because of them. No one ever just walked in through the front door at a new job and instantly became a part of the team. This kind of thing took time. We all have memories of a person, be it ourselves or others, who tried to indoctrinate themselves too quickly into the status quo. *What memories arose for you?* Was it an ill-timed unprofessional joke that made you turn sour to a person? An overly familiar stranger who wouldn't shut up? Some overly confident inept sham of a person who you had to keep tidying up the pieces after? At the end of the day, no one liked being disliked and it's rather unfortunate that some people find it so easy to be unpopular, rather like Mrs McDowley.

Collin walked them down a series of new corridors. A series of jars ran across a series of shelves. Each jar had the pickled remains of some undead fiend or dangerous beast. It was unclear if these were decorations, trophies or pieces of evidence from assorted crime scenes. Several agency workers busied themselves with their work. The occasional one greeting Collin as he went. This workspace, despite being ornate and magical, felt very similar to your usual workplaces back on Earth.

Suddenly Kiko found her skin crawling as she saw the figure of a person she preferred to avoid at all costs. Kara cast a worried look over her awkward friend. She knew how the approaching man made Kiko feel.

Llewelyn Daniels.

There was no apparent reason on the surface for Kiko's destain for this tall, gaunt man. There was no clear indication in his appearance as to why she disliked him so much. No indicator as to why she'd want to run out of the room any time he'd entered it. On the surface, he seemed like a well dressed and respectable man. However, the reason he made her feel uneasy was less due to his appearance and more the fact of how he acted when he was around her. He became the worlds most unbearable drooling fool.

"Oh, uh, hello Kiko. I like what… you… you've done with your.. with you… your hair!" His voice was shaky and uncertain, like winter's ice on the first day of spring.

And there it was. The reason for the destain. He was so awkward! A single bony hand combed through her hair rather pathetically. "Um… new shamp-shampoo…?"

Kiko nodded then proceeded to pretend to ignore him as she pulled away. This caused Llewelyn to turn bright red and he started stuttering about something or other. Hypothetically, if Llewelyn had been an avid ship enthusiast and spent every weekend and morsel of his free time at whatever dock, marina or shipyard that took his fancy. He would have been totally oblivious to the one ship that always on display. *The HMS Friend Ship.* And to be fair even the captain of the HMS Friend Ship would find it weird if a person twice their age kept touching their hair and would contemplate throwing you overboard. It mattered not if you were a man or a woman, the unwanted advances of any man or woman twice your age was always uncomfortable. Especially if that person was your father's age, could never make eye contact with you, continually got tongue-tied and kept staring at the floor whenever you walked into a room as a crimson red blush flooded their cheeks.

"Oh, mister Daniels, I was actually on my way to come see you and introduce you to Kara…" Collin interrupted.

"We've already met…" Kara gave a look of annoyance, knowing that Kiko was too polite to say anything to defend herself about being touched.

A short Halfling woman appeared from behind Llewelyn. And introduced herself as Claire. As Claire and Llewelyn discussed the occupational chance of a lifetime with Kara, Kiko took the chance to leave her friend to settle in. But also as to not be in the same room as Llewelyn.

"Uh, Kiko can you hold on a second?" Her father's voice cut over the debates of new work etiquette as he took his daughter to one side. "I was talking to your supervisor, we were thinking it would be a good idea if you had Kara shadow you today. Show her the ropes as it were..." He said in a whisper. His long pause seemed to indicate that this was a question and not a statement.

"I mean sure, I'd love to." Kiko replied gingerly after an awkward pause.

There may be some people out there who will be surprised to learn that this decision of having Kiko as a mentor had very little to do with her friendship with Kara. Despite having only been with the Arcane Intelligence Agency for a little over a year herself, Kiko had already established herself with strong foundations as a proactive and useful member of the team. She was logical and forthright. *Her peers had found her helpful with a pinch of a cheery demeanour.* The power behind her familial name had helped open doors, this much was true. But I doubt this was the entire reasoning behind it. Their job here was still of utmost importance. You don't just give someone an important job because of who their brother is. *Right?*

Kiko was so well respected by the TBI that she was one of the few allowed free reign with the ever-elusive Temporal Teleportation spell. Most of the other TBI agents had to use a special timekeeping device for their travellings of the fourth dimension. Kiko was not like other people though. She seemed to have a natural gift when it came to understanding time as a construct. Complex theoretical thought pieces on rhetorical temporal musings were as easy for her to learn and understand as riding a bike was to an Olympic athlete. A combination of her warm personality, brains and famous name meant that she was usually the agency's 'go-to girl' if they wanted to impress a new person. A way of showboating who they had on the payroll, although admittedly it was more due to who her brother was. Kiko was famous enough to be impressive to the people that knew what she represented, but not so magnificent as to appear daunting. If Vincent was Coca-Cola, then she was Pepsi. *I mean Pepsi is fine, right?* I mean some people... even prefer... Pepsi... apparently... right?

Her skills had unlocked doors for her far earlier than they would have been otherwise. Kiko had even been allowed passage to six other planets to commune with the aliens on Earthly matters. One small step for mankind was a much bigger step when aided by magic. Undoubtedly there is at least one reader right now angered by the concept of alien life. After all this story, up until this point, has had a very standard Fantasy genre feel to it if I do say so myself. They probably dislike the idea of magic mixing with the musings of science fiction. Like trying to mix orange juice with toothpaste or a toaster with a bathtub. *Martians and wizards don't usually share the same friendship circles.* But if there was more than one life across the multiverse, then why exactly wouldn't there be life across the vacuum of space? More than one planet had life, much like how there was more than one universe. What was so great about this world (*where all the people in it all complained about having nine-to-five jobs and depression or anxiety.*) that made them so obstinate about accepting alien life?

Avid gardeners will tell you that maintaining your own garden is great, but you do need to keep an eye on your neighbours'. It's swell that you might have award-winning rose bushes, but next door just filled their garden with a busted up sofa, the remains of a car and keep throwing empty beer cans everywhere. *Plus I don't think their dog has any more space left to defecate in.* Good luck maintaining your property value next to that! Likewise, why would the Arcane Intelligence Agency waste time making sure that all of the comings and goings of Earth followed their rules if they didn't keep tabs on everyone else?

Kiko had once visited the Martians, who were not actually green by the way, as well as other planets you may or may not have heard of. She had seen the vastness of space and her place within it. The scale of it all was amazing. This was something she had over Vincent. He had always been too busy playing the hero, to leave the comfort of Earth. Which was fine. It meant she had space travel all to herself. Something of her own. Cassandra had made sure Vincent didn't step on Kiko's toes on this matter too. She had never seen her daughter as happy or excited as the day she had first returned from interplanetary travel.

CHAPTER FOUR

THE BEGINNER'S GUIDE TO NECROMANCY

Anyone choosing to ignore the request and the end of the second chapter (*and willingly skipped chapter three*...) are about to ruin the story for themselves. Kiko and Vincent were now dead. Kara now had to decide whether or not breaking the law was now more important than repaying the debt now owed to the Attetsons for housing her for so long. *Two-thirds of Cassandra's adult children lay dead at her feet. Who would tell Muhren?* This was of course a lie. Hopefully, anyone who skipped chapter three was thrown off by that misdirection. Also hopefully, any readers that did read the third chapter but still fell for that red herring aren't too angry. Hopefully, none of you decides to jump the shark or jump straight to that moment in your own life when you close this book for good. Anyone still reading potentially learned something from this. A cheap joke I chose to make at the end of the second chapter had the potential to derail the entire narrative structure. If this book was a house (*it's not – it's still just a book!*) the roof could have collapsed due to the immense beating the fourth wall just took. Luckily, if you're still here then the foundations I've built were strong enough to retain your interest. But building a strong foundation takes time. Building a foundation requires patience. Building a foundation requires familiarity, friendship and for trust to blossom. *For anyone who cannot tell, I'm not talking about writing a book or building a house.* I'm talking about the stresses of a workplace. Almost all of us have done so, to work somewhere and have a job. To work as part of a team that works alongside you. And in case my repeatedly using the word '*work*' wasn't '*working*' for you, I hope we can '*work*' towards a better '*working*' environment, where we can all get along and '*work*' together. If not I will 'work' towards using 'work' less in future sentences. Does this promise '*work*' for you? Or are you starting to doubt that the word '*work*' was even a working word within the confines of the English language?

In her own way, Kara was struggling to come to terms with the offer of a lifetime that had been presented to her. *The idea of this perfect job was stressing her out.* As does the fruition for most people's ambitions. In this way, Kara was very much like us. The fear was never '*not getting what we wanted*' but rather '*what if we fail when we get it?*' Personal expectations were usually a persons undoing.

Also, I've gone an entire paragraph without mention the word work. *This line was a part of its own paragraph, so me saying it then didn't count.* But for anyone who re-read the last paragraph to double-check if I was telling the truth, might begin to understand why Kara kept replaying the events that had occurred earlier today in Collin's office. As happy as she was that her parents had not been lying in wait, ready to spring out on her and drag her home to Titan Point, a subsidiary of Raven Rock Enterprises, it still didn't feel real. But if this offer to roam the world as a member of a Death Squad turned out to be a joke, then perhaps her parents draggin' her away would have been a less cruel alternative.

The cold wet floor of the crypt was slippery underfoot. As far as inductions to workplaces went the Arcane Intelligence Agency didn't hold back. As it turns out they were rather fond of the deep end and throwing you right in it. Like an overzealous lifeguard. Sink or swim. Whereas a retail-based job may ask you to press buttons on a till, or a chef may be asked to cook some food, if your job relied on you to fight (*and hopefully kill!*) things for a living, then there was only really one form of suitable training. Or in this case, evaluation. *You had to kill something.* This is an oversimplification, what you had to prove was a '*proficiency to work well under pressure*' and '*an ability to follow and complete tasks within a respectable time frame.*' Curriculum Vitaes were not critically vital for the job if you could prove yourself to be capable of the tasks required.

No manual teaches you how to keep your head, both literally and metaphorically, when a werewolf is chasing you. There was no training video on how to exorcise a demon out of a child's body. These were skills a person either had or simply did not. *(Also I lied, there were several manuals and training videos on workplace safety in regards to not being killed by the monsters and ghouls. I was being hyperbolic. Although these videos and guides served more as a tool to prevent potential lawsuits or legal action.)*

So here Kara was with her friend in tow. The task was simple enough in theory, and the reward was definitely worth the risk.

Japan was having a rather unfortunate run of luck lately. There had been several reportings of people disrupting and interrupting funerals. And I don't just mean that someone was gatecrashing, even though that would be a pretty awful occurrence in itself! The thing that was awkward about these interruptions had been that the person who was causing the mayhem was the same person that was supposed to be lying dead in the coffin. The very same person everyone had come to see for one last final time. *To say goodbye.* These coffin-dodging cadavers were bad for three reasons. The first being that the Japanese were very much into the whole *'honourable life, honourable death'* thing. Perverting the afterlife and making someone come back to life was just about the highest insult imaginable to them. It was an affront to their entire culture. *It robbed them of their honour.* The second reason it was bad was that it also made the funeral homes look bad. But more than this; funerals (*given their very nature*) were already like a big old box of emotional dynamite on a short fuse. Emotions that were ready to explode at any given notice. A shared, not so secret, wall of grief ready to crack open at a moment's notice. *Tensions were already high.* This power keg of sorrow was bad enough without your grandmother leaping out of her coffin and trying to eat your brains through a straw. *(Not that zombies normally used straws, but you get the idea.)* The third reason zombies are bad is because they are both scary and gross.

People were always confused to see zombies outside of Halloween. As if there was had been a super-special bond that had existed between the undead and All Hallows' Eve. Halloween shared the role of being an international winter's holiday with Christmas. People were well aware of the expression that said of how *'a dog was for life and not just for Christmas.'* The same, in theory, was true for the necromantic arts. This was not to say that if you raised the dead then you had to keep it, feed it and take care of it like a responsible pet owner. But that the act of raising the dead was not restricted to being on just one day of the year. *Yet people were always surprised to hear about people raising zombies outside of October.* In the last two months, there had been an estimated three hundred reportings of the arisen dead across all of Japan. This proved two things, the first being that a lot of people died a lot of the time. It was almost endless. *(Just like the Australian soap opera, Neighbours.)* Across the world, twenty-three people had died in the time it had just taken for you to read this one sentence. That was another thirteen. The only guarantee in life was that it would end one day. *(Unlike Neighbours.)* That it should end. *(That was not a dig at Neighbours, I was talking about life.)* To interfere with death was perverse. It was unnatural. *It was disrespectful.*

Unnatural acts, such as necromancy, were so awful that they seemed to stain the air. To alter the very fabric of reality. *You could feel it.* You could almost smell it or taste it in the air. As if the very universe itself had hated it so much that every atom of its existence had tried to flee from the evil act whenever anyone tried to raise the dead. The act of necromantic spell casting always resulted in the surrounding area feeling extremely eery and falling very silent. It felt wrong. Wrong in the roots. Wrong in the air. *Wrong in your bones.* As if all of nature had run away from the threat of it. Like the silence found after birds flew away from a sudden gunshot in the night.

Necromancy also tended to kill all of the blossoming plants and flowers nearby. The only plants not affected by this were Nightshade and Death Blossom. *This was probably why these flowers had such ominous-sounding names.* But these clues had been enough intel for the Arcane Intelligence Agency to be able to surmise where these necromancers were hiding. The people they were looking for were believed to be deep within the Aokigahara. For those in the know, they knew that this forest went by the nickname *'the Forest of the Dead.'* With such an on the nose sobriquet, it should have probably been more obvious to look here sooner than they had done so.

The Aokigahara lay at the foot of Mount Fuji. This forest was a maze of trees. *(Like most forests are.)* But unlike most forests, this one lay upon a ground of cracked volcanic rock. Despite what a title like Mount Fuji may suggest, it wasn't actually a mountain at all. *It was a volcano.* The volcanic earth and soil had allowed a plenitude of strong, healthy trees to grow. Which in itself isn't an issue. But due to the nature of the land here being very shallow, it had led to the ground being a tangled network of exposed roots. *A minefield of tripping hazards.* Careless travellers could quickly cause themselves injury if they were not careful. The density of the trees also absorbed almost all nearby sounds; so it was easy to get lost. You would literally be unable to see the forest for the trees. The Aokigahara also had a bad reputation. For some unknown reason, people would travel across all of Japan to come here. They came here to end it all. *Suicide.* This word of mouth also brought tourists and thrill-seekers. *Hopefully not to take photos of those battling suicidal thoughts.*

It would probably warrant mentioning that not all who died here did so intentionally. Some died from accidents or getting lost. *Oh, and some died from running afoul of the necromancers.*

"It's so creepy down here!" Kiko complained while examining the cobwebbed interior of her stony new environment.

"You're such a girl!" Kara replied laughing to herself mockingly.

"But... I am a girl..?" Kiko said after a moment of confusion. "And so are you!"

This statement was true. However, not all girls were afraid of the dark. *Some thrived off of it.* Kara was one such girl. She was so caught up in the excitement of her surroundings that she had almost forgotten how nervous she had been earlier. Well, almost. But not quite. Which was weird. Normally people would be more nervous, not less so, when exploring an underground crypt in the fabled Suicide Forest. Especially when searching for the signs of undead zombies or black mages.

I guess some people just like the macabre.

The girls had stumbled upon the entrance to this underground catacomb almost by accident. Truth be told they weren't even all too sure that this underground structure was even a crypt. The entrance had been little more than a heavy cast iron manhole cover. But a potential underground crypt sounded cooler *(and more impressive!)* than a potential underground sewage system. It invoked more interesting ideas and imagery and would tell a better story.

The entrance had been hidden under a lifetime of dirt and grime that had fallen from the imposing overhanging trees. Either by the passing of time or by the deliberate hand of man as an attempt to hide what lay beneath. This entrance had led them to an underpass of dimly lit circular stone hallways and tunnels. The ground was slippery and cracked. On more than one occasion Kiko had stumbled and almost slipped. *Kara was doing fine, thanks for asking.* The walls felt like they may have once been ornate, but if they had been it was a long time ago. An untold duration of neglect had left them overwhelmed by the returning onset of nature. A series of roots from the forest had ruptured through the ceiling, like a series of vultures' talons puncturing through the rotten earthy flesh. *Nature was bleeding in.* Reclaiming the lost lands of man.

A sinister coldness nipped at the bone and dug into the skin. The occasional drip of earthy water dropped down onto them. Each drop of trickling dirt made Kiko even more aware of how much she detested being down here. *Why did creepy people always hang out in creepy places?* I mean it was only like eighty miles to Tokyo. Why did none of these creeps ever go to a spa, national garden or quaint little local market? *Maybe catch a movie and a dinner somewhere nice?* Why did they always go to places that smelt like stale mould and regret?

One clear thing was that someone had been here recently. Whoever it was had lit a series of sconces that clung to the walls as they passed through. These torches cut through the dank sapphire light. Hopefully, they would also lead them to whoever lay within. Hopefully whoever lay within was who they were looking for. Otherwise, the encounter that was about to follow would be awkward for everyone involved. Worst case scenario was that the girls may be about to jump out on some underground groundskeeper. Some poor maintenance guy just doing his job. It feels weird addressing a maintenance worker as a worst-case scenario when compared to necromancers. This isn't a dig at maintenance workers, because the truth of the matter was that the actual worst-case scenario was that an innocent may get hurt. *Or even killed.* And who would want to cause harm to an innocent bystander?

The terrible time Kiko was having was amplified as a throng of ravens erupted in flight around the scouting girls from down within the dark tunnel beyond. A frantic flurried fog of feathers and an outbreak of blustery beaks. Somewhere within the heart of this wave of wings and tide of caws, Kiko was a shrieking, cowering ball. Hunched over in a fetal position. This urge to stop and drop was counterintuitive when compared to Kara's far superior attempt to avoid the influx of spontaneous birds. Kara had chosen to pin herself flat against the right wall and use a torch as a natural shield.

The ravens had no interest in being burned, so left her alone. It took a few seconds for the ravens to pass. Afterwards, Kara almost looked cool with her newfound torch. *Like an old tomb-raider or archaeologist from an old eighties film.* All she needed was a cool hat to complete the look. On the other hand, Kiko looked like a cowering mess of windswept, messy red hair and scratches.

"Shut up." Kiko said as she 'allowed' Kara to help her up.

"I didn't say anything!" Kara replied with a faked tone of confusion.

"I hate you." Kiko hoaxed as she tried straightening her hair unsuccessfully.

"No, you don't." A smile broke across Kara's face. "You're just *egging* me on."

"Don't!"

"I think today is going im-*peck*-ably well!"

"Stop it!" With that, Kiko stormed off.

"Oh come on, it's my first day on the job Kiko. I'm just *winging* it!" Kara shouted after her affronted friend.

There was something about being underground that made people forget all sense of scale. It was easy to get turned around or lost in the dark and lose track of the distance travelled. The taunting bird jokes had continued for some time. For Kiko, this had made the time spent travelling together feel longer, as she was doing it with the worlds *worst* jester. For Kara, this was going fairly quickly because she was hilarious and having a great time.

Kiko was also currently distracted as she remembered the first time she had ever seen a reanimated corpse. *She had been the ripe old age of ten.* This walking bag of rotten flesh and wriggling worms had just ambled up into her back garden. It had done so with a similar lack of care as a person would have expected to witness from a neighbour's cat. This zombie had seemed completely oblivious to everything and uninterested in all other life as it had repeatedly walked up to and bounced off the Attetson's garden fence. Attention had been brought to this bumbling corpse as Kiko's terrified scream cut through the house. Kiko had to sleep with the light on for two years after what she had witnessed that day.

It was exactly eight minutes and thirty-two seconds later when the girls had discovered a great chamber within this underground labyrinth. This chamber was far larger than any of the rooms or tunnels that they had seen so far. A great number of candles lit up and encircled a series of pillars that held up a crumbling old roof. This failing roof had been supported in places by these cracked wooden scaffolding and splintered structures that seemed to buckle under the great weight of the forest above. A bassy hum of chanting men echoed through the confined darkness. These two men wore red robes and pretentious white masks. These robes hid almost their entire figure beneath them. These robes were also weirdly rather clean when you considered the unclean surroundings.

Necromancy had a strange place within the pantheon of the other arcane schools. Whereas the rest had evolved into magical actions of maximised efficiency. Of substance over style. Necromancy had seemed to go a different way entirely. It seemed like it was all about the style. *To look cool.* It was unclear if it was due to the kind of people that the necrotic arts attracted or if it was some intrinsic part of the whole routine, but Necromancy was always somewhat showy. Casting rituals were always ornate and elaborate. Robes and other clothing were always picked with a needlepoint accuracy to exuberate their appearance. Despite the grotesque nature of the casting school, they always look good doing it. Okay, well they didn't look '*good.*' They looked evil. *But they dressed well for it.*

The floor of this room was stained a deep blood red. Two hollowed out and gutted wolves lay to the side. From behind the brazier where the two girls hid they could also see a sizeable pile of bones and skulls. Like a junkyard for the abandoned dead. Disregarded waste with no more value left. Disposed of with about as much care as dirt swept aside with a dustpan and brush.

An arrow of pure light pierced the altar of bones and skulls that stood between the two hooded figures.

Kiko glanced over to Kara just in time to see a similar bow of pure light disappear. They had travelled this far. If patience was a virtue then Kara was virtually lacking in it. Besides, what could possibly be gained by waiting any longer? They were here now, so they might as well just get on with it.

"You're under arrest!" Kara barked into the room with a glistening authority.

...

"You're under arrest...?" Kiko questioned with a blistered, hissing bewilderment and perplexed disbelief.

She then watched as a skull of pure fire smacked against her over-ambitious, Half-Elven friend.

She watched as Kara was raised off her feet.

She watched as Kara crumpled through a wooden support and collapsed under the debris of splintered planks and tumbling rocks.

The hands of fear clasped at Kiko's heart. She watched for an eternity as the nails of disbelief, horror and dread sunk in. Why wasn't Kara getting up?

Get up!

GET UP!

"Ow..." Kara groaned to herself. "That... sucked!"

As Kara returned to her feet she noticed a blue light. This light was being cast from an ornate energy shield Kiko had conjured. This shield was taking a considerable beating from a horrifically painful-looking barrage of spells.

"Under arrest?" Kiko questioned for a second time. She had rather sounded like a hissing cat.

"Okay... Alright... My bad..." Kara said gasping for breath. "What's the plan?"

The plan had been to listen and wait for an opening. But when did a plan ever go to plan? *If plan A was so good, then why did everyone need a plan B, C and D?*

"The Demon mother shall rise again!" One of the hooded men shouted at the two girls. The only problem with this was they couldn't actually hear him over the cracking of dark spells clashing against the mystical barrier. It was like when someone tried speaking to you when you're walking past a construction site or at a really loud music venue.

"Is he saying something?" Kara asked Kiko in a state of deafened confusion.

"The Demon mother shall rise where the Angels lie!"

"What?" Kara asked a second time to a shrugging Kiko. Whatever it was it probably wasn't important.

The chamber ahead seemed to have a load-bearing support column in the centre of it. This semi-wood-semi-rock support looked as if it was struggling under the weight of the bowing ceiling. Kiko surmised that one good hit was all it would take for the whole thing tumbling down.

"...and she will blot out the sun. She will rip all love and hope from the hearts of man. She..." The masked necromancer was still going, not stopping for breath. There was one thing that would finally make him shut up though. For a split second, the sensational illuminations of Kiko's shield disappeared as another singular bright arrow pierced into the central column.

I'd safely imagine that almost everyone reading this has experienced being caught in a hailstorm at least once in their lives. For anyone who hasn't, imagine trying to get home after a stressful, busy day. Imagine walking down your street. *Easy right?* Now imagine walking down this street as someone was following you around and pelting hundreds of little rocks of ice at the back of your head. Constantly. Relentlessly. This is what a hailstorm is like. If you can imagine or recall the feel of a hailstorm, then imagine that instead of hundreds of tiny pellets of ice that this hailstorm was bombarding you with was actually a flurry of rocks and boulders the size of your face.

Imagine seeing a ceiling collapse around you as you stood beneath it.

If you can imagine such a thing then you could probably also begin to understand the look of fear in both of these necromancers' eyes as the roof of this chamber came tumbling and crashing around them. You would probably also understand why they had chosen to run away. *To be fair, you'd probably do the same too.*

A red flash erupted from them as they fled.

A rotten hand burst through the soil as a corpse dragged itself back into existence. Another two corpses followed suit. These three walking-dead looked archaic and ancient. The smell of putrid rotten flesh filled the air and invaded the lungs. These bloodless, tattered bodies slumped under the weight of rusted and flaking samurai armours. All dragging equally corroded and dilapidated katanas in the dirt behind them as they lifelessly ambled along. These decaying constructs were all attired with round metal conical hats. *(Otherwise known as rice picker hats.)* All three hats were cracked and aged. These hats secreted their faces under a deep shadow; the lights from the braziers and torches were insufficient in lighting them fully. The centremost zombie's hat was adorned with a jewel-eyed dragon on the very top of it. This metal dragon's tail ran down the side and formed the very brim of the hat itself. To make things easier, we'll call this Feudal Japanese zombie '*Central.*'

The zombie to the left of him had a giant crack down the side of his hat which caused the side of its skeletal face to be lit up like a bolt of lightning on a clear, dead night sky. We'll call this one '*Lefty*!'

The undead to the right of him wore a Men-Yoroi mask. This full-faced, bronze mask depicted a demonic face with two big black pointy horns and two big black pointy teeth. The ironic thing was that the face that now lay behind this mask was probably a thousand times more horrific than the mask itself. Unsurprisingly, we'll call him '*Righty.*'

Kiko wasn't much in the way of a fighter. You never really got the chance to work on your muscles by carrying books all day. *Not even the really heavy ones.* However, Kara was a fighter. As part of the De'Carusso upbringing Kara had been raised to be as cold and brutal as possible. Whereas Kiko was the thinker, Kara was the warrior. This was why the Bureau of

Necrological Investigations had wanted to recruit her. As such she had met Lefty pretty much straight on in battle with unwavering intent.

Two axes were summoned to her in a cloud of purple smoke. Both axes were that of a steely metal carved into the shape of howling wolf heads. From within these open jaws protruded the actual axe blades themselves. The tops of the heads fused into the haft and ran down it in a circular pattern reminiscent of a spinal column. With a terrible clash of metal-on-metal these axes had been caught by the long blade of Lefty's sword. He had blocked a series of blows in quick procession. *Son of a bitch, that was annoying!* Despite being dead for half of a millennium he was still pretty quick on his feet. So she decided to do something he would probably not expect. In all likelihood, Lefty hadn't expected it because the reality of the situation was kind of gross. *Like really gross.* With a step to her left, she pushed her whole body weight into headbutting him as hard as she could right between the eyes.

Lefty's head snapped back and popped all over her. Like the world's worst champagne; all lumpy, rotten and slimy. Think rotten pickled eggs and decaying fish. Think of a thick red jam, Kara's green eyes shone out like emeralds from amongst all that red. Zombie dust, brains and bodily goos were many things. But as it turned out, flattering was not one of them. *They also smelled really bad.* Like a blue cheese soaked in vinegar on a hot day. *Like blue cheese soaked in vinegar on a hot day in a junk-yard across the road from a zoo that only housed skunks.* I'm not entirely sure if it was determination or adrenaline that had stopped Kara from just vomiting up every meal she had ever eaten in her entire life. Maybe she just had a really strong stomach for this kind of thing. Or maybe she was just really gross.

Kiko ducked and zipped around Kara as a red ribbony light she summoned awkwardly deflected the blows from both the Righty and Central undead. This light quickly found itself wrapping around Righty's leg and trying to hold it down in place. I say '*try*' because Righty was basically being held together by nothing more than pure determination and will at this point, and the strength required to hold his leg down was something much stronger than the leg could realistically take. *So it simply popped off.* This caused him to fall straight down with about as much elegance and grace as you'd expect from a five-hundred-year-old zombie with one leg. *(This being not a lot!)* This lack of grace was not helped by Kara, who upon seeing an opening cracked her axe straight into his falling jaw. Cleaving his whole face into two pieces.

Central, otherwise known as the last remaining zombie, grabbed Kiko by her red hair and flung her to the ground. Kiko felt herself let out a feeble yelp as her body cracked against the cold hard ground. She had fully expected the fall to have been quickly followed by swift stabbing pains, but weirdly nothing had happened.

There was a loud snapping sound as Kara grabbed the zombie's hand, breaking two of his bony fingers as she did so. Before he could do anything about it she had kicked out his leg from beneath him. As he fell Kara had cracked his head upwards against one of the support beams as he ricocheted away from the force of her rising knee. When he had tried to rise again she had gone to kick him once more and accidentally stomped clean through his chest... *Shit!* She felt the terrible shudder of his snapping and splintering rib cage travel up the muscles of her leg. *(If you can, try recalling the sensation of how it felt when you stepped on a snail. That distinct sound and feel of its shell cracking underfoot. Now try multiplying that sensation by a thousand, it still wouldn't even come close to how this felt.)* Her foot had broken through his torso, yet he was still trying to rise once more. Her leg was now stuck!

The sight of this careless and coldly determined cadaver slowly trying to pull himself up her leg, completely unphased by the gaping hole she had made in his ribcage, freaked Kara out with a fear that froze her into a complete standstill. In her panic, she had tried to free herself from her undead foot trap. Her failure to succeed had made her lose her balance and she fell, face to face with a mouth of snapping undead teeth. Kiko erupted a fireball erupted over the face of the last zombie, washing away any remaining rotten facial features under a wave of heated flames. The zombie fell silent as Kara jabbed a nearby flag pole through its eye socket, seemingly out of spite or revenge.

"*Shit!*" Kara turned on the spot as a moment of realisation sunk in around her and chased after the two retreating necromancers down the stone corridors. Kiko chased after her. This had better not affect Kara getting her dream job! The drum beats of adrenaline pounded in her ears and pain gripped into her muscles. But she wasn't ever about to stop running. Not now. Not ever.

About a minute had passed for these two girls as they followed the trail of the two no-good doers by the time they had stumbled back upon them. However, much to both of their surprise, they had not found them quite as how they had expected. *They were laying unconscious at the feet of a very familiar, very perfect gentleman.*

Vincent Attetson. *The golden child.*

"Ah! Girls. So nice you could join us!" He said patronisingly as a big smile broke across his face and he opened his arms towards them.

Kiko felt a pang of confusion upon seeing her bother down here. *Why was he here?* What possible reason could he have for being in the Aokigahara? *Had he been keeping tabs on them?* If so that was extremely patronising! She wasn't a child and certainly did not need babysitting. A deep-seated whittling rage quivered at her heart. She had a lot to say about this intrusion, yet she said nothing.

"Kiko, are you alright? You know I worry about you?" He grabbed Kiko around the arms, catching her mid-fall as she suddenly gave way. Out of nowhere, the room had begun to spin as a feeling of light-headed dizziness swept over her. The adrenaline of fighting zombies had faded and faded fast, withering like a flower in the winter. Leaving in its wake a rush of tiredness and discomfort. It was probably for the best Vincent had turned up when he had, she was doubtful of how much use she would have been in a second fight. It was strange. These waves of exhaustion always came out of the blue. Like a surprising punch to the gut that knocked the wind clean out of her without any warning at all.

"They were mine!" Kara snarled, pointing to the two men who lay unconscious on the ground.

"Clearly not?" Vincent's smile dissolved into a frown of derision. "I know you want to play the part of some bad-ass hero. I know you have so much to prove to the world, Kara." He pointed towards Kara as if she could somehow be unaware that she was speaking to him. "But next time you go running into a fight with the undead with your stupid axes, can you please try and not get my sister killed?"

"Killed?" Kiko chirped. "I'm fine! What are y..."

"Yes, you are." Another smile broke across his face. "Thanks to me..."

"Thanks to you?" Kiko snapped back as the deep-seated rage returned once more. Who the hell did he think he was speaking to? A clapping broke across the chamber as Collin had appeared from the darkness.

"Stop antagonising your sister." He gave a patronising sigh to Vincent. "I really do worry one day she might teleport you to the archean aeon and leave you there." He winked to his daughter jokingly. "And as for you, Kara..."

Kara froze as she awaited the result of her evaluation.

Chapter Five

MARVIN'S

As a general rule of thumb, worlds rarely revolved around two people. And this world was no exception. *Yes, it took two to tango, sure, but it always took several more people to make life really worth living.* The concept of a world not revolving around two people may also be obvious to any narcissists out there, but I fear that might admittedly be for the wrong reason. See, the world also doesn't revolve around one person. *Sorry to any narcissists I may shock with this revelation.*

Hopefully, by now you have a fair understanding of what Kiko and Kara are like as people. So this feels like a good time to segue into a breakdown of this Earth they called home. Of how a single planet can be home to so many different races that cohabited together in relative peace. Where each one of these races originally came from and the events of history that defined them. If for no other reason than to help you understand the role that these two (*Kiko and Kara!*) played in their world just a little bit better. No one is an island, alone at sea. Even if we don't like to admit it, we all absorb tiny bits of the world around us and reflect it back to the world in our personalities and personas. We define who we are based on how we all subjectively experience life. *In this way, the world becomes a part of us and we become a part of the world we live in.*

The easiest of the races to start with were the Dwarves. The thirteenth Earth had three great mountains were spread out all over the world, Thrúll, Thrów and Thren. These three mountains were home to the original ancient Dwarves of old. Thrúll was in Australia, Thrów was African and Thren lay between China and Russia. Although being entirely separate entities, they all evolved in an almost identical manner. Either history loved to repeat itself, or the Dwarves were very simplistic and predictable. *(I'll let you decide which one of these it is for yourselves!)* Each of these three mountains had a secondary, now extinct, species living on them. The avian humanoids known as the Alkonost. In all three versions of history, the Alkonost were said to have shared a mutually beneficial relationship with the Dwarves. Their mountains were seen as paradises of great wealth. The Alkonost defended these great mountains from any airborne threats and the Dwarves defended the mountains from underground menaces. This had allowed these two species to coexist, right up until all three versions of the ancient Dwarves befell hardship. In all three societies the Dwarves became the victims of bad luck. *Cold winters, famines etc.* When faced with their struggles each of these races of Dwarf marched up to the top of their respective mountains and ate the Alkonost or enslaved them. No one was quite sure whether or not this counted as an act of cannibalism or not. However, their meat was said to be so tender and tasty that it would drive you mad from just a single bite. That's all. Just one. It was reported that these dwarves were fuelled by an immense state of something not too dissimilar to blood lust after eating the Alkonost meat. Some even locked themselves away and refused to eat any other type of food until dying of starvation. However, this did mean that almost all traces of the Alkonost were either destroyed or consumed by around 200 BC. *So, well to the done Dwarves!*

Seeing how badly these Dwarves had treated the Alkonost, and how they'd driven the Alkonost into extinction, the other species and races of the Earth decided that it was probably best to never trust a Dwarf. And time and time again, the Dwarves proved them right for choosing to do so. Nowadays it's very rare to see a Dwarf in any position of power or authority. Especially if it meant them having superiority over anyone who wasn't in themselves a Dwarf.

The Orcs had a rather unique place within the rosters of life. That is if you considered the world *'unique'* interchangeable with the words *'brutally aggressive and utterly terrifying.'* These tall brutes had a *'special'* origin. Most people assumed Greenland to be named after grass. However this was not the case. Anyone who has been to Greenland knows there's more ice than grass to be found there. It was originally named the Land of the Green, owing to the green-skinned creatures that lived there. These Orcs were short on temper but high on testosterone, which rarely ended well for anyone who fancied popping by for a visit. *Things really did not end well for the tenth-century European settlers who thought they had found a new place to call home in Greenland.* All they had found here was an extremely territorial barrage of green giants who didn't much care for sharing. When these settlers fled (*Because why wouldn't you run away from Orcs?*) they had unwittingly brought back whole armies of Orcs that had clung to the outsides of their ships for the hundreds of miles, as they fled back to their original homes of assumed safety. *Orcs were the only recorded species that had ever invaded the lands of those who had sought to invade theirs.* It took almost two hundred years for the Orcs to accept they had been discovered by everyone else and that they should probably share their toys with the other kids, so to speak. During this time they had fought with everything that had a pulse. Even occasionally fighting things without one as well. *Never anger an Orc.*

Perhaps the most dominant species (*besides for all the humans kicking about the place!*) were the noble Elves. The extremely proud, elegant and beautiful Elves. The also extremely rich, snobbish and elitist Elves. It was originally said that they spawned from great forests that had once spanned over all of Europe and parts of the Asian continent. The intellect and cunning of the Elves usually resulted in them coming out on top in all of their dealings with the other races. That combined with their cunning, guile and knack for leadership had aided Europe into becoming the capital of the world's trade for well over a millennia.

On this Earth, Christopher Columbus's had discovered America, much like on our own Earth. However, this world's bloodshed wasn't quite so clear cut as it was on our Earth. As it turns out a secondary race of Elves had dwelled deep within the trees of the Amazon forest and, like the Orcs, they didn't take kindly to the idea of random people just turning up and saying '*See this? This is mine now; I've just decided so.*' Things did not go well for the European settlers when they had chosen to provoke these feral Woodland Elves. Here on this world, Thanks Giving Day was actually in celebration of the day that these Wood-Elves had decided to stop hunting and killing the settlers. A celebration and an act of gratitude for the fact that these new Elves had eventually allowed these settlers to stay. That by the mercy of whatever gods these Wood-Elves believed in, they had simply decided to just stop killing everyone all the time. Even though this ferocity had been a testament to Elven supremacy, it apparently didn't count for much of anything. Not according to the original Elves of Europe, who had hated their Amazonian counterparts. Because despite being completely Elven in their own right, these new Wood-Elves were not the *'correct'* type of Elf. So it didn't count. Think upon it kind of like a bitter mother in-law, no one was quite good enough when compared to their own special little Elven heritage.

Humans had spread like wildfire across this globe, much as we have on our own world. However, these humans had brought another variant along with them. If humans were to be considered a proud noble steed, Halflings were like a stumpy little off-breed of Shetland pony. *Just plodding along.* Plodding, and usually eating. These Halflings were said to have originated in Eastern Europe. But truth was, a Halfling was just the result of a Human living in a state of indefinite existential poverty for too long. Generations upon generations of malnourishment and poor living conditions had resulted in these once human-beings now being considerably shorter, stumpier and more robust. As a result, they were a fairly common sight. After all, poverty is far more common than wealth. It was almost (*but not quite*) as common as that one woman who always insists she's being 'naughty' every time she fails a diet or that one guy who always tries to be one better than you. *You could probably think of an example of one such guy, but I could think of two.*

It mattered not what race or creed you were on this planet. Much like on our own the only way you'd survive to the finishing line was based on who you knew. Friendship was a great and powerful thing when done right. If any two friends were to stop and think about just exactly how many other people there are on the planet; they might just begin to realise how unlikely it was that they had ever met in the first place. It was even more of a miracle that they had found enough in common to warrant being aware of each other enough to call each other *'friends.'*

The strongest friendships were usually forged by one of two things. The first being a figurative *'drawing of swords together'* against a shared enemy or adversary. Some shared obstacle or menace that had to be overcome. Some *'thing'* that needed to be defeated. And by fighting together against this common enemy, lifelong allies would be made. This enemy varied from friendship to friendship. You could be a soldier at war. It could be a person you and a friend shared a hatred of. It could be a boss that no one likes. It could even be a place or time, like a dreaded shift at work that you would have to unite over to overcome or even a shared destain for a subject or teacher at school. But in all possible scenarios there needed to be a shared cause. Some '*thing*' so horrible that it inadvertently brought the people together as one when it was defeated.

The second way to make friends was considerably easier. Food.

Everyone loved to eat food, however not all food. It was said that you don't make friends with salad. (*Unless you're a vegan...*) There is a secret rule that the best types of food to make someone like you was either sweet and sugary or full of carbs. *(Bonus points if it was in any way alcoholic, if you were past a certain age.)* These were literal recipes for success. If in doubt just stick to pizzas and beer. *(Or if you're too young for beer, drink something else!)*

And here we now find ourselves returning to Kiko and Kara. They were on their way to celebrate a job well done. Well, well done enough to be deemed as a success. Admittedly Vincent had flown in at the last second and reaped all the rewards that were available from the Arcane Intelligence Agency. After all, capturing the culprits was a far more important feat than killing a couple of zombies. However, killing them had been deemed enough of a success to warrant a certain De'Carusso finding herself with a certain dream job. The girls had chosen to celebrate this victory the way most friends usually celebrate. *They were going to stuff their faces with food.*

Liarath was a fairly sleepy town. It was small and it was quaint, but not necessarily in a bad way. Some people preferred those sorts of places. As I said before, the world becomes a part of us and we become a part of it. In this way, Liarath was as much a part of Kiko as she was a part of the town. Down off of the centre square, under the old oak tree was where she had shared her first awkward, sweaty kiss with the head of the local chess team, James Buckland, when she was fourteen years old. It had been a very cumbersome and inelegant affair for all involved. They had both been wearing braces at the time which had gotten stuck and intertwined on each other. *I'm told it was extremely embarrassing for both of them.* Kiko had actually met Kara at a local magical gathering at the Town Hall when she was eight years old. They had initially fallen out over extremely contrasting views about something long since forgotten. But when Kiko had stormed off and gotten her hair stuck, trapped in the chain-link of a swing set, Kara had been the first to come to help her. The rest was history, as they say. In their teenage years, they had hung out in alleyways and parks with similarly minded friends. For Kara, this served as an escape from her family, likewise, although for extremely different reasons, the same had been true for Kiko. One such park, Loch Monumen, was where Kiko had gotten drunk for the first time. In fact, Kiko had gotten so drunk she had fallen into the loch. *(And for anyone unsure of what a loch is, try saying 'lake' with a Scottish accent.)*

But there was one place that the girls loved to visit the most when they were in Liarath. A cafe that went by the name of '*Marvin's.*' Marvin's was a fairly charming little place. It was relativity small, but in a way that gave it a loveable rustic feel rather than a cramped or tight one. A big part of Marvin's appeal was in no small way thanks to Marvin himself. Even if he wasn't human, and I don't mean that in a way that would suggest him to be an Elf, a Dwarf or any other creature that you might be expecting. But I'll get to him later, for anyone that's interested.

Kiko's interest in this cafe was in no small way due to the tall, dark-haired and mysterious waiter who worked there. For Kara, this interest was in no small way helped by her repeatedly having seen Kiko do her best, unintentionally hilarious, impression of a tomato every time she had tried to speak to the tall, dark and handsome waiter. *(For anyone unaware of how exactly you impersonate a tomato, it's fairly simple. All you have to do is turn bright red and not be able to say anything. For extra credit, you even could try getting tongue-tied and lost for words whilst you stare at the floor.)*

On this day, as the girls made their way to Marvin's Cafe, Kiko had seen a person. Which in itself isn't an unusual occurrence, I'll gladly accept that. A tall, fairly happy-looking person. A big, fairly happy old person who was currently waving frantically at her. Which was strange, because Kiko didn't recognise her. Running off an instinct of not wishing to be rude or insulting, Kiko found herself impulsively waving back to the kind stranger. Kara gave a confused look to her friend before a secondary person emerged from behind Kiko and greeted the old person with open arms. Kiko froze as a wave of embarrassment washed over her. She glanced sideways hoping her friend hadn't seen what she had just done. Kara had. *Oh boy, she definitely had.*

"*You're such a dork!*" Kara said under a playful laugh, shaking her head in a mischievously mocking manner as she grabbed her friend by the arm and dragged her inside the cafe.

And there he was. One of the few people who could make Kiko forget how to speak entirely. The tall man who stood behind the counter, serving food to the customers, owned this whole place. This cafe served just about the best food you could ever imagine eating. However, Marvin's wasn't named after the man who owned it. As I said before this cafe was named after another curious creature that worked here. This being the eight-limbed octopus, Marvin, who was currently chilling out on Samuel Turner's shoulder. Samuel being the waiter who had commonly caused Kiko's social awkwardness to flourish like a well-aged wine. The strange thing about Marvin, despite the elephant in the room of him being an octopus with a job, was that it was unclear if he was actually magical or not. Not every creature needed to be endowed with magic to be special or noteworthy; being special was an attribute not defined by you as an individual, but rather by contrasting you against your surroundings. *Trust me, there was a plenitude of boring wizards out there.*

Octopuses were a weirdly intelligent species. They were also weirdly in tune with their surroundings. Anyone who has ever owned or worked near one would agree with me. If an octopus is unhappy with you, he'll let you know. *They're not famous for being shy!* There have been countless reports of Octopuses refusing to eat fish that they had believed to have been off. Whereas a cat or dog will meow or bark at you, an octopus will remove itself from its tank, grab the offending fish and throw it back at you. *Like a celebrity diva that was angered that you had brought her fizzy bottled water instead of still water.* Likewise, there was once an octopus, in an aquarium, that had learned all of the guards' night-time patrols. Down to the finest second. This eight-legged poacher had learned all of their routines. As such he had fancied himself as something of a cat-burglar *(Or a cat-opus burglar, if you're inclined to being hilarious!)* and broke an entry into his neighbouring tanks. The aquarium had no idea why all of their fish had begun to go missing. But over time they had noticed a pattern. All the missing fish had been within the vantage point of this hungry boy's tank. Upon reviewing the CCTV footage they saw the octopus patiently waiting for the first guard to pass on by, open the lid to his tank and quietly slide across the floor, like a sloppy spider rag of the sea. After waiting for the second guard to pass, he opened the desired tank and dropped in to have a late-night fishy snack. *(Like you when you raid the fridge at two am!)* He would then wait for other guards to pass again before closing the tank lid behind him, sliding back across the floor and going back to bed.

Even weirder than this was the story of an Australian octopus who was said to have been able to predict football results with an astonishing degree of accuracy. His name was Paul. In exchange for correctly calculating the game's result, Paul was offered food as a reward. He liked being rewarded so kept getting the results right.

Samuel, being fully aware of the powers of the octopus, had decided to use it as a gimmick that worked in both of their favours. Like Paul, Marvin worked for food. Using his intuitiveness to predict what meals potential customers would want without them having to say anything. If Marvin predicted correctly, or had a happy customer, he was tipped with a fish for a job well done. Needless to say, people were eager to test his instinctive prowess. To witness first hand if this was eight-limbed soothsayer was really able to win over the hearts of their taste-buds and stomachs alike. To be fair to Marvin, he faired fairly well. *There was a valuable life lesson buried in here somewhere.* Any young lads who were interested in winning the favour of the fairer sex, people were only ever really interested in good food. Keep a person well fed and they'd like you more. As such, business was relatively booming, thanks to the instincts of this intuitive Cephalopoda.

Marvin had deduced Kara was in the need of finely poached eggs on an avocado & feta based toast, with a freshly roasted pumpkin spiced latte. Kiko, on the other hand, was apparently in need of carrot cake and a giant, creamy strawberry milkshake. Both seemed happy with the choices made for them, like they always did, so Marvin received two lots of fish.

The girls had found themselves sitting at a table with two of their friends in this picturesque diner. One friend was a young man who went by the name Osiris Kelley. Osiris was consistently happy and commonly effervescent. A happy joker who rarely went by the name Osiris. For some reason, he preferred to be called Ozzy. Perhaps because it was quicker and easier to say, or maybe because Osiris was a terribly ornate name that people rarely went by anymore. *(My apologies to anyone by the name of Osiris that I may have just offended!)*

There was also a key aspect of his appearance that social normalcy dictates that I have to specify. He was a person of colour. As much as this may be of intrinsic importance to some people out there, this will be the only time that I mention anyone's skin colour. I'll also rarely mention things like height, sexual orientation or favourite television show. *Any reader anywhere in the world is welcome to interpret or visualise any character any way they like.* In fact I encourage it. However you choose to interpret a character neither validates or invalidates their true nature or their story. Truth be told, sometimes over describing a character robs the reader of their power and creative licenses. Like whenever a book gets made into a movie and ultimately gets it all wrong. Casting a certain actor can ruin the image of a character for millions of people across the world. Casting the wrong actor can even lead to mass protests and complaints.

Next to Ozzy sat Penelope. A pink-haired Halfling girl. Penelope was an obnoxious person with a repellent outlook on life. Kiko had found her brattish and rude. Penelope fancied herself a punk, although this was most likely only until the next bigger, cooler fashion scene came along. *Penelope was so rude and spoiled she barely deserved the time it took to describe her.* Everything she owned had been bought for her. At the age of twenty-four, she had never worked a single day of her life, yet went out of her way to throw shade at how other people, especially anyone in a low paying job, worked around her. In the two years of Marvin's diner being here, she had been the only person to complain. Not about the food, she had never actually eaten any, but rather about the lack of hygiene of allowing a '*squid*' to have a job. *Now I think about it, maybe I just don't like Penelope because she had been rude about Marvin.* But then again, you shouldn't belittle or insult someone who was trying their best to better themselves. Even if they are an eight-limbed water dweller. Everyone was just trying to survive.

And that was the kind of person Penelope was. The kind who gossiped about everyone and everything. *(If you find yourself sat at a table of friends, and every time a person leaves, they talk about that person; you do realise they do the exact same thing about you when you leave, right?)*

Kara produced a red bag as if from nowhere as she sat down. Now there was always something special that occurred whenever an author or writer mentioned something as being red. For some unknown reason, all English Literature teachers were unable to accept that something could ever just happen to have coincidentally have been the colour red. Red, for some reason, always had to represent some rage or angst from the characters past or twisted torment in their future. *Some anger or hatred.* A colour based indication of malcontent. However, when most writers say something is red it usually has little more connotation to it than it being the colour that the item was. There's usually little more to it than that. This isn't to say over-reading into a subtext was inherently a bad thing. In fact it was usually welcomed with open arms. Not only as it allowed a writer to write less, but it also invited the reader to engage with the content more thoroughly. To really think about what was happening. *Why do you think Kara chose a red bag?*

As much as Kara would like the idea of people assuming this bag was a subliminal message to how angry she was, or if it was foreshadowing a future event. Unfortunately, the truth was a lot less grandiose. There was no ulterior motive on the day she had happened across this bag in the shops. The truth of the matter was, rather embarrassingly, it had matched her socks she had been wearing that day. That's all. *(An English Literature teacher might insist that the red of her socks were a metaphor for her secret pain and hidden rage, and you know what? I might actually agree with them. Who really understands what the hell goes through the mind of a person when they buy socks?)*

From this red bag, which totally represented all the hidden rages and angst of the universe, she produced a purse. It wasn't red. *Sorry Literature Teachers.*

The schools of magic were split up into several schools. You've already been exposed to Necromancy, so I guess I should inform you of the others. The Arcane Elements were the foundations of most of the damage based spells. All of the Arcane Elements were said to have been gifted to the universe by a great and ancient series of gods at the dawn of the universe. The fire giant Surtr had gifted us with fire. Shiva, the ice queen, had obviously given us ice. Most people knew Thor had given us thunder and electricity. Gaia had given us the druid-crafts and all magics to do with the Earth. Posiedon had taught of the secrets of the sea and the waters.

Legends spoke of the gift of magic being given to the people to help fight back against a terrible darkness. This of course meant the Demons and other monsters. After a great Angel had betrayed the gods and bled evil into their worlds. But that's a story for another time.

Inti, the god of light, had led to the rise of restoration based magics. Like the rising sun, light always found a way to bring life. Titanius Maximillia was the first mage said to have discovered how to wield the light to help his fallen brothers. Loki, the trickster had given us alteration based magics. The power to change our appearances or how others thought. Both acts being incredibly useful and powerful when used at the right time.

There may be some who believed that in a universe of magic that it would be the utmost form of power. This however was not the case. It was universally, or rather multiversally understood, that money always seemed to find a way to creep to the top of every social ladder when it came to dictating importance. Power, in all its forms and manifestations, is always claimed and controlled. *In this way, magic was no different to money.* Strict rules and laws governed what you could and could not do with magic. You '*could*' provide the starving masses with magically summoned food, but this would mean a certain individual would go bankrupt. *Apparently, the wealth of one individual outranked the suffering of a thousand individuals.* So that simply meant that you were not allowed to do so.

So if you wanted food or any commercial luxury of life, you had to buy it. In this way, this universe was very similar to our own. Last Tuesday the girls had done one such food shop of their very own. Kiko had almost died from embarrassment when Kara had shouted at a slow elderly couple for standing in front of them for too long and blocking the carrying baskets for what had felt like an eternity. Both had grabbed their own baskets for shopping in. *(They do have some independence after all!)* Looking inside their baskets served as an interesting insight to them both. Kiko had stocked up on essential five-a-days and quirky foods of nutritional value. She had also seen about five books that had caught her interest, but alas only had space to carry three. *Even magical people had to make sacrifices from time to time.* After this self-sacrifice, Kiko had decided she deserved a strawberry smoothie. But there had been a small problem, there was only one left in stock! This singular smoothie was alone. By itself at the back of the highest shelf of a cold, double-doored fridge. Like I'd said earlier, Kiko deserved this smoothie. So she decided to climb the shelves to get it. *This was her mission now.* Nothing else mattered. Somehow, in the process of clumsily acquiring this fruity drink, she had also managed to '*twang*' both of her funny bones (*the bones in her elbows*) simultaneously on the glass doors of the fridge as they closed on her. Anyone who has caught their funny bone before knows how it feels.

Kara's basket had consisted of snacks, alcohol and an ungodly amount of burgers. Kara really liked burgers, a thing that her friends teased her over on several occasions. She was actually chowing down on one now back at

Marvin's. The eggs and avocado toast had apparently not been enough to quell the hunger of her celebrations of victory.

"I can't believe you're eating food made by that..." Penelope sneered as she indicated towards Marvin.

"I can't believe you're always here if you hate it so much..." Kiko caught Penelope in a death glare.

"Oh, Samuel?!" Penelope called over to the waiter. "I think Kiko has something to say!"

When Samuel had come over Kiko had found herself almost choking on a mouthful of her cake. Samuel had long black hair, steely blue eyes and a chiselled jawline like a stoic Greek statue. Not that Kiko was able to look at him in the face right now. She was too busy trying to dislodge carrot cake from her tonsils as her gaze became locked directly onto the tabletop.

"Oh, I'm so, so sorry Sammy. I'm clearly mistaken. She has nothing to say." Penelope sneered as she took a sip from her recently unsealed can of drink.

"Wow! Penelope that was a bit cold, man!" Ozzy said with a tone of a fake laugh as him and Kara shared a look of dismissive destain about Penelope. "So tell me, little miss Death Squad. Do you get a uniform?"

Kara glanced over to Kiko, who shook her head as if to say *'no'* as she dislodged cake from the back of her throat with her fingers.

And so these four friends sat for a few hours swapping stories and opinions about life. Penelope had nothing nice to say, so I won't waste my breath. Kara was discussing what her future employment may entail. *Oh, and hopefully it was obvious that she wasn't just sat here in public still soaked in zombie's guts.* She had cleaned and washed herself thoroughly. *Twice for good measure.* Those zombie parts were lost somewhere in the pipes and sewage of the world. Out of sight and out of mind. Ozzy had recently met a girl and was excitedly nervous about telling him how he felt, and I think we all know how that feels like. However, Kiko had added little in the way of interaction herself. She was too focused on why Vincent had been there in the Aokigahara. *Did he really have that little faith in her to get things done?* If this lack of trust wasn't bad enough, he had also stolen all the credit for the capture of the Necromancers and made the whole thing about himself. *Like he always did.* The smell of that underground chamber still hung in her mind and she swore she had seen a worm crawling through the eye of one of those undead samurai. Kiko also gave a concerned thought to how she always seemed to get light-headed and faint at the worst of times. How it always seemed to invalidate her and made her seem weak. *(Marvin had sensed her unease and was now staring right at her. Was she unhappy with her food? Would this mean no more fish?)* She didn't get it. One minute she was fine, the next she wasn't. Annoyingly, Vincent was always there to *'help.'* This only served to concrete the notion of her being a *'helpless victim'* and a *'damsel in distress.'* These weird power fluctuations always left her as quickly as they had arrived. She never knew if she was coming or going.

Coming or going...

Coming or going....

Come on we're going...

"Kiko? Come one. we're going..." Ozzy gave his ginger friend a quizzical look as he outstretched a hand to her.

Chapter Six

THE MAN WHO SPOKE TO GHOSTS

Evil is not natural. It's not born.
It's something forged.
Like a great weapon.

And that is exactly what I am.
I am a weapon.

I am decay and I am rot.

The Demons made me into this. This weapon.
Their weapon.
Their soldier.

This life is all I can remember. They took everything from me.
The Demons ripped me from my mother's arms.
They took me away from my home.
They killed my family. They broke my people.
Purged my entire planet.
They raised me as a weapon. Taught me to hate. Taught me to kill.
To kill for them.

As far as they're aware, that is all I am.
They think I am theirs.

The fools.

They took everything from me. Even my name.
I know I had a name once.
Even if I've forgotten the sound of it. I had one; once upon a long time ago.
But it is long lost to me, I cannot remember it.
I have not heard it on the lips of others for so long.

Oh, so, so long.

The people of the Arcane Intelligence Agency call me Llewelyn Daniels.

They think I am one of the faithful. An ever faithful and dutiful employee.
But that name is only as real as the life they believe 'Llewelyn' to live.
I am not one of their agents.

But I am a spell caster.

Or rather I was. Long long ago.
Oh how I long for the day that I can reveal my true self once more,
to have revenge on that pompous agency and all of its people.

That day will come.

It comes sooner than any of them even realise.

Those fools, in their agency, have no idea that
the dark side lies in wait for them.

The Demon forces have never been stronger.
The Arcane Intelligence Agency knows nothing.
They stand there, in the light, and think themselves better than the shadows.

But they do not know. They have no idea. None at all.
In their arrogance, they have found only blindness.

For she lives.

The demons wait for her.
She lives once more.

The great Demon Queen.
The Queen of the Damned.
The legion mother.

Lilith.

She has awoken.

And she calls for us all.
Even me.

I was once a tool for her great power. Long, so long ago.
Lilith presumes me her faithful lap dog.
But how could she?
How dare she? After everything that happened...
Her people took everything from me!

I do not mean my life from before, I care not for what could have been.
But once I had power. So much power, thanks to the Demons.
I had done everything asked of me. I played my
part; and what do you think they did?

The Demons betrayed me.

They cast me aside and abandoned me.
Like a whore in the morning time.
And why?

All over a singular and silly mistake. Such a small error.
One small lack of judgement was all it took for them to throw me out.
I had once been the queen's apprentice.

The Dark Hand, they called me.

Now I have nothing. Nothing!
And now they dare to call me?
Me!

*I have languished in the dark for a thousand years,
thinking of nothing but revenge against the Demons.
I thought of nothing but my return to power.*

*Evil is little more than a deeply routed will to survive, regardless of the cost.
And I am a survivor.
I am the greatest survivor of them all.*

*It has been so long, so long clinging to the dark.
But I am a survivor.
And I promise you I will survive in the chaos yet to unfold.*

*I will be the last survivor at any cost.
I cling to the shadows like a spider.
Lies are my only friend now.*

*I will rise once more. And it will be mine.
I will have it all.
Power.*

*My comeuppance against the Demons and the Agency alike.
Oh, how beautiful it will be!
Against the whole damned universe if it dares stand against me.*

Please make no mistake, I hate them with every fibre of my being.

*I will play both sides against each other.
Like a great game.
Oh, what fun!
What fun!*

*I'm ten steps ahead and no one else has even figured
out what game we are playing yet.*

*I have no fealty to either side. But there's no harm
in both of them believing that I do.
They both look down on me, the AIA and the demon-kind alike.*

But I know more than both of them.
I know what's coming.
A great war. The greatest war.

The Arcanium Wars.

I know of how the Angels shall be ripped from all of their
heavens and how the Demons will be torn from the fire.
Forced to fight in the great war. I will play them off against each other!
Both the Angels and the Demons will go to war and both will die.
But not me.

You don't know what's coming.
Oh, what fun!
What fun lies in store at the end of your pathetic planet.

Whilst both sides fall. Whilst they all die.
I will climb. I will rise.

I am the great survivor

Revenge.
It will be mine. I will have my revenge.

But for the war to start, I must play the part expected of me.
To be he who casts the first dice.

It's ironic, the greatest war of all time. Started by me, the Fallen soldier.
Gathering the other fallen soldiers.

It's almost poetic.

There is so much that the Arcane Intelligence Agency does not know.
So, so much; and not just about me.
It's this lack of knowledge from the AIA that brings me here.
To the bitterly cold Antarctic circle.

The 'non consenting spirits' are so pathetic. They truly hurt to look at.

*Where is their backbone?
Instead of fighting for what is rightly theirs, they accept having nothing.*

They accept being treated like nothing.

*Clinging to the dark and desolate places of the world
and calling it home. They make me sick!
What sort of self-respecting creature would choose
to willingly live all the way out here?*

In these forgotten communes. It's pitiful.

*I feel sick in my stomach as I look across this
barren tundra at their lousy camp.
Why do they even have camps? They never sleep, eat or feel tired.
They feel nothing!
Ever!*

*Perhaps that's why they're okay with being out here in all of this ice and
snow? They make me sick to my core in a way I never knew possible.*

*To be fair, I do empathise with these worthless worms a little.
But only a little...
I know how it feels. To be a dutiful soldier to your masters.*

*To serve a higher purpose. To be cast aside by those you fought to protect.
To be dropped and forgotten now that you have no further use.
To be an oh-so dutiful soldier to your masters!
We were all weapons for greater powers...*

*I thought myself of value, I was a fool. Just like them.
I was nothing more than a puppet wrapped in string.
But now my strings are cut. I am free.*

*I made that choice. Me! Upon my own merit!
They could have done the same!*

How could they all collectively accept such abandonment and exclusion?

Pathetic.

*But if I am to play my part for the unsuspecting Demon Queen,
then all of these dearest forgotten soldiers must first play theirs.*

After all, this is why I'm here, in this endless wintered dive.

*Did you know why this funny little breed of spirit is special, little one?
The Arcane Intelligence Agency does not. But I do.*

*Because their funny little species didn't get a choice in being ghosts.
Because the choice wasn't theirs, as the gates
of heaven and hell were closed.
Somehow they were allowed to keep their soul.*

*They never chose to be ghosts and prowl the Earth for eternity.
So they never actually had their souls taken from them.
You don't realise do you, the power of the soul?*

*But the Demons do, and they want it.
They want all that power for their great weapon.*

Something they believe can break time like an egg.

So that's why I've been summoned here.

*I am a hunter. They are the hunted.
They are filth. They are the forgotten. They are powerless.*

But that will soon change.

*I watch as my illusionary spell is lowered, revealing my metal arm.
In my metal hand is the Cube of Equinox.*

*A single contained moment of a black hole.
In the palm of my hand.*

*I feel all of their struggles, squirming against me as
I catch them all in my web of green light.
They are fighting the inevitable.*

As I look out across this wasteland of confused spirits.
Oh, if only you could see the pitiful looks upon their faces.

I see the terror in their eyes and it brings such a smile to my face.

It is good.

One hundred ghostly bodies floating around me, unable to escape.
Like fish on a snared line.
Like a hundred hanged men without the noose.

Their cries for help are as meaningless to me as their attempts to break free.

I see one look at my arm of steel.

I will have revenge for that too.
My lost arm.

Against the Attetson child!
The great Attetson child.
She took it from me. She took it!
The child of time!
The great time witch!

I see! Oh, how I see her! I see her every day.

She is the reason why I have chosen to target the
great Arcane Intelligence Agency!
I see her better than she sees herself. For I know what she will become.
We have been at this a long time, me and her.

I know what she will become.
My past is her future!

She will live! I can feel her coming.
I feel her presence. The great child of time.
The one who will rise and fight the demons and push back all the dark.
Oh, how I see her!

I can see her, she's so close.
So close.

My dearest Kiko.
Kiko Attetson!

The foolish girl has no idea the part she will play in the war to come.
It's so strange seeing her before her rise to greatness.
Before our fights of the future.
Before she took my arm from me.

Like a caterpillar before the butterfly.
Like a blank canvas before the paint.

How blind she is. She does not see it.
Both her greatness or who I truly am.

Oh, but she will find out soon enough...

Oh, how I have waited for her time to rise.
Like a great phoenix of time from the ashes of disaster.

I have been hiding for years.
I'm waiting. Always waiting.
They all expect nothing.

I know what she doesn't.
The secret of the cancer of that monster that calls itself her brother.

I look forward to seeing the truth break her.

Oh, far, far I will sink fuelled by my singular
hatred of what she will one day become.
I know what lies in wait for you, Time Witch.
I will relish in every moment of your upcoming pain.

I will watch you rise and I will carry myself off of your successes.

Kiko, her agency and all the Demons will die.

Then my revenge against all of them will be complete.

When they are all dead, when I have my absolute revenge.

*I will feel the crack of Kiko's skull under my heel.
And have no doubt, it will feel good!*

*I imagine it every time I talk to her under my
disguise as the pathetuc 'Llewelyn Jones.'*

*I am the Dark Hand.
And I see all.*

*Evil is not natural. It's not born.
It's something forged.*

But I like to think I'm something more.

*I wish there was a word to describe the rush of power I'm feeling as all of those soulful spirits enter the Cube of Equinox. I wish there was a word to describe the feeling of glee I will feel when I present this gift to the demon-kind, knowing that soon they will all die.
Thanks to me!*

*I have been waiting.
Improving over time.
Like a fine wine.*

Chapter Seven

CHOICES

Kiko looked out over a messy table of scattered and half-opened books. Albeit that this wasn't exactly an unusual sight, this was far from a normal situation. Excluding the fact that the books she usually read were interesting, fun or in some way unputdownable and these books were heavy, clunky, dusty and tediously written. *It did not help that she was also reading for work.* I think everyone knows that contrasting feeling of doing something because you have to, say for school or a job, against doing something that you do for a hobby or because it's of interest to you.

Kiko's office was a rather cramped room, especially when compared to her fathers. It was also a lot more basic in terms of its design. There was a purple feature wall contrasting against three white. Three was also the number of blue chairs that were here. A three-tier black glass-shelved bookcase ran the distance of the feature wall. These shelves housed a wide array of books, hence why it was called a bookshelf. If I was to say that these books were arranged in any form of meaningful order, then I'd be lying. However there was a waving Maneki-Neko cat (*one of those Asian, golden waving cat ornaments.*) sat on the middle shelf, if that counts for anything. A series of Matryoshka dolls (*Russian babushka dolls.*) sat on her desk. These were painted to look like a series of famous wizards from history. On the ceiling, there was a series of six magical lanterns which lit the room. There was also a small laptop on top of her desk. (*What? Why wouldn't she have one? Just because she casts magic? Think about how crazy that would be. Oh look at me, I can summon an elephant from thin air, but I can't use technology. She's not your grandparents!*)

Six weeks had passed since Kara had joined the Bureau of Necrological Investigations. During that time she had adapted to her new job pretty well. Like a duck to water, some might say.

Kiko was currently investigating a weird international occurrence. There had been a series of strange disappearances. Mass reporting were trickling in from all over the world. All of the non consenting spirits had disappeared from most of the major cities around the world. The first had been noticed in the New York subways. The sewers of Oslo had also been cleared. The catacombs of Paris were now reportedly empty.

And no one knew why. *(Okay, well we know why they're disapearing. But that's besides the point. It's not like you can tell anyone!)* And this was exactly the problem Kiko faced now. No one was coming forward. For a species that had existed for almost a hundred years, no one knew anything about them. Like seriously. Besides the fact 'they exist' and 'they are here' all other recorded materials on them were vague and rhetorical at best. They were malicious and false at worse. For the past few minutes, Kiko had found her attention falling upon a small insect that was running over one of her book covers. She wasn't sure why she was staring at him. Maybe he was helping her focus. *Or maybe she was procrastinating?* She knew not of how he had gotten in or even what he was. Was he even a he? By no means was she an expert in bugs. *She was no entomologist.* A series of green legs ran over *'Allen Hartwell's Ghosts: a Spiritual Guide.'* Unfortunately, this book had fallen under the category of *'malicious'* writings. It was barely worth the paper it was printed on. How could it be that a whole order of creatures could exist amongst us for so long and not a single person had tried to actually interact with them or even give them as much as a second thought?

Her blood boiled and her skin crawled as she had read story after story of how poorly these deceased were treated. Swept away like dirt under a rug. *Out of sight and out of mind.* The fact that there wasn't a single person who seemed to care or know anything of substance about them was sickening. No one seemed to notice them anymore. But what was worse, no one even seemed to care. *How could no one care about a whole species?* These ghosts had once been people and were now treated like cockroaches.

From all accounts, these ghosts weren't special. None were of any great importance. Especially not anymore. They were rarely vengeful, spiteful or interested in causing pain or suffering to the living like other spectres and spirits were. There were no recordings of them being in any way powerful or particularly exceptional or distinctive in any way. There was nothing to suggest what they might be currently be doing. They all just seemed to bumble and drift like non-corporeal tumbleweeds caught in the winds of life. There had been no record of them really doing anything or going anywhere. Not ever. They all just seemed to keep themselves to themselves. *So where were had they gone now?* In a best-case scenario, they might finally be passing through to the other side. Into their afterlives perhaps? *Maybe Heaven and Hell finally realised their oversight?* Maybe they'd all decided to go on holiday at the same time? However, life was rarely so easy or so kind. Good things rarely happened for no reason. *There was always a hidden agenda.* Some selfish riddle that needed solving. Something beneath the surface. Some form of motive. There was always something. But the non consenting ghosts were harmless. Hurting them would be like taking candy from a baby. Not in the sense that it would be easy, but why on Earth would you want to steal candy from a baby? Who does that? Kiko found herself banging her head off the side of her table in frustration.

'Thud.'

"Ow."

But there were no leads. Nada. Everything Kiko had was circumstantial at best. Kiko rubbed her forehead and readjusted her glasses. *Okay, no leads was a bit of an exaggeration.* There was one. By chance, luck or coincidence an old CCTV camera had managed to get a grainy shot of what appeared to be a hooded man that had been seen near the non consenting spirits compound in Sheffield. Unfortunately, the world wasn't running short on men who wore hooded tops. Truth be told this, was a fairly common occurrence, so this potential evidence had offered nothing in the way of anything useful.

But it did give a starting location for an investigation. Maybe, if she was super lucky, this individual might have dropped a detailed note with all of his motifs and intentions. *'Wouldn't that be nice?'* Kiko thought to herself. A manifesto, like an evil dude's monologue in a story. Some clear indication as to why he was doing this. Hell, right now she would happily settle for any indication as to what any of this all was. *But wouldn't it be lovely if the world worked like that?* If you could skip to the final chapter and get all the answers. - Please don't do that! - She ran her fingers through her tousled hair whilst lost in thought. It was at this moment, as her fingers ran through her dirty hair, that a mortifying realisation struck. *Her hair felt gross.* Like really gross. *Oh no!* She had been so busy with work that she had forgotten to shower either last night or this morning. Kiko discretely gave herself a little '*sniff-sniff*' to assess how bad everything was. *She was fine.* Everything was okay. She smelled alright, nothing a quick squirt of deodorant…

'*Oh shit!*'

Great! Llewelyn was in her office. Staring at her.

'*What a creep!*'

Kiko awkwardly allowed her arm to fall to her side, hoping that if she provided nothing in the way of an answer as to what she was currently doing sniffing her armpit, that he would offer nothing in the way of a question. Although she did wish that the ground would swallow her whole, both due to embarrassment and the fact it would mean she wouldn't be in the same room as creepy old Llewellyn Jones anymore. To be fair, Llewelyn also wished Kiko would fall through the floor and disappear, never to be seen again. *But Kiko didn't know this.* He wished for a lot of bad things to happen to her. *But she didn't know that either.* As much as she tried to fight it, she felt a heated flush fill her cheeks. She was now blushing.

"Um, can I help you?" Kiko asked as she thought of the deodorant can in her bottom drawer.

"Yes, I was just wondering…" Llewelyn glanced over the rubble of books scattered across her table. "Any leads…?" He shot Kiko a momentary concerned look before smiling broadly.

Why was Llewelyn asking about this? Llewelyn had never just popped by to ask about cases. It wasn't in his nature. If he was in the habit of continually dropping by, Kiko would have switched offices by now. *Oh god, what if she had to swap offices around now?* What if this was the start of a daily visit? *Oh god no!* He was usually always too busy… doing… *what the hell was his job?* Kiko's mind went blank. He obviously did something. Yeah. She was pretty sure his role was something to do with the research offices upstairs. So why was he in the Temporal Bureau of Investigations? *Why was he here?*

"Nope. No leads. Sorry!" Kiko gave a short, fake smile before Kara burst through her door.

"Oh thank God!" Kiko accidentally said out loud.

"Hey, Kiko. Is your brother's meal thing still on tomorrow night?" Kara asked as her head protruded from around the door as if floating in mid-air.

To commemorate Vincent's defeat over the Succubus in chapter one, Liverpool had given him a ceremonial key to the city. To celebrate this, Cassandra was throwing a party of her own at the Attetson household. For anyone wanting to attend, the address is sixteen Diamondpeak Avenue, Liarath, Scotland. But as I have said before, it's not in this universe. *So good luck actually getting there in time.* But also during the entire time you were reading that and whilst Kara had been asking Kiko the original question about the party, Kiko had been subtly glaring and discretely indicating towards Llewelyn with an expression of enlarged, angry eyeballs that seemed to cry out *'get me the hell out of here! Now!'*

"Uh, yeah… as… far as I… know…!" Kiko replied still discretely nodding with her head towards her unwelcome visitor.

"Okay, cool. I won't be back tonight. I got to go to Caerphilly on account of some vampires." Kara seemed to pause for dramatic effect. *"Guess I best go Caerphilly!"* A big smile broke across her face as she waited for her applause.

There was none.

But still, she waited.

Nothing.

Just two people staring at her blankly with annoyed expressions on their faces.

"Oh to hell with you two! *That was funny!"* Kara retreated with a vexed look on her face.

"So… you're by yourself tonight then?" Llewelyn asked.

"*Nope!*" Kiko shot off from her desk and made for the door. "I'm, um, going to Sheffield."

"Why?" Llewelyn shot her a panic-stricken look. She noticed that one, even if she misunderstood the reason behind it.

'To get away from you.' She thought to herself. "No reason..." Was what she had actually said out loud as she grabbed the deodorant from the bottom drawer.

Llewelyn repeated Kiko's last statement back to her as a question as his arm rose to block Kiko's exit through the door.

"You know, I've never understood why you keep Kara around." Llewelyn's slow and measured words cut through the room as he watched for a reaction. "All she does is slow you down. It must be such a burden having someone living off of your kindness and generosity all the time. It must be so hard." A fake smile of his own adorned his face. "Like a parasite, feeding of your kindness and generosity. Besides she's a bad influence on you. She's so... *belligerent.* Plus her family is nothing but trouble."

"No, no. She's no trouble at all, sir." Kiko chirped as she ducked under his arm. A heated rage bit at her soul. How dare he comment on any of her friends. "Goodbye, Llewelyn!"

And with that, she was gone. She zipped around the corner with the determination of a greyhound at a racing track. That rage was still gnawing at her. *Just who the hell did he think he was to come into her office and discussing her relationships with her friends?* Who did he think he was, passing comments on her and her friendships? She ought to go back and punch him in his stupid throat! Some poor and entirely innocent bystander received a hearty kick for being in the wrong place at the wrong time. Poor bin, it wasn't his fault! Oh and even better, now it looked like Kiko was going to Sheffield... Even if she didn't actually want to go.

Sheffield is a city in the English county of South Yorkshire. When you know that it's English then there's not a whole lot else left to say. It shares the same weird mix of really old and brand new buildings like every English city does. One building can be from the 1800s, the next had finally finished being built yesterday. The one after that could be Victorian. The one after that one could be from the 1980s. There was no rhyme or reason as to how the streets were made. One person could call it majestic, the next could call it quaint. *Another could call it messy, or ad-libbed.* The only thing for certain was that it was raining. It was the north of England after all. So here Kiko walked the streets, under the protection of her dutiful umbrella. It had little pictures of sheep on it, if you're curious. She had been here in the rain for about an hour asking passer-bys if they had seen the guy in the picture. No one had. Maybe it was because the CCTV image of the hooded man was pixelated and blurry. *Maybe it was because it vaguely pictured a non-descriptive, hooded individual.* There wasn't a lot to go on. The TBI Identification badge that Kiko had hung off a chain around her neck had given rise to some attention from the locals. A free warm cup of tea being the highlight of these interactions. Anything that helped to beat the cold rain was considered a win. Potentially being thousands of miles away from Llewelyn was also a win. What a creep! *'I've never understood why you keep Kara around.'* How dare he pass judgement on someone she cared about. Besides, since when was it a crime to help a friend? And Kara wasn't a damsel in distress. Kiko was no white knight either. Friends just helped other friends out. It's just a thing that they do. If you liked a person, and if you were able to give them a helping hand; you did. *What was the alternative?* Allowing a person she viewed as a sister to sleep on the street? That wasn't about to happen any time soon. *To allow a person she loved to keep living in a house where she knew that person was being tormented?* No chance.

'Parasite.'

'Belligerent.'

Kara was one of the few people who had ever had Kiko's back. Perhaps if the world was a little less judgemental then everyone would be just that little bit better off. Free from the pressures of watching, judgemental eyes. *Kiko considered pinning the whole ghostly disappearances on Llewelyn.* Just out of spite. To just tell her superiors that it was all Llewelyn's fault. That he had some great big master plan. Just to make him squirm. To put him under the spotlight and have people judge him for once.

But there was a problem, besides the fact that Llewelyn was far too pathetic to have a secret mystery life, Kiko had far too much integrity to ever do something like that. It was just fun to think about. Plus it was better than focussing on the rain. *If only she knew the truth about how Llewelyn spent his spare time…*

Anger and rage have the uncanny and rather unique ability to blind a person. We become too focused on our fury to see the world as it is. To see what is happening under our very noses. To this end, Kiko was no different to you and me. As she stood there in the pouring rain, feeling sorry for herself and irritated by Llewelyn's rubbernecking, she had failed to notice a group of black-robed individuals sneak past her. *Good going Kiko!* These three individuals consisted of two men and a girl. If Kiko wasn't so busy planning her one-woman pity party, perhaps she would have seen them struggling with a series of oversized suitcases. If she wasn't so preoccupied with her busy schedule of sulking she might have noticed their hushed tones and concealed movements as they tried carefully to avoid her attention.

These three were members of the Coven de'la Praxus. The Coven de'la Praxus were Demon worshippers. These children of beguiled darkness loved the demon-kind with an all-consuming passion. They revered them like gods. *(Which was ironic if you knew of how the Demons came to be!)* I guess if you had to be fair to the members of the coven, these Demons had never allowed for anything less than one hundred percent devotion one hundred percent of the time. Like a narcissistic lover, they always expected all of your attention. Sorry, no… *They demanded it!* These cultists showed their affection to the Fallen in the way of rituals and blood sacrifices. Both virginal and goat based. *Occasionally a virginal goat, but only on very special occasions!* This was a death demonstrated devotion, even if the Demons never actually gained much from these rituals happening. Demons were already extremely powerful. No nutrients or sustenance were derived from these sacrifices. It wasn't an essential part of life like eating was. But it was fun to watch though. For them, a sacrifice was comparable to a night out at the cinema. *A simple act of voyeuristic pleasure.* They loved to watch as the power of life was stripped from the defenceless.

If you were to say that the Coven de'la Praxus were in a *'relationship'* with the Demon-kind, then the act of a blood sacrifice wouldn't be all too dissimilar to giving a girlfriend a bouquet of flowers. Yes, such an act was extremely cliché and a couple of flowers wouldn't save you from having the very soul ripped out of your body if you'd done something wrong or if the mood randomly struck. *But you'd best be sure there was no way you were about to open that door empty-handed.* It wasn't worth the risk. Never, ever, turn up empty-handed. This is not to say that being a cultist was without its merit. The bountiful gifts that were offered in exchange for servitude were deemed by many to be worth the risk of the occasional flaying or curse. Dealings and trades with the Demon-kind had been given rise to both the vampires and the werewolves, as well as a wide array of other human-based creatures. At the cost of exactly one mortal soul, you were given eternal life and immense power. For many, this trade was cost-effective. *I mean what good was a soul anyway?* All it did was allow you access into Heaven and provide you with a moral compass and a conscience. *No biggie!*

To a normal, sane person a Demon was just about the worst thing in the universe. *Yes, even worse than a dentist or a traffic warden.* But only just! All the monsters and all the evil of the universe was said to have been caused in some way by the Demons, but that is a story for another time. This trio crept right past Kiko. When all three of these cultists were out of sight, they ran as fast as they could. Straight up to a nearby bank. *People sneaked around people of law enforcement and ran at banks all the time, right?* I'm sure it was nothing… Kiko took a sip from her cup of tea that the passing elderly Orcish woman had given her earlier. 'Boom.' The sound of a far off explosion erupted through the wet sky! The shock wave had caused an alarmed Kiko to spit her tea back up, and not just through her mouth. Here she stood with her nose and throat burning from the red hot liquid and her ruined now snotty cup of tea. This combined with the self-sniffing earlier, today was not a good day for dignity. There was a quiet thunk as the cup bopped against the ground and the tea became quickly washed away with the rain. Kiko sprinted towards the sound of the eruption. Fighting her umbrella every step of the way.

"Here, take this." She thrust the umbrella onto a passer-by as she flashed him her TBI ID badge and ran off at full speed, pulling a new, freshly summoned hood close around her face from under her blue coat. This Dwarf had been happy with his free umbrella and quickly scampered away with it in his tight greedy grasp.

I'm not entirely sure why you would need to, but if you ever need to find the source of an explosion, here is some advice. *Watch the nearby people.* Just take a second and watch how they run. Watch which direction they are all running in and run the opposite way. Run against the crowds. If anything was true of the people of Earth, they were not keen on the idea of dying. Truth be told, they rather hated the idea, even the ones who joked about it.

The survival instinct was just too strong. So whenever there was a source of danger then the majority of people would run in the opposite direction. *Run.* Run for their lives. Be it an explosion at your local bank, a gunshot in the night or villagers running away from a fiery wolf attacking people in pre-revolutionary France; people always knew to run away. To stay safe, even if it only bought them a few more seconds to their precious lives. So this is exactly what Kiko did, even though she was technically running in the wrong direction. She was hunting for the source of the explosion. Admittedly in this case she had seen a building with all of its windows blown out and smoke billowing out of the door. *That was also a clear giveaway!*

Before Kiko had a chance to enter the bank, a police officer had been sent flying out through the front door, through the swelling clouds of smoke. He landed in a crumpled pile on the ground at the base of the concrete steps. This had been enough to make Kiko stop dead in her tracks. No, not out of fear. But to check if this man was alright. To see if he was still alive.

Luckily he was, but just barely.

Sometimes in life we were given moments that would define us forever. These times and events would shape us for the rest of our lives. Not only who we are as people but also how we viewed ourselves or the world around us. We never knew when these moments were coming. In truth, we only realised how crucial that those moments were after the fact. *The curse of hindsight.* That ability to see the domino effect of that defining moment and the series of choices that followed afterwards. After all, that's what life was. It was just a series of events and the series of choices we made because of them. We can either choose to do the right or noble thing, or we can choose to act selfishly to further our own agenda. Most people when faced with a neutral question of '*what would you do if...*' always said that they would do the right thing. But in the heat of the moment this rarely ended up being the case.

Kiko often pondered two things in life. The first being, what if all the Ancient Greek sculptures were actually just victims of Gorgons? (*The most famous of the Gorgons being Medusa.*) The second being, what would she do when faced with these character-defining crossroads? Would she zig or would she zag? Would she find the strength to be a hero, like Vincent, or would she crumble under the pressure?

Sometimes life gave way to scenarios where there were no good or right choices. *Only slightly less bad ones.* Sometimes in life, if we were really, really lucky, these moments would give us the ability to redefine ourselves forever; usually for the better. Diane Dawnstar had not had the easiest of lives. By the age of sixteen she had lost both of her parents and had a run-in with a bad crowd. To most people the idea of a bad crowd would entail drugs, late-night loitering and smoking. For Diane, this meant being stuck with the Coven de'la Praxus. *A life of twisted, unspeakable horrors.* She had no love for her fellow cultists, but it beat the alternative. Starving to death living alone on the streets. She had not actively chosen this life of sacrifices and Demonic gods, there had just been nothing in the way of an alternative. She had been swept off her feet by the tide of life and was now stuck a million miles away from the shoreline. *Joining the sharks had been a better choice than either drowning or being eaten by them.* But now it also meant that she couldn't just swim away. Hell hath no fury like a Demon scorned. Truth be told she was terrified of them all. The Demons and the cultists alike. But it wasn't like there was a long line of people offering a better alternative. She had no money or qualifications to fall back upon either. *So what options did she really have?* What else could she do? She was trapped within her own existence. Life had become her jailer.

This morning began the same way most did, but little did Diane realise that today was going to be one of those days that would change her life forever. Recently Diane and her two brothers had been involved in an interesting array of events. The term '*interesting*' being a completely valid way to describe the occurrences which had befallen them. Well, that's if you thought the term '*interesting*' could be interchangeable with the term '*a complete and utter failure.*' Diane had been fully aware of how '*interesting*' things had been for them lately. Louie Dawnstar, her eldest brother, was the leader of the group. He was also a victim, but perhaps not in the way how you might initially think. In his youth, he had been a victim of just about the world's worst outbreak of acne. But besides this, he was also a victim of bad luck. This wasn't his fault though, it never was. As far as he was concerned it wasn't even bad luck. It was all merely down to the lack of conviction that Diane and Matthew had usually shown. Life would turn around, all they needed was a win to turn everything around. This dry spell had been going on for a while now. Being short on wins had left the Dawnstars running low on favour with the Coven de'la Praxus and were now completely out of cash.

However, there had been a seemingly simple solution. All they had to do was rob a bank. Naturally. You know, because that was a completely normal thing a person does. It was so obvious that Diane's protests had been little more than an annoyance. Louie's reasoning was true and simple enough as a concept. They had no money, and money lived in banks. If you wanted to see an exotic animal, you went to a zoo. *So where else would you go for money?* This cash was all that they needed to grease the wheels of success. Before they all knew it, they would be living the life of luxury. This primitive observation of the financial world was derivative, to say the least. Yet somehow the thing that both Louie and Matthew had found hilarious was Diane's insistence that the only way she would get involved was if they promised that no one would end up getting hurt. This negotiation was, gauging by their laughter, just about the funniest thing that either one had heard in their entire lives.

Matthew was, what some might refer to as, a stone-cold idiot. He was always the first in line if something sounded like a genuinely bad idea. If being a moron was an Olympic sport he would have most likely have been disqualified before the competition had even started, for trying to eat the gold medal like it was a chocolate coin. The whole reason these three siblings were even associated with the Coven de'la Praxus was entirely because of him. He was the one who had run afoul of the cultists in the first place when he had tied to steal from them. This had been about two years ago. Maybe three. Louie, being the ever vigilant leader he was, tried to regain control of the situation. One thing had led to another like it always does. *Only this time, it had resulted in one very dead vicar and six nuns that had been left in such a condition that even the best and most dedicated forensic team in the world would not be able to identify the remains of them.*

It was said that all the blood he had seen on that rueful night still haunted the dreams of the Detective, Gavin Daniels. Some even said that it was this unsolved murder mystery that had led to him retiring the badge and turning to a life on the bottle.

Speaking of bottles. It should be safe to say that Diane bottling up her true feelings about the cult offered very little in the way of a defence for murder, and a jury of her peers would most likely agree. *A man and six women were dead.* There was no escaping this fact. *Their blood was on her hands just as much as it was on the hands of her brothers.* I would like to think that Diane was aware of this too. But as little substance this serves as a defence for murder, it does serve as an example of how our actions define us. *She could have refused the coven.* To be fair, she would have probably died for doing so. *But at least she wouldn't have to live this life of endless and eternal guilt and she wouldn't be branded as a murder.* The worst bit was she didn't even have anyone to turn to about all this. Her own brothers felt like total strangers and she really missed her parents.

The fancy bank's marble flooring was in blinding contrast to the cracked concretes of the abandoned warehouse where the three cultists had spent the night. Gone were the rusty metal shelves, in their place stood grand oak desks. The scurrying of rodents in the night had been swapped with the hustle and bustle of people going about their day to day lives. The dim illumination from the outside lamppost was now a series of ornate halogen lights. The agreement of 'fine but no one gets hurt' was short-lived. Matthew, being the eternal genius that he was, had decided upon entering the bank that the best way to get everyone's attention would naturally need to be the biggest and grandest way imaginable. *And nothing was bigger or louder than an explosion.* Luckily he had been smart enough to pack some in the suitcases. A thick swirling mist of smoke and ash circulated the air and burdened the lungs. It stung at the eyes like a grainy pepper spray whilst also underhandedly lowering any available visibility in the bank, wrapping the room behind a smoke-filled blanket. *You could taste the dust in the air.* You could feel the airborne dirt between your teeth; it was thick and almost chewable. Crumbs of determined and demented debris clung to the outside of Kiko's black-rimmed glasses, like little grey gremlins. These grey specks hung on tight as if they were needy children hanging off their mother's coattails.

A warbling cacophony of terrified screams and panic-stricken cries arose from within the clouds of settling debris. This terrible orchestra of woe and tears came from the greyscaled, cowering masses that clung to the sides of the once-great room, trying their collective best to keep a low profile. To stay safe, but more importantly, to stay alive.

Through the dizzying distraction of her overwhelmed senses, Kiko could make out the shape of an obscured black-robed individual darting manically through the mayhem, laughing vulgarly as he disappeared. As she turned she saw another shadow retreating into the thick haze leaving nothing but wisps in the grey cloud behind him. As she lost focus on that man she could feel another person emerge behind her, trying to catch her off guard. *And another one after that.* All were still laughing with a pure-hearted malcontent. Circling her like hyenas prowling a wildebeest on the great African plains.

"You made a mistake coming here!" A man's voice called out from the shadows.

"Yeah, we're real dangerous, we are. Big mistake!" Another voice replied.

"You don't want to do this!" Kiko warned her mysterious aggressors, as best she could with an uncertain voice as she still tried to assess the situation.

How many people were here? How many of them were innocent? How would she be able to deal with them all without endangering the lives of everyone else?

Truth be told, it was Kiko that was the one who didn't want to do this. Being outnumbered and potentially outgunned by an unknown number of dangerous individuals meant that it was incredibly unlikely that she would be able to apprehend any of them without endangering the lives of any of the innocent bystanders. Their survival was of the utmost importance to her. Maybe if she had a clear line of sight on any of these robed people, things would be different. But with the poor visibility, she might accidentally hit one of those not-so-guilty people instead. Obviously, she wouldn't want to do be doing that.

Clearly, the biggest issue was this unnaturally thick fog. A simple spell would dispel it. But that wasn't the issue. *A simple spell would also leave her open and vulnerable to an attack.* What good would it be, being able to see, if all you were able to see was that you'd left yourself open to a sudden fireball or thunderbolt coming directly towards you? Kiko wasn't particularly keen on the idea of getting hurt in the process either. Starting a fight with an unseen enemy she knew nothing about would also be bad for her health. This left her with only one solution. If she was to survive this, she'd have to be smart. *She would have to reason with these people.* As she pondered her best course of action a suitcase emerged from the muddled mists, directly towards her. With a flick of her wrist, she cast a temporal displacement spell. One second this suitcase had been here in present times. *The next it was hurtling through the air of a 1920's San Francisco night sky.*

Tommy Brown was a somewhat nervous and clumsy egg. He was always the jitterbug. Especially when he was around Mary Garcia. Mary was a hotsy-totsy doll with the most amazing set o' gams you ever saw. This little firecracker caught Tommy's attention one morning at his local diner. This being where she worked. Every morning Tommy would swing by and order the same breakfast. Two eggs, easy done, with a side of bacon and coffee. Black with two sugars. He thought she was the bee's knees and that she was one swell gal! It was somewhere around about his fiftieth consecutive breakfast that Tommy had dug deep and found the courage to ask her out on an actual, real-life bonafide date. *He was surprised that she had said yes!* Later that night the two found themselves alone in his father's pickup truck. Tommy was praying for the courage to kiss the beautiful girl whilst Mary, somewhat ironically, had been praying for him to find the courage to kiss the girl as well. Whilst they awkwardly sat there in the dark, trying to figure out that they had both wanted the same thing, a temporally displaced suitcase broke out in the night sky behind the star crossed lovers and erupted into a furious explosion some forty feet above them.

It was somewhat ironic that Kiko's suddenly displaced explosion in the night's sky had been what had finally brought these two together. The circle of fate worked in funny ways. Tommy Brown had actually died during the events of World War Two, thinking of nothing but his beloved Mary and the day they would be reunited. *And although Kiko didn't know it, he had been one of the non consenting spirits that had been kidnapped by the Dark Hand here in Sheffield.* Life always had a funny way of panning out. It was almost as if the universe had a sense of humour. *If it did, it was definitely a twisted one.* Kiko had been somewhat responsible for finally bringing Tommy the love of his life, and Tommy had been somewhat responsible for bringing Kiko to Sheffield, where she had been responsible for bringing him closer to the love of his life. It was almost like a self-fulfilling prophecy.

But who actually started it all off? Tommy by being kidnapped as a ghost or Kiko by displacing the suitcase packed with explosives? You've got to love a paradox. Matthew Dawnstar looked dumbfounded at the disappearance of his poorly disguised bomb.

"Where did it go?" He asked a shrugging Louie, who stood it the wreckage of the former bank.

"I wouldn't do that again, that's not going to work on me!" Kiko bluffed with all the bravo she could muster.

This bluff was actually a cold faced lie. The temporal displacement spell had almost run her dry. The spell had required a lot of power (*both the power of sending the packed bomb away and the power required running the complex temporal equation that made sure this bomb didn't randomly appear somewhere where people would get hurt.*) and as such Kiko didn't have much magical energy left in her for a fight.

"Trust me. You don't want to hurt these people, I can see it in your eyes. You don't want to have to live with yourself if you have their blood on your hands! I know you're scared, and that things in your life haven't gone to plan."

Kiko raised an open hand towards her assailants. Reasoning with them was the only option she had left. Hopefully it would work!

"There's a handful of ways in which I could stop you right now." She cast an uneasy look towards Matthew and then towards Diane. She knew she was lying. She just hoped they didn't. "But I honestly don't think I have to. You're almost there, I can see it in you. The uncertainty. You're conflicted. Listen, I just want you to think. Just for a moment. *Can you do that?* Please, just for a moment. *Just think.*"

People say that evil is a choice, that people have to choose to be evil. This sentiment felt reductive to Kiko. People were good at their cores. *Kiko honestly believed that.* She believed it with all of her heart. She also believed that sometimes people get treated unfairly and lose their way. After all, life can be cruel. *All some people needed was a helping hand and a nudge back in the right direction.* To be put back on the right track and brought back into the light. A reminder that there was still good in the world. A little forgiveness goes a long way. All they needed was a small push in the right direction. When given the chance to do the right thing, they would. But only if you allowed them to do so. Sometimes all that was needed was a small act of kindness to get the ball rolling.

"Do you really want to do this? *Do you really want to be this?* This person who hurts other people? *Or do you want to be more?* To draw a line in the sand and decide no one should suffer the way you've suffered?"

Kiko also knew, deep down, that if you spoke to people with respect then you were more likely to be treated with respect in return. Speaking down to, invalidating or belittling a person would achieve nothing more than more conflict. Threats or violence would only cause an escalation. *If you're aggressive to someone then you limit how they'll react to you.* But if you approach someone with a variety of options and they choose to reply with aggression? Then you know exactly what kind of person they are.

"You have to make the choice, be the person you choose to be. Not the one people decide for you to be. I can't make the choice for you, but I can see you're doubting this lifestyle. So start here. *Change*. Choose today. *Choose right now.* You could walk right out that door, that door right there. Just leave and no one else gets hurt."

"We can't just leave!" Diane called back in disbelief. "Do you think they'll let us go after all we have done?" Tears welled in the corners of her brown eyes. "They'll never forgive. They'll never forget!"

"Wow, okay. *Sure*. Well if that's all it takes, then I forgive you. But more than that, I promise to help you. Lay down your arms. Promise to turn your life around and will give you my word. I'll help you. In any way that I can." A fond smile softly shone from Kiko's face. "After all you've done, if all it takes to turn your life around is a little mercy. Then that's what I'll give you. *Mercy*. If you need kindness, I'll give that too. *I forgive you.*"

Come on. One. *Just one.* That's all it took. One single person was all that was needed to make a change. A solitary voice to say '*no.*' To refuse to the world the way it was. One person to rise up and be the change they wanted to see in the world. They just needed to be brave enough to welcome it. *To embrace the choice and be the agent of their own destiny...*

"Aww bless, what a lovely little speech. But I'm afraid we'll 'ave to decline!" Louie cackled to his brother as he dipped into a sarcastic bow.

"That's absolutely fine. But, heads up, I *clearly* wasn't talking to you..."

Louie's mocking laughter was cut short as a brass handrail 'twanged' around the side of his head, knocking him unconscious. Before Matthew could do anything about Diane's betrayal, Kiko had lifted him into the air with a wave of her hand, freezing him in mid-air.

"Handcuff him and then we'll talk."

Chapter Eight

THE HOUSE OF THE DAMNED

"Can I actually trust you?" Diane's cold and uncertain words broke through an uncomfortable silence. The realisation that she had sold both of her brothers out to a complete stranger had just sunk in. And it had sunk in hard, as she recalled the events in the bank earlier that day. The choice that had changed her life. Now was the moment of truth. Would this choice be for the better or for worse? If this ginger witch was lying, then Diane would have nothing. No one. *'Oh no!'* What had she done? A distraught fear raced through her. A few fanciful sounding words of a better tomorrow was all it had taken for her to betray her family. *Her brothers.* Sure, they were not the best of people. But those two brothers of hers were the best she had. *They were all she had.*

"I'm guessing trust is in short supply within the Praxus, 'ey?" Kiko said with an unsure, jokey smile as she slid a strawberry milkshake across the table to her doubtful new friend.

Kiko had decided to take Diane to the only place she could think of where this girl might feel slightly comfortable. To Marvin's, a place where Kiko had always felt welcome. Diane gave a doubtful look to her pink milked beverage. Then gave a secondary look over to the eight-limbed waiter who had served it. The chairs here were hard and uncomfortable and, as it turned out, Diane found the appearance of octopuses deeply unsettling. *Diane didn't even know that she suffered from chapodiphobia.* So at least that was one lesson learned from today, I guess.

"Well, it's not poisoned. If that's what you're worried about." Kiko gave another smile before taking a sip from her own drink.

Diane did not follow suit. Childhood was a time of simplicity and unbridled happiness. Or rather, that's what it was supposed to be. This is not the case for a lot of people. For a lot of you. Fear and doubt have a special place in the hearts of those poor unfortunate people who experience pain and hardship at a young age. Truth be told, many spend a lifetime trying to escape from the negative thoughts in their heads. A lifetime trying to prove to themselves that they are good enough. This pain changes them in a way that no one else on the planet will ever really understand. Childhood was a time of untold joy. A simpler time of innocence and boundless wonder. It's through this innocence and wonder that a child learns about the world and their role within it. A child learns who they are *(and their value)* by how we treat them. These formative years were supposed to be a time for good things to happen. For these children to flourish. A time where feeling safe and loved was supposed to rule from on high with an unfaltering authority. After all, children are defenceless and they need to be defended. By showing a child love, we teach them that they deserve to be loved. When we feed them, we teach them that they deserve to be fed. So what happens when a young child experiences pain or cruelty? *What do we teach them then?* What are we teaching them of their own personal value, as well as what to expect from life? Unfortunately, the answers to all these questions are rarely anything good.

Regrettably, Diane had been one of these dispossessed children. The catalyst for all this pain and doubt had not been the death of her parents. Neither parent had been exactly reliable during the thirteen years of life she had shared with them. Long before their deaths, Diane's life had taught her she was a nobody. *To never expect anything from anyone.* That she had no value. That she was worthless. The worst bit of it all was that she had actually accepted this role in life. Kiko couldn't help but find herself examining the teenager that sat opposite her. Her skin was mural of tattooed symbols, partially healed brandings and carved out scars. Markings from the Coven de'la Praxus. This multitude of markings on Diane's flesh was the aftermath of a series of dark rituals and sacrifices. They were woven into the surface of her skin as if someone had read from the *'Beginners Guide to Crop Circles'* and had decided to recreate it in human form. Some markings Kiko had recognised, others she did not. But they all looked incredibly painful. Kiko doubted any had been done in a clean or safe environment.

Diane had clearly gone through some bad times. Some of these markings looked fairly recent, based on the swelling around the wounds.

"Did they hurt?" Kiko found herself asking as she indicated towards the pagan symbol for winter that had been carved into Diane's right forearm.

Diane's response was to hide her arm under the table, either ashamed or embarrassed by Kiko drawing attention to them.

"Why are we here?" Diane asked as she glanced out the window.

"You tell me." Kiko replied, perhaps more bluntly than she'd intended.

Kiko felt bad for the girl that she had plucked from the bank. This girl seemed to think Kiko had the faintest clue what was going to happen next. As if she had some grand master-plan. *Truth be told, she hadn't expected Diane to take her up on her offer.* This wasn't to say Kiko had been lying before. That wasn't even remotely close to what had happened. I mean, she had certainly hoped that Diane would listen to her and Kiko was happy that she did. She just hadn't planned for what to do in the event of the little *'cult girl'* deciding to listen to her. And now it wasn't like she could exactly admit that she was clueless. The stakes were too high. But Kiko couldn't help but silently admit to herself that she had no idea what she was doing. She would never admit it out loud, but she was making it up as she going along. It felt wrong to see this girl so dependent upon her. It felt like a facade. But it didn't matter. Kiko had enough sense to know that in this current place, at this current time, that none of her trepidations mattered. Helping Diane find her way to a better life was the only thing that mattered right now.

"I dunno, man." Diane snapped with as much teenage angst as she could muster at that moment, before staring at her knees and picking at a rip in the fabric around the knee. Her anxious nails pecked at the strands like a feeding chicken. "I'm just sick of hurting people, y'know? I don't... I don't want to keep on being *this*." She vaguely gestured towards her current appearance.

A muted minute passed before she continued.

"But for the record, I don't trust you." Diane shot Kiko a look so bitter that it would make ice feel cold. "Not yet. I've met people like you before. The kind of people who only want you around if they think they can get something from you." Kiko went to speak but Diane spoke over her. "I know you're looking into those soldier-ghosts disappearances. I ain't stupid..." Diane pushed her drink to one side. "I know stuff about that! I know who is responsible. But I want your help getting revenge first."

The bluntness with which Diane had spoken to her had offended Kiko a bit. But it was somewhat understandable. What Diane had proposed next had been simple enough. In theory, it was a trade. A quid pro quo. What she had wanted was revenge against the Coven de'la Praxus. She needed it.

"It is the only thing that can bring me any peace." She explained.

If she also got redemption or absolution at the same time? Even better. As well as payback against the cult that had ruined her life, she wanted to be cleared of all crimes she had committed in the name of those evil cultists. She wanted to have a fresh start. A new beginning unburdened with her past life. If she got these things then she would tell Kiko who had been stealing the non consenting spirits away. She had a name, but she also claimed to know the motive behind the ghostly disappearances. As far as the quest for revenge went, there was a pocket dimension that the Coven de'la Praxus used as a safe house. (*Some children like to play with bubbles. If you were to imagine the entire thirteenth universe as a big-old-squishy-bubble, a pocket dimension would be like a smaller bubbles that can get stuck to the side of the bigger one. This was a painfully inaccurate and outright overly simplified analogy of what a pocket dimension was. However, it was innocuous enough as a concept, whilst also being close enough in reality to what a pocket dimension was, that if this description helped you understand what a pocket dimension represented, then go nuts. I won't be the one to stop you from thinking upon it this way.*) In this secreted dimension they had hidden away a series of children. Some of these children were being kept here to be turned into future Cultists; like an evil recruitment drive. Some of these children were less fortunate and were going to be sacrificed in the names of a variety of great evils.

Diane's demands were simple enough as a proposal. Not only would both girls be getting something they both wanted, but it would also spell a great professional success for Kiko at the same time. Naturally, the Arcane

Intelligence Agency were not too fond of the Coven de'la Praxus. If losing access to this pocket dimension was going to hurt the Praxus in any way, then it would simultaneously shine favourably on Kiko in the process. However, Kiko couldn't actually authorise Diane's absolution herself. She lacked the power to do so. It would be well above her pay grade. There was only one person that Kiko knew of who had that kind of clearance within the Arcane Intelligence Agency. So she found herself doing what most people do when they needed some help. *She called her mother.*

Cassandra Attetson sat in sharp contrast against the quaint and rustic cafe. As she passed a judgemental eye over the strange establishment, she could see why her daughter had always spoken so highly of it. It was definitely a *'unique'* premise for a business model. Even if there was no way on Earth Cassandra would let an octopus touch anything she was about to eat. There had been a strange expression of motherly pride mixed with a pained frustration on Cassandra's face when her daughter had told her how she had single-handedly thwarted a bank robbery whilst outnumbered three to one, and then how she had allowed one of the key perpetrators of the bank heist to just simply walk away from an active crime scene with her on what had amounted to little more than a whim. Regardless of Kiko's intent, this was still technically harbouring a fugitive. That was still a crime. The AIA did not look fondly on their employees who broke the law, even if it was for moments of good intention. However, they did make exceptions in exceptional circumstances.

It was rather lucky then that this raven-haired girl had claimed to have had useful intel. Cassandra was permitted, due to her station within the AIA, to authorise such deal of absolution. To her own surprise, Cassandra had even found herself sweetening the pot. Upon these children being saved from the dangers of the Praxus and the sharing of this intel about the spirits' disappearance, she would be absolved from the failed bank heist, due to the fact she had helped apprehend her brothers at the crime scene, and from the murder of the vicar and his nuns, as she had been forthright with the information. Her continued willingness to divulge any and all information about the Coven de'la Praxus, their routines, any secrets she also knew about them, including either known names, associates or locations of their operations would also result in her being enrolled into one of the Arcane Intelligence Agency's witness protection programmes. Mainly to keep her safe from any form of reprisal.

Diane being entered into this protection programme also meant that Kiko wasn't about to get into a whole lot of trouble for allowing a fugitive to escape from an active crime scene. *So that was also good!* Hearing the calm and collected manner in which Cassandra had dealt with Diane had somehow made Kiko respect her mother even more than she already did. This newfound respect had surprised Kiko, who had no idea it had been possible for her to respect her mother more than she had done so. *Yet here she was.* I guess that was the beauty of mothers, they achieved impossible tasks and rose to new heights with almost every passing day.

Somehow Cassandra had even managed to bring a sort of sedated peace to the young Diane, who was now eating a bowl of French fries that the Attetson mother had ordered for her. Although by the time Diane had finished pouring extra ingredients into the mix, the bowl had potentially ended up being more tomato ketchup and vinegar than actual chip. Diane had squirted the sauce and vinegar for what must have been a good ten seconds each. *No, not all of the sauce had landed in the bowl before you ask.* Kiko had assumed the bottom of the bowl to be like the bottom of the world's worst swimming pool, full of vinegar and sauce. Kiko couldn't recall ever meeting anyone who had liked ketchup this much before. Nonetheless, it was nice to see Diane acting like a child. Even if it was just for a single moment. It couldn't help but bring a smile to Kiko's face.

Kiko gave no argument to being told that Cassandra would be joining the two girls to the pocket dimension.

"There's no way you're going there by yourself!" Cassandra had stated in a calm yet demanding tone that rung with unquestionable authority. "I'm going with you, or there's no deal."

The truth of the matter was that Kiko had been relieved by her mother's decision to come along. If Cassandra had not made it clear that she was also coming along, Kiko would have probably asked for her to do so. She had no intention of doing this by herself. *To do so would have been crazy.*

The entrance into the cultist's pocket dimension was a spell, of sorts, opposed to being an actual door somewhere on the planet. The three had left Marvin's and quickly found a quiet place for Diane to cast her portal spell. Diane took a singular, simple piece of white chalk from her jeans' pocket and started drawing on a nearby wall. She began by outlining what appeared to be a curve-topped door. To reach the top of her design Diane had to extend to her full height, both on the tips of her toes and to the full length of her outstretched arm. She then drew, what Kiko had wrongly assumed to be, a great three-pointed pagan symbol in the centre. At the precise moment Diane had finished the central symbol it transformed itself into a bright outline of a horribly distorted, screaming – yet still muted – face that was made of pure light. The doorway suddenly came alive as a myriad of other neon based symbols of light erupted into existence and twisted themselves around this gaunt expressionate face, within the confines of the door. These markings varied from witchy pentagrams to other demonic scratchings. From ornate runes to ancient markings from the Elvish, Dwarven and Orcish alphabets. Within mere moments of these markings' arrival, they had found themselves transforming once more. This time these luminous markings had ruptured into the resplendent outlines of a whole range of evil-looking, mystical creatures. They all seemed to come alive and move around the pagan illumination as if they were all a part of a great, yet still muted, tribal dance. The outline of a series of shining imps, centaurs and goblin-like creatures danced and flayed and ripped at each other across this devilish masterpiece, as waves of what had appeared to be flames seemed to lap around them. A pair of symmetrical neon snakes climbed the outside of the border of the door and wrapped themselves around it. The line-work even seemed to crack and constrict beneath their mighty grip. This had caused the border of the door-line to glow with a bright hot light as all of the blank space inside this outer line suddenly turned into a deep blood red. All of the animated neon art and markings quickly stopped moving and turned into a rich black that seemed to scorch the very top of the wall as the horrible face collapsed in on itself. Leaving a gaping hole within the actual wall itself that had now filled the entirety of where this luminous demonic mural had recently occupied. Within the hole itself was now a fiery portal that seemed to lead somewhere.

"Okay, now that was pretty cool!" Kiko chortled out loud to her mother as she stood pointing towards the once dancing art piece with a goofy smile cracked across her face.

The name given to the distant land that had lain in waiting for them on the other side of this portal was what was often referred to as a 'Demonscape.' Demonscapes were minor alternative realities that existed just outside of this one. When the Demon races and their Queen, Lilith, had seen what the old gods had created (*this being all the nauseating planets and the entirety of life those planets had brought with them.*) the Demons had detested it all so, so much that they took it upon themselves to create a whole range of twisted and evil pockets of reality, all of their own to live in. They did this mainly as an act of mockery. *A cursed reflection to insult what the gods had created.* A jab to show that the gods were not the only ones with the power to create, that they could create things as well. The largest of these planes had been the Howling Halls. This being the dimension many had confused for Hell. Hell was actually the dimension where bad people got tortured in their afterlife, as a form of punishment. The Halls of the Howling Horde was where the vast majority of the Demons, Ghouls and a whole host of other heinous beasts had lived.

However, this dimension where Kiko, her mother and Diane were currently stood in, was not the Halls of the Howling Horde. This pocket dimension was a lot smaller and a great deal less terrifying. They had found themselves upon the top of a tall cliff. The ground here was a rich, brownish-red that sort of looked like clay. It felt coarse and dry under their feet as they walked through this nefarious hellscape. Occasionally, and also rather unsettlingly, the surface of this dirt would crack and splinter under their feet as they walked as if they were walking over the surface of a frozen river.

The sky felt like it was hanging down close around them. It was a majestic canvas of swirling brooding blues and inky indigos that bled into shades of cherry reds and stunning scarlets. A series of dark green clouds also drifted through it. Above their heads floated an endless series of derelict, ebony Viking Longboats. It was almost as if the trio were deep under the sea, looking up at a great flotilla of motionless ships. Most of these hundred ships were in a state of decay, to the point where not one of these dark ships had managed to remain fully intact. They had all been left to suffer at the neglectful hands of the abandonment of time in one way or another. Great ornate figureheads mounted the bow of each ship, the majority of these figureheads were carvings of spine-chilling dragons, but other figureheads were kicking around. All of these Longboats were made of wood and had metalwork holding them together. Gloriously tattered sails billowed despite the lack of wind. This had almost made the boats feel alive. Unbeknownst to the girls, these great ships had been unmanned for hundreds, if not thousands of years.

Off in the far distance, they could see the remnants of old rope bridges on the horizon around them. Most of these bridges had collapsed and decayed over time. These bridges had once connected a multitude of rocky mountains into a large ornate circular landmass. This cliff the girls were on now was a part of the great sequence. A large body of water filled the void between these mountains. Despite no one saying it, they had all agreed it was probably best not to try and swim in the depths. *This was probably a good idea.* Wherever this place was, it had most likely been a place of great beauty, once upon a time. However, that had clearly been a long time ago. Nowadays this mountainous ring was a place that was hauntingly quiet and unnervingly still. *The literal personification of the tranquil calm before a violent storm.* A large two-storey, Edwardian styled house stood in juxtaposition to the rest of the stoic Norse aesthetic. The complete contrast of this regal looking house against its ominous surroundings had caused all sensations of eeriness to multiply to no end. The two dormer bay windows that had protruded on the front of the house from the black slated gable roof, had almost looked like a giant pair of eyes. I guess that would make the black wooden door look like a mouth. If the analogy of this house looking like a face was to continue, then the skin of this house was that of grey stone. Another series of windows stood on either side of the door. All of the windows and doors were surrounded by simple, yet elegant, black woodwork, which would have normally contrasted nicely against the stone. *You know, if this house had not been in a Demonscape with floating Viking longboats in the sky.*

Upon them entering this ornate looking house, all of those feelings of eeriness and unease had worsened and had now become excruciatingly exacerbated. It seemed as if the very air itself was now thick with the sense of imminent danger. The hairs stood up on the back of Kiko's neck as she stood inside this old vacuous building. No matter what she did, she could not shake a feeling deep inside her. This palpitating, tingling doubt. *This tickling dread in the back of her head.* It felt to her as if the house had somehow come to life and that it did not like them being there. Not one bit. It was as if their arrival had been an affront to every brick, window, door, pipe and floorboard around her. The walls seemed to pulsate with an angry energy that bled into your soul and that the floorboards creaked with an unbound vexation and desire to inflict pain. It felt like the house was breathing, or rather like it had given a tremendous, bellowing sigh upon their arrival. *Or maybe it was all in her head?*

The house itself, if you could pardon the expression, was a complete shit-hole. It was vile. A disgusting cesspit of mouldering decay. Discarded furnishings lay abandoned, rotting away across the entirety of the building. Tattered, faded wallpaper decorated the cracked walls. Chipped black painted clung to the remnants of the ageing floorboards. This house was a repellent display of stomach-churning nausea. The dilapidated interior of this uninviting abode was unequivocally worsened when you considered the unwilling inhabitants who lived here. The children unfortunate enough to call it home. Four young children, approximately aged from ten to fourteen, were found sat huddled together in what one might have assumed to have been the kitchen, aeons ago. There had been no food here to lead to this conclusion, it had all long since rotted away into little more than the dusty musings of distant memory. But there had been a rusted up, beaten in cooker. *Not that it still worked.* This house had also been home to about a hundred or so rats and a whole array of cockroaches and woodlice, as well as a variety of other squirming critters. It was probably a safe assumption that these creatures had been what the children were relying on for nutrients. *Yes, that was just a fancy way of saying that these children had been eating rats and insects.* But one does what they must to stay alive. Regardless of the cost to comfort or the taste on their tongues.

Kiko ran to the nearest wall and pulled a stethoscope out from within the seemingly bottomless pocket on her coat with a fervent yank. She then began using it to listen at the wall, as if it had been a patient at her hospital and Kiko was now a pious doctor about to do a routine examination, or if Kiko was now a wily thief prowling in the night. Listening to the ticks and clicks of a rotary combination lock on a safe, like the safe cracking cat-burglars of olden days. *At least this second analogy would have meant that Diane would no longer be the only wannabe bank robber here anymore.*

"Your daughter is really weird!" Diane said as she gave Cassandra a doubtful (*and also slightly condescending...*) look as Kiko intently listened to the bricks.

"There's... something in the... walls!" Kiko exclaimed as she continued with her examination, completely ignorant towards Diane's flippant remark. "Some... sort of... spirit..." She continued. "Living in the walls." She gave a concerned look towards her mother as she listened. "It sounds... big... and... angry..."

Until three months ago Gabriella Rodríguez had been living a pleasant little life before she had been kidnapped by the Coven de'la Praxus at her eleventh birthday party on the streets of a sunny Barcelona. Jürgen Schmidt, a fourteen-year-old German boy, had been stolen away when he was returning home from school. Isabelle and Adam Evan-Thompson were a pair of ten-year-old twins from England. These were the names of the children present here, in this damned house. It was probably worth mentioning that one of these children had arrived here with two eyes, but currently only had one. *I won't divulge the details of what happened.* Some stories were just simply too uncouth to be repeated in a civilised conversation. Just know that not every sacrifice makes you a martyr.

Kiko leapt away from the wall and began burning a ball of sage, again taken from within her deep pockets. The act of burning sage was commonly referred to as smudging. Smudging was a good way to repress the negative energy that poltergeists fed on.

"Now would be a really good time to leave!" Kiko proclaimed with a subdued panic.

Diane grabbed at Gabriella and Adam whilst Cassandra tried to calm Jürgen and Isabelle with a conjured ball of light.

"We're here to help. But we have to go right now." Cassandra said whilst giving a strong yet reassuring smile. "You've all done so well. *I'm so proud of you all.* I just need you to be strong for a few more minutes." She held both hands out to the terrified children. *"Can you do that for me?"* She asked as she faked a smile once more.

Diane, Adam and Gabriella dashed the door. Cassandra, Jürgen and Isabelle were right behind them with Kiko following at the rear, still trying every trick she could think of to push back the spirit that she had felt living here. There are no words in the English language for what Kiko had felt when she had listened to the walls of this great house. But as this is a book written in the English language means I still have to try.

Imagine rage. Imagine hatred. Remember how it feels. *How it really feels.* I want you to feel it now. Deep inside of you. Eating at you like a great snake churning away inside of you and snapping at your gut. That stoked fire burning a scorching inferno in the centre of your heart. How that heat sets everything you have ablaze with a vehement, violent ferociousness. That tempted indignation that rises from under your shoulder blades. That fury that locks all of your muscles into stone. The steely grip of your clenched fist crushing in on itself. The pounding drum in your chest that you can hear in your ears. The tight clenching of your jaw. Now add the desire to inflict nothing but pain. That desire to crush everything around you under your heel. A detestable loathing for all life. A feverish scream of untold fury. The abnormally abhorrent and acute determination to devastate and destroy. The quivering desire of absolution. An endless longing to break all that has ever been good in the world. To rip inside its chest and snap, crack and pop everything inside. An intense, everlasting yearning for all of the light of the universe to go dark. To rip at the very foundations of the Earth. To shatter the land and send it all cascading into the murky depth of the sea. A suffocating sense of cold as if you were lost on top of a mountain. Desperate and alone as your very flesh pleads for you to find salvation from the gnawing blizzard that bites at your bones. That hopeless sense of dread that picks at your soul like a desperate vulture determined to consume you before your time. A thousand troubled screams from a thousand wailing widows. The choking taste of blood from starved madmen chewing upon tiny broken shards of glass that puncture the gums as he bites down, lancing the tongue and snapping the teeth with a determination reminiscent of a tapeworm burrowing through the skin. *This is what Kiko had heard.* This is what was here. This is what was now awake. This is what was now coming. This is what was rising in the walls. This is what was under every floorboard. This is what was in every nook and cranny of this vile house of irrefutable injustice.

He was awake and he was coming for what was his.

The Stolen children.

"You're making him angry! He won't let us leave!" Gabriella screamed as she stopped dead in her tracks just before crossing the threshold of the door.

Diane grabbed this little niña by the arm and tried to pull her out of this despicable residence. She heaved and pulled with all of her might. But it made no difference. The girl's feet were planted like roots, Diane could not move her. It was as if something was pulling her back into the house. A repugnant deluge of black ink dug into Diane's arm under the skin like an endless cascade of rusted nails and scratching fingertips that seared at her flesh as if she was a prize pig at a family barbecue. Diane screamed from the pain as Gabriella was lifted off her feet and hurled towards the rear wall of the property. Kiko leapt with as much agile determination as she could muster to try and grab the flying child as she fell, but she was unsuccessful. In her failure, Kiko had been batted away by the impact of Gabriella's falling body and flipped with a painful thud to the now bleeding ground. Gabriella cascaded against the other children, like a human bowling ball crashing against a series of pins. All four children were now pinned against the back wall, squirming like rabbits caught in a bear trap.

All three of the would-be rescuers found themselves being exiled from the property. All three had felt a hard hand slap against their ribs that had pushed them away. All three fell to the ground outside the Edwardian house.

Kiko looked up in an aghast horror to see that the walls of this once tangible hell house had, in a way, faded away into a sort of transparent and semi spectral state. The building had become incorporeal and translucent as it rose upon a pair of great white shoulders. Two colourless, behemoth arms snapped out of the dirt as a whole torso pulled itself from the crumbling mountain top as this Mephistophelian creature released a bellowing guttural howl. This ear-popping scream almost sounded like the foghorn from a ship on a winter's night.

Now would be a good time to point out that like Demons, ghosts also have a wide and varied variety of subspecies. The most common variant of ghost being when something dies. You can have ghost Humans, Elves Dwarves, cats, dogs, cows and chicken. All the original living host needed was the will to not accept death. This giant spectral house was what was referred to as a *'Lar Dos Mortos'*. A literal translation of this being *'the house of the dead.'* Although this name isn't entirely accurate, houses aren't alive. But they can absorb energy, rather like a sponge. Some events are so horrible that they can stain the very fabric of reality. All that is needed is for a clever little Necromancer to pop by and '*poof.*' All that latent energy is converted. Condensed down and given sentience. Some negative experiences can bleed into the walls and all the Necromancer has to do is come by and give it life. *Like an evil midwife delivering a living ghost house unto the world.* The most famous of the Lar Dos Mortos was the home of one H. H. Holmes. Holmes was a serial killer, circa the late 1800s. Holmes had hired a series of different contractors to build him a property. Due to the continual replacement of the workers, Holmes was the only man alive who knew the layout of his house. He used his unique knowledge of the building to hide a series of rooms, halls and entire floors. In these secret places, he had tortured almost two hundred victims. All of them died. All of that death made for the perfect candidate to be converted into a Lar Dos Mortos.

The vampire hunt in Caerphilly had gone well and was over fairly quickly. Kara had now found herself enduring a rather dull water cooler conversation with the usually indignant Mrs McDowley. The same slug-like woman who had given Kara her physical on her first day with the Arcane Intelligence Agency. Due to a misunderstanding, Mrs McDowley had now believed that Kara had shared her keen interest in botany and gardening. *Kara absolutely, one hundred percent, did not.* But that couldn't save her from the barrage of tips and tricks on how to grow the perfect plants that was now coming her way. All Kara could do was nod politely and blindly agree if a pause should arise. Good lord, how Kara had wished to be suddenly whisked away anywhere else.

Perhaps she should have been more careful about what she wished for.

A nervous hand had grabbed Kara by the arm as Kiko teleported her here into this Demonscape. Kiko knew Kara has handy in a fight. For Kara, the conversation with Mrs McDowley had been awful. Sure, Kara had wished for anything to drag her away to anywhere else. *However, this wasn't quite what she had had in mind.* Truth be told, now that she had found herself stood her with a Lar Dos Mortos bearing down upon her, Kara silently wondered if the conversation about the correct way to trim hedges had actually been all that bad after all. But it was too late, she was here for the long haul.

Diane gave a hearty yelp as one of the Viking Longboats came hurtling down from on high and crashed down around her. The skies of this Demonplane had awoken and a downpour of archaic sea vessels was now falling like a nautical avalanche around them. *As if the big demonic house had not been enough to contend with by itself.* Kiko had screamed as another ship landed directly behind her. Kara had almost died from another. Cassandra would have rather died than admit that her minor dodging of one of these falling ships, a simple step to the side, had caused her to feel an extreme amount of pain in her lower back. Don't get old, guys. *It's just an extended period of your back hurting every time you tried to move.*

Despite being nearly phonetically identical, the fact it's raining Viking Longboats should never be confused with the Weather Girls' 1982 pop-song classic *'It's Raining Men.'* This song had reached the number one slot in almost the entire world's Top Ten charts upon its initial release during the eighties. This had been a somewhat understandable occurrence. Despite this event being entirely meteorologically impossible, it had made for a rather catchy tune. The song had also found itself being covered by Geri Halliwell in 2001. Geri Halliwell had once been a member of the extremely popular nineties pop group, the Spice Girls. The Spice Girls motto during this time had been *'Girl Power.'* This had led to them having a very popular career with a certain target audience. Having had such an emotive catchphrase, I occasionally wonder what the Spice Girls would have made of these four women right here, right now. Kiko, Kara, Cassandra and Diane. The reason for this, you see, was that because tonight, for the first time in history, it was raining giant demonic Viking Longboats.

Permanently getting rid of a ghost was usually something resembling a straightforward task. Traditionally all it would usually have required was for you to either reason with the spirit (*and get it to give up*) or you would have to exhume the spirit's physical (*dead in the ground*) body and salt and burn it. But that would only work if there had been a physical body to burn. This house had never truly been alive, so there was nothing to exhume. There was nothing dead and buried. There was also little chance that the Lar Dos Mortos would listen to reason. *(I mean, you were always welcome to try, but it most likely would not end well!)*

A flurry of Kara's magical arrows had done nothing to this deplorable Demon disguised domicile. Instead of these arrows of light hurting this ghost's giant torso when they had broken through the skin, all they had done was make the Lar Dos Mortos laugh. Its laughter was that of a sinister depravity. It replied to Kara's attack with one of its own design. Cassandra had just been fast enough to stop a behemothian closed fist from crushing the life out of Kara. Cassandra struggled and strained as her left had maintained a sizeable, shielding orb over her, Kiko's and Kara's heads, which momentarily held the colossal spirit's hand at bay. The Lar Dos Mortos's hand had collided with such force against this magical shield that it created a loud shock wave and had caused chunks of its rotten hand to loosen and fall around the girls. Cassandra's feet dug into the ground with all of the strength and defiance that she had as she pushed back. Her heart beat with a steadfast resolve. A determined will to never submit. *To never give in.* Not necessarily for herself, but to keep these three girls safe.

The ground cracked under her as she pushed back against the power of the mammothian undead house. To her surprise, she had felt the angry tugging of a skeletal arm that had broken free from the ground under her and was now grabbing at her leg. Cassandra looked across the battlefield to see an endless series of skeleton-like creatures pulling themselves out of the freshly cracked dirt. *As if the Lar Dos Mortos hadn't been enough to contend with!* Her left arm felt as if it might be breaking under the strain of holding this undead's lofty attack away from Kara and Kiko. Her right hand had quickly summoned a series of grey metal spears to rise as if from the very ground itself. These steely javelins impaled through the Lar Dos Mortos's wrist causing it to retract and writhe in tremendous pain. With another flick of her wrist, she summoned a shotgun and threw it at Diane. *This was not just any old shotgun!* This was a pure gold shotgun that had six barrels that were clustered together. The front rather looked like a honeycomb. Cassandra had also summoned a great supply of ammunition at Diane's feet.

"Kiko, Diane, you two deal with crowd control!" She barked with the level of authority you'd have expected from a general at war. "Kara! You and me, we got the big guy!"

Kara nodded.

"I need you to buy me some time!" Cassandra continued as she began wrapping an improvised splint around her arm which had actually snapped from the pressure of holding off an entire house at bay.

"What do you mean I need to buy you some time? Are you alri-?" Kara's concern was cut short as Cassandra tackled her out of the way of another great swing from the Lar Dos Mortos.

"Pay more attention to your surroundings and less attention to how I'm doing!" Cassandra snapped as she cradled her arm.

Kiko looked out across an infinitude of skeletal humanoids. An endless wave of featureless faces bit at her with ferocious teeth and attempted to scratch her with their bleached bony fingers. This writhing tide of gnashing horror was constant. An unrelenting alabaster army of uncaring undead, so determined to kill these unwelcome invaders that none of the freshly risen soldiers cared if they were crushing one another. And they were. Perhaps if they had all been as smart as they were determined to kill, they might have been more efficient when achieving their goals. Their desperation had made them easier to deal with, as they were all clamouring over each other. It was rather like shooting fish in a barrel. *At least for now.* One little slip up would easily result in the girls being a feast for a thousand biting teeth. Being ripped apart limb by limb under a sheet of bones and death. Or crushed to death by the flailing arms from the giant torso of the Lar Dos Mortos, that was sticking out of the ground.

One such oversized limb came tumbling down towards Cassandra and crushed her frail human body as if she had been little more than a grape.

'Pop!' No more Cassandra...

Or rather, one such oversized limb came tumbling down towards her and had intended to crush Cassandra's frail human body as if she had been little more than a grape. But instead, it had been stopped by something. *Something incredibly strong.* That something was a human body. Kiko span around on the spot to see her brother, Vincent, floating above them, some ten feet in the air. He had taken the entirety of the tremendous punch from the Lar Dos Mortos and saved his mother's life! It was as if this strike from the Lar Dos Mortos had been nothing more than a fly landing on his shoulder. Vincent felt a tremendous rage boil within him as he noticed his mother's broken arm. His long, black coat billowed perfectly as he landed into a pose that some referred to as the superhero landing. If asked, Vincent would politely deny and play down all comments that had compared him to a superhero. Vincent had always sworn to be little more than a *'normal guy'* doing the *'right thing.'* That he was neither any more special nor powerful than you and me. *This still couldn't change the fact that Kiko had once seen him knock a dragon unconscious with a single uppercut!* Or the fact that he had about a hundred or so different titles that people like to refer to him by. Vincent, *'the Vanquisher of Valdoon,'* never actually liked to use these titles. There wasn't enough space for him to write them all down whenever he would fill out his name on a form. And people would only ever refer to him by one title at a time; as no one had the time, or energy, to say each one, one after another. Vincent, *'the Defender of the Wakeless Void,'* felt a tremendous panic wash over him as he found himself examining his mother's makeshift splint that encased her arm. This monster would pay for that! And he responded the only way he knew how. He burst into the air once more like a rocket and walloped the towering Lar Dos Mortos right between the eyes. (*So, technically right between the bedroom windows then,*

I guess...?) The Lar Dos Mortos recoiled from the force behind the great hit and released a deep wail.

"Vincent be careful! There are still children inside!" Cassandra howled with a wide-eyed stare.

"THERE ARE WHAT INSIDE?" Kara proclaimed as she summoned her bow of light once more.

The arrow she had shot had a silvery, silk-like rope attached to it, rather like a thick spider's web. She had used this to grapple up the dark wooden door that constituted as the Lar Dos Mortos's mouth. She buried one of her axe blades deep within the wall of its face for something to hold onto as she tried to pry the door off of its hinge as it thrashed around. To her surprise, she had found Vincent, *'the Slayer of Calvackoom,'* landing next to her to give her a helping hand. No Seriously! *He literally began punching at the door.* Together they knocked the great door off its hinges and went deep inside the belly of the beast. A few moments later Kara reappeared with the four children. But where was Vincent, *'the Saviour Incarnate?'*

The Lar Dos Mortos let out a blood-curdling cry as its head *(technically house)* was effortlessly lifted clean off of its shoulders. Vincent hung in the air for a second before launching the ghostly building-head directly at the retreating skeleton army, crushing a great deal of them as they fled.

Thank god Vincent was there to save the day once more!

Approximately an hour had passed. The children had been rushed to hospital and their worrying parents had been informed. This hospital was also where Cassandra was getting her arm seen to. Vincent and Kara had both returned to work with a renewed respect for each other and how they'd both had instantaneously reacted upon hearing that children were at the risk of danger. Diane watched out from the curbside where she was sat, as an unmarked van appeared to take her to her new life with the AIA's witness protection programme. She was sat here with her arm wrapped around her new friend, Kiko.

"A deal is a deal!" Diane said as she gently tightened her grip around the girl who had saved her life. "All those World War Two ghosts that have been disappearing? I know who's doing it. They're being kidnapped, Kiko. The

Demons want them for a weapon they think can break time. There's this creepy looking dude with a metal hand. He's the one you want. They call him the Dark Hand."

Kiko froze for a moment, that was a lot of information to take in all at once.

The Dark Hand? Who was that? *What did it mean to break time?* The information was definitely helpful, but Kiko had had a long day. This way of new information floored her. It was almost too much for her brain to take in and process. She just wanted to sleep. If this was true, then this was the exact sort of lead she had needed. Thanks to Diane Sheffield hadn't been an entire bust. So Kiko thanked Diane before escorting her to the van. Diane gave Kiko another big hug, the kind that makes it hard to breathe.

"Oh, one more thing. You need to be careful, Kiko. The Dark Hand already knows who you are. *He hates you Kiko and he wants you dead."*

Chapter Nine

EVERYONE LOVES A PARTY!

Diane had given Kiko a lot to think about with her revelations about the Dark Hand and his involvement with the non consenting spirits' disappearance. Not only did Kiko now have a name, but she had also been given something that resembled a motive. But only one thought had continued to revolve in her brain like a mysterious carousel; who the hell was the Dark Hand?

She had never heard of this *'Dark Hand'* before, so she had decided to ask some of the more senior members of the Arcane Intelligence Agency to see what they knew. The most useful answer had come directly from her boss, Jallasper Winterblaze. He was an elderly Elf who was the head agent of the entire Temporal Bureau of Investigations. This also meant that he tended to be extremely busy all of the time. Mister Winterblaze was a fairly reserved and courtly gentleman that was getting on in his years. His hair was well kept and as white as snow, as was his well-trimmed beard. He was a usually polite gentleman, but short on patience. He also had a fond love for pinstriped suits and all forms of steam-powered and gear based mechanisms. This old Elve's steampunk-themed office had more closely resembled the insides of an old steam train, filled with cogs and contraptions, than it had the office one would normally expect from a senior agent at the world's foremost magical policing network.

Mister Winterblaze had been the one who had told Kiko about the known origins of the Dark Hand. How he had been a faithful servant of the

Demon Queen, Lilith, up until a point where he had betrayed her because of his insatiable greed and lust for power. Apparently Lilith had not been appreciative of his desires to steal power from her and exiled him from her dimension as punishment for his actions. Winterblaze had shown a weird mix of confusion and concern upon hearing the Dark Hand's name being mentioned for the first time in over fifty years. He warned Kiko to show caution and demanded that she focus purely on this case of abducted spirits, because if it had been in any way true that the Dark Hand was involved in these kidnappings, then only bad things were to follow. Especially if it was true that it involved a weapon that could break time. When it came to answers about the Dark Hand, Winterblaze had been a lot more helpful than Llewelyn had been. When Kiko had asked him if he knew anything about the Dark Hand, he had simply replied by choking on (*and subsequently spitting*) his coffee all over himself and his office. Kiko had assumed this was due to some level of ineptitude on his part. *Obviously, we know the real reason why Llewelyn acted in such a shocked manner upon hearing Kiko ask what he knew about the Dark Hand, his alter ego.*

There were so many contrasting thoughts, theories and questions about the whos and the whys racing through Kiko's brain that it had become hard for her to focus on any of them long enough to create a tangible thought process out of any of it. Her thoughts were becoming jumbled and confusingly crowded. *She felt herself becoming overwhelmed by it all.* There had always been a simple, yet slightly unorthodox, method that Kiko had adopted over the years whenever her thoughts and stresses had become too much for her to handle. A straightforward and therapeutic act that she had found to be both relaxing and to bring a sense of clarity to her mind afterwards. *She would redecorate her bedroom.* Whereas some would feel the need to meditate or do yoga to refocus their minds and to think clearer, she would roll up her sleeves and paint her walls as a means to deal with any of her psychological and worldly problems. It would force the world to stop around her, as she locked herself away in her room. It gave her time to stop and catch her breath. To think things through from a different angle. To re-evaluate her life whilst she was too distracted to think about anything else. Plus, they say that a change was as good for the soul as a rest was.

A dollop of navy paint washed over a freshly primed white wall. All of Kiko's possessions had been exiled into the centre of the room under a series of old white blankets. A secreted kingdom from a lifetime of trinkets and nostalgic keepsakes. These items had included a wide array of books, clothes, photographs and a certain *'Mister Theodore,'* the old and battered stuffed teddy bear that she could never bring herself to get rid of. Regardless of how wrecked he was.

Music was also a very important part of this process as well. They say you can tell a lot about a person by the music that they listened to. Apparently it revealed a slither of their soul to the world for all to see. Perhaps unsurprisingly, Kara liked to listen to the meaty riffs of Classic Rock, Metal and Pop Punk. Cassandra and Collin had shared a love for Country music and Power Ballads. Vincent had always been *'too busy for music.'* But this hadn't stopped Kiko from accidentally walking in on him singing his heart out to soundtracks from several different musicals over the years. There may be some people out there who would be surprised to learn that Kiko's favourite choice of music to listen to was gangster rap and hip-hop. Despite her scrawny, book-wormy appearance, she could often be found tearing up the dance floor to any and all rap songs about some G. living in the Hood with his money, his guns and his bitches. To be fair, her dancing had usually been reminiscent of a drunken giraffe riding a skateboard. A series of flailing arms, struts and an absurdly off-putting amount of randomly pointing at the poor innocent people attempting to dance near her.

This being the style of music that she had chosen to listen to again for the millionth time today as she decorated. An old, battered Walkman cassette player floated in the air behind her as she worked. It was currently being held together by nothing short of pure determination, dried paint spillings and duct tape. It was currently blaring mad beats about thug life in the Hood directly (*and loudly*) through a pair of retro, over-the-head headphones and straight into Kiko's ears. She bopped and weaved like a flamboyant boxer as she painted, lost to her favourite beats. If anyone had seen her *'dancing'* it would have most likely been a cause for ridicule. *Actually no.* That's not true, I take that back. Everyone in this house had seen this spectacle of struts, sways and bops far too many times by now for it to be anything less than part of the daily routine of life. Even if it was something that was terribly cringe-inducing to behold.

The word *'DARKHAND'* had been painted upon the colours of the old wall, as a method of keeping her mind somewhat focused on her mission. Even if it had currently read as *'RKHAND'* as it had continually lost ground to the encroaching navy paint line that was quickly consuming it, as Kiko methodically painted her way up and down, up and down, up and down the walls in time with her music.

Cassandra was currently busy in the house below as she was getting ready for yet another party to celebrate the magnificence that was Vincent Attetson and his defeat of the Succubus that had attacked Liverpool a few weeks prior. She had taken a great deal of offence at Kiko's decision to decorate her room today instead of helping her arrange the house for the evening's festivities. But in Kiko's defence, things usually lost their appeal the more often they happened. This had been the sixth, or maybe even the seventh, party to celebrate one of Vincent's many accomplishments in the last two years alone. It didn't help that for each one of these parties, Cassandra had insisted that she needed to outdo the one prior. She was her own worst enemy when it came to putting on a show. She was also her biggest critic. Nothing she ever did had ever been quite good enough.

But nonetheless, Kiko had little interest in adding to the facade that would boost Vincent's ego anymore. She had been hard pushed to find a place in their spacious home to store his oversized ego as it was already. This was not to say the Kiko wasn't happy for her brother, of course she was. As such she would definitely be attending the party later on tonight and joining in with the celebrations. But she still had her own life to live in the meantime and saw very little reason why she should put her life on hold for yet another one of those grandiose spectacles her mother liked to call a *'party.'* The whole world would have to revolve around Vincent without her for the time being. *Another line of vibrantly blue paint made its lasting mark on the wall.*

To her surprise, Kiko had realised Vincent was actually painting alongside her, even if she had no idea how long he had been there for. She quickly removed her headphones and looked towards her brother, confused as to why he had been lending a helping hand in the first place. It wasn't usually in his nature to help. *What did he want?*

"What's a Rkhand?" Vincent asked jokingly of the partially painted-over writing on the wall.

"Oh, that?" Kiko asked as she glanced at her handiwork. "Oh, that's just someone from a case that Mister Winterblaze has me looking into. His name is the Dark Hand." She replied with a coy attitude. "Apparently he's like a Demon lord or something, I dunno..." Kiko's reply had been one of a calculated coolness. She gave a sideways glance to her brother in a discrete attempt to gauge what his reaction might be. A part of Kiko had wanted him to be jealous of her for working directly under the head of the TBI. An even larger part of her wanted him to be proud of his little sister and the work she had been accomplishing lately. *She wanted him to acknowledge her.* Just once. She would even settle for him thinking this new case of hers was '*bad-ass.*'

"Oh wow. That's big." Vincent replied as he continued to paint without breaking his stride.

What the freaking hell was that? *'Big?'* Had that been the words of jealousy or had that been a tone of pride? *'Big?' 'BIG?'* What the hell kind of reaction was that? *Who the hell referred to things as big?* He hadn't been ordering his preferred size of coffee or takeaway meal! *Oh my god!* What a freak. Kiko was now straining her neck backwards to attempt another measuring of Vincent's demeanour about what she had just told him as the insecurities of her sibling rivalry whispered in her ear.

"It's about time that the Temporal Bureau realised how talented you are, sis'. I'm proud of you." He turned to her and gave her a big smile.

…

A shocked splosh of blue paint fell from Kiko's paintbrush and stained the floor as she stood there frozen in an amazed state of dumbfounded speechlessness. Kiko's whole world seemed to momentarily freeze.

"Yeah." She cleared her throat and tried to pretend that she had been unaffected by and indifferent to his words. "I mean, yeah! Maybe one day I'll even get a party of my own, right?" She playfully taunted towards her brother with a jovial wink.

"Yaayyyy!" Vincent sighed sarcastically. *"God, always gotta have a party!"* He said under another heavily sarcastic tone. This reply had confused Kiko somewhat.

"I thought you loved all that?" She gave him a curious look. Could this mean that she had been wrong about her brother for all these years?

"Oh good god no, I hate it." He replied whilst laughing. "They're just so awkward! Do you know the other day, I saw this little girl getting attacked by some demon-thing, and I almost didn't step in to save her?" His jokey demeanour sank into one of a serious nature. "I genuinely second-guessed myself for a moment if it was worth it because I knew how mom would react."

Kiko watched her brother as a wave of tender concern washed over her. *What was happening?* They never spoke like this? They were never this open and honest with each other. Why was he being like this? Oh no! *Was he dying?* Vincent had mistaken Kiko's look of concern for him and his well being for a look of derision on whether or not he had actually saved the little girl or not.

"I mean, of course I saved her." He gave a nervous laugh. "But I almost didn't go through with it. It was just the idea of, y'know… *yet another Attetson celebration.*" He trailed off as he stared blankly into the wall. "You know Kiko, Sometimes I get the feeling you hate me."

"No, don't be stupid. You're my brother and I love you so very much! I'm proud of you and everything you've done." That was what Kiko had intended to say to this accusation of hatred. But for some unknown reason, the words tasted like a lie. Sorry, no. Not a lie. *Like a cheap cliché.* As she found herself standing there, she realised that she had nothing to say on the matter. Sure, sometimes she had felt trapped under his shadow and it had led to her feeling extremely frustrated with him and his entire persona. She felt as if every *'normal'* victory she had ever achieved had felt small when compared to his successes. *But that didn't equate to her hating him.* Not even for a single second. She was proud of his achievements. *But perhaps she had been in the wrong all this time?* She had never once asked how he was. She had never checked in on the man who had seemed to live the perfect life. She had never even felt the need to do so. It hadn't occurred to her, not even once in over twenty years. She also realised that her brother had just asked her if she hated him and she still had not replied yet. *Oh good god!* It had been quite a while. *She really should say something!*

"I'm sorry… but what's going on?" She gingerly enquired. For some reason this was the best reply she could muster. "Are you okay, dude?"

Whenever people achieve great things in life it is often forgotten that they are still just ordinary people at the end of the day. Regardless of their fame, power or title. They were still just real people with real emotions. People with flaws, fears and doubts. *Like me and you.* In this way, even the highest flung celebrity could be plagued by the same ailments as a down-on-their-luck homeless person. It was often said that success could be just as bitter-sweet as failure. People often joked that at least rich people could cry in their Ferraris. This flippant attitude was often needlessly cruel. Since when did having physical ownership over property negate human rights? You have things in your possession that, let's say, a homeless person does not. Does the simple fact that you own something they did not mean that you were no longer entitled to feel anxious, sad, hurt or paranoid about things in your personal life? *Of course not.* Yet somehow, when a person is seen as successful we seem to forget that there is a real person in there, somewhere under all that gold. As it turns out, this had been the case for Vincent. The man who had fought with demigods, dragons, Demons and a whole plethora of other oversized nasties. The man that had become famous for saving the entire planet at least sixteen different occasions in the last decade alone. All of that success had rewarded him with a lifetime supply of fame and glory.

And he hated it.

He had a monster living under his skin. It had stolen his face and robbed him of his life. Fame was a curse that had dragged him into the spotlight. All he had wanted to do was to be closer with his baby sister, who he had loved more than anything else in the entire world. But all of that fame and success had driven a great wedge between them. *A great cavernous void that seemed impossible to cross.* Vincent was fully aware of the resentment Kiko had felt towards him for the way that everyone else had doted upon him. He knew how conflicted this resentment made her and how it cut her up like a big guilty knife inside her gut. How it tormented her with shame; this guilt of her secret jealousy. He knew she loved him. *(Or at least he really, really, really hoped that she did!)* He wanted to be more honest with her. *He yearned to tell her about the secret monster that was within him.* But he could not overcome his self-doubt. He was riddled with it. Like we all are. He was afraid that this honesty would drive a further wedge between them. All of the self-doubt, pain and suffering from carrying the fame of the entire world upon his shoulders for so long had exhausted him. He had never known the correct words to say to Kiko. *He never knew how to reveal his inner monster.* He was scared of how she would view him if she knew the truth about him and how weak he really was. So he had always kept a straight face when he was around her and he kept her at arm's length. He had once decided that it had somehow kept her safe, although, in reality, it had probably just been to protect himself. Recently he had begun to realise how much he had regretted doing so. *He had begun to question if it was all worth it.* He figured that it was never too late to try and start again with someone. To start from the beginning and to at least try and do it right this time. It had taken seeing Kiko and his mother almost dying at the hands of the Lar Dos Mortos to make him see what was important to him. He had also heard how Kiko had defused a bank robbery by herself with nothing more than words of compassion. *He realised he could do with some compassion in his life.*

"I hope you realise, Kiko, that I don't like any of this. This endless parading." He looked his sister dead in the eyes. "I know you've always felt put out by how mom and dad treated me. I know that's why Muhren left." His voice began to break. "And I am sorry for it all. I guess what I'm trying to say is... I'm sorry." He quickly looked away as tears began to form. "I'm sorry for everything."

Emotions can sometimes be somewhat like a great light, this is to say that the emotions in our head can feel blinding. And blinded is what Kiko felt right now. *What the hell was happening?* Kiko had found herself dumbstruck once more. Completely lost for words. Nothing was computing, it was like her entire existence had just shut down. A muted shock gripped her bones as a sense of sadness carried its way through her veins. Every word she had ever learned how to say throughout her entire life was now seemingly lost to her. I mean, what could she even say to that? There was no word in any language that could do her emotions the justice that they deserved. This was an even more impressive statement when you realised that Kiko fluently spoke eight different languages. Yet somehow, despite having a vocabulary nearly eight times larger than your average person, she still couldn't find the words. *Nothing.* It was like her entire soul and dropped out of her body.

Kiko quickly grabbed Vincent's hand as he made his way to sheepishly exit the room.

"Thank you." She whispered as a single tear escaped down her cheek.

He found himself responding with a weak smile before clearing his throat and acting all manly. *Because emotions suck.*

"I need to get ready for the party. Can we talk afterwards?" He sheepishly asked as he looked towards the floor with an uncomfortable air.

"Of course!"

It had been some two hours of quiet contemplation later before Kara had barged into the room carrying with her a long flowing red dress.

"Cass' says it's time to get ready!" Kara informed as she thrust the red dress into Kiko's arms. "Wasn't your room blue like a year ago?" A puzzled, borderline moronic, look was draped across her face as she examined the walls with confusion.

Kiko quickly squirrelled her way into the fancy red dress that her mother had picked out for her. It was an off the shoulder, refined bodycon design of ruby red silks that effortlessly contoured itself to the shape of her body. It had somehow made her seem taller and more striking than she normally looked. *She looked stunning.* The deep reds of the fabric, and the way in which it was cut, was reminiscent of the blossoming petals of a crimson rose on the first day of spring. A fancy black trim ran across the seams and highlights of the bodice in the decoration of little black flowers. The dress flowed in such a way that it drew attention to a slit just off the front that had allowed for her to walk. The dress had also somehow been the perfect shade of red to suit her ginger hair (*which she wore down to the side*) so that neither shade had become washed out.

Despite being a design of regal beauty, *Kiko had absolutely hated it.* She hated how the long flowing fabrics had required her to wear a pair of matching red heels. She hated how tight the dress was around her ribcage. She hated how aggressive the colour was and how it inevitably would draw attention to her. And she hated how much of her leg the slit revealed as she walked. Regardless of how much Kiko despised this dress, this could not stop the involuntary '*oh damn*' that had escaped Kara's lips when she had seen how elegant and beautiful her lifelong friend had looked in it.

"Hey! How come you're not all dressed up?" Kiko asked with an annoyed tone to her voice as she realised that Kara was still wearing her trademark leather jacket and black jeans from before.

"Nuh-uh!" Kara proclaimed in a child-like manner as she pointed to a studded earring that was pinned to her earlobe. "That's pure diamond that is!" As if a fancy pair of earrings had constituted as dressing up fancy. "Oop! Just one more thing!"

And with that Kara jumped up off Kiko's bed, walked up to her and removed her thick-rimmed glasses. Kiko's world instantly became blurry and out of focus. *She hated that too!*

"Perfect!"

And, to be fair, Kiko looked it. Despite her scrawny frame and penchant for strange clothing, Kiko scrubbed up well when the situation called for it. Although the ironic thing was that she didn't even know that she looked good. She had been too busy being preoccupied with how far this devil dress had pushed her out of her comfort zone (*and assuming that this change had made her look hideous*) to consider that she might actually look good in it. To her, she was a walking embarrassment. Nothing more than a crimson billboard on long legs to gather the attention of wandering eyes. A travesty of garishness that would incite ridicule.

But she was strong and she was determined. *So she would endure.*

She took a single defiant step towards the door.

And naturally lost her balance thanks to the new heels and poor vision thanks to the lack of glasses. Falling face first, straight into the wall. Collapsing like a house of cards on a windy day.

I think by now we all knew that Cassandra liked to put on a good show and that she had excelled at lavish displays of splendour and gravitas. *Tonight was no exception.* The downstairs of their house had been literally transformed into something that rather resembled a great, ornate cathedral of high stony, chiselled arches and pillars. Anyone aware of the Dwarven architecture of old would say that Cassandra's magical redesign of her house was reminiscent of the Great Dwarven Citadels of Thrúll, Thrów and

Thren. A masterfully crafted mural had been painted onto the ornate gold ceiling that hung some forty feet above your head. This painting detailed Vincent's past deeds. The vastitude of demons, aliens, vampires, dragons and werewolves that he had defeated over the years. Impressive chandeliers hung from thin air and dimly lit the ornate chambers with a low light above you as you walked through the bustling crowds. The ground beneath your feet was that of thick glass, that served as a window to red-dyed waters that lay beneath. Through this glass could be seen a menagerie of aquatic life blubbing around on the tides of their day to day life. The term 'aquatic life' wasn't just limited to the fish, jellyfish and dolphins. In these well-lit depths you could also see Water Imps, Merpeople and Glasslings. (*Glasslings were eel-like creatures that had luminous spines (that shone through their semi-transparent skin) and long horns that stuck out the top of their heads. They looked somewhat like legless, underwater Unicorns.*)

Small groups of musicians were gathered on compact black metal stages. These stages were round and stood appropriately four foot from the ground and allowed the music they played to carry over the crowds of happy partiers. These musicians were all playing gentle traditional Japanese string music in majestic unison. The caterers for this event had been a plethora of fairies. They hoisted great big (*average-sized!*) serving trays above their heads and flew mouth-watering appetiser directly into the hands of the discerning party-goers.

The actual attendees of this party had included a great number of presidents, prime ministers, otherworldly leaders and lesser politicians looking to make a name for themselves. A great number of agents from the Arcane Intelligence Agency were here as well. These crowds had also attracted the attention of semi-famous actors, musicians and other socially parasitic would-be celebrities. These '*celebrities*' had been hunting for the next big social gathering to attach their brand image to. Some ostentatious event to garnish the attention of the tabloids and boost their careers by appearing on the pages of some cheap gossip magazine. But to be fair, who could blame them for wanting to be here? *For many, this was the closest they would get to being in the presence of a god.*

Somehow the entirety of the downstairs of Kiko's home had ballooned in size to fit this utopia inside. Needless to say, this had not been how her home had looked on the other three-hundred and sixty-four days of the year. They had actually lived in a normal-ish house the rest of the time, and not in some sweeping cavern of grand pillars with a floor stolen from an overly pretentious aquarium. The last party Cassandra had thrown resulted in the downstairs of their home transforming into a knock-off Moroccan palace. The time before that, the party had had an ice theme which had resulted in what could only really be described as a snowy tundra invading their living space.

Encrazed children ran through the bustling crowds, stirred with the merriment of youthful games. They galloped and they danced as their hearts heaved with excitement; their elbows clipping against the occasional miffed adult as they ran on by. Alcohol was flowing this night like a waterfall in a thunderstorm. These intoxicated adults swapped intensely detailed stories and drunken tales of life with other inebriated adults who listened attentively as they sloshed drinks down their gullets. The heaviest of these drinkers were of course the Dwarves. *But honestly, such a sentence wasn't really a surprise now, was it?* Hardly a hardier laugh could be heard from within the braying rabble of high-spirited party goers. A great number of Elves were also in attendance tonight. They were little more than a huddled amassed assembly of eyebrows raised in unison as they cast a discerningly condemnatory and judgemental glare over the other, more jovial, attendees and their sophomoric ways. The Orcs that were here hadn't quite gotten to the point where everything was a drunken challenge for a fight, but the night was still young. *Give it time.* Time once had it that the best race to have at a party was the Halflings. And some things would never change. These little people loved a good celebration and were naturally talented when it came to having fun. They played with the children, they drank with the Dwarves. They even danced with the Orcs and had made a few of the Elves join in too.

The air was alive with the rousing, pulsating energy from all of these great races and people merging together as one. I suppose that was why people loved to party; it was an excuse to bring everyone together. A reason to stand in unison and to momentarily discard the things that separated us as people and caused bitter divides. True, it was only a matter of time before someone would become offended. *But for now, things were good.* The world was severely lacking in good, so everyone made the most of it whilst they could. This was why Cassandra spent so much time when planning these events. For the chance to unite everyone and bring them together. For all the unlikely friendships and unions that were forged at her events. The relationships that would form that would have been extremely unlikely if not for her and her involvement.

But one thing could definitely be said about tonight's affair. No man alive, be he Human, Elf, Dwarf, Orc or Halfling, was quite sure of how any of the red themes, the grand Stone architecture or aquatic life had connected themselves to either Liverpool or Succubi attack they had suffered. *Perhaps you could think of what the connection had been?*

Kiko awkwardly scuffed her way down the marble staircase with support from Kara. Regardless of how many of these transformations she'd seen, Kiko had always felt weirded out by seeing the downstairs of her house change so drastically with each party. Funnily enough, speaking of a drastic change, it had seemed that every head at this party had been turned when she had entered it; amazed by the transformation of her own. It was amazing the difference a bit of clothing could make to a person's appearance. Cassandra hurried her way towards her daughter and sighed at the clumps of blue paint that were ruining Kiko's hair and smudged all over the side of her face. With a snap of Cassandra's fingers, Kiko was clean and ready to be set free.

The girls made their way to a cluster of their friends. This group had included the jovial Ozzy and cantankerous, pink-haired Penelope that had shared in Kara's victory brunch at Marvin's when she had first been employed by the Bureau of Necrological Investigations.

Some while later there had been a thunderous din of cheering when the guest of honour had finally arrived. Vincent was finally here, his arms linked with his girlfriend, Kaya Kiribati. Kaya was a household name in her own right. The sort of celebrity who was famous for... for doing *something...?* But no one was exactly sure what that was. *I think she may have been a model once?* Or was she in a band...? She had big, bouncy raven-black hair and dark hazel eyes. Her smile was almost as wide as her waist. *(Which for a smile was pretty wide but less so for a waistline!)* She was famously pleasant. Especially when around cameras. She was also rather vacantly minded and not too bright when engaged in direct conversation. The picturesque couple beckoned and waved to the impressed crowds. They had a level of refinery one might have expected to see from a member of a royal family.

A few hours had passed. Kiko and Kara now found themselves deep within Collin's study. This room was a kingdom of varnished woods and timeless trinkets and curious artefacts. Bizarre statues of ancient cultures lined the shelves of a tall shelving unit. A tall bookcase housed a wide array of fancy-looking books. The sounds of the downstairs party wafted through the floorboards below.

"I still can't believe he said all that stuff to you!" Kara proclaimed as she hunted through a pile of jackets that lay on top of the desk. The conversation Kiko had shared with her brother earlier that day was still playing on her mind. She was currently sat on the edge of her father's desk. Crossed legged and still wrapped in the velvet red dress.

"I know!" She replied as she examined her hands. She didn't have anything on them, she was just nervous from all of the contemplating she was currently doing about her relationship with her brother. "We've never really had a friendship like that, y'know? We have never really had a heart-to-heart before!"

The reason for the girls being here, opposed to still being at the party, was rather straightforward. See, Kara was a smoker. And right now she desperately wanted the sweet release of a quick blast of nicotine. But she had found herself without any tobacco. *This was a problem.* See, you can't smoke without tobacco. *(Well can, but shut up! You'll get me in trouble!)* Kara knew that Vincent had shared an addiction to this smokey habit as well. She knew that this study had been where he had stashed his jacket. For those who don't smoke there is always an inherent urge to look down on those who chose to do so. For those who don't smoke (*for argument's sake let's call them 'Clean Lungs'*), it was just about the most baffling thing a human could willingly choose to partake in. If your body was a temple, why would people willingly inhale dangerous toxins that would inevitably destroy this temple? *'Clean Lungs'* loved to be condescending towards smokers for their choice of habit. But the reason why smokers chose to infect themselves was fairly straightforward; it felt good. *And who doesn't like things that feel good?* Some smokers also thought it looked cool. *And who didn't want to look cool?* It also made you hack up your lungs with odious coughing fits that could wake a sleeping giant. *And who wouldn't want to hack up their lungs with odious coughing fits that could wake a sleeping giant?* You also wouldn't be able to run great distances anymore without being short-breathed. It also made your breath smell like an old ashtray at the dust factory. *But at least it felt good for like a whole three seconds.* That moment of relief was deemed enough by all smokers to make the risks seem worth it. *(But each and every smoker also knew that they were secretly immune to getting ill. And even if they got ill, then they might as well keep smoking. Because they already had cancer, so what was the point of stopping now? Besides, nobody liked a quitter!)*

The goal was simple. Steal some of Vincent's tobacco without him realising. Kara grasped at his coat and a small box fell from within one of its pockets. Quietly thudding on the surface of the hard oak floor. It was a small black box, approximately two inches wide. On the rear side was two small hinges. There was always something about a sealed container that piqued intrigue. As such, being curious as to what Vincent was hiding inside, Kara naturally opened it without a moment's hesitation.

It was a ring.

The ring was pure gold and it had a diamond inserted right into the top. This diamond was so big that it had made the ones in Kara's earrings seem tiny in comparison. *Which was fine*, it wasn't a competition. The size of the diamond didn't mean anything, likewise, it wouldn't mean anything when Kara would later remove her diamond earrings and discretely hide them in her pocket until the night was over! *She wasn't ashamed of her tiny diamonds. Shut up, stop over analysing and move on!*

This ring had been why Vincent had been so open with his sister earlier today! He was going to ask Kaya to marry him. They had been together for three years now and the time had felt right. It had also felt like the right time to build bridges with his sister. *Love had the strangest way of making us all think clearer.* To bring everyone together and want to live as one.

"What is it?" Kiko asked as she lifted herself off of the desk for a better view.

"I know Vincent's dirty little secret!" Kara said jokingly as she turned with a big smile on her face to show Kiko what her brother had intended to do.

'WHACK!!' The ring fell back to Earth as the girls disappeared suddenly without a single warning!

An abrupt and sudden terrible light had engulfed the two gossiping girls. An awfully noxious smell penetrated their noses as a wave of nauseousness made the entire room spin out of control. Their knees buckled and their eyes burned. The room of oaks and books swirled away, like water down a sinkhole. In its place was a horribly cold metal room. The wooden floor was ripped out from beneath their feet without warning and swapped around them for a much smaller room. *A room of metal and plastics.* The room was super cramped and vibrated under their feet. The girls shared a terrified and alarmed look. *Where were they?* It was eerily quiet and it was difficult to move. *Were they now in some sort of prison?* The sounds of the party had been washed away and replaced with the noise of a gentle hum that seemed to be coming from the walls.

A sudden deep sickness gripped Kiko's stomach as the burning sensation of vomit hung in the back of her throat. She stood for a moment fighting the urge to simply pass out on the spot. She looked out at the confinement of silver walls. What the hell had just happened? *Where were they?*

As it turns out, they were in the depths of space. Not that they knew it yet. They were in a spacecraft that was about to go to war with an army of soulless cyborgs. But they didn't know that either! But why were they here? What was happening? Why were they in space? Will Kiko get to be a maid of honour at Kaya and Vincent's wedding?

Keep reading to find out.

Chapter Ten

THE GODSHIP COMETH.

Space was always the final frontier. This was given to the fact that regardless of how far any fledgling or experienced astronaut chose to travel, there was always more space to be found. Some far off undiscovered constellation, nebula or galaxy was always one step ahead. These eager pathfinders were never short on new discoveries of further life to stumble upon. These trailblazing interplanetary pioneers would never run out of universe to feed their appetites. This was both a good and bad thing from both an objective and subjective viewpoint. Yes, the universe would offer you everything. - *It literally housed all stuff in existence.* - All of time and space. Some far off new land, a paradise of unimaginable wealth. An endless bastion of new life, colours, shapes, sizes and stories to either be learned or told anew. It also offered nothing in the way of closure. *If you were in a relationship with the universe every day would bring a new exciting date.*

For breakfast you could go cliff diving off the mountains of Allapraxia, brunch was swimming in the seas of Delta Twenty Three, lunch is travelling the jungles of Bantio searching for the ever-elusive *'Lesser Silver Spiked Staramander.'* Stopping for breath meant you missed witnessing the last of the Zeta Praxis Nebula as it was consumed by a black hole. Two hundred billion sentient species had once called it home, and where were you? You had dinner reservations with the Marsh Land Ashes, but you had also double booked and missed that the Nekrith had conquered Mars. When you got home from your date with the universe you had realised that you had eighty-three billion missed calls. Despite being with you the entire day, the universe had somehow found the time to call you. *They'd rung once every*

0.000001 seconds. As you slept you kept getting prodded awake. Despite clearly being asleep the universe thought you'd want to sit down and watch a five hour documentary about that one time the Betalans had discovered how to make cheese. Again when trying to sleep you had to refuse a freshly cooked meal of some sort of squid that puffed purple gas. Even if not asleep there was no way you'd be eating '*that*.' When your alarm wakes you up you see that the universe has planned yet another exciting day. This being the two hundredth day in a row.

If you didn't set boundaries the universe would consume you whole. *It was never meant to be witnessed entirely by a single creature.* Imagine if you will, a table of every item you have ever eaten in your life. This was the universe. If you were to gorge on it all at once you'd very much not be okay. Eating a single good meal was better than eating every meal you had ever eaten all at once. Many of these pathfinders found themselves stressed, exhausted and in need of a hot bath. But, good lord, no one was taking these experiences from them. Seeing something was better than seeing nothing at all and the pathfinders who stayed were the ones who had learned to pace themselves. Those who didn't learn this trick had lost their appetites and returned home with tails between their legs and tales of slipping sanity.

Here we find ourselves at our neighbouring galaxy, Andromeda. Three thousand years from now a spaceship found itself in orbit around the planet of Revantide. *This ship went by the name of HMS Edinheim.* Revantide had found itself on hard times in a war against an endless enemy. Edinheim housed over two thousand crew who called it home. These space sailors did what they could to keep afloat in the seas of space. There is obviously no sea in space, by the way. *Space was not wet.* So that was a terrible comparison. If you went overboard, or left the ship in any way, without the correct equipment on then you would die. A movie would tell you that this death would be quick. *A movie lied.* Vikings didn't have horns on their helmets and dying in space took time. If you chose to pop out for a quick '*space-cigarette*' you'd first involuntarily defecate yourself as the vacuum of space pushed all of the gas (*and everything else!*) out of you. You'd begin to choke due to the lack of oxygen. *This lack of oxygen also meant your lighter would not work.* Which was a shame, as this both meant no cigarette for you, but also that there was no source of heat to keep you warm, not that a single small lighter could do much against absolute zero. Whilst you were projectile vomiting your very soul out from your body alongside yesterday's breakfast, your blood would begin to freeze rather quickly. The near-instant change in internal temperature would result in seizures. So here you are, *a defecating bag of frozen puke*. With your skin bloated from the expanded, frozen blood. You look out as the last backup processes of your brain gives way. As everything turns black you see your mother, as she tells you for the hundredth time that day that you should have stopped smoking. *It was bad for your health.* And how a mother always knows best.

Kiko frantically tried to figure out this grey metal room as best she could. She held her hand over her wrist, making a magical projection emerge as she did so. The translucent words that had appeared to her were temporal coordinates. This being a date stamp and a series of numbers that worked to indicate where any lost or accidental temporal wanderer may have wandered off to. To avoid any wondering wanderer worrying where they may be. *Sometimes the answers were worse than not knowing.* Currently, Kiko and Kara, based on the numbers, had jumped three thousand years into the future and according to these numbers, *they were in space!* Thus evident by the shiny metal room they were currently stood in. This room vibrated gently underfoot from the whir of the endless web of machinery all around. Long gone were all the comforts of their home life. The world of Earth and the entirety of the Milky Way sat far, far away. Yet here the girls were, stood within this bubble of artificial black metals and white plastics. Undoubtedly the myriad of blinking lights and screens that mounted the walls meant something to the initiated, but to Kiko it was little more than a jargon of outlandish scientific gobbledygook. The air itself was unnaturally humid within this man-made landscape. This was probably a result of all the machinery that lay beneath the surface of the walls.

"Where the hell are we?" Kara asked an uncomfortably close Kiko who was invading her personal space in a big way. Wherever this room was, it was far too small for two people! This much was clear.

"I'd, say based on the lack of space, we are in some sort of supply closest." Kiko tried replying tugging on her annoying dress, whilst narrowly avoiding Kara's cramped elbow as they both tried fighting for the space to move.

"We're not in a.." Kiko's face was too close for comfort. "We're not in a supply closet!" Kara nudged Kiko's attention to the toilet that stood to the side of the room as she tried separating her spinal column from the washbasin that was almost splitting her in twain. "I meant 'where' are we?"

This was clearly a vessel of some kind, you could tell by the gravity. The residents of Earth had grown accustomed to the feel of land underfoot and the stable gravity that it provided them. When not having a nice stable landmass to stand themselves upon, Earthlings could instantly feel it in their bones.

"Promise... promise... you won't freak out." Kiko negotiated whilst trying to find her footing within this awfully cramped room.

"Why would I need to freak out Kiko?" Kara had now stood boldly upright, aware that was something to be aware of. *(Free word of advice, if you ever need to keep someone calm, never start by telling them to keep calm. It never works.)*

"We may or may not be..." The two locked eyes for a split second. "... in space."

Kara burst through the bathroom door in a panic into the much larger room that was adjacent to it. In this room was approximately thirty people. Whilst very simplistic, this ship was still of spectacular beauty! *This ship stood as a testament as to how far man had come.* Both in a literal sense of distance travelled and as a metaphor for how far they've advanced as a species. The technology of man had risen far beyond our days of toasters, calculators and smartphones. The HMS Edinheim was exquisitely pristine. *Unusually so.* Like, there was not a single drop of dirt anywhere to be seen. Kiko was unsure if these halls of glistening, immaculate perfection stood as the result of some poor, exhausted cleaner working his fingers to the bone, or if it was all a part of some self-regulating, automated machine that wasn't even breaking a sweat. But either way, someone was doing a bang-up job. Everything sparkled as if it was brand new. However, those thirty or so people didn't seem too impressed with either Kiko or Kara. Given their clean-cut white plastic microfibre uniforms, adorned with differentiating insignias and all the guns that were displayed on the wall, it was safe to approximate that this was a military vessel of some kind. *Hence the guns.* Guns like the one that was now jabbing Kara in the back as she and Kiko were being led to the captain's offices on board the HMS Edinheim. Given that these two were wearing a regal red dress and rough leathers between them, it was safe to approximate that the girls were not military.

Things were moving so fast for the girls that neither one had had the chance to gather their thoughts or reflect on why they were here at all. One second they had been on Earth, in the twenty-first century. Partying away. The next second, they were several thousand years in the future. Being held up at gunpoint by angry soldiers in space. Travelling through time wasn't a particularly new act for Kiko, true, but this was the first time she had done so against her will and with no knowledge as to why she was here. *It was also the first time she had had a gun pointed at her.* For the record, she didn't like it. And for the record again, she was also not entirely sure where here actually was. Her spell had told her she was in the Andromeda galaxy and that the year was 5015. But sometimes facts just breed the need for more questions. The most worrying question was why did she feel so exhausted? It was like all of the life had been drained from her. *Being led around in this stupid red dress wasn't helping things either.* These gunned men led them into a small office. Like the rest of the HMS Edinheim, it was well ordered and rather respectable. An ornate gold emblem mounted the wall behind a silver desk. It rather looked like an eagle, but with a long neck and with a much longer beak. Neither girl had remembered seeing anything quite like it on Earth. *The simplest reason for this was because it wasn't from Earth.* This bird wasn't even from our solar system. Gold emblems ran throughout the fancy desk and decorated the walls. The sound of the lights burred from within the ceiling above them.

"Now just who the bloody hell do you think you pair are trying to fool, eh?" An elderly, muscular, grey crew-cut haired gentleman now stood before them. Some people might be surprised to learn that this Captain was of Elven descent, as if for some reason you couldn't have Elves in space. Here he stood pressing all of his weight down through his palms and onto his desk, spitting as he spoke. One such saliva droplet pelted across the left lens of Kiko's glasses which had protected her eye from what it had seen incoming. *Gross!*

"Again, sir. *Mister...?*" Kiko froze waiting for the response of a name. In the heat of all that was happening, she had somehow managed to forget his name. Perhaps she was too focused on the chains that were now trapping her and Kara to their chairs. Maybe she was still distracted by how impractical this dress would be in a fight.

"*Captain...* Orellan!" The pause seemed to indicate that he was rather fond of his fancy title and Kiko couldn't help but feel that he probably should be referred to by it for the remainder of the conversation. Unless heads were to roll, and no one wanted that.

"*Captain*... Orellan." Kiko reassured him as calmly as she could. "Once again I must insist upon you sir, uh, captain, that I am a member of the Temporal Bureau of Investigations. I came here by accident. Me and... my associate, we're..." She paused as she struggled to think of a reason for them being there that might keep them alive. She had nothing. "Well, we really have no idea how or why we are here! *We're not lying...*" Kiko's explanation and attempt at reassurance had fallen on deaf ears.

"And I know you are a liar, girl. Even if you are TBI. *Which I doubt!* This is a military ship, you have no jurisdiction here!" The captain growled, leaning in close towards his stowaways. He smelled like stale coffee and cigarettes.

"Like I said, sir..." Kiko tried once more.

"I AM TALKING." Orellan cut Kiko short. Sorry, Captain Orellan. One of his subordinates slammed the barrel of her gun against the top of the lavish table as if to send a message. "We have nothing on board warranting any of you magical lot interfering! *So I say to you that you're a liar!* You are a Nekrith spy! Sent to catch us off guard! I will not be caught off guard!"

Why were they here? What was happening? What the hell was a Nekrith? *Why was everyone being so rude?* How had all this happened? *Since when did Elves have military jobs in space?* When can Kiko get rid of this impractical dress?

Nothing made sense. This Elven Captain and his dark-haired lieutenant showed about as much prowess or interest in level headed conversation as one might expect from a soldier. *(No offence, soldiers, but let's get real for a second, would you rather sit down and have a nice little chat about something or would you rather roll up your sleeves and get shit done your way? The proper way.)* Their indifference to the confusion shown by their magical stowaways did little to help the girls figure out their surroundings. The weirdest part of this whole series of unfolding events was how Kiko had so little of her power left. Her battery was run almost empty. But she hadn't used any fatiguing or demanding spells since her time at the bank where she'd met Diane Dawnstar. *So why were her powers on the fritz?*

"I'm sorry?" Kara asked cautiously as she watched the nearby gun. *"But what's a Nekrith?"* Being from Earth three thousand years prior, it was hardly surprising that she had no idea of this alien metallic horror. Like Kiko, Kara could think of no reason as to why they were here. One minute they had been enjoying the party at the Attetson household, joking about Vincent. *Huh, Kara still hadn't had the time to tell Kiko about the ring...* The next they were here. Kara was doing her best to follow Kiko's lead. Time travel was her forte. She didn't doubt for a single second that if the situation arose, Kiko would act accordingly. She just worried that her friend might see the wrong side of a smoking barrel before she had the chance to act.

The Nekrith of which this captain spoke came from the planet Nekrithia. This Nekrithian horde was intergalactically feared. Mothers told their children tales of Nekrith ships landing in the night as an attempt to scare them into good behaviour. Soldiers huddled around campfires telling tales of woeful defeat, of whole planets and races stolen away and broken before daybreak. Whole planets shivered and squirmed at the merest mention of their name. The Nekrith were mostly cybernetic in their physiological design. These giant and spindly robotic creatures stood at nearly eight-foot-tall. They had long thick wired necks, approximately the width of a standard household mug. *Their faces were the only feature that you could tell them apart by.* Each and every time a creature fell to the Nekrith they were dragged away if they were compatible or alive enough to be converted. They were to become new Nekrith. These fallen creatures would eventually find their skulls sitting in a nest of cold exposed wires within a transparent plastic casing. *All emotion and organs were sifted, pulped and fed back to them for organic nutrients.* These freshly baked Nekrith would then return the favour, conquering others to share a likewise robotic fate.

The Nekrith homeworld, Nekrithia, was hidden to all. It was said they were protecting an ancient artefact of their god upon this planet and converting the universe in his name. But on account of everyone either dying or running away, no one had thought to ask for more detail. *So this was probably little more than a rumour or superstition.*

However, this was not the answer the captain had chosen to give Kara. Instead, he had chosen to laugh. Because of course, everyone knew of the Nekrith! *Not knowing who they were would be like not knowing how to engage in light-speed travel.* Everyone knew of the Fall of Wintermire, the Scorching of the Blackwood Gardens and the war that never seemed to end.

This confirmed it. *These two idiots were spies!*

Captain Orellan was a pious, man. His religion was one of war. The battlefield was his church, where bullets flew like the words of God. The unworthy or the weak fell where he had been blessed with the privilege of standing to see another day, to continue spreading his word of God. It had been some thirty years that he had spent within the Andromeda war zone. Any friends that he had arrived with were long dead and buried. Their names were now lost to him, from both heart and mind. The faces of the dead being little more than grains of sand in the desert. There were so many of them now.

This is not to say he did not care, he cared a great deal.

If he had not cared, why would he continue to fight? Fighting is worthless without something to fight for. He did so in the hope no one else would have to raise a gun in the years to come. He saw his metallic foe for what it was; the end of all life. *The Nekrith did not care.* They did not stop. Whole planets fell in their wake. If something was not done, all life would see through the eyes of an emotionless Nekrithian motherboard. A cold, desolate existence designed only to kill. Their red glowing eyes searching for all non Nekrithian life to exterminate. *To convert or destroy.*

Many years ago, the planet of the Blackwood Gardens had been a utopia. The blue-skinned monks welcomed all with open arms and with open hearts. Deep within their forest-dwelling temples, they had sought only to teach, to help and to mend. A Blackwood Gardener had navy-like skin and a set of four violet eyes. Having so many eyes had only helped them to be able to see more of the destruction that befell them when the Nekrithian ships landed. Brother La-ahamell watched from under his red hooded robes as the metal, skeletal-like Nekrith knocked down the ornate metal doors of his home, the Reserve. He had watched how these hoards of steel lanky cyborgs had flooded his streets. He had seen the sight of laser beams and blaster bolts laying his friends down to die. He had heard the screams of his fallen children dying around him. He had felt the hands of his son within his own as they were snatched apart. He had been powerless to save him. *To save anyone.*

He listened as the sounds of drills bored through his skull behind his ears. He heard the sound as great saws sliced through his bones. He heard the sounds as the plastic casing closed in around his face.

Brother La-ahamell had been converted into a Nekrith. And now he watched from under his plastic visor as he turned his rifle on the unpure Black Gardeners. He felt unbridled satisfaction as he pulled the trigger. Laser bolts slammed into the backs of the weak as they retreated. He watched as his metal hands, arms, legs and feet scaled the walls like a spider hunting his childlike prey. He joined the hoards of his cold, steely brothers as they flooded the streets. He felt nothing as he watched families torn apart.

"All hail the Nekrith." His harsh, static voice erupted when the Black Gardens had no more fruits left to bear. This barren planet had been shredded to its last life. *Where was next?*

Any readers confused by Brother La-ahamell turning on his people may be eased to learn that he did not do so of his own free will. He was at one with the Nekrith Hybrid Network. And like all machines, he now obeyed its masters will.

Captain Orellan had seen this type of conversion happen time and time again. He knew who the enemy was and he knew that they had to be stopped. HMS Edinheim operated under the New Andromeda Republic, the last stand of life against the robotic dead. This was what had brought him and his ship to Revantide. This planet that HMS Edinheim orbited had sent out a distress signal. So here a fleet of the New Andromeda Republic's finest waited. *Ready for war.*

Some readers may surmise that the sciences behind the Nekrith were very similar to the magic of a necromancer. *It's true.* It was a solid observation that the act of necromancy and whatever operated the Nekrith armies both pulled on the strings of the dead. Using their bodies against the original host's will. Neither a zombie nor the Nekrith thought of anything other than their master's goals. Both wanted to kill everything that was not like them. It was never known whether or not the Nekrith operated off of the fuellings of some dark magic, or if they were ever even aware of magic's existence at all. All sciences and technologies would be deemed magical if you went far back enough through time, casting yourself long before these things were ever created. A person who had never seen such a piece of technology before would think you were a god or had some bastion of magical prowess. Any person who used the device past the point of its expiration date would be impatiently awaiting a future upgraded release because this one *'kinda sucked.'*

As far as Kiko was concerned the only thing that kinda sucked right now was that it would take her almost two hours to regenerate enough magic to be able to get her and Kara back home safely. Whatever had happened to make them appear here had drained her of the magic that it would now require for them to leave again. Until such a point where she was recharged, she would have to play nice for this lug headed captain and hope nothing would happen that would get them killed. In the mean time it also wouldn't be a bad idea to figure out why they were here in the first place. *Had something dragged them here for a reason?*

The HMS Edinheim shook violently and alarms began to blare. Captain Orellan and the female officer (*Who had slammed her gun against the table earlier.*) shared a look of pure panic. A red flashing light filled the room as another soldier barged into the interrupted interrogation.

"Sir, they're here! The Nekrith ha-" Blood painted the walls as this officer's head popped like crimson champagne.

The dark-haired lieutenant ran into the corridor and opened fire upon her attackers. She watched as one of the several approaching Nekrith walked forward with a minigun. The term minigun was a worryingly inaccurate misnomer. If anyone has been unfortunate enough to see one then they would know that these guns are actually very sizeable. *They're not 'mini' at all.* To be able to lift one would require a fair bit of strength. If anyone was unlucky enough to see one fire upon them, they would not be able to tell you that these guns could fire an impressive fifty rounds per second. I say *'would not'* because they would be very much 'dead.' The kind of dead that would freak out a trypophobe. This is to say your corpse would resemble Swiss cheese. (Your corpse would be filled with holes!) As a side note, any people suffering from trypophobia or thanatophobia should avoid any war zone with fast-firing guns. To be fair, this advice also holds up equally as well for anyone who happens to not suffer from either phobia as well. *Bullets and laser bolts tended to be bad for your health regardless of your fears.*

Lieutenant Amirah Miller, this being the name of the lieutenant who was about to have a minigun fired upon her, had about twenty years of service with the New Andromeda Republic. This dark-haired thirty-year-old had spent almost her entire life in the armed forces, and yes this does mean she had been recruited at the ripe old age of ten. *At this age she had witnessed first-hand what happens when the Nekrith suddenly drops in on you.* Amirah now looked certain death in the eye as the minigun began unloading rounds at her.

Her whole life flashed before her eyes. Childhood was supposed to be an amazing time. The formative years for everyone being a period of innocence, love, fun and exploration. A time to be safe and well cared for. This is a right all children deserve to have. So it is a sad moment in time when a child is robbed of this. To witness horror and have their childhood innocence snatched away and to be thrust into the mindset of adulthood prematurely. This was the case for Amirah. If Diane Dawnstar's experiences as a child had sculpted her into being a murderer, *then this meant Amirah was the child of war.* The will to stand up and fight was in her blood. It was a part of her soul. At a young age she had witnessed as her brother was slain in cold blood by the menacing alien machines of war. She was also robbed of any time to mourn for his death, as her parents had died similar deaths in the following week. Amirah lived a very serious life and rarely had cause to smile.

However, seeing a whole fleet of Nekrith being annihilated in a single swoop by rebounding laser beams brought a smile to her face. To her surprise, she had not died to the minigun wielding Nekrithian soldier. *That had been a pretty good surprise.* As she looked to her side she had seen that one of her prisoners was now stood right in front of her. This red-haired girl had somehow summoned a shield of pure blue light around them. This shield had caused the barrage of bullets to ricochet back at their assailants, the Nekrith robots. Not only did she get to see something that she had truly hated die, but the lights of the lasers had also momentarily reminded her of the fireworks from her homeworld. *This being a happy memory from before all of this endless loss.* She hated to admit that she might have been wrong, this ginger girl might just be alright after all. For anyone confused as to who this girl was, it was clearly Kiko. *(How was that not obvious?)* Kiko stood bolt upright and clicked her fingers. This had caused her red dress to instantly disappear and be replaced with the clothes she had felt more comfortable in. With a billowing whip, she pulled her blue coat out of thin air and threw it back on in a display of ebullient defiance. *The red dress was finally gone!* Captain Orellan on the other hand stood wide-mouthed and aghast at how easily he had just seen one of his prisoners break free of her restraints. The blonde one was still sat staring at him with a furious glare.

"Reckon you can untie me now?" Kara said sarcastically as she raised her bound hands towards him.

"So the great big massive robot things have great big massive guns now?" Kiko smiled softly as she helped Amirah back onto her feet. *"My name is Kiko Attetson, and I think you really need my help."*

The Nekrith were here and the girls were about to witness first-hand why the entire Andromeda galaxy had feared them so much. The Halls and corridors of this now broken ship were washed with the broken and bleeding soldiers of the New Andromeda Republic. Whoever it was that said '*in space, no one could hear you scream*' had clearly never been here before. The HMS Edinheim was now swarming with Nekrith. It was like a poorly planned picnic that had become victim to a horde of ravaging ants. *You know, if ants were eight-foot-tall and carried big metal guns.* The dying screams of the soldiers flooded the ship like an infection. Waves upon waves of soldiers crashed against the rocks of the Nekrith army. Crumbling under a firing range of laser beams and blaster bolts. Their cold bodies lying motionless at their feet.

The Nekrith were as emotionless as they were ruthless. Decimating their foes with a perfected swiftness and precision. All inferior creatures were considered an enemy of the Nekrith and were to be destroyed. The Nekrith were designed to be the most superior beings in existence, eradicating all other life forms or converting them to their cause. As they were a race unburdened with morals or ethics, this had led to them having mastered war unlike any who unlucky enough to stand against them. All they wanted was to see you dead, they cared not how it happened. *And they always got what they wanted.*

The once clean HMS Edinheim had now become a blistering mess of destruction. Pipes hissed like broken bagpipes, as unknown gasses leaked from them into the battleground. Burn marks from blaster bolts charred the once white walls with a darkened hew. Broken screens sparked and whizzed under a laboured mechanical breath. A furious frenzy of laser beams glistened through this dying space-traversing construct. If it was not for all the dead people that lay slumped across the ground, all the lights cast by the laser beams might have almost looked like the lights of a late-night rave. However with all the dead bodies scattered across this starcruiser, it probably looked like a late-night rave on the morning after some great big space party; the dead being like the leftover partiers, sleeping on the dance floor.

The battle raged as a flurry of soldiers tried pushing back their metal enemies. The voices of the Nekrith had a strange static sound, rather like that of an old radio. *(You know, if old radios would ever scream taunts of death and destruction at you, wishing the death of all life.)* Their voices were deep and horrifically chilling. They were almost hollow sounding and were a little bit raspy. There was also a distinctively guttural sound, like the rev of an old muscle car's engine.

As it turned out having two female wizards with you when you fought off a robotic invasion had been rather helpful. The Nekrith had not planned for magic, I mean who would. So for all of the high tech gadgets that were built directly into them *(that worked wonders against the type of guns you only expect to find in science fiction movies.)* offered about as much protection against the magics the girls used as holding a paper bag in front of your face would if you had just asked a championship boxer to wail on your face.

Kiko held out her hand as she summoned a stained glass icosahedron into existence. *(An icosahedron being a shape with twenty sides. Anyone confused as to what stained glass is, need only think of the windows at a church.)* These paintings of glass usually told a story. The glass ball Kiko had just summoned was no different. Trapped within this magical ball was an Arcane Element. In this case, it was ice. The stained glass which enwrapped it told the story of how this cold element had first come into existence. Each panel of the icosahedron being like the panel of a comic book. This icy-white icosahedron told of the goddess of ice, Shiva. It told of how her followers had angered the fire god, Surtr, and how she had gifted them the secrets of ice to build walls that kept his fires out. This ball of encased ice sped down the hallway of the HMS Edinheim. A cluster of Nekrith were frozen alive under this engulfing blizzardly blanket. *(Okay, maybe not 'alive.' They were still undead robots, but they weren't going anywhere anytime soon.)*

For the second time today Captain Orellan had found himself in a state of bewilderment as he looked upon the frozen statues of his lifelong enemies. This confusion was only furthered when he saw Kara transform a Nekrith into something much smaller and squishier as she stepped on it. As she tried awkwardly scraping the pink goo off of the bottom of her boot, she had seen the most beautiful object she had ever seen in her entire life. Something more glorious than anything else in existence. Every morsel of her being cried out in a union of ecstasy as the pupils in her eyes expanded as if she was a household cat about to pounce on a small bird.

"Yes!!!" She bellowed with a maniacal laugh.

I don't think Kiko will ever forget the day that she had witnessed her Half-Elven friend, Kara, chase down a battalion of alien robotic soldiers with her very own rocket launcher. *Her devilish chuckle as they exploded in her wake.* The unbridled glee in her eyes. The thrill of Kara's laughter as the explosions erupted around her. It's worth mentioning only two out of the five of the rockets hit any Nekrithian soldiers. *But this didn't matter to Kara.* Not one bit.

"Bet you're glad you didn't kill us now, eh?" Kara mused passive-aggressively, as she stood posing with her new rocket launcher. *(Damn she looked good!)*

The captain, the lieutenant and the two girls fought their way past the first wave of robotic invaders with relative ease. However, this intergalactic space battle was not going well, even with the help of two spell casters. The HMS Edinheim was ruptured. Like the corpse of a great metal herbivore floating alone in the emptiness of space, being swarmed by a throng of cybernetic carnivorous rats.

"We need to secure the engine room, lieutenant." Orellan ordered Lieutenant Amirah. "Take these two with you!"

But before anyone could go anywhere or do anything, Kara had found herself distracted. She now happened upon a window, for the first time since arriving in space. *And there it was.* She could not help but stare out at the vastness of it. The endless black. The eternal infinitude. At the planet below. She felt a wave of awe wash over her. It was beautiful. It was amazing. To be stood so high above a planet that you could see it as one single entity. All that splendour and beauty. It was breathtaking.

It was said that when you saw an orbiting planet for the first time that you finally got to see the scale of your place (*and importance*) in the universe. A sense of understanding of the magnificence of it all and the tiny part you played in everything. For some this had driven them crazy as a sense of worthlessness soured all of their lifelong achievements with a vinegary doubt. Others would become dumbfounded by the beauty and feel a great sense of freedom. As the clouds swirled all over this blue and green planet, it almost looked like all the pictures she had seen of Earth. Of her home. The only real difference was that this planet looked a little less blue. Beyond this green rocked world she saw stars burning in the endless vacuum of space. *She was awestruck.* It was all so magnificent. She felt at peace seeing the grandeur of it all.

Some moments later Kara and Kiko had found themselves in the engine room. Little did they know that the secrets within would turn the stomach and break the heart. For you see, the members of the New Andromeda Republic were smart. They were smart and desperate. *This was never a good mix.*

In the far off reaches, at the beginning of time. When everything was new there was said to be a single species. *They were called the Divines.* These creatures were of immense and untold power. It was also said that they had nowhere to call home. No planet to lay their sleeping heads. The reason for this was rather simple, they were the planets. Or rather, they would one day become them. As hard as it may be to believe, there was once no planets. Not a single one. *So where did they all come from?* Almost all life-bearing planets were once a Divine and their Earth was one of them. But the Divines did not look like planets, not originally. It was said that at first, they had resembled giant newborn babies, or rather giant grey fetuses. Each one was of these demigods was said to have been the size of a traditional van. It was said that at the dawn of time these giant infant-like creatures had travelled the virginal universe. When they found places they were happy with, usually being in places near a star, they would draw towards them all of the nearby debris and rock. As they did so they were cocooned in the forming planets. Over time they would become one single entity. *They would merge and become the heart of the planet itself.* After this metamorphosis, life from the baby Divine would seep into the soils of the world. In the case of the Earth, this had led to the evolution of trees, plants and, one day even dinosaurs all living off its power; its very life source. Druids were right, mother nature was technically a thing. Some people called it God, the bringer of all life. *(Even though the Divines transcend the confides of gender normality. It was neither a man nor a woman. It was a big baby wrapped in a ball of rock and gasses.)*

However, in the case of the HMS Edinheim, a Divine had been used for something much worse. It was little more than an oversized battery. This *'would-be demi-god'* had been brought down to being nothing more than a glorified phone charger. A cacophony of wires had protruded from its back, connecting it to a huge glass dome that encased it like a test tube.

"Is… is that a *baby…?"* Kara asked wide-eyed with horror as she pointed towards the crispy grey blob. She couldn't quite wrap her head around what she was seeing. This giant, grey, fetal-like creature seemed to be like some form of a rat in a laboratory. Kara had never seen anything quite like this before. *It was so ugly!* What the hell was it? This *'thing'* looked like an oversized fetus with grey, slimy skin and two giant shut eyes. Kiko knew exactly what this thing was. *A Divine was a gift from the gods of old.* A fiery primal rage grabbed at her shoulders.

"It can't be?" Kiko ran up to the Divine's giant glass container. She could see water bubbling through the glass. "Do you have any idea of what that thing is, lieutenant?" Kiko glared at Amirah with an ablazed passionate rage. "By all rights, that thing is a god. And you… and you've… perverted it into *this?*"

The Divines were said to have been created by the gods, the same ones that had gifted us with magics. A Divine's single purpose in life was to bring life to the huddled masses yearning to breathe free. They fed off of solar energy and other cosmic radiations and in turn, they would grow strong over time. Eventually, they would become planets and life would flourish. *But this?* This was unnatural! If for no other reason than that giant baby demi-god was alive. It could feel every wire that had been stabbed into it. Kiko felt a rage burn away inside her, quite unlike anything she had ever felt in her entire life before. Kiko dashed towards the lieutenant.

"You and your captain, you talk of your fears of the Nekrith invaders. Becoming corrupted into something against your will!" She beckoned to the giant fetus. *"A Divine is pure life!* A creature destined to travel the universe. To bring hope and joy wherever it goes! And you've done this to it?" She paused for breath. "This is sick!"An act of heresy against the natural order of the universe that was completely devoid of empathy. Or at least that's what it was to Kiko.

"This was necessary!" The dark-haired lieutenant bit back. "You weren't there! How dare you judge us! We have fought against the Nekrith for generations! Do you have any idea of how many planets have been lost?" Amirah shoved Kiko. "There is not a night I don't hear the screams of the dead. I see their faces everywhere I go. Besides, that *'Divine'* over there.." She pointed towards the incubated infantile powerhouse. "The Nekrith tried converting it too. If it wasn't for us, it would be dead!"

Instead of allowing this powerhouse of energy to die, the New Andromeda Republic had decided to put it to good use. Where would the sense be in simply letting it die? At least this way this demi-god's suffering could save lives. One creature's suffering didn't out way the suffering of an entire galaxy, but this was an equation that Lieutenant Amirah Miller could easily live with.

Kara stood between them, with the empty rocket launcher still strapped to her back. To her, this creature was little more than an oversized fetus. She had never really seen Kiko lose her cool like this before. As much as she had been impressed to see it, she couldn't help but feel confused as to why a giant space-baby warranted such anger. *I mean, come on, just look at how ugly it is.*

"This is no time to fight one another." Kara started as she made her way between Kiko and the Lieutenant. "Yes, the baby *'thing'* is really creepy. Yes, using any living thing as a power source is *super weird*." She patted Amirah on the shoulder. "But I don't think I care enough to be distracted from the *literal killer robots*, are you?" Kara turned to Amirah who shook her head. "And you?" Kiko looked to the floor. *"And you?"* Kara repeated before Kiko ultimately brought herself to uttering a pitiful sounding *'no'* as she shuffled her feet.

The sound of Captain Orellan's voice broke out through on a nearby radio. *"Lieutenant Miller, have you secured the engine room? Over."* She replied with confirmation. *"Is the cargo secure?"* This assumedly meaning the

Divine. She replied with confirmation once more. *"Good. The Revantiders have gotten word of our stowaways and have asked to speak to the ginger girl and her friend immediately. We're readying a landing party now!"*

Kiko and Kara shared a look of confusion. It looked Like Kara would get to see Revantide up close after all.

"Reckon I could get a refill?" Kara asked as she indicated towards the rocket launcher still on her back.

Chapter Eleven

THE NEKRITH INVASION

"I can sense your kindness and that you are driven by the desire to help these troubled people, these sufferers of war. I know you are from another time and place, Kiko Attetson. I can see you are driven by an urge, thinking you can help fix these broken people when you can."

Kiko and Kara were sat in a luscious green forest upon Revantide. They had found themselves sat in an opening of trees with a village elder that Amirah had all too recently introduced them to. This being so recently that they had not gotten around to exchanging names yet, let alone the musings of being other-worldly.

"But I know that there is more to you. You are logical, yes, always logical. I know that you sense the powers that flow through this world. I see the true intent behind your actions. You speak of being for the people. A saviour of the lost and the broken. I know you better than you think, charlatan. Intelligent people assume themselves far above those around them. You think I do not know your true intent. You know that Revantide is lost. You feel it deep within. *You seek only to save the source of its power.* To bring it home to your own time, with the only people you believe have the right to possess such a thing."

Kiko was dumbfounded and left speechless as she sat crossed-legged on top of her coat. Yes, it was all true. The Arcane Intelligence Agency had a policy that all artefacts of extreme magical power had to be catalogued and removed, given unto them. The Arcane Intelligence Agency would do whatever it deemed best with these items, either to use them, lock them away or destroy them for the betterment of all life.

As a side note, all powerful artefacts were spread across the entire known universe. They were considered too powerful to be allowed to be grouped together. Any one planet with a surplus of either would either become too powerful or be perpetually targeted for its riches. It was also commonly agreed that all creatures were too dumb to be trusted. The items that the Arcane Intelligence Agency had kept a track of were separated through time by the Temporal Bureau of Investigations. These usually being on different planets of allied races or ones under Earth's control.

"There is a darkness in you." The elder turned towards Kara. "I know you hear its voice in your eternal waking nightmare, child of Ragnarök. You hide your fears well, little one. As the walls of doubt and despair creep ever closer in around you. Through stormy dark seas, you wade. You run from the fire, even though you still hear the calling. *You are drowning and you are burned.* You fight not for the betterment of others around you or to live to see another day, but as some pretence to prove that you feel no fear in your heart. The need to prove yourself to everyone. *Darkness has reached deep inside you.* It has become a part of who you are and you cannot return. Every day brings you closer to it. You go to war with the world because you're afraid to stand against the beast inside of yourself."

Kara felt a single tear run down her face as she sat with her insecurities exposed to the entire universe for all to see. "But there is still light in you yet, child. As long as you feed it, it will grow."

Kara sat wounded upon her newly found rocket launcher, which she currently used as a chair. *(It was probably not a good idea to use a rocket launcher as a chair!)*

'This is so weird!' Kara was filled with a wide-eyed sense of wonder and amazement. This was a brand new planet! New grass underfoot! New air in her lungs! New, well, everything! Revantide was amazing! It was beautiful! It was charming! It was magnificent! Grasslands, forests and rocky Everglades stretched as far as the eye could see. Ravishing greenery swirled all around them like a living series of emeralds. Strange bird-like creatures flew effortlessly overhead. Weird small brown balls of sentient fuzz leapt and hopped all around them. Equally as excited by their visitors' strange appearance as their visitors were of them. *These little guys were so full of joy!* One such fur bag jumped into Kiko's hands. From under all the hair she could discern two big round eyes and a wide smiling mouth. This delightful critter made Kiko find herself having a small chuckle. Its innocence was almost overwhelmingly endearing. This creature, which was called a Queckar by the way, would certainly not fair well against what was to come.

But there was something else, something different over the horizon. Yes, the Nekrith threat was imminent, but there was something new and something powerful here. All attuned magic users could feel the existence of power magical artefacts in the air. They could sense it in the deepest waters. Hear it calling over the tallest mountain. The closest comparable feeling you'd understand to this sensation was when you were really tired. You've had a long busy day of whatever activity that has exhausted you. This whole day of activities has left you wanting nothing more than to sleep in your warm and comfy bed, so in you crawl. The troubles of the world seem to melt and fade away. Sinking and falling into a peaceful slumber. *FALLING*! A sudden jolt ruptures across your entire body. As if somehow you were about to fall through your bed for a thousand miles. This alarming sudden feeling of plummeting through an instantaneous abyss that washes over you. That is how this felt to be near such an item of power. Your body knows it's out there. Somewhere. A sinking feeling you feel in your bones.

There was some unseen secret over the horizon, calling out.

A band of Revantiders had congregated in a small camp. Red tents bustled in the breeze. Children ran around in a merriment of games, rather like the children at Vincent's party back on Earth, which was either thousands of years prior or an hour or so ago depending on how you looked at it. People of the community seemed to bind together helping each other complete their everyday tasks. Revantiders had an appearance similar to that of a Human, if you were willing to ignore the grey skin and white eyes. *They were also all as bald as a rock.* This being in extreme contrast to the bounding Queckars that played with the children. *'Perhaps the Queckars had stolen all the hair?'* Kiko pondered to herself.

Amirah had a troubled look to her as she watched the sky. The sounds of the far off battle were not to be heard. Yet. But still, she carried her gun, ready to shoot at any given moment. She had not died yet today and had no intention of doing so. At least not without a fight. She looked at her new, weirdly dressed, associates with wonderment. *Who were they and why were they here?* Maybe the Amaranth would know? The Amaranth was one of Revantide's last remaining wise men. He was born to a line of ancestors who, according to legend, had been said to have made an offering to the planet. In exchange for what was taken it was said that they were given the truth. The ability to see it in everything. Every word, action and atom. To them, life was a canvas of art and they could see the true meaning behind every stroke of paint on it. They had found the Amaranth in a clearance of a nearby forest, meditating on what lay in store for his planet. Like his brethren, he had grey skin. He was garbed in a fine red cloak, almost silk-like in appearance. His grey skin was worn and bumpy, like the bark of a tree and a blue light seemed to shimmer dimly underneath the cracks. This light also shone from his eyes and his mouth when he spoke. He was covered in a wide array of necklaces, bracelets and other trinkets of jewellery. *(Most likely offerings from the people of Revantide.)* His face had carvings and etchings dug into it. It was impossible to tell if this was a part of his face or if it was some grandiose mask. It was smoother than the rest of his body, sure. But there was no ridge to indicate an edge of a mask or mark to suggest where it had been fused onto him. His head rose into two flat peaks, kind of reminiscent of a hammerhead shark or the split in a big tree. This feature was unlike any they had seen on the other Revantiders.

The girls sat in bemused bewilderment. Not long after being told to sit down, they had now been left feeling like children who had been told off for trying to steal the cookie jar. This was far worse for dearest Kara, who had so cruelly and coldly had her darkness exposed to the world. She often worried about being something bad. A bringer of damnation and malediction. Often did her parents tell her she was the undoer of all things. The Ragnarök child.

For anyone unaware of Ragnarök; ancient Norse gods believed this to be the end of all things. The final destruction of the gods. A great battle that extinguished all life. *A time of cruel winters and death to all.* For some people, the thought of Ragnarök was the same as a Monday morning as they woke up for work. However, the fresh horrors of Ragnarök that awaited the mourning crowds were much, much worse than the first morning of the working week. The weak would be broken and cast aside as the World Tree was torn asunder. The World Tree was what the ancient Norse believed the universe was, a series of lands supported by the strength of a strong, beautiful tree. Much like the trees of the forest the girls were in now.

A gathering of Queckars had gathered around the four as they talked and gazed longingly at them. Their curious beady eyes staring intently before the end of their world came in a crash of blazing defeat.

"There is no time left for ceremony anymore. No, there's no time left at all." The Amaranth spoke again. "As a keeper of the Revanspear, I grant it safe passage unto you, the children of time." Kiko and Kara shared a look of confusion as to what a Revanspear was. "To be stolen is a better fate than to be destroyed. However, it lies not here, and away you must travel. Deep, deep into the heart of the world." The Amaranth arose. "I shall be your guide and Amirah shall be your shield."

"But what about all those people? We have to save as many as we can!" Kara looked at all the nearby Queckars that lived life so joyously and had given her such happiness to witness.

"All things end." The Amaranth explained. "Revantide's time has come. But fortunately, our prayers were answered and the child who walks through time has answered our callings."

"So you summoned us here?" Kiko asked, wondering if this was what had led the pair here to this featured future of the end of a world.

"You greatly overestimate the extent of my powers and you humble me." The Amaranth beckoned the trio to follow. "I see it was a brother that sent you here. I see he is scared of the truth. He worries you know of the monster beneath the man."

Kiko was alarmed. *A brother?* What did that mean? *Which one?* This wise man, this *'Keeper,'* was clearly not as insightful as he would have had himself believe. There was no way either Muhren or Vincent would do anything to hurt her. *She knew how much she loved both of her brothers and she knew they loved her back.* This was impossible. *A lie.* The only monster beneath the man was this soothsayer and his honeyed words which did nothing but hurt people. Despite this clearly being lies, she couldn't help but recall Kara's final words before they had appeared on the HMS Edinheim.

"I know Vincent's dirty little secret..."

The splendid forests of Revantide were vast and walking through them was a delight. Or rather it would have been if these visitors were not all so entirely aware of the metal menace in the skies. These once clear skies were now full of clouds and it was now snowing. The clap and roar of thunder could be heard far overhead. *Except that this wasn't snow and that wasn't thunder.* The ships of the New Andromeda Republic were being blown up above them. What sounded like thunder was the sounds of a great war just out of orbit. The snow was the ash and death of the ships as they broke up in the atmosphere. *Death was literally raining down on them.*

All the fantastic creatures of Revantide had run away. They had crept into their holes and burrows. Hopefully, some may yet survive all this. Besides the deafening skies, the land was left quiet. It was horrible.

"Are you intending to carry that empty Marrak-Class missile launcher with you for the entire day?" Lieutenant Amirah asked Kara.

"Oh, uh Kiko, will I ever let this go?" Kara asked as she passed a glance to Kiko.

"No..." Kiko answered through a sigh.

A crack of commotion broke out above the racket of space's battle. They looked up to see a spaceship as it broke through the cloudline. *The sonic boom was deafening.* Amirah felt sick to her stomach as she saw the HMS Edinheim hurtling down, crashing between two nearby mountains. Broken across the mountainside. Birds and other flight based creatures fled in a horrified hysteria. The HMS Edinheim was no more, a testament to what lay in store.

It was some twenty minutes later until the next event of note took place. Across the planet, the Nekrith had landed. The Revantiders were powerless against their cold, metal foe. One such Nekrithian ship had caught sight of our four travellers out in the wilds. A piercing whirring noise ripped through the air as Nekrithian thrusters burst through the approaching night. The whirs lowered as the ship turned to land. Amirah immediately launched herself in behind a nearby boulder. Everyone else did similarly. Off in the distance, they saw as one of their foes stood on top of a boulder of its own. The setting 'sun' had caught directly behind it, giving this Nekrith the appearance of some sort of unnatural, demonic-robot like spider against the light. This six-limbed devil in a metal casing was not alone. Four shiny peers stood alongside it. Kara quickly stood up and as she did so a bow and arrow of pure light seemed to draw itself out of nowhere. A single arrow hurtled down the battlements. There was the sound of a far off *'thunk'* as the spider-like Nekrith folded in on itself and collapsed on its back, like some arachnid that had just been effortlessly swatted with a newspaper. Amirah smiled at Kiko and her Half-Elven friend. *You know, I don't think Amirah has smiled quite this much for a very long time.*

The battle that ensued was over fairly quickly. Despite the Amaranth providing no offensive capabilities of his own and Amirah's bullets being little more than water off of a duck's back. As it turned out the two arcane girls shared a natural proclivity when it came to stopping these Nekrith. Their robotic shields and gizmos were no match for these masters of the supernatural arts. Kiko had crushed one in a gravity well. Kara leapt into a roll and cleaved one in two with one of her axes as the other blade had lopped off another Nekrith's leg. Before that Nekrith could do anything about the missing limb, a ball of fire had erupted across its face causing it to explode as Kiko had summoned another of the arcane elements. Clearly, this one had been of fire. *(This red glassed icosahedron told of the Demon Mother, Lilith. Of how she had tricked the early ancestors of the Earth with a new form of light to push back the night. It warned of how her new gift was a trap and the deaths caused by the fires.)*

As the final machine tried to lay down some suppressive fire, Kiko had catapulted this previously lopped off robo-leg straight at it. This limb was now poking out from one of the Nekrith's eyes as it lay twitching. This Nekrith, in one last desperate act of defiance, *threw a grenade up into the air!* Kiko and Kara watched helplessly as Amirah was now lost in a ball of fire. The skin was ripped clean off her face as shrapnel consumed her!

Kiko gave a horrendous shriek as time seemed to stand still at this horror. Kiko then stood confused as she saw time unstitch itself. The lights of the fiery act undid itself as a blue light shone around her. The fire was being undone. She watched bewildered as Amirah's face glued itself back together. Life had been returned much like how the grenade and had now been returned to its sender. Time had rewound. *Which was impossible!*

Kiko saw for a second time as the grenade was let loose. There was a gust of wind as it was sent hurtling off into the distance. A far off explosion could be heard as Kara hacked at the last Nekrith. Amirah was still in one piece.

What had just happened was impossible. Time could not be rewritten. Something didn't feel right. Kiko had not felt right since leaving Earth. Everything seemed… clearer. She felt refreshed for some reason. As if for the first time, in almost forever, she had been freed from a headache she had never realise ever existed. Kiko chose to say nothing about what had just happened and she remained to do so for the rest of the journey. A journey that had had a certain Amaranth watching her the entire way. He knew what was really happening, but also knew it was not his place to say.

Eventually, they arrived at a cave mouth. This doorway into the abyss was framed by a metal border. Inside this cave was a web of steely hallways, which stood in contrast with the outside world. Gone was all the greenery of nature and in its place was a well-constructed monument hidden under the rocks. A burrow of simple and elegant hallways. In the floor was etched a series of small symmetrical hexagons which bobbed when you stepped on them. The walls were plain, except for a single white light that ran down both sides down the tunnels and into the rooms. This structure had been built thousands of years ago by the ancient Revantiders. It was timeless. Both eery and beautiful in design. A monument of splendour to their love for the artefact that lay within. These tunnels spanned the whole upper crust of the planet. It was an archaic subway of plate. All of the doors were approximately teen-foot-tall and were triangular in shape. These triangles were broken up by a series of smaller triangles of light. The doors opened from their centre most point and unfolded for entry.

Statues of old Revantiders were seen from time to time as they walked through. Each series of these statues told a story, or so it would seem. Unbeknownst to the trio, this story told of the Keepers. The ones who had first found the Revanspear and the gift of sight that this spear had bestowed. Some statues had told of great evils that the spear had undone. Some told of the knowledge of secret wealth the Revanspear had birthed. The gang had walked for so long down these hallways that it had made their feet hurt. Any and all sounds of the outside defeat were lost to them now, drowned out by metal and rock. They were alone in the expanse beneath the planet. The white lights were still running down the walls seamlessly beside them. The light cast gave the hallways an ominous yet beautiful glow. *Nothing felt real.*

The hexagons under their feet still rocked under their weight, but nothing gave way. It was almost like the planet wanted them to be here and was holding them up on these micro-platforms accordingly.

After a while, they had reached the largest room they had seen so far. The white lights were replaced by a red glow. This room was somewhere close to a mile in diameter. The walls were hidden behind an army of statues, similar to the ones they had seen throughout. Ornate chairs and machinery were built directly into the floor. All of this stuff was facing directly towards the centre, and this was where the Amaranth was quickly headed.

A sudden explosion erupted sending the Amaranth and an array of chairs flying in all directions. The Nekrith had arrived once more and they had returned in a great number. *It seemed like some days you just couldn't escape an alien invasion, no matter how hard you tried.* It was here on this planet, so many miles from home, where the girls now found themselves fighting for their lives. If you had told either Kara or Kiko that they would have spent their day in the far off reaches of the Andromeda galaxy, being constantly fired upon by cybernetic monsters; they would have probably volunteered to stay in bed instead. But here they were, cowering behind chairs and machinery which they did not fully understand. Fighting for survival against an enemy they didn't fully comprehend.

Statues cracked and the floor shook as a battalion of Nekrith tried to close in around them. Lasers lit the room and broke the furniture. Fires quickly arose.

"We can't stay here!" Amirah ordered as she shot at her foes. "You have to go!"

"We're not going anywhere!" One of Kara's light arrows cut through Nekrithian armour.

"If you stay here we will all die!" She threw a grenade similar to the one that had failed to kill her earlier. "Go! I'll buy you time!"

"We're not leaving you here to die!" Kiko barked as one of her fireballs engulfed the doorway the Nekrith were entering through.

"That's an order!"

"We don't work for you!" Kara remarked as the debris of a statue landed next to her.

"We won't let you die for nothing!" Kiko demanded. "This planet is a lost cause. Come with us, we can save you. We'll take you back with us. Pick your battles, lieutenant. The fight is lost! Don't be a fool. *Don't die for nothing!*"

"I stand where I fall and I shall fight to the end!" Amirah caused one of the approachers to lose an arm. "If I see my brother this day, I shall deem it worth it! You will not rob me of a noble death, Kiko!"

"This isn't noble! This is-" Kiko was cut short by a section of roof that came hurtling down.

"Kiko! We need to go!" Kara exclaimed. "She's made her choice."

And with that the two girls vanished, teleporting further into the room. Amirah stood defiantly for as long as she could. *Given how badly she was outnumbered this will not be all that long.* The centremost part of the room was equidistant from all the walls. A series of stairs rose and at the top was the prize, a spear of pure metal. Although this description of it being spear-like was inaccurate. Much like the misnomer surrounding the name 'minigun' the girls had seen on the HMS Edinheim, this Revanspear wasn't actually a spear. It had a resemblance much more similar to that of a staff. At the base was an ornately carved golden seal. All across the handle were further tribal carvings. The top of the staff opened up, like the pages of a book. Arising from this point was a series of spikes, that wrapped around a stone. These spikes looked either like fingers of a hand mid grasp, or rather like a series of roots that were entangling the centre stone. This stone was semi-translucent. From within this rock, a reddish emerald fog could be seen turning away. It also seemed to be floating free from the staff. A secondary entity also floated freely. Above the wrapping vine fingers was a tetrahedron. Carved within all its visible side was an all-seeing eye. The tetrahedron itself was black, but the eyes were encased with a red stone. The Revanspear was resting in the open hands of a great statue; this figure was sat stooped over it. A metal robe hid all of its facial features. As Kiko extended an arm to grab the spear-that-wasn't-a-spear-but-was-actually-a-staff, Kara grabbed her arm cautiously.

"Kiko, look..." Her friend indicated to a plaque that was in front of the Revanspear.

*'Upon our darkest of days,
at the end of our ways,
A child of time approaches.*

*As the hand of death encroaches,
She will walk these halls,
When the last Keeper falls.*

*Seeking answers,
To all life's cancers,*

*We saw your arrival,
And we wish you no deprival.
This spear of Revantide is yours.*

*We hope it brings the cures,
Of opening secret doors,
For all your upcoming wars.*

*Beware your brother's betrayal,
His intention for you was intended to be fatal.*

*Beware the change,
However strange.*

*A brother dead,
A secret not yet said.*

*Beware the fires lost,
And the demon's cost.*

*Run now, child of time,
Avenge the crime.*

*Go now little Attetson,
Back to the Earth and Sun.
Good luck, Kiko.'*

Why did ancient civilisations always love things that rhymed? Why did they always speak in riddles? Likewise how and why did they know of Kiko? She looked at a Kara that shared her panic-stricken look.

"A brother dead?" Kara asked.

Before Kiko could get an answer in, a Nekrithian blast of energy knocked the flooring away from underneath them as the two girls fell into the dark abyss. Kara watched as she, her friend and her rocket launcher faded into darkness.

Chapter Twelve

THE REVANTIDE WOMAN

The war was not going well. This was hardly surprising; after all war was little more than the manner in which the strong chose to speak with the rest of the universe. *How they delivered themselves upon the weak.* Their words being acts of physical violence they used to get their own way. Where a more empathetic entity would try to use reason and understanding to act out their will, war used brute force and fear. To break you into submission. To take. All you needed to understand in war was *'you'd do as you were told.'* The reasoning was that if you tried to say no then you'd get hurt. If life was a playground of children, war was the bully. Systematically targeting other children for their lunch money. If one bully clashed with another bully their fights would be legendary. *Kids would be talking about this for weeks!* However, if the bullies teamed up and started working together, children would simply stop going to this playground. *Obviously.* People rarely liked being called names or being punched in the face and having their money taken from them. *Or invaded, shot at and have their house blown up around them.*

This metaphor was a gross simplification for the state that the Andromeda galaxy had currently found itself in. This new kid, the Nekrith, had perfected the act of bullying to the point that this galaxy was like a deserted playground. *No one wanted to play here anymore.* Those who could flee had done so, leaving the weaker planets defenceless and ripe for the picking in their wake. The New Andromeda Republic was this galaxy's last defence and they were quickly losing ground to defend. Revantide was a thing of beauty. Like a kaleidoscope of butterflies floating on a cool summer's breeze. What was currently happening to these *'butterflies'* was comparable to being hit by a train travelling at a hundred miles per hour. Do you know what happens to a butterfly when it's hit by a train? The same thing that happens to everything else. It gets unequivocally *'Donald Ducked.'*

And right now Revantide was getting Donald Ducked harder than an awkward teen on prom night.

Nothing made sense. One minute Kiko and Kara were joking around at home in a state of contented joyfulness, the next they had been at war with an alien enemy. Wandering across space and distant planets during a time that should have been several millenniums away.

The distorted echo of an explosion from above loosened some rubble off of a cave ceiling and it rained down onto the cold, wet, rocky floor. Some of it spattered on Kara's face and muddied her hair. An intense ringing flooded her ears as she tried pulling herself up out of the dirt. An intense pain whelmed in her lungs as she breathed. Her fingers pulled through her messy, matted hair; which tugged at the roots. Her eyes tried in vain to adjust to the darkness around her. As she stood there, or rather knelt there, all she could discern was a small glimmer of light off in the distance and the sound of trickling water. Every other shape, colour and sound was muted to her.

Where was she? Why was she in so much pain? She felt a sharp stinging across her trembling arms. She felt weak as if all the life had been dragged out of her. She could remember falling. She could feel the icy rock under her toes... *Where were her shoes...?* She had most definitely been wearing them earlier. Who had taken her shoes? Why had somebody... Kiko? *Kiko!* Where was Kiko?

Kara tried calling out into the darkness for the reassuring replies of her pseudo-sister. But as she tried a sharp pain ripped through her vocal chords. As she lay there, hunched over, gagging and rasping from the agony that was her burning throat, she felt herself spitting up something all over her hands and into the darkness. *That had better have not have been blood!*

It was always a strange sensation when a bright light flooded absolute darkness like the bursting of a dam. *It was almost painful.* It was definitely blinding. It also was disorientating. It was unpleasant and jarring. It was also a favourite way for mothers to awaken those children of hers who she had deemed as oversleeping or wasting the valuable morning hours.

Light flooded the chamber, just this time it wasn't from someone opening a pair of curtains. No matter how hard she tried, nothing Kara did helped her eyes to concentrate on the hazy figure that was now stood in the doorway. All she could make out was its blurry form overlapping in upon itself as her eyes slipped in and out of focus. It was kind of like being at the optician's when they keep changing the lenses over and ask you to read from the eye chart. *(You know, if you were broken and almost dying, soaked in your own blood. And if this opticians was on an alien planet, during a time of war and was also deep underground.)* The change in light was too extreme, it was all-consuming and disorientating. A loud clang filled the room as a tray of food fell against a cold and wet metal floor. The only thing Kara could make out was that she wasn't actually in a cave after all, but instead, she was trapped in some sort of metal structure. *If that was any better of a place to be...?*

As she tried calling out to the stranger a second stinging discomfort stabbed at her throat. The cry for help that had actually escaped her body was pathetic and feeble. She had tried to stand, but her legs gave way. *She crawled weakly across the metal floor.* Dizzying confusion swept across her mind. The dirt on the ground dug in under her fingernails and her toes frantically skidded across the wet floor underfoot, as she desperately dragged her broken body towards this indifferent stranger. This undisclosed form. Mutedly she begged and pathetically pleaded to the shadowed figureless blur. Her calls for help fell on deaf ears and seemed to stir no emotions as this thing turned away from her.

Darkness returned to rule the room once more as the door was slammed shut again. *This darkness ruled all.* Tears of fear ran down her face as Kara slumped in a ball of defeat against the door. Panic pounded and pulsated in her heart as the realisation of a powerless isolation began to harden from within. *Where was Kiko?* Kara was helpless and alone. Who was that? *Where was she?* Torments and imaginings of the realisation of isolation clawed at her soul. Here she was, all alone again. Crying into the void like she had done as a child.

Darkness had returned. *The darkness had won.*

"You are always alone. Darkness is eternal. I am eternal."

'No, you are just the voice inside my head! You're not real!'

"I do not need to bargain, pathetic child. You cannot hide from me."

'You have no power over me! I am free of you!'

"I do not beseech, plead or reason.

I am the Darkness."

'Go away!'

Kara clutched at the sides of her head in a fervent grasp of hysteric despair as she rocked.

"You beg and cry yourself to sleep, thinking such an act matters."

'Leave me alone!'

"That it makes a difference."

'Shut up! Shut up! Shut up!'

"It makes none, my Ragnarök Child."

'I am not your child of Ragnarök!'

"There is no going back to how things once were... You are alone. Always alone."

'No! No! Please, no more!'

"From here to the end."

'I just want to be free, for a moment's peace!'

"You drove them all away by the very nature of your existence.

You deserve this."

'I was a child! I deserved better!'

"All of this."

'No! You're wrong!'

"None love that which is undeserving to be loved."

'Shut up! Leave me alone!'

"You turned your back on the darkness, Kara. Look around you now, it is all you have."

'You're wrong!'

"You will die here."

Thoughts and voices ripped at her mind as she slowly began losing consciousness once more, despite how hard she fought against it. The darkness of the room began to fade away from her.

Tugging, tugging tugging. She could feel something? The rhythm of something jerking and wrenching. It was tugging, pulling and yanking roughly at the side of her head. *Tugging. Tugging. Tugging.* Awareness returned unto her as she felt a keen prickling pain pulling at the roots of her scalp. The realisation that something was combing her hair had jolted awareness back across her entire comatose body almost instantaneously. Her eyes flashed wide open. The air momentarily froze as she realised a pair of long black humanoid legs were wrapped around her from behind. These legs were cracked and rough like used charcoal. An uneven and flaky arm was enfolded across her torso, keeping her upright. *Something large was cradling her.* Like a spider. *Deep raspy breaths wetted the back of her neck.* Kara could feel the breaths deep within her ears. The sensation of its awful hand was still to be felt as it passed through her hair. All of her senses were on fire as she slowly drifted her eyes over her foul surroundings. This room had what seemed to be a metal table to the side, she seemed to be lying here with this thing on top of what resembled a bed. Rotted lumps and faded picture frames adorned her surroundings. *A godawful smell flitted through the air.* A metal floor ran off in all directions, but the walls seemed to consist entirely of smooth rock. *But let's be honest, you're not interested in the décor right now, are you?*

Kara broke free of the ebony limbs and turned to face her ensnarer. This act of defiance was less impressive when you bore in mind how desperately she was using the table to keep herself upright.

Two diluted white eyes shone out from across the features of a cracked and dry face. This dark navy-like face was broken and irregular. A hive of scars lay interwoven across the features on the right side of this thing's face. Lank balding hair hung loosely from the scalp. The skin was almost ripped away entirely from around this side of the right side of her jaw, allowing pools of saliva to collect and cascade onto its body. This *'body'* seemed affronted by Kara's separation as it slowly rose. The dry skin shuddered as the bones creaked and cracked from within. A desperate and confused rage seemed to drape across this humanoid's face as a black hand slowly reached out to Kara. What few fingernails that were left were broken, jagged and coarse. Like the remnants of a house fire poking out from the debris. A dry rasping breath drowned out all the other sounds. A maddened feral groan was released after every third or so breath as the desperate and confused rage folded into an expression of delirious yearning. *The bitter, desperate hand was still outstretched.*

In her folly, Kara had tried to strike away the hand of this dark entity. Truth be told, this was probably a bad idea. *(Like a really, really bad idea!)* A white-hot flash of pain broke out across Kara's wrist as a sickening cracking sound came from within it. Imagine the sound of several carrots being snapped. Now imagine that sound coming from your wrist.

With an unnerving speed, this thing had snapped her arm back and was now holding her off the ground by her wrist as its other hand reached around her mouth. Bony blackened fingers wrapped around her face. Kara's muffled screams were nothing against this thing's blood-curdling shrieks. The gaunt being lent in as if to whisper into Kara's ear.

"DAAAAAAUGHTER no!" A hiss-like howl ripped through Kara's ear as both hands tightened. "Mother is sad! Mother angry!" This guttural sounding attempt at words fell upon terrified ears.

A few seconds had passed before this awful thing fled hastily out of the door. Slamming it shut with such a force that the sound wave reverberated back off the walls. Kara fell to the floor, sobbing once again. As she fell she accidentally kicked the food tray and sent it flying across the floor. Here she sat clutching her injured arm as she rocked back and forth.

Now, I'm not entirely sure that there is a fitting explanation for what had just happened that could do justice for just how scared this poor, little Kara now was. See, you need to realise Kara has witnessed a lot of trauma in her lifetime. Despite her relatively young age. I genuinely worry for her well-being, currently Kara did too. Obviously. *And I hope you are secretly worried too.* If she had known the secret truths as to what this woman was it would have broken her heart. If you, dear reader, knew what had led this woman to being in this state and why she was now so broken, both of mind and body, you'd probably stop reading. *Either out of despair, disgust or fear.* I have no interest in regaling you with such horror. But I will invite you to share your opinion. *Who do you think she is?* Why is she doing this? What does your heart tell you?

I'll tell you the obvious, in case you missed it. Kiko and Kara had fallen together. They had been deep underground. *So where could they have fallen to?* Probably deeper underground, right? Where was Kiko and why wasn't she here with Kara? Why was Kara alone right now? There was no way Kiko would allow any of this to happen. Not for one second. Not for a single moment. *Was she still alive?* Had this *'thing'* taken her? Was she also being held captive? Kiko would have done everything in her power to help her friend. *Where was the Revanspear?* What had happened with the Nekrith? What did the Revanspear riddle mean? *What was going to happen next?* What kind of structure has metal floors and rocky walls? *What was this room?* I want you to really think about all of these questions. After all, any answer might have a chance of saving Kara's life. Because, honestly, do you even think she can survive this? *She can barely stand.* She can't speak or cry for help. People who can't stand, fall. By literal definition. This woman was clearly stronger and faster than her. Does anyone even know she's here? *Would anyone know where to come looking for her?*

Fear always had the ability to warp a person's perception of time. Perhaps this was because it was nigh on impossible to gauge its passing if all you were doing was crying. So as Kara sat here, she was completely unaware as to how much, or little, time had passed. Kara had not had the best of relationships with her actual mother, Elizabeth, never mind this pseudo, would-be other-mother. Elizabeth was always cold and uncaring, just like her husband Edwin De'Carusso. The grand halls of Titan Point were not a place one went when seeking expressions of love. *Even if you are the only daughter of the family.*

So as the fresh thoughts of horror Kara currently faced raced through her distraught mind, they awoke with them forgotten memories of a time long since repressed. Dark thoughts always found a way to bore through the mind like a great drill. Awakening other emotions as it went. Before you knew it, it wasn't just one bad thought. *It was a few hundred.* This brew of nightmares became overwhelming. Here this child of Ragnarök sat in her room of rocks. Unaware of the passing of time.

One thought kept breaking through, like a lighthouse at night.

'Kiko will find me.'

"Will she though? Are you sure?"

A cold hard metal plate pressed against the side of Kara's jaw as she snapped back to reality. *She had fallen asleep!* How could she have been so stupid as to fall asleep? Two bloodless eyes watched as an ungrateful child refused the offerings of food. An ebony hand grasped at Kara's hair and pulled. Kara had almost been choked by the tidings of food that had been enforced down her throat as she had tried to scream. *Crushing food tided against an anxious gasping for air.* This retching was in no small way aided by both the scent and the taste of the food. Or what was maybe once food, long ago. Think sour trout and curdled milk but with the consistency and texture of porridge. *Maybe it had never actually been edible?* It was impossible to tell by the taste.

The Revantide mother seemed to take great delight in the hilarity of seeing Kara struggle down her food and began thrashing and leaping with strides of en-crazed jubilation across the small room. Bounding like a salmon swimming upstream. One of these bounds sent her crashing against the table. No sooner had she fallen against it than she had span around, fuelled by a terrible and tremendous rage and attacked the table with a single strike. The table bounced off the opposite wall before almost landing directly on top of Kara. Who, if not for the fact she'd curled up into a ball to escape, would have most likely have been crushed. However, this fetal position had offered little in the way of protection from the Revantide mother, who seemed to blame her for the whole event and leapt on her and was now screaming over her.

Kara felt the spray of saliva engulf the side of her cowering face and pooling inside her ear. The arm that her face was hiding behind felt more like a waterfall of heavy, trickling spit than an actual arm at this point.

The door slammed shut again with a resounding crack. This slam shuddered over Kara's crying body as it lay cowering in the corner. Defeated. Terrified. Alone.

Life had never been easy in Titan Point. Elizabeth and Edwin had never much cared for acts of sentiment. Elizabeth, the white-haired Elf was as beautiful and as cold as a crisp winter's morning. Edwin was about as power-hungry as a power-hungry Human could be. For him, the value of life was measured by how far it had allowed for him to progress his wealth and value. Another step up the ladder. To him all life was unimportant. The only pride the working masses had needed to feel was the sense of satisfaction of making him more successful. *To make him more powerful.* All life was little more than the cogs of a great machine. His great machine. His two sons, Alistair and Sebastian, understood their families value and had never wasted a single second on the musings of stuff like guilt or ethics. *Why would they?* Kara had always been little more than this proverbial thorn in their side. She had always worried about the feelings of others and the effect her family had on the world. She had always slowed down the great wheel of progress to discus things like ethics and to question their code of conduct.

This value she placed on seemingly unimportant lives had always left her feeling castrated and alone from the rest of her family. This separation from her own family had strengthened her bond with Kiko, who in herself understood how it felt to be living in someone else's shadow.

A few more hours had passed when a small trickle of brilliant light flooded Kara's prison. From the crack in the opening door, Kara saw a familiar entanglement of red knotted hair and black-rimmed glasses.

"Kara!" Kiko exclaimed as she held a hand out to her long lost friend. Kara tried to rise to her feet but had been unable to do so.

She felt the gentle hum in her bones as Kiko cast some sort of healing spell upon her. Kiko's skin was muddied and bruised. But despite her unkempt appearance her oldest of friends had seemed more confident than Kara could ever recall observing in her before.

Kara felt the strength of life return to her. It was almost like a drug. She could feel the adrenaline coursing through her veins. Her bones felt like iron as the power came back to her legs. The ringing of tinnitus ceased allowing her to think clearly again. The fire in her throat had been extinguished allowing her to speak once more. *She felt the vigour return to her as she rose.* Like a great rose in the lights of the summer sun. This analogy being extra pertinent when you bore in mind that the De'Carusso family crest was that of a red rose wrapped around a green snake. There are some out there who may assume that this snake was winning against the rose. *This was not the case.* Great golden thorns ruptured through the snake's skin and pierced through to the other side. Their family motto was *'We Do Not Break. We Rise.'* An ideology they followed intently.

This was a lesson that this Revantide woman was about to learn and she was going to learn this lesson the hard way. The De'Carussos were like metal. *They did not break.* They did not bend. They did not falter. If backed into a corner, if they were ever pushed down, if their faces were forced into the mud. This would not stop them. They would rise once more. Always rising, like the sun. Forged anew. No matter how hard they fell. *They always got back up.* And it had never ended well for whosoever decided it was a good idea to put a De'Carusso down. (*One such example was in the 1990s. Kara's grandfather, Albert, had a doctor executed for diagnosing him as dead. He wasn't dead, but he was that level of old where it was hard to tell the difference.*)

Kiko watched with a confused facial expression as Kara rose to her feet and walked past her without saying a word.

"A thank you would be nice by the way!" Kiko sarcastically called after her. "Also, I'm fine! Thanks for asking!"

A loud crashing noise spilt in from an adjacent room. By the time Kiko had entered the place from which the noise had commenced, Kara could be seen. She was standing, huffing and panting with rage over a quivering husk of some humanoid figure. *She had one of her axes in her hand.* This charred anthropoid was trying to crawl away from her. It looked terrified.

"Kara...?" Kiko's confused voice cut through the tense silence. She was unsure what had happened to her blonde Half-Elven friend during their time apart.

Kara realised she didn't feel right as she there over her captor. She should want revenge. Every fibre of her being called out to be avenged. *A bloody retribution birthed from a steely blade.* Reprisal achieved in the De'Carusso way. The way she was supposed to. By blood. *'We Do Not Break.* We *Rise.'* The words she had heard thousands of times over. *'We rise and crush whoever it was who tried to make us bend the knee.'* So this thing that had attacked her deserved everything she was about to get. But as she stood here over her imprisoner, she felt no rage.

She felt pity.

As Kara looked over this Revantide woman, she was surprised to realise that she saw neither a foe nor an enemy. Weirdly, she saw herself. *She saw what it felt like to cower.* To tremble. To recoil and hide away in fear of a totalitarianistic father. This realisation snapped her out of her feral rage. *What was she doing?* She hated her father. *So why was she allowing his voice to guide her?* This wasn't her. There was a flaw with the eye-for-an-eye strategy. What happens in this great new world of half-blinded people after you've hurt everyone who has ever hurt you? When everything is perfect and just in the world and everything is precisely how you want it to be. What happens to the people like you? When the tally of those you've hurt out of revenge, come seeking revenge of their own? At what point do you stop being justified in your actions? When does the weight of it all shift and you become the bad guy? How are you going to protect your brilliant life of vindication from the next self-entitled aggressor?

All those nights spent talking with the Attetson family had taught her one thing. Sometimes a little mercy can go a long way. Sometimes a thing can seem important at the time. But what about in a year? What about in ten years? After the heat of the moment has passed and it all becomes memories. *Will it still be as important?* Will you be happy with how you reacted at the time? How do you want to remember your own life? How do you want to be remembered by others, as an angry aggressor or a reasonable person?

It was all a choice.

And deep down Kara knew what her choice was.

She leant over and pressed a finger against the side of this woman's ghoulish head. Her skin felt dry and scaly. As she did so a faint light shone over the Revantide woman. As this light shone, her ghastly feral mannerisms faded into something more human. More refined. What Kara had chosen to do was to cast a healing spell of her own. Not one for the body, but for the mind. Freeing the Revantide woman of whatever had made her lose control. She had agency once more.

"Kill... me..." The woman's voice cracked under the weight of her newly regained freedom.

Kara looked froze as a puzzled look cracked across her face before she stood up once more.

The Revantide Woman gave a longing look to Kara's axe.

Chapter Thirteen

THE WAX MAN

There was a crack of magical amber light as the cold rocky walls of Revantide's cave system were replaced with the surroundings of a more familiar series of Earthly brown tower blocks. The sounds of far off sirens and city chatter filled the crisp night air. A setting sun reflected in the windows of the nearby buildings, casting a blood-red glow. A cluttering of disposed of trash lay scattered all around them. A testament to man's waste. A pile of black bags smothered a defeated skip and a weather-worn sofa lay abandoned, stained brown by the rain and who knows what else. Crisp (*potato chip!*) packets and cans rustled in the cool night breeze.

This place was a dump, this much was true. But at least it was Earth. *It was home.* Or at least something close enough to their actual home to bring a modicum of peace. And that made it more beautiful than you could ever imagine. There was always something to be said about returning to a place that you recognised after some form of hardship. *The comfort of familiarity.* The sights and sounds of a subconsciously designated and recognised safe-space to trigger a sense of complacency and security. This could be you returning home after a bad break-up with the love of your life and being comforted by a parent. Likewise, you could find comfort in a selection of the same five songs you have listened to from ten years ago. Maybe it was a certain meal, movie or even a friend. But there was always something. In this way, this dilapidated council estate meant that the wars of Revantide were over. The horrendous horrors of the Nekrith were behind them. However if asked, the nearby residents of this 1970s Cockney council block would say that their ordeals would be far from over. Rumours had spread of a gas leak. This gas leak had apparently caused mass hallucinations of terrible visions and nightmarish shapes. A headless child had tormented the sixth floor. On the third floor, a lodger swore he had seen his kitchen full of hanged, hysterically laughing corpses. A woman on the fourth had been chased by a balding man with rotting skin full of maggots. This had led the nearby citizens to avoid this concrete cesspool.

"Ugh... Kiko? Where are we?" Kara pulled her scarf over her nose to cover the smell of the black bags and skips.

"Um... Earth... London... 1973..." Kiko replied shortly after checking against her temporal coordinates.

"1973?" Kara snapped back. She had had a rough time of it lately and just wanted to go home!

"At least it's Earth..." Kiko shrugged.

Even if it was the wrong decade, at least it was the right planet. This act of teleporting was similar to throwing a dart through the very fabric of the time vortex itself and trying to hit a dartboard from three thousand years ago! *Yes, Kiko had missed the bullseye.* She would happily admit that. But she would also like to see you do better. *Can you teleport yourself through time?* No? *So shut up then, no one likes a back seat driver.*

A scream of a child broke out over the night.

"Ugh! What now!" Kara grumbled out loud, drained by the time she had spent with the Revantide woman and the choice she had just made. She was in no mood for whatever 'this' was

A young boy sprinted around the corner. His footsteps echoed against the dirty landscape. This terrified child was running straight for them. If this wasn't alarming enough of a greeting, he had also begun to scream for '*help*' at the top of his lungs. He seemed to be dressed in a set of blue and white striped pyjamas. This brown-haired boy seemed no older than ten years old.

As this child dashed hastily towards the girls he happened to cross over a seemingly quotidian and ordinary-looking puddle. At the precise moment of him doing so a pair of white, wax-like and colourless arms discharged from underneath the flooded surface with a horrifying speed. *A pair of bitter, lengthy fingers enclosed around his arms.* And with as little time as it had taken for these arms to emerge, they had now disappeared. Dragging this petrified and screaming child down into the depths with them as they submerged themselves out of sight, drowning his little screams into a hollowed silence.

Kiko raced forward and tried to grab at the boy, with Kara not too far behind her. It had not been too long, if she was quick they'd still be able to grab him and pull him back out from the depths! Kiko struck at the surface of the puddle to reach into the abyss beneath, just to discover that this puddle was as shallow as, well, a puddle. *There was no boy.* There was also no way a little boy could have ever fitted in there, regardless of how 'little' he was. As she turned to look to Kara for advice she felt a hand pull at the back of her collar. The yanking sensation dragged her to her knees, ripping the skin on them as she landed. *A milky white set of hands now grasped at her face!* She felt a burning sensation from the back of her head as blood trickled down the back of her neck. Kiko pushed back with all the strength she could muster as a head began to emerge from the waters. The pang of stones dug into her palms as she fruitlessly continued trying to push herself away.

This bloated feminine face had bulging yellowy eyes. Her complexion was cracked like an old weathered canvas, her skin like old paint that flaked off with age. Her lips were chapped, cracked and frayed. A black sludge that was as dark as her lank hair gushed out of her yellow-toothed mouth as she bellowed into an ear-piercing shriek. The smell of rotting fish and putrid puss filled Kiko's nostrils. With all of her available might, she pulled away from this aqueous adolescent nightmare girl. As she did so she had accidentally overexerted herself and fell flat on her back! *As she arose she realised that she was now in a small room.* The alleyway had somehow disappeared from around her. Dirt and mould crept up the faded and ripped wallpaper. Old decomposed curtains blocked the light from the windows. Putrescent wall-hangings were either hung askew or lay abandoned on the floor. An old music box played a tune the best it could from under a lifetime of rust. The hairs rose on the back of Kiko's neck and a shiver went down her spine as she fixated upon a discoloured black door.

'Open it.'

'No, don't open it.'

'You have no choice.'

'It's not safe.'

'I mean, it's probably not safe in here either...'

'There's no other way out!'

The voices of doubt and indecision grappled in Kiko's mind as she raised a trembling, bleeding hand towards the brass and round door handle.

Kara rushed towards the drowning child, with Kiko just in front of her. With everything they had just witnessed on an alien planet, this wasn't the homecoming she had hoped for. But regardless, if this was how a demon or ghost wanted to die, she was okay with that. She would more than happily oblige. A blinding pain shot through her side as *a giant spider burst forth from nowhere* and tackled her into the side of the skip. There was a terrible *'twang'* as her head rebounded off of the side of it. Black waste bags collapsed in around her, submerging her beneath them (*and their smelly juices*) as the spider's long, spindly legs stabbed aggressively through the trash. *This eight-legged monstrosity was trying to wrap her up in a big ball!* Kara quickly rose to her feet and batted the black bags to one side with an axe ready to swing at this heaving arachnid that had just blind-sided her. But there was no '*thing*' and no '*one*' to be seen…. Not even Kiko…!

'Oh no! It's happening again!'

"*Of course it's happening again, I deserve this.*"

'I don't want to be alone!'

"*Ha-ha! She thinks she deserves the company of others!*"

'Why does this keep happening?'

"*Because you deserve this, Kara.*"

'No! Stop it! Leave me alone!'

"*You will never escape the voices in your head, Kara.* You will never escape me!"

'*Leave me alone!*'

"It is time to grow up, Kara. Time to accept how alone you truly are!"

'I'm not alone!'

"Oh no? Then where is everyone?"

'Get out of my head!'

"Where is Kiko?"

'What is wrong with me?'

Thoughts rushed through her mind as she recalled her imprisonment with the Revantide psycho. As these thoughts span in her head like a carousel, so too she span, looking for a sign of anyone that was to be seen. The 1970s trash décor quickly faded away into the visage of a sodden bogland. Wet mud and dying grass closed in around her. *A single great tree stood in front of her.* This tree was thick and it was old. Its bark was grey and cracked. This tree looked impossibly old. Far too old to be from a 1970s London council estate. It hadn't been here a moment ago, so where had it come from? *Hung on it were close to fifteen hanging corpses!* The knotted ropes of the hangman's noose wrapped around each of their broken necks. Here they hung, lifeless and emotionless. *A swarm of cold cadaverous.* It was a horrible sight to behold. Suddenly a raging fire broke out across the branches of the tree and engulfing it whole. Lighting the dark sky orange with its mighty blaze. The fallen corpses began to wriggle and writhe, like unearthed worms dug up by a spade, as they all broke out into several blood-curdling screams. *The sudden sight of this tree and its fire had caused Kara to fall backwards.* As she did so she cracked her head on a tombstone and fell into an open grave. Down and down she fell, screaming all the way into this bottomless pit.

Some readers may be confused as to what was currently happening. On the thirteenth Earth, there existed an extremely rare creature quite unlike anything else. The fabled Pesadilla-niño, or nightmare child, was an ancient creature that was said to torment the Spanish mountains of Monte Perdido. Or rather, this mountain range was this creatures' most frequented hunting grounds. Truth be told they could be found anywhere and anywhen. Although that revelation was a lot more terrifying than the idea of them being isolated to one Spanish mountain, so people rarely mentioned it. No one was sure what they looked like as these tricksters could change their shape at will. These reality-warping telepathic demons could create micro pockets of existence, in which a whole manner of living nightmares could be created. These micro pockets of existence were not all too dissimilar to Demonscapes. The fear they created in their victims with these illusions was purely delectable to the Pesadilla-niño, it was like an endless box of chocolates on which it would gorge itself. *Like a child in a sweet shop.* Any victim would be accused of suffering from psychosis, paranoia, being dissociative or lying. They may also blame the occasional gas leak. From within its created reality the Pesadilla-niño controlled everything. Unlike a Jinn (*or a Genie*) which burrowed into your mind and created realities in your subconscious as it feasted off your flesh, the Pesadilla-niño created illusions in the real world. This wasn't some dream from which you could escape by simply opening your eyes. The Pesadilla-niño would create illusions to scare you and feast on your fears until you died. If you were afraid of spiders, you'd be trapped in a house made from spiders as a giant spider (*Which was also made up of smaller spiders by the way!*) would chase you. Can you even begin to imagine how many spider legs that would be, just twitching away? Scared of clowns? Well '*it's*' a night at the world's scariest Haunted House for you then. The Pesadilla-niño would even disguise its own appearance. The spider that had tackled Kara was the Pesadilla-niño. The face in the puddle was the Pesadilla-niño as well. So was the balding man with rotting skin full of maggots and the headless child who had tormented the sixth floor before the girls' arrival.

What horrors do you suppose the Pesadilla-niño would inflict on you?

Both Kiko and Kara blundered into the same room at the same time. *(Kiko had entered through the front door, Kara had fallen from the ceiling.)* The two ran for each other and compared rushed, horrified accounts of what they had both just witnessed. To their surprise, this room was surprisingly faded. As if colour had never existed in here. It had almost felt like the whole room was draped in a sepia tone filter. The room was approximately thirty-foot wide in all directions and devoid of any other characteristic than the fact that it was made of wood, except for four symmetrical windows that adorned each of the walls which allowed a small trickle of light to enter. *A sudden multitude of furious bangs erupted from beneath the floorboards as the floor of this wooden room quickly became overran with hundreds, if not thousands, of horrible bulky rats!*

They poured down from the rafters like water from a ruptured pipe. Glass smashed and rained down as they clamoured desperately in their droves over the frames of the broken windows. The walls split and buckled as they emerged from deep cracks within. They pulled themselves up through the gaps between the floorboards. This swarm of bloodthirsty vermin surged in such a great number that it had become impossible to see the floor beneath the all-consuming sludge of their blackened furs.

Hundreds, if not thousands, of pairs of ruby red eyes locking on with a hateful glare from their bodies of jet black fur. Hundreds, if not thousands, of scurrying claws clamouring over and digging into each other as they ran. Hundreds, if not thousands, of dirty rats squeaking away in a frantic unison. *Can you even begin to imagine how it all must have sounded?* How it must have felt to have such an influx of rodents run straight for you?

The onset of these hideous rodents was as horrendous as it was sudden. The floor cracked and splintered as the walls bulged outwards under the weight of the swarming hoarded tidal wave of rushing vermin. Kiko quickly summoned a ball of light from her hands, almost instinctively. It seemed to do the trick, for now. The heinous horde seemed to be stopped in its tracks as if they had been scared of the light. The rats snapped and snarled at them as the light shimmered in their hateful little eyes, like a shimmering of rubies within the sea of ebony fur and gnashing yellow teeth. Terrible claws swiped angrily at the light in a feral rage as these nasty critters swarmed over one another as they crawled and scurried, desperate to find a way to their prey.

Kiko's heart pounded in her chest and throbbed in her ears. Her chest rose heavily with each terrified breath. *What was going on?* Something didn't feel right. Besides the obvious room of endless rats, which she had despised with her entire soul, something about all this didn't quite add up. The endless conveyor belt of nightmarish visions. It didn't feel real, which most likely meant it wasn't. She watched out over the sea of eager hungry rodents. *Where had they come from?* She felt the blood run down the back of her neck. Kiko tried to suppress the thoughts which quickly arose. The idea of all of these awful creatures ripping and tearing her apart from this wound, until she was little more than a flayed corpse, stripped to the bone. *Why did it have to be rats?* She hated rats!

Her heart stopped for a split second as her summoned light began to fade. *'Oh no, oh no!'* She held her breath and focused with unbridled attention. The squeaking and squabbling of the rodents seemed to fade away into a blur. She waited with a furious concentration.

The room went black.

Kara's screams bellowed as Kiko quickly summoned another light around them. The encroaching rats had closed in further around her! *Shit!* They had lost ground to them. Their beady eyes and snapping jaws inching ever closer. She couldn't help but feel that she was delaying the inevitable. The inescapable fate of tooth and claw. But as she wasn't exactly keen on the idea of being completely swarmed by rats, she didn't mind buying each and every second of extra light that she could muster. *All Kiko had needed was a little extra time.* A chance to put together enough pieces of the puzzle for her to be able to figure out the true aggressor behind these awful attacks. If she knew what was attacking them, then she would know how to fight back. Kara had said that a giant spider had attacked her at the same time that white figure had grabbed Kiko. There had been no record of giant spiders assisting or working alongside anyone besides Goblins. Even then, this alliance wasn't one of choice. The giant spiders weren't pets, they were wild and unpredictable tools that were equally as likely to eat a Goblin as any of the Goblin's foes. The Goblins had been (*barely, but just*) smart enough to figure out a way to utilise the ferocity of these oversized arachnids to drive away invaders, without losing too many of their own in the process. So the idea of the spider aiding the puddle-person was unlikely.

Kiko's light began to *fade*. She thought over how she had been instantly teleported to the inside of a house after pulling herself away from the awful face. *Hang on, that interior had been almost identical to the interior of the Lar Dos Mortos!* Man, she hated that ghostly house! Even the slightest memory of it made her run cold. No wait, hang on. Kiko distinctively remembered Kara telling her of a time when she had been no older than six, and her father had executed a band of unfaithful workers by having them hanged from a nearby tree for all to see. Kara had told Kiko once of how terrifying she had found it. *Time was running out!* Could it be that something was using their fears against them?

Time had run out. The room went black once more.

Kiko forced another ball of light into existence, her breath heavy and laboured. The snarling mound of lapping rodents had jumped forth and was now too close for comfort! Her heart pounded as she looked at their numerous claws. *No, wait!* She was terrified of rats too! So this fitted her forming hypothesis. Something was using their fears against them! Kara was also scared of spiders, so now the giant spider made sense!

'Oh crap, the boy!' Kiko suddenly found herself worried about the little child they had seen. Was he okay? *'No! Focus!'* There was no time to worry about the fate of anyone else right now. Time was running out. She wouldn't be able to help him if she was dead. As she looked out over the vermin tide, she doubted there would be enough time for her to recast her spell again. *Shut the hell up and focus!*

Focus right now, harder than you have focused on anything in your entire life, Kiko.

Focus, because your life and the fate of Kara and the young boy hang in the balance. What monster or Demon uses fear to hunt its prey? Nightmare-lashers were Demonic worms that burrowed deep in your brain and projected visions into your head. No, but they required you to be comatose! If it was a Nightmare-lasher she would be too close to death to make a difference anyway. So there was no use in focusing on that as there was nothing she would be able to do to save her life. Plus this would mean that this version of Kara wasn't real either as everything would be a dream. This didn't feel like a dream... but she supposed that all dreams felt real at the time... *so maybe?* She knew it couldn't be a Mimic, as they could only change their appearance and could not summon creatures to enact their bidding. She recalled stories of the Djin and how they...

The room fell dark once more.

In a blistering panic Kiko summoned an anguished light, one last time. She felt lost for breath as she saw that the ebony swarm of death was a few mere inches away! One brave rat leapt through the light and bit into Kiko's leg. A deep and terrible pain rang out as dirty, yellowed teeth punctured through the surface of the flesh on her thigh and sunk deep into her muscle, causing crimson blood to cascade forth. With a terrified yelp and tremendous flick of her leg, the rat was launched across the dark room, lost to the countless number of identically minded, nasty little carriers of her quickly approaching demise. Kara's hand was wrapped tightly around Kiko's arm. Kiko could feel Kara's whole body trembling behind her.

The Pesadilla-niño! Kiko had figured it out! The only creature that made sense. *But it was too late.*

The light had faded…

Kiko felt them scurrying up her legs. She felt their claws dig into her skin as they ascended up her torso, ripping and gouging away. A thousand ratty toes tore at the skin as an overwhelming mountain or vermin was now piling in on top of them. A myriad of scurrying, rat-like talons ran across the surface of their clothes, through their hair and tugged at the roots. *(In a sensation far too similar, for Kara's comfort, as to that which she had just experienced with the Revantide woman, moments before. God, Kara wished she still had her rocket launcher!)*

Kiko and Kara tried to fight them off, but there was just simply too many of them. They waded, batted, screamed and brawled their attempted ways to freedom. *But there was none to be found.* For every dirty little rat they managed to fling off, another five took its place. In no time at all, they were quickly overrun. From within a myriad of creeping rodents Kiko heard as the ground beneath Kara's feet gave way! Kara fell, but had managed to grab at the decaying floor just before it had been too late! *She kicked with her feet and pulled with all of her strength.* But she was still being swarmed by an endless parade of rats. Kara yelped and she screamed as she held on tight for dear life. Her heart pounded and her body ached, yet still these rats swarmed all over her, not giving her a seconds peace. She looked up to see the rat-infested form of Kiko, washed in a heaving pile of thrashing rodents, as her knees buckled under the immense weight and she fell to the endless tide of rats that had engulfed the entirety of her being.

The all too familiar voice of Kara's inner darkness returned once more. The deep, horrible voice of doubt cut her deeply once more.

"How pathetic. You are still the weak little girl you have always been. Forever the child, weak and feeble. How embarrassing and what a waste of time you have been. All that time and effort wasted in training you. All of their endeavours to make you into the perfect fighter... And here you are, dying to rats. If only your father could see you now. He would see that he was right about you. You are weak. Is this really how you intend to repay their hard work and sacrifice? By dying like any old commoner in the dirt... You were supposed to be better than this. You are undeserving of the De'Carusso name. You are filth, Kara. A disgusting waste. Thank you for wasting everyone's time."

Kara had not overcome all of her ordeals with the Revantide woman just to die in a shitty rat-infested room in London! *'Screw that! Not Happening!'* With a tremendous back-flip she shot herself into the air, this sent rats plummeting in every direction as they lost their grip on her. *(She was still a Half-Elf, so feats of agility were rather easy for her!)* As Kara landed she did so with a tremendous purple light that emitted from her torso. This energy burst forth from her and filled the room with the ferocity of a thousand thunderstorms. No rat, rodent or vermin was safe from its blast of ruination as they were all pelted against the walls. Kiko coughed and spluttered as Kara helped her back to her feet. All of these vile critters exploded on impact as they landed. *(Which was good!)* From each of their fat corpses an inundation of hundreds of spiders rushed forth. *(Which was bad!)* Kara screamed and jumped in behind Kiko and swore profusely.

"No! No! No! No! No! No!" She cried as she buried her face deep within Kiko's coat.

Kiko swung her arms open and three magical symbols appeared in thin air around her. *(Her sudden movement had caused her coat to billow around her and Kara.)* These were the Elven symbols for '*fuel*,' '*heat*' and '*oxygen*.' Each symbol was approximately six inches wide and was circled in a wreath of pure golden light. As Kiko drew her arms back into a close, these three symbols followed suit. All three converged, stacked in front of one another directly in front of Kiko. With a determined frown she hit the frontmost symbol, heat, with a tremendous slap from her right hand and launched it straight into the symbol for fuel. Then these two symbols collided with oxygen. Do you know what you get when you combine heat, fuel and oxygen? *You get fire.* Do you know what is great for killing spiders? *Fire.*

The room lit up as a sudden jet-stream of flame erupted from Kiko's palms and ignited across the pale room with an orange hue. She had looked like a flamethrower and she rather felt like one too. A million scurrying spiders had been no match for her endless flaming inferno. They were all burned to a crisp and ignited in the wake of her heated rays. An endless field of embered, twitching barbecued spider legs were now curled up in balls around the girls' feet as Kara began mercilessly stomping left, right and centre. The spiders made a hard crunching sound as they crumbled under her impassioned trampling. *Man, she really hated spiders.*

"Die! Die! Die! Die!" This release of Kara's pent up aggression had felt almost therapeutic. Even if it was extremely messy and noisy. The crunching noise of the roasted arachnids was rather reminiscent of the sound a young child made as they ate cereal with their mouth open. *(Granted the cereal probably tasted better than these charcoaled spider carcasses. Of course, unless that cereal was a store-branded bran flakes. Then it was debatable!)*

"I know what we're dealing with!" Kiko proclaimed, coughing and spluttering after her ordeal.

"It's a Pesadilla-niño." Kara replied with a cold tone as she carefully watched at her uncharacteristically quiet surroundings.

Kiko had a semi-surprised and slightly crestfallen air to her that Kara had already figured out the monster without her help.

"Oh."

"Yeah, it's kinda obvious…" Kara snapped. It had been a long couple of days and she wasn't in the mood for Kiko's games of assumed intellectual superiority and acting like she was the only smart person in any given room at any given time. Kiko wasn't the only person with a functioning brain after all.

"But what the hell was that flame-shit about?" Kara questioned as she shoved her ginger friend, annoyed by how long it had taken for her to act with a spell that would have been useful long before they had been swarmed by a thousand stinking rats. "Why did you wait so long to use it?! Why didn't you 'shoot fire' at the r-"

"Don't shove me!" Kiko replies sternly as she pushed Kara back with a shove of her own. It had been a long three nights that she had spent sleeping rough and hunting across the surface of Revantide for Kara whilst trying to protect Revantide's refugees from the Nekrith. Kiko wasn't in the mood for being pushed around like a little rag-doll in yet another one of Kara's great tantrums. Kara wasn't the only one with a lot on her plate right now! *At least she didn't have literal aliens warning her about her brother!*

Truth be told Kara had been more than slightly surprised about Kiko pushing her back for once. She had spent almost her entire life seeing Kiko being walked over and saying nothing about it. It was nice to see her actually fight back for once. Kara had respected it; even if the shove had been pretty feeble.

Fear was a strange thing. There was nothing quite like it for fogging the mind and diluting your focus. Even the most resolute person would occasionally stumble when the all too familiar prickle of fear sank in. As such people usually found themselves acting in strange and unusual ways, doing things they would not normally do with a rational mind. Some even found themselves betraying the very essence of their soul when faced with moments of great fear. Honest people would lie, seemingly brave people would run away and the best of friends would turn on one another; as was starting to happen now.

"You know what, Kara? You're not the only one who went through weird shit on Revantide. If you don't wanna talk about it, trust me, that's absolutely fine! But if you think I'm just going to let you push me around, you've got another thing co-"

Kiko's impassioned speech of respect was cut short by an intense burning smell. The girls had been so distracted by shoving and arguing (*and also feeling sorry for themselves*) that they had failed to notice that the sepia-toned room they were in had defaulted back to the appearance of its 1970s council block flat attire. The tacky plastic furniture and matching cheap decor of this cramped room had ignited under Kiko's flames. Soft furnishings blazed under a red-hot, sweltering blaze as the hard woods and plastics bubbled and boiled. These fires were now billowing around them like a dangerous bonfire.

Kiko was now distracted from her argument with Kara as she cast a troubled glance over the ablazed furnishings, the dancing flames reflecting off her glasses. A sudden gushing, gurgling sound arose as Kara ripped a nearby water pipe out of the wall with a levitation spell. The pipe (*which had been minding its own business at the time*) now found itself (*rather rudely*) exposed to the room as its cooling liquids from within lapped over the inferno and quickly put it to sleep.

Kara looked down at her ruined shoes and sighed deeply. The sooner today was over, the better!

"Come on, let's go." She said with a semi-defeated tone as she waded through the brown waters.

Kara loved those shoes. *Today really sucked!*

The pair silently left the ruined room and found themselves in one of the long, desolate hallways from the block of flats. Endless brown doors and thick, off-yellow cheap plastic light shades were visible on both sides of this nightmare of brown striped wallpaper. To be fair to the cheap decor, it was in fashion at the time. *(For some unknown reason, society as a whole had looked at the colour brown and said 'yes please.' They then proceeded to make everything as faded and beige as possible. And for some reason everything had to have a pattern either printed or sewn into it. Regardless of whether or not the design had actually looked good. These patterns were usually square or circular in design.)* Thick metal numbers hung on each of the doors, each door led to the different tiny flat that lay behind it. Like a really lame, straight and narrow maze of secreted residential life that smelled like stale cream and old cigarettes. Down the very bottom of the corridor the girls saw the young boy who they had seen just moments before. He was alive, but visibly scared. His brown terrified eyes locked on them for a single second before he dashed off around the corner in a terror-struck panic as fast as he could.

"No-no-no-no!" Kara called out after the kid with a tired and semi-defeated tone, as Kiko sprinted after him. "Don't run! Where are you going?" She sighed the sigh of a terrible frustration as she glared down the hall after him. *"Come back here you little bastard!* We're just trying to save you! Ugh!"

To her surprise one of the doors near her slowly drifted open with a creeping squeal from the hinges. The noise was shrill and elongated. *Kara slowly turned to face it.* From within the dark interior of this room could be seen the shape of another much younger child stood within a slither of glistening moonlight that shone in from the semi obstructed window behind her. As Kara's eyes adjusted to the low light levels she quickly realised that this child wasn't a child at all. *It was a creepy porcelain doll.* Her skin was as pale as snow, as hard as ice and cracked in several places. A series of maggots crept their way over her bone-china surface. *Her eyes were balls of dark and emotionless glass.* She wore a dress that was ripped and dirty. It bulged and billowed under the movement of the many maggots beneath. She also had a single dilapidated dolly-shoe at the end of one of her chubby, non-human legs. *There was a devilish grin of red lips carved directly onto her face.* Oh, and she also carried a big ol' butcher's knife.

"Nope! *No thanks.*" Kara said with a fake smile as she pulled the door closed and quickly made her way after Kiko and the boy.

It had taken no time at all for Kiko to catch up with the high-tailing boy, she was quite a bit taller than him after all.

"No, please! Please! Please, no!" He screamed in pure terror as she grabbed his wrist. Kiko quickly let go.

"Hey, hey! It's okay!" She held her hands up in a way both to indicate that she was '*unarmed*' and bore him no ill will, but also to try and calm him down from his current state of unfaltering hysterics. "You're alright! I don't want to hurt you."

The boy shook and trembled like a leaf in a winter's breeze. His breaths were deep and rapid. His movements were rushed and sporadic. His brown eyes darted in a mad panic.

"My name is Kiko, what's y-"

Kiko was cut short by a small porcelain doll bouncing off the wall behind her as it rebounded from one of Kara's kicks. Its knife clattered off to the side.

"Not so tough now are you?" Kara taunted aggressively as she stood over her small foe.

The doll tried to rise once more, laughing as it did so. So Kara booted it down the corridor with the biggest punt she could muster. She popped into a quick mocking pose as if to cause further insult to her fallen adversary. This had been a mistake, as all she had done was leave herself wide open to an act of reprisal. The doll seemed to instantaneously melt in thin air into a thick, white and viscid liquid. This sudden onslaught of bleached, syrupy wax quickly found itself forming into the shape of a tall, fat and balding man in the blink of an eye. With a single powerful uppercut (*which had completely caught Kara off guard!*) he impacted upon her jawline with an irrepressible seething rage, knocking her clean off her feet.

This '*man*' was approximately six-foot tall. His skin was like a hot melted white wax. His form was somehow solid yet flimsy. His skin seemed to drip whenever he moved. With every step parts of him seemed to jitter and flake away, these loosened bits of debris would then reform themselves to him as they fell, either being absorbed directly into his body or sliding across the ground to return. His thunderous footsteps rang out and echoed through the hall as he stomped towards Kiko and the child with an unparalleled desire for sadism. A furious, wide-eyed and bloodshot glare was broken across his pale face. Shallow breaths and snarls escaped through his rotten, yellow teeth. He was a lumbering mass of rage and malcontent. And he was bearing straight down upon them. *To Kiko's surprise his face was that of Vincent's.*

A thick heaving hand grabbed at her throat and slammed her against the wall as Vincent's face looked down on her choking body.

"Aw, what's the matter, Shadow Dweller? Come-on-come-on-come-on. You spent all those years prattling and complaining behind my back, nipping at my heels. Always grumbling in the shadows and resentful. Now here is your chance. You've always had something to say; so say it!"

The would-be Vincent sarcastically lent in close to Kiko to mockingly listen to her rasping suffocation. She kicked and pulled against him, struggling for air as his hand was still closed around her throat. Her tongue felt thick and uncomfortable in her mouth as saliva built up around it. Her bloodshot eyes flicked manically trying to see a way out. Her breaths were desperate and panicked.

She frantically dug her nails into the wall and into his lumpy plastic skin, trying to find an escape. Her boots desperately skidded and banged off of the wall and wildly kicked at him as she tried to break free from his tight grip. *Nothing was working.*

"Naw, darling little Kiko. After a lifetime of tantrums about no one paying you enough attention, what's the matter? After all this time, surely you don't have '*nothing*' to say?"

He laughed as she still frantically fought him off. Here she was gurgling and gasping for air as the room began to fade to a deadly black. Her ears rang out with a high-pitched squeal as her face began to turn a purplish red. Her dashing eyes began to slow as they expanded from the trapped blood in and around her swelling face. A single tear escaped down the right side of her face.

"You have always been a nothing and a nobody. You remember your feelings of being undervalued? It never had anything to do with me. You turned me into the bad guy to hide your own pathetic inability to-"

A sudden brilliant and blistering light of pure white ruptured forth from deep within Kiko's chest as the Revanspear leapt out of her, as if from nowhere! Its pyramid of eyes span frantically. A searing light of truth and deliverance. Kiko gave an alarmed and puzzled stare towards the blazing spear as she felt the grip loosen from around her throat. One of the spears many infuriated eyes locked onto the waxy figure that resembled Vincent as he melted away to reveal the figure that lay beneath.

The true form of the shocked and screaming Pesadilla-niño had been revealed. It was tall and gaunt. Its skin was dry as a desert and looked like that of an old withered corpse of tanned browns and dirt. From both of his shoulders, a metal shape protruded. This shape was a semi-circle of rusted metal that rose and joined over its head. It had six points that stuck out of it that rather resembled the shape of a flattened crown or the primitive outline of a metal sun. The creature's eyes were hollowed out and it had a large hooked nose. Several thick nails protruded from both of its arms and the creature's thin body was draped in a wine-red cloth. Both the creature and Kiko had seemed equally surprised by the sudden (*and fortuitous*) return of the Revanspear.

Indignant and defiantly radiant lights of truth shone from within the metal spear and cast itself upon the Pesadilla-niño who had found its power of illusions had been undone. The creature that dwelled in the shadows had been brought into the light.

With a hiss, it dropped Kiko and disappeared into a fog. The spear (*and subsequentially Kiko*) clattered against the carpeted floor. Kiko quickly grabbed the spear and ran to Kara. As she got to her collapsed friend, a bony hand grabbed at the pair and flung them far down the corridor. They landed with a 'flump.' The pair watched in horror as the Pesadilla-niño grabbed the boy and they both disappeared into nothingness.

Kiko went running after them, but Kara grabbed her arm.

"Kiko, no. We're in no state to fight." She looked up at her ginger friend as she continued pleading. "We will die!"

And she was right. Even with the Revanspear, they would be no match for the creature, not in their current state anyway. If they continued to fight they would all die. Where was the sense in that? But if they left then there would be no way of tracking the kid back down. If they had been at full strength then they might have been better prepared for a fight. But after several days of stress and abuse, Kiko found herself saying something she would have never thought she would ever say.

"Fine." A deep light consumed them as they abandoned the 1970s and they returned home.

The worst bit about them leaving the young boy to his fate? *They didn't even know his name.*

Chapter Fourteen

THE LONG NIGHT

Kiko and Kara's joyous return to their hometown (*and home-time*) was ramshackled by the bitter stabbings of guilt they now felt deep within their hearts as they pondered over the abandoned kid's fate. The most probable ending for him being that he had died that night, or soon after. On the one hand, an argument could be made that it was preposterous to feel bad about someone who would have died some fifty years earlier. If he was still alive then he would have been a lot older than they were now and would most likely (*Or rather hopefully!*) bear them no ill-will. But for these two, this night of horrors had not been half a century earlier. It had been the grand total of a whole five minutes. What had become of him? Maybe he had escaped and one day told the story of the day he had met Kiko and Kara to kids of his own. Or maybe he was little more than an abandoned skeleton, somewhere beneath the streets of old London town.

After a long pause of reflective despair upon their return to present-day Liarath, Kara put her hand on Kiko's shoulder and uttered the most commonly spoken Earthling sentence of all time.

"I'm going to the pub. *Coming?*"

The people of Earth shared a special relationship with pubs. If churches had been where a person went to seek life lessons on how to live a proper and moral life, full of strict rules, commandment and mandates, then a pub was where they would quickly find themselves afterwards when they had decided that the pious life was boring and that they wanted to cut free and live a little. The concept of a '*pub*' went by different names. Be it a bar, a boozer, a club, a free-house, an Inn, a public-house, saloon or tavern, the principle rule was the same; patrons frequented these buildings in their droves to purchase drinks. And no, these drinks were not water. Consuming alcoholic beverages was the foremost favourite pastime of the entire planet. This is because people like how it makes them feel. *Most of the drinking populace did so because it's fun.* Alcohol lowered inhibitions, which was just a fancy way to say that it made people less focused on how dangerous or stupid stuff was and made them more willing to do fun stuff. This included dancing as if no one was watching, telling a lot more jokes or trying to back-flip for the first time, because why not? Some people drank because it gave them newfound courage. To try asking a person out on a date that they would never have had the courage to ask sober, or to jump out of a really tall tree into a pile of stinging nettles because, again, why not? Some people drank because they wanted to forget and suppress horrid memories from their life. *This was why Kara had chosen to drink tonight.* The time spent in Revantide combined with her trip to the 1970s had been enough to make anyone want to turn to the bottle to find solace.

When the desire to get '*plastered*' (*really drunk*) struck the pair had often found themselves frequenting the Inn of the Drunk Dutchess. The sign outside this old stone free-house told the painted story of an oversized and cherry-cheeked woman with a wide smile on her face as she held a slopping glass tankard of ale high with pride. She wore an old-timey ballgown, which she held pinned down with her other hand from the unwanted advances of an over-eager balding Halfling. The door to the Drunken Dutchess was big, it was old and it was heavy. As such it would often stick and require a hearty series of tugs and pushes to open. It would also squeak deeply on its hinges every time it was opened. Hidden behind this door was a tavern of ruby red walls and black wooden furnishings. Directly in front of the door, at the rear end of a large room of stools, chairs and tables, sat the long ebony bar. Behind the bar was another series of paintings of the Dutchess, beating up the bald Halfling who had tried peaking up her dress and kicking him out. The door to the right of this room led to a substantial dance floor, where local bands would play music for the drunken regulars. They would play on top of a rather special and unique stage that sat in the far corner. The reason why this stage was special was because it wasn't powered by electricity. *It was powered by fairy magic.*

Beneath the top of the thick wooden stage hid a secreted word of pistons and gizmos that kicked into life with a wheeze and a groan upon the whims of the fairies that oversaw them. These pistons would power large bronze dishes that worked in a very similar manner to a microphone. These dishes would automatically cast a spell that absorbed the sound, which would be carried down a series of thick see-through cables. *(The sound would light up so you could literally see it move.)* These cables were connected to a series of bronze statues, carved into the shape of frogs. These frogs would then broadcast the music to the dancing crowds. These fairies loved all things music-related, so would even drop fairy dust over the attending patrons. This dust caused them to fall into a euphoric state that would make the music feel even better, due to raised endorphins and dopamine levels. *No one was quite sure whether this practice of spiking people with mind-altering substances was entirely legal or not, but no one ever really questioned it.*

The door to the left of the bar led to the beer garden, smoking area and toilets.

Kiko and Kara found themselves sitting at a table with their friends Penelope, Ozzy and Bailey Matthews. Bailey was another of their friends. He had long blonde hair and a body of defined muscles. He was a bit dim but with a heart of gold.

"Where the hell have you guys been?" Ozzy asked as he shot the two a troubled look.

"What do you mean?" Kiko called over the cheerful drunken din of the nearby drunkards as she sat down with her drink of vodka and lemonade.

"What do I...? It's been five days Kiko! Where have you two been?" Ozzy enquired with a miffed tone.

So apparently it hadn't been the exact night on which they had left. *Oops!*

"You know how it is." Kara vaguely replied whilst she shot Kiko a glare as she sat down with her pint of ale. "Killer hangover, dude. We just laid low for a few days. Lost track of time. Didn't we, Kiko?"

She went to kick Kiko from under the table. Penelope yelped as something hard struck her leg. So they had lost five days, but that was the problem with time travel. *It was always a tiny bit unreliable and slightly unpredictable.*

To be fair, it was also really hard and rather quite difficult. At least that was Kiko's excuse. Whereas Kara's speciality just required her to swing a blade at the side of some monster's head, Kiko's speciality took a great deal of effort, training and finesse. *Any old idiot could stab someone.* It took a certain level of skill to travel the fourth dimension. Something that Kara would never understand. Or, again, that was just Kiko's thoughts on it. She gave a look towards Penelope who was rubbing a large lumpy bruise on her leg.

'Oh my god, did Kara just try to kick me?'

Kiko shot a look of a thousand daggers towards the blonde Half-Elf.

'Bitch!'

Ozzy and Bailey had tried pushing Kara for more information on their disappearance.

"So what did we miss?" Kara asked as she tried to distract them once more. The two girls had shared a silent agreement on it not being worth the drama of explaining the truth of their sudden vanishing. Space travel and alien invasions would have invited a wave of endless questioning. Something that neither girl had wanted. That and the fact neither one wanted to admit that they'd just abandoned a little boy to his horrible fate.

"I fell off of my skateboard and ripped the skin off elbow!" Bailey said with the same enthusiasm of a happy golden retriever as he shoved his arm directly under Kara's nose. "See?"

Kara cast a disgusted glance towards his scarred arm. She was still a De'Carusso at the end of the day, and at the end of that day had still found a deep destain for any acts of uncouth *'over-sharing.'* As such, she slapped his elbow away from her face as if it had been a bothersome fly.

This had caused a playful argument to start between the two. This argument had led to the entire group deciding to dance to the music of some local band. *This decision had led to more drinking.* The drinking had led to more dancing and more drinking. This elevated level of alcohol flowing into their bodies had resulted in the inevitable desire to eat fatty and greasy street foods. This need to feed had led them to the nearest kebab house. *(A 'restaurant' that sold takeaway meats and extras. Most were little more than glorified street meat vendors.)* Here the gang had acquired the perfectly satisfying mix of thick meats and fried potatoes to satisfy their drunken cravings.

Kiko had gone for the classic lamb doner kebab, which she drunkenly picked at as she pretended her arm was a 'mother ostrich' feeding her mouth. Kara had, of course, chosen a quarter pounder burger, with fried onions and mushrooms, a dollop of ketchup and a side of French-fries; the grease of which soaked through the bread and ran down her fingers as she drunkenly munched her way through it with a tender look of affection, and without a single care in the world. *(Never underestimate the award-winning power combo of alcohol and food!)* Penelope, despite swearing blind that she was a vegetarian, was currently chowing down on a slice of doner meat and chips whilst heartedly laughing at Kiko's arm-bird impersonations. The boys had both gone for chicken kebabs. All were extremely greasy and all were extremely filling. *What else could a drunken person possibly want?*

"Oh, do you know what they should do next?" Ozzy had asked as he led them straight back to the Drunken Dutchess for more alcoholic beverages.

At some point during this night, the group of inebriated friends had united in a shared agreement that Kara should play her violin to the crowds! Kara was regarded as a musical virtuoso, this stemmed from a childhood of forced violin lessons. Being a De'Carusso, she was of course forced into being unquestionably perfect at it. *(A simple missed note or mistake would mean several hours more practice until her fingers bled.)* And to be fair, she was now flawless at it. But there was a small problem; the ability to play music well required you to be able to show and convey your emotions. You had to '*feel*' what you were playing, otherwise it was just random noise. *(Think of any band or song you like, now just imagine if all the band did was to stand there in an emotionless manner.)* Showing emotion wasn't something Kara liked to do, *(Truth be told, she hated it!)* so she actively avoided doing so. Like Kiko with her red party dress, the idea of a thousand staring and judgemental eyes made her feel uncomfortable. It was much easier to live a life of sarcastic jokes and passive aggression that hid your true feelings about something than it was to ever be honest and open up about something. But the problem with this approach to life is that, like Kara, '*healthy expressions of self*' became harder with each joke told. Eventually your true emotions end up hiding on a proverbial island behind a thick wall of fake hubris and pent up aggression. This making being emotionally honest a thing that was even harder to do. So she rarely ever picked up the violin. Besides, some skills were better kept as a secret.

"Do it! Do it! Do it! Do it!" Their voices called out as Kara's friends circled around her, chanting.

Peer pressure was a common go-to for breaking a person down into making them do whatever it was that you wanted them to do.

"Ugh! Fine!" Kara snapped back as she drunkenly summoned an ebony metal violin from thin air.

The reason why peer pressure was so popular was that it almost always worked. Kara took a determined step towards the stage with her violin gripped tight in her hand and -'*BANG*!'-'FLIP!'-'THWACK!'- she drunkenly tripped over a nearby female Halfling in a dramatic fashion and fell flat on her face, sprawling across the newly silenced dance floor.

Now, I'm not sure if what occurred next was due to Kara's repressed anger caused by the time she had spent with the Revantide woman and her frustrated feelings towards leaving the child with the Pesadilla-niño, or if it was due to a lack of understanding created by her high alcohol consumption, but as a looming Orc was stood over her, trying to help her back up onto her feet, she mistakenly thought he had started a fight with her. The words of Kara's family ideology stabbed at her once more. 'We Do Not Break. We Rise.' With a sudden and impressive flip Kara was back on her feet and she grabbed the Orcish man by the scruff of his neck. *She then punched him straight in his big green face!* The band stopped playing their instruments (*because they had never actually stopped playing, and this was a thing Kara's drunk friends had never quite stopped to consider when they were pestering her to play. The band would probably never have been okay with the idea of her joining them!*) as everyone now looked at her. The room was silent from shock.

The band's lead-singer lent closely into his microphone as he shouted:

"One, two, three, four!"

And with this, he led his band into playing a fast-paced song that held the perfect tempo for a bar-room brawl. The room erupted with a fury of noise and violence as the Orc's friends fought Kara and some of the other local boys. Everyone joined in, in one way or another. Those who didn't join in the fight continued to happily dance around the fracas of flying glasses, launched fists and flailing legs. They seemed to be encouraged by the aggression shown and danced even harder, wrapping around them like a great swirling, painted void of blurred colours and spilling beers, cheers and jeers as the music urged them on.

Kiko stumbled and staggered her way through the commotion of the blundering scuffle towards Kara. Kara was currently enjoying the thrill of the fight as she kept two of these men at bay with relative ease. One guy worked at the local butcher's and the other was an estate agent… she was a trained monster hunter. This was not a fair fight, not by a long shot. Kiko grabbed her overly aggressive friend by the arm and Kara span to face her. Upon this happening, the estate agent saw an opening and clocked Kara right in the jaw! She dropped to the ground as the room fell silent once more. *Watching and waiting with anticipation.* Everyone eagerly held their breath to see what the Half-Elf, who had started the tussle would, do next. Somewhat surprisingly, she grabbed the estate agent's arm and thrust it straight up into the air in an act of celebration, whilst also raising her other hand. *It was as if he had been a boxer who had just defeated his opponent and won the championship belt.* Kara cheered loudly to the crowd of inebriated onlookers. The whole room broke into a unified maddening scream of whooping celebration before everyone continued on with the rest of their night as if nothing had happened. The fight was over as quickly as it had started.

Kiko irritatedly grabbed at Kara's arm and swiftly dragged her outside to the pub's smoking area.

"What the hell was that?" Kiko asked with inquisitive indignation.

"What? He attacked me!" Kara retorted with a shrugging sneer of tempered indignation as she lit a cigarette and took a long drag.

"No! You tripped over some Halfling woman! *The Orc guy was just trying to help you back up!*"

"Oh? *Oops*!" Kara laughed as she tried not to choke on the smoke in her lungs. "Oof, that's embarrassing!"

Kara's aloof response triggered a deep sense of animosity in the intoxicated Kiko, who decided to punch her blonde friend in the arm. Kara's jokey demeanour quickly faded into a cold glare of unrestrained anger as she looked down towards her arm. Her two eyebrows sunk low on her face and furrowed the skin above her nose as she looked back towards her scrawny framed friend with her trademarked wild mop of uncontrollable hair. *'What the hell was that?'* A sudden, and entirely never felt before the urge to slap Kiko in her face arose. *'Who the hell did she think she was?'* No one ever hits Kara De'Carusso and gets away with it! This caused an argument to break out between the two. Kiko was still annoyed about being shoved earlier that day whilst being bewildered by how Kara had just set upon some poor, unsuspecting group of people over something so trivial as falling over. Kara was angry over being hit and how Kiko was always so up-tight all the damn time. After a few minutes of drunken shouting and angry pointing, the pair had found themselves crying overly apologetically about shoving each other earlier, for having shouted and for doing anything that had hurt the other in any way. Sudden bouts of rash, and often contrasting, emotion was not uncommon amongst the overly drunk.

It wasn't long after this that the decision to go home was made. The warm glow of comfort created by the idea of finally being able to rest in nice warm beds was deeply relieving. The longest day, the day that never seemed to have an end was finally going to be over. A good night's sleep was the best form of closure. Something that could serve as an end to the previous day of horrors and serves as the gateway to a better tomorrow. That's what they both felt now as they made their way home. The reassurance that sleep would usher in a brand new day. *A better day.* A day without alien planets or Nekrith invasions. No threats of abductions, kidnappings, or living nightmare monsters.

Within the throws of a stumbling drunken attempt of silently stealthing through her sleeping home, Kiko flung her bedroom door open. All she wanted right now was her warm and cosy bed. Her memory foam, king-sized mattress and thick, snug duvet. Her eyelids hung heavily over her eyes and her feet felt like slabs of concrete on the end of her tired legs. She had yearned for the rest of a comfortable rest on each of the three nights spent sleeping rough on Revantide. And the moment was finally upon her. *It was finally time.*

Time for Kiko to realise that she had never actually finished decorating her room and all of her possessions were sat under a thick white sheet, piled up high on top of her bed.

She unveiled a sorrowful sigh of all-consuming despondency as she looked upon it all. Her heart sank like a ship in icy waters. The piled belongings genuinely hurt to look at. Vitality was draining from her like the air set loose from a punctured tire and the last thing she wanted to do was to fight her way to her bed. She didn't have the energy. *This sucked so much!* She thought she might cry. So with a heavy heart, she subsided to the bleak acceptance of sleeping on the couch.

Kiko reluctantly dragged herself back downstairs. The land of glass floors and stone pillars of the party had subsided back into her normal living area. The bright lights of her fridge flooded the kitchen and reflected like headlights upon her glasses. The sudden pang of an uninhibited sweet-tooth had arisen, seeking sugary comfort like a hungry dog, as she came looking for an edible based resolution to her sleepless sorrow. Kiko's exile to the distant lands of the couch was not something she had intended to partake in without the consumption of some snack to help comfort the blow of yet another awkward night's sleep.

"I wonder how many sleepless nights it takes before your skin cracks like the Amaranth's?" She joking asked the contents of the fridge before a sorrowful remembrance of his fate sunk in. How he lay upon the grounds of that ornate room, broken and abandoned like a rag-doll. Kiko then thought of how he had warned her of her brother's intentions.

Suddenly her tired eyes locked onto a beautiful and pulchritudinous looking carrot cake. It looked so captivatingly enticing just sitting there on the glass shelf. *It was utterly alluring and seemed to beckon towards her with a captivating call.* A rich, thick and creamy icing sat delicately upon a base of exquisitely tanned and crumbly hazel browns. Gentle orange coloured flakes resonated from within the mix, like the glow from a myriad of warm candlelights on a gentle night. Kiko's mouth salivated with thick anticipation as her eyes widened with unkempt elation. Kiko had no recollection of having bought a cake recently. Clearly past Kiko had a keen eye and a good taste when it came to acquiring snacky foods. She applauded her past self as she darted towards the nearby cupboard for a plate.

To her surprise when she turned back around she saw a shirtless Bailey was standing in her kitchen with nothing but a towel wrapped around his waist. Kiko found herself startled by his sudden and overtly informal attire.

"Um, Bailey? *What the hell are you doing in my house?"* She snapped at her supposed intruder.

"Yo, Kara invited me over. Hope that's coolio?" He replied with a big smile.

'Ugh, gross! The fewer questions asked about that, the better!' Kiko thought to herself as she grabbed her precious cake. It was hers and she wasn't going to share.

"Kara sent me down for some food. Before we-"

"Do not finish that sentence!" Kiko warned dangerously. The truths of what may (*or may not*) happen behind closed doors would be enough to put her off eating food for life. *She will stab Bailey with the pointy end of her fork if he ruins this meal for her.* She will. She most definitely will. *It would be wise not to test her!*

Kiko quickly fled to her non-permanent sleeping place as she parked her butt on the couch. It was just her and her cake now. No one else was around. *It was just the two of them.*

Her fork sunk effortlessly through the soft icing and into the flaky mix beneath. A rich and creamy golden icing tenderly awoke her yearning taste buds as the flavours of gentle, yet impactful, spices swaddled her tongue in a tender blanket of moist, soft, flaky crumbs and delectably crunchy nuts. She was unsure if it was because of the alcohol in her system, or if it was because of the stressful time she had had lately, but this was heaven. This mouthful of the cake was nothing less than a perfect moment. *It was quickly followed by another.* And another. Most of the cake had disappeared when Kara's voice called through the door.

"Hey, Kiko? Have you seen my carrot cake anywhere?"

'Shit!' A sudden guilty gulp of dry cake forcefully slid down the back of Kiko's stressed gullet as her two panic ladened eyes quickly widened. She stared silently into the room as she stood perfectly still. Her eyes watered as she forced down the gulp, mid-chew. She withdrew the guilty, crumbed fork from her mouth.

"Mmnnng-phrow!" She called out. *'Shit! Shit! Shit!'* "Um, no!" Kiko replied as she watched the door with fervent unease, with a slice of stolen cake still balancing precariously on the plate in her hand. Kara would be furious if she opened the door. Kiko watched with an abated breath of suspended trepidation. There was the sudden relief of the sound of Kara's footsteps retreating upstairs.

'Phew!'

Life was a curious thing. It was random and it was unpredictable. It was strange how a person could seemingly achieve nothing for years on end. Having had nothing of significance happen for as long as they could remember. Then almost as if from nowhere, out of the blue there would be a series of days, weeks or even months where everything would seemingly happen all at once. One minute, there you were, minding your own business, the next you were in space. Perhaps you could relate to this feeling in your own lives? *(Although maybe not the bit about being in space...)* This had been the case for Kiko. It felt strange to think about how much stuff had happened since fighting the necromancers in the Aokigahara forest almost two months ago. How she had single-handedly stopped a bank robbery and helped to save those four children from the Demonscape. She thought of the brilliant heart-to-heart moment she had shared with her brother. She then thought of how such a simple and life-defining moment was instantly ruined by her being warned to be wary of him on an alien planet by the Amaranth. She recalled the several nights that she had slept rough on Revantide, helping rebel soldiers fight off the Nekrith as she hunted for Kara. *She was fully aware that this was a lot of stuff that had happened in a short space of time.* She wondered why so much stuff was happening in such quick succession; she had no idea why it was all happening now. The unfolding of time was a mystery to everyone, even to time travellers. A soft smile broke across her face; she was just glad that Kara had been there by her side every step of the way. A good friend always made things seem more bearable. *Even if that friend did start fights in random pubs.* As Kiko sat in her room she looked over the ornate Revanspear and thought over how it had undone the powers of the Pesadilla-niño the day before. This spear was such a weird and unusual thing to behold; Kiko found herself knowing exactly what she had needed to do with the magical spear next.

Jallasper Winterblaze's office was a treasure trove of twisting gears and trinkets. A vast paradise of whirring cogs and clockwork machinery. All of these cogs and gears worked together to power a giant ornate clock that ticked away, mounted into the wall behind him. Luckily all of these clockwork parts were situated behind thick glass walls. Otherwise the sound of ticks, clicks and whirs would have been unbearable to listen to. Kiko looked out across his vast desk which Winterblaze was sat behind with a troubled look on his old, pointy-eared face. A small clockwork bird 'chirped' away from inside an ornate cage; it was approximately three inches in height and (*Based on how happy it was jumping around and tweeting away.*) seemed rather content and unaware that it wasn't actually a real bird.

The Revanspear was now laying across the top of Winterblaze's desk and he was staring at it. His two long index fingers were pressed up against his lips as his elbows supported his weight on the edge of his desk. He was lost in thought as he let loose a slow ponderous "hmmmmmmmmm..."

He had assumed that there would have been more updates about the non consenting spirits' disappearances when a red-eyed Kiko had found herself barging into his office without an invitation. The reason why Kiko's eyes had been red was because of the night she had spent trying to sleep on the couch. This had proven to be fruitless, as all she had done was lay there for the entire night. Thinking of the child she had failed and replaying the Revantider's prophecy about her brother in her head on an endless loop. Wondering. Wondering what it all meant. *'A brother dead?'* When last she checked both of her brothers were still alive. *'A secret not yet said.'* What was the secret?

Right now she was so very, very tired. She thought she might die from exhaustion. Even if she was being a tad melodramatic, Kiko did feel as if she could collapse at any given moment. This was probably due to her hangover. But she understood the importance of informing the Arcane Intelligence Agency of the strange artefact that had found its way into her possession. She didn't want a repeat of the situation with Diane where something she did might get her accused of withholding information from the agency. To be accused of aiding and abetting or harbouring dangerous goods; or anything else the organisation may try to throw her way. She had been through a lot lately and she was too tired to be accused of anything else. She had told her boss, Winterblaze, about everything. (*No! Of course not about the ancient Revantide prophecy (or technically, I guess the future Revantide prophecy...?) about her brother! What are you, some kind of idiot filled idiot from the idiotic planet of idiots? Vincent was a great and powerful hero! You can't just accuse famous heroes without evidence! Could you imagine the absolute shit-show that it would cause if she started throwing around accusations all willy-nilly? You absolute moron. 'Some far off planet told me to beware of my brother's betrayal, his intention for me might be fatal!' No! Of course she didn't. No one would have believed her! It would have sounded like little more than the prattling of a jealous sibling. Besides she had no actual proof to work off of. The reasoning of 'an alien species three thousand years in the future said you can't be trusted' felt flimsy at best. So she purposely left that bit out!*)

Winterblaze wondered to himself (*inside the brain that lay behind his bushy eyebrows*) on what the link was between her being 'expressly ordered to only investigate the ghostly disappearances' and her 'gallivanting around on an alien planet.'

"So there I was, with the Pesadilla-niño pinning me down. This '*thing*' pops out of me, shining like a lighthouse, and then suddenly all of the Pesadilla-niño's illusions had completely disappeared and it ran away." Kiko recapped, whilst deliberately not mentioning the child she had failed.

"It seems to me that what you have here is a '*Truth Revealing Artefact.*' I assume you are aware of Loki's principles of alteration?"

The conversation that had followed next was rather dull and full of expository dialogue. So if it's alright with you we'll just skip right past it. It was basically just a battle of intellectual egos proving who was smarter and who knew the most. A pissing contest to see which of these two had been the most knowledgeable about alteration based magics. (*Or which had known the most facts about life as a whole.*) These bravado fuelled exchanges were a commonplace occurrence whenever two (*or more*) people of above-average intelligence met. See, slightly smart people were used to being the smartest person in a room. Usually just by the fact that they were normally surrounded by morons. Even if they would never admit it, these smart people had rather liked how it felt to be thought upon as being 'smart.' This would lead to them feeling challenged in the presence of any other person who was also of an above-average intelligence. Whereas strong people would fight it out with their fists to find out who was stronger, smart people fought with words; in a game of endless one-upmanship and a perpetual escalation of continual 'well of course I knew that, but did you know...' until one person ultimately came out on top. *(Either for not knowing something or for being caught out for trying to lie about something that they had pretended to know stuff about to try and save face.)* These conversations, if you could even call them that, usually boiled down to the childish equivalent of *'nyah-nyah nyah-nyah-nyah, I know more than you do!'*

Ultimately Kiko had found herself coming up short against Winterblaze. What with her being a twenty-three-year-old with a small amount of life experience, against the three hundred years worth of intel the old Elf had under his sleeve, it was hardly surprising. Ultimately it had been assumed that the overall purpose of Revanspear was to undo any spell that altered a person's perspective or created disguises. As much as this was a somewhat solid (*and almost accurate*) summarisation of what the Revanspear was capable of, it paled in comparison to the spear's full capabilities.

The entire purpose of the Revanspear was to reveal the unseen. Yes, this included being able to cut the bonds between magical illusions and their caster, like a doctor snipping the umbilical cord on a newborn. *This was what had happened to the Pesadilla-niño.* The spear had '*blocked*' its link to the horrors that it summoned. But it was also capable of so much more. Anyone who took the time to attune themselves with the spear would ultimately gain the ability to see the truth behind any spoken lie and (*if they were really lucky*) would even be gifted glimpses of the future. *So if you were cheating on your partner, you had better start running if you ever saw them with the Revanspear!*

The Revanspear hated all lies. As such, it forced the darkness of any deception directly into the light. But the spear also cared not for the reason behind the act. So it would even '*reveal truths*' that would be to your detriment. It couldn't discern between, let's say, '*a Fear Demon conjuring Machiavellian illusions to torment your soul*' and if you were to '*make yourself invisible to avoid a serial killer.*' It would negate the effects of both.

But all of this exposition was something that the Arcane Intelligence Agency would have to figure out for themselves. As such it was decided that the Revanspear would stay with them, at least until they had figured out what its purpose was for.

Given the rather stressful time both Kiko and Kara had had lately, Winterblaze found himself authorising the pair to take the rest of the day off. To be fair, Kara had never actually asked for permission to not attend her work today. She had also not bothered to inform anyone of her decision. She had just chosen to stay home, hiding away from the world in her comfy and ever so warm bed. But that was to change, as Kiko insisted that they leave the house for a while. Mainly so she could be away from Vincent.

Kara and Kiko had found themselves partaking in an ingrained tradition from their teenage years. Any teenager who claims they don't know this tradition is a liar. They had gone to one of the nearby local parks to loiter like hooligans. Kara had brought bottles of cool, refreshing cider, Kiko brought two bags of greasy chips and the two converged on the nearby park bench, ready to consume. A prattling of quacking ducks went to war over their kingdom of discarded bread crumbs in a nearby pond. The sounds of a gang of kids playing an improvised game of football rang off in the distance as a multitude of dog walkers strained and pulled against the tugging of over-eager 'walkies.' The smell of vinegar wafted through the air, from the warm chips upon a brisk breeze that bit at the skin. These imperfect chips were being washed down perfectly by the cool and refreshing taste of crisp cider. Kara had gone for her usual pear flavoured cider, whereas Kiko had received her favourite, a sticky toffee pudding flavoured one.

Here these two sat, looking out over their green surroundings of normal people living out their normal lives. It was beautiful to behold and they couldn't help but notice how weird their lives had become lately in comparison.

"Have you noticed a lot of strange stuff has been happening lately?" Kiko enquired as she made quick work of her latest chip-victim.

"Oh my god, yes!" Kara proclaimed as she lifted both arms in the air with a suddenly revealed frustration, almost losing her chips to the ever-watching eyes of one nearby determined (and chip starved) duck.

"Quack, quack!" Which roughly translated into an impatient: *'Give me a ducking chip!'*

This wasn't an entirely *'accurate'* translation...

"What the hell is going on?" Kara continued to proclaim. The chips almost fell once more. "Like, seriously! In just the last few days; there was that weird demon-house-thing, then there was your brother's engagement ring. Then I got kidnapped on an alien planet. Which totally sucked by the way! *Oh!* That stupid spear-thing and that B.S. prophecy about your brother. How did they know your name? Oh and let's not forget about that freaky fear Demon! It's been like three freakin' days!"

Yes, it was true that this had been a lot of strange things to happen, especially in such a short period of time. But only one part of Kara's recap had actually caught Kiko's attention.

"I'm sorry... my brother's what now...?" She enquired with a highly confused tone.

Somehow Kara had not gotten around to informing Kiko about the engagement ring that she had found on the fateful night of the party before they had rather rudely found themselves stranded on the HMS Edinheim. Kara had also somehow forgotten the fact that she had not informed Kiko about the very important detail of her brother's intended engagement ring yet. *'Oops!'*

"Oh, yeah. I saw he had an engagement ring the other day. Did I not tell you?" She casually enquired, being fully aware that she had not. Kara had hoped that playing coy about the whole thing would save her from being shouted at for not telling her friend this important fact sooner. "Y'know, before we were getting shot at by literal alien robots! *It's just so crazy, right?* The worst bit is that if I tried totell anyone, they'd just call me crazy! Why is so much weird stuff happening to us all of a sudden?"

As Kara took a sip of her cider, this had given Kiko a chance to reply. Kiko was only fixated on that one piece of information that had been kept from her. *(She already knew the rest.)*

"I'm sorry, my brother is what?" She repeated for a second time. Still shocked to her core by the sudden revelation. This proposal-to-be must have been why he had been acting so strangely before the party! It must have been! What other possible explanation could there have been for his sudden desire to be more open with her? *At least this meant he wasn't dying!*

"I'm not sure it's that big of a deal." Kara claimed as she ate another chip. "I'm more worried about why an alien race is telling you to be careful about him!"

"No, shut up. I don't care about that! Vincent's going to ask Kaya to marry him? Oh! That's amazing!" Kiko gave a short squeal as she flapped her arms.

"Ow!" Kara replied as she rubbed the ear that been closest to Kiko.

Kiko couldn't help but feel ecstatic. She had a lot of love for Kaya and thought that she was amazing. So the fact that she would one day be her sister-in-law was extra-amazing. It was so amazing in fact that it had made Kiko forget about the entire lack of trust she had felt for her brother just moments before.

Marriage was a rather special thing. How it could bring together two entirely separate families and unite them as one. Look across any wedding venue and you'll see it. How a shared love for the happy couple has united them all into one great big unison. Regardless of how different and sometimes bizarrely contrasting the two mixing families can be, they were all here for the same reason. They were here to witness first-hand the power of love. How love had brought these two people together and how their shared love for each other would guide them towards their future; to create a family of their own and all of the exciting new possibilities that it may bring. Or at least that was Kiko's view on marriages and weddings. To Kara, it was nothing more than a grandiose excuse to parade one's self around for attention. An ornate event to justify narcissistic tendencies and to lavishly try and out-do your peers. Every couple shared a love for each other, it wasn't a competition. Yet every bride wanted the whitest dress and the biggest venue. If your family and friends really loved you then they would have been happy to see you get married, regardless of the venue and your desire for peacocking, because all they would have wanted was to see you happy. At least that was Kara's hot-take on marriage. *What's yours opinion on it?*

The two girls continued to discuss their contrasting views on marriage. Kaya Kiribati had always been deemed as rather 'lacking' when it came to the people that Cassandra had deemed good enough for her eldest child. So the one thing that the girls had agreed upon was that Cassandra would not take the news well. I mean she would definitely pretend to. But any and all support and happiness shown would most likely be insincere. Not that it really mattered, was anyone ever truly like by their in-laws?

The conversation had changed into one of the Revanspear and the powers Kiko believed it to hold. A thing Kara had found deeply interesting. This picturesque moment of green fields, ducks and playing children, that was seemingly taken from the back of a postcard, had quickly found itself being soured (*This was still Scotland after all!*) as an overly aggressive squawking seagull dive-bombed the ever-loving-shit clean out off Kiko's poorly defended chips. The furious flurry of white flapping wings and showering chips had even made Kiko knock her cider over as she was rudely jolted back to reality.

Two poor, puppy-dog-inflated eyes eventually found themselves locking onto Kara and her intact portion of chips.

"Come on man, share your food with me?" Kiko pleaded as best as she could.

"Ummm...?" Kara seemed to contemplate for a moment. "No!"

She quickly snapped the lid shut on her own chips as she watched towards the sky, now fully aware of the threat of potential food-stealing birds. *(Both of the seagull and Kiko variety!)* Kara bolted off, doubled over like a demented hunchback defending her food and drink from any would-be dangers! *Either through her life or her death, she swore that no one would rob her of her chips.* Not a single one.

A few hours later the two had girls found themselves back at the Attetson household. Collin and Cassandra were just about to sit down to a late afternoon lunch of burgers. They offered a seat at the table to both of the girls. Kiko politely declined, but burgers being the best thing in existence ever, Kara quickly accepted and sat at the table.

"But you've already had chips?!" Kiko snapped in an en-bittered vexation upon her friend's refusal to share her food earlier.

"Yeah, but I've not had burgers yet..." Kara replied with a playful taunt.

"Oh, uh, Kiko? A courier came from the Arcane Intelligence Agency with something for you. We left it in your room." Cassandra interrupted as she began serving the food.

Kiko quickly returned to her room to find the Revanspear had been returned to her. There was a thick note folded up on top of it, tied up with string. Kiko picked it up and read it.

"Dear K. Attetson.

I hope this note finds you well. Upon investigating the staff and enquiring with the people Revantide, we have decided that the 'Revanspear' is harmless enough and should be returned to you. Perhaps it will assist you with your investigation into the Dark Hand and the disappearances of the non consenting spirits.

Llewelyn Jones."

What the hell was she going to do with the spear? It wasn't like she could just carry it everywhere with her! Although the Revanspear had proven itself useful this far. So logic dictated it would be useful in her investigation into the disappearances. An investigation that she had just realised she had forgotten entirely about! That's probably not good. Kiko grabbed the spear and fled back down the stairs, fuelled by the desire to continue hunting for the ghosts before anyone realised her faux pas. She hurried down the steps in a manner reminiscent of a schoolchild running late for a lesson.

She cut quickly through the dining room, where Kara and Vincent were sat eating with the older Attetson parents. Kiko shot a troubled look towards her brother as she ran through.

'Wham!'

She had almost dislocated her shoulder and nearly fallen flat on her back as the Revanspear stopped dead in its tracks, bolted into place. It had seemed to lock onto Vincent with a keen intent as it began to shake violently. *Kiko and Kara shared a concerned look as they recalled what the spear had done to the Pesadilla-niño the day before.*

"What's with the eye-staff-thing?" Collin asked as he pointed towards the Revanspear.

"Um, it's supposed to reveal hidden things... and... lies..." Kara said as she slowly rose to her feet.

A revealing light flooded across Vincent as his face and body disappeared away to reveal something truly awful that lay beneath. *In a sudden instant, Vincent was gone.* In his place now sat a tall feral looking humanoid creature of brown matted furs. Long dangling arms with terribly pointy and jagged elbows rested on top of the family's table. His three-fingered hands, with long white claws, were wrapped around a semi-eaten burger. Two buckled legs rested under the table. It sat hunched over and confused. Sat on its face were six red eyes, like that of an insect, that shone out from the disgusting fur. He also had no visible nose or ears. Two long, curved prominent teeth sat on either side of this creature's insectoid-like mouth. Two great, twitching antennas stuck out from the top of the creature's head and four very small wings stuck out from its back.

"What?" Asked the sudden horrifying creature that was now chilling in the Attetson dining room and eating their food. "Why is everyone staring at me...?" The lank creature looked across the room. "Do I have something on my face?"

The face that all parents knew. The face all that parents feared. Whereas most of the Fairy-folk were usually fairly benign and magnanimous creatures, nary a bad thought or malicious intention between the whole lot of them, Irish folklore told the tale of a uniquely grotesque fairy that roamed the lands and combed their green countrysides; hunting their lands for the most innocent of victim imaginable. Irish gipsies were well aware of the threat of the child-snatching 'Changeling.'

It takes a certain level of depravity to do anything bad to a baby. This stems from how utterly and hopelessly defenceless they are. There is no thrill or acclaim to be found in hurting one because they can literally do nothing to protect themselves. There is no challenge in hurting something so vulnerable or helpless. Yet these appallingly loathsome Changelings managed to do exactly this with an unsettling ease. Truth be told, they thrived on it as a culture.

In a simple essence, Changelings were rather like the Cuckoo bird. Because like how a Cuckoo bird places its egg into the nests of other bird's to be raised by them, the vile Changelings replaces newborn babies with themselves, to be raised by those parents. Now I know what you're thinking; a newborn baby looks nothing like a furry, brown, bug-eyed fairy. *(Besides the fact that 'Yes, some do. Your baby isn't as Earth alteringly beautiful as you think it is. It is literally only a face a mother could love. You're just biased about the new thing you made. Get over yourselves!')* The insipidus Changeling has the uncanny ability to alter its entire physical appearance to match the defenceless newborn infant cooing away in its crib. The skulking Changeling makes itself into a carbon copy of the original darling sprog. They do this for a rather simple reason, to trick these new mothers and fathers into feeding them, nurturing them and raising them as their own. They steal the love of these unsuspecting doting parents and use it to grow strong as well as stealing the entire life that should have belonged to the baby. *What do you suppose happens to the original baby?* It's kind of obvious. The Changeling's ghastly ruse is barbaric, but it is also wrought with peril. The entirety of the Changeling's well-being depends upon not being caught. Owing to the very nature of the subterfuge as to how the Changeling managed to gain entry into the family home, this said family would never respond well upon the realisation of the monster that had stolen their child's life. It always ends in violence. Every single time. *Hell hath no fury like a parent defending their child.* And they have no qualms about avenging the death of their newborn. *I mean who would blame them?*

Can you imagine how that would feel? That child you loved more than anything in the world. You had raised it. You had fed it. You loved it with all your heart. *With every beat.* But it wasn't actually your child. *It merely stole their face.* It was the thing that had killed your child and consumed it whole. Their body, their life and their entire future. Snapped away in a second. And you, you had raised it. You'd fed it. You had let it into your house and you had loved it with every fibre of your being.

This is why all parents hated the Changelings. *They despised them.* With every cell in their existence. They were perverse, detestable, skulking fiends. The worst thieves a heart could bear to imagine. Twisted bringers of sorrow and despair that fed upon the unquestionable love of innocent, unexpected families. *They betrayed the very meaning of this love.* Bastardising it for their own sick personal gain. When a fox is hungry, they eat a chicken. They care not for the age of it; they're hungry, so they eat. Whilst this isn't perhaps the nicest thing in the world, it is understandable. We know and understand why creatures hunt. We share the same need to eat. But this isn't what the Changeling does. Simply eating the baby and fleeing, whilst of course being awful, has boundaries. There's a limitation put in place. The parents would instantaneously be faced with the awful reality. They would be allowed to grieve for their fallen child. But the Changeling even robs them of this, because nothing has changed. Regardless of what face a Changeling wears, a parent has still lost a child. They just don't know it. But the worst bit is (...*even though they don't know it*...) that their child's murder is right there, right in front of them.

This is what was now standing in the Attetson kitchen. The real Vincent Attetson had died many years ago. As a baby in an ill-prepared hospital. The true Vincent had been defenceless and ripe for the picking. His killer had stolen his name, his face, his entire life and his family.

Can you even began to comprehend what the Attetson family (*plus Kara*) were currently witnessing in front of them? *This sudden change.* And how it must have felt to realise that the person they always thought of as Vincent wasn't even a person, but a murderous creature? Think of a person you love and trust. *Have you thought of someone?* Can you see that person in your mind's eye? Are they a friend? Are they a family member? *Now imagine that this person wasn't actually who they seed to be, but instead was an evil monster deep beneath the surface.* Someone with a secret life of subterfuge. That this someone you had trusted with everything and had loved with all of your heart had lied to you for your entire life. For every moment of your entire existence you had been played for a fool. No doubt somewhere right now an ex-wife is making a joke about how 'she doesn't need to imagine what this feels like because she married one such monster and is much happier now since her divorce.' Well done, how original. *Very droll.*

Now, I know some of you reading this might be surprised by this revelation. Some may feel like I've pulled the rug out from underneath you or that this came out from nowhere. But I did warn you before about what he was. Just before the party that celebrated *'Vincent'* and his victory against the Succubus.

If you can recall I said: *'He had a monster living under his skin. It had stolen his face and robbed him of his life. Fame was a curse that had dragged him into the spotlight.'* It turns out the monster was literal and I wasn't just being hyperbolic about fame. Fancy that. Although I suspect this fame had been a great curse to the Changeling. As previously stated, his survival depended upon him keeping a low profile about who he really was deep inside. Having everyone on the planet know your name must have made that extremely difficult. *So why run the risk?*

It should also be said, that even though he was actually a *'monster in Vincent's clothing,'* the Changeling did love Kiko. If you can remember I also went on to say: *'He wanted to be more honest with her. To tell her about the secret monster that was within him. But he was riddled with self-doubt. He was afraid that this honesty would drive a further wedge between them. The self-doubt, the pain and his suffering from carrying the weight of the entire world for so long. He had never known the correct words to say to Kiko. He never knew how to reveal his inner monster. He was scared of how she would view him if she knew the truth about how weak he really was.'*

Kiko was now stood wide-mouthed and aghast. The Revanspear had done what it was always supposed to do. *'To reveal the unseen.'* She had never expected, not even for a single second, to see her brother change into a Demon fairy. Yet the Revantide prophecy raced through her. *'A brother dead, a secret not yet said.'* It all made sense now, even if Kiko wasn't willing to accept it. Like slotting together the pieces of a puzzle. The last words before her and Kara's exile to the alien planet. The last words Kara had uttered.

"I know Vincent's dirty little secret!"

Kara had meant his proposed engagement to the empty-headed Kaya Kiribati. Clearly, a certain sneaking Vincent had overheard Kiko and Kara gossiping. In his panic about his actual truth, being a Changeling, he had gotten his wires crossed and sent them away to furthest reaches of space to keep his sordid secret safe. But ironically this had been his undoing. *He had unwittingly brought them one thing that would spell this vile usurper's undoing.*

Kara was a fairly simple person, all things considered. She was quick to act and never quick to consider the consequences of her actions. If she thought someone was attacking her in a pub? She fought back. *If she saw a monster?* She acted accordingly. She had seen a monster sitting there, right here, right now, next to her in the dining room. The fact that it had recently worn Vincent's face did not phase her in any great way. The jolt of instinct lashed at her heart; so she did what she was trained to do. With a single huge swipe from her wolf bladed axe, the bug-eyed Changeling's head had been removed from its body and rolled across the kitchen table. *'Splat!'* Cassandra's freshly cooked brunch had been ruined under the flooding of her pseudo-son's black blood which spouted out as if it was the water from an unattended hose pipe. It soaked her clothes, Collin's clothes, and all of the nearby soft furnishings. Cassandra let loose the harrowing scream of a thousand bitter sorrows.

I'm sure that will end well... right?

Chapter Fifteen

THE TIMES THEY ARE A' CHANGING

It had been a cold wet night at Saint Moira's hospital when a singularly minded and determined Kiko teleported onto the scene. She was determined to find the answers to the questions that haunted her and ate away at her heart. Somehow this desperation for answers had managed to hold her overwhelming grief at bay. *But this grief was still lying in wait.* A swarm of ants and vultures ready to strip her heart bear at a moment's notice. The pain was being held back for now, but all it needed was for a single second of weakness and then it would be set free. Kiko found herself appearing to this old, red-bricked hospital exactly 13,402,883 minutes (*approximately twenty-five years*) before the rueful day on which she had witnessed the death of that imposter who had worn Vincent's face and changed her life forever.

She did not believe that her '*brother*' had been a Changeling. She could not. The reality of the situation was just too hard to accept. That the brother she had known for her entire life had actually been some random run-of-the-mill monster and not her brother at all. Some ever-present pretender who laughed and mocked at the Attetson stupidity. Kiko refused this version of reality. *It was a lie.* Of course it was! *It had to be... right?* Of I mean, seriously, come on now. Think. What were the odds that Kiko's entire family would have failed to notice that an actual and genuine monster had been living with them for a quarter of a century? It was far more likely that Vincent had recently run afoul of some creature in their own time and was in desperate need of Kiko's help. So Kiko ran back through time to prove that no monster was about to jump out from behind the bushes and kill her brother. If a multi-bug-eyed monster wanted to try, he would quickly find himself regretting it! But she knew that the real Vincent was still alive and well in her own time. And the sooner everyone stopped worrying over this misdirection of him having secretly been a Changeling for the last twenty-five years, the sooner all efforts would go into trying to find her missing AND ALIVE brother.

Saint Moira's had been the hospital where Cassandra had given birth to Vincent. Or rather, it was about to be. Any moment now she would burst through the front doors, so time was of the essence. This also seemed like it was the most logical place to start hunting for imaginary Changelings. I mean it wasn't like the Changeling would be able to steal a child directly from the womb. Kiko knew that Changelings usually stole babies before their first birthday. *(Wait, was her plan to watch over her brother for an entire year? Um, I'm sorry, that feels a bit excessive! But then again I suppose people went to extraordinary lengths to prove the truth...)* It mattered not how long it might take to disprove the Changeling theory, she would simply pop right back to the time from whence she left. It would be as if no time had passed at all. But she would have proof that Vincent was Vincent. That he always had been and always will be the one and only Vincent Attetson.

Saint Moira's was an old Victorian hospital that stood appropriately five miles from Liarath. It had been where Cassandra's mother had given birth to her, and her mother before her. It was somewhat of a tradition. Kiko and her other brother had been born here too. Currently, the rain lashed against the thick, black-rimmed windows as doctors and nurses alike ran through their busy night. Some were busy saving lives, some were just avoiding the rain. It was approximately nine pm and it was surprisingly cold. Kiko had stolen a set of blue scrubs. The reason for her doing so was simple, people would stop and question a girl stomping through the hospital on her one-woman mission if she was wearing a big blue coat. But no one would question why a nurse was at a hospital. It was where they were supposed to be after all. So it was practical and it made sense. Even if it was a ghastly plain and unflattering cut of cloth. She hurried through the medicated crowds, avoiding eye contact with the passing patients and medical workers the best she could. She read the overhead plastic signs as she tried to get her bearings. Kiko knew she needed to go to the maternity wing, she just didn't know where it was... This hospital was huge. It was like an endless maze of archaic decor, full of sick and dying people. A multitude of gurneys and stretchers wheeled patients off in different directions. All around her were people coughing, sneezing and sniffing away. So here she hunted and prowled, searching for this horrible Changeling that also hunted and prowled in its own way. Eventually she had found the maternity wing. But to her surprise, something had happened next that she did not intend. A sudden hand grabbed at her as a doctor dragged her into one of the numerous rooms.

"We're having some problems in here with this birth. *We need all hands on deck!"* The doctor barked as a deep stress radiated from within his Orcish eyes. He thrust a pair of plastic gloves and a surgical mask into Kiko's hands. "Come with me!"

A deep confusion grabbed her. She wasn't actually a nurse! *What the hell was she going to be able to do?* What the hell lay behind that door? She didn't want to help someone give birth! Couldn't this stupid Orc see she had more important business to attend to! Kiko was here to save her brother, not to play nurse! A pained screamed broke free from behind the green door. It sounded like a person was being split in two. *(This is because a person was technically being split in two. Childbirth is an amazing thing! Sorry, that was a typo! Childbirth is an amazingly terrifying and painful thing!)*

Kiko's two wide eyes locked on the door that sealed away the untold horrors.

'I don't want to go in there!' Was all she really thought right now. *'You can't make me!'* A pure terror grinded her flesh. 'Oh god, oh god, oh god.' A sick feeling burned in her gut. *'Aaaaaaaaah!'*

The Orc shoved her in through the door. What was this nurse playing at!

As Kiko stumbled through the door she was surprised to see a pair of faces she had partially recognised. *Crap!* It was her parents. *They looked so young!* Kiko quickly wrapped her face behind her surgical mask before either one of her one-day-to-be parents had the chance to see her face. This was not so they wouldn't recognise her because she would not be born for like another two years. It was just a practical decision to avoid a lifetime of them questioning why their future, growing daughter bore an uncanny resemblance to one of the midwives that had helped them with the birth of their firstborn son. It would stop a lifetime of longward glances of speculation at their only daughter. The reverse of this situation was also something she had wanted to avoid. The conversation of *'hey, I'm your daughter from the future and I'm here because there may, or may not, be a Changeling about to eat your newborn baby'* felt like it may cause more trouble than it was worth.

The Orcish doctor gave this red-haired nurse another angry glare. *What the hell was this nurse playing at?*

However, the reality of the current situation at hand had found itself sinking in hard and fast. She had not actually planned nor intended to be present for the birth. She had especially not intended to be on the business end of the ordeal. Oh god, *she didn't want to touch anything!* Never, not once, had Kiko ever wanted to see this angle of her mother. Grunting and screaming with her legs up on stirrups. *Pushing a flesh melon out of her you-know-where.* No child should ever have to see this; sorry Kiko... *Great!* Now not only would any and all future conversations with her mother be soured by the potential death of her brother, now she would have this disgusting sight trapped in her brain forever and ever. Good lord, it was sickening. *That was her mother!* Whoever it was that had called childbirth beautiful had clearly not seen it from this angle! Cassandra, red-faced like an angry lobster, and Collin, as pale as a sheet in a snowstorm.

The Orcish doctor shoved Kiko once more.

"What are you doing?" He barked. "Get in there and help!"

So she did. And it was awful. Vile. The images she had seen in this room would live with her forever and ever. One night, three years from now, she would undoubtedly be laying there trying to sleep when her brain will remind her: *'Hey, remember that time you had to see your mother give birth? Do you remember the screams and the yelling?'* And she would never be able to sleep again. Kiko wondered if she would need to start buying books on how to deal with insomnia. Any form of eye contact with her mother would definitely be out of the question. *Sunday lunches would never be the same.* Not for a long assed time.

Although she had gotten to witness the first moments of her brother and his first cry, so that was something rather special. Even if he did look like a baby that had just been dipped headfirst into a Mexican Chili dish. Kiko also knew at this moment that she would never give birth. Why bother going through the anguish of trying to remove a human-shaped bowling ball from your *'downstairs?'* Why would anyone choose to willingly go through so much pain?

Although... little baby Vincent was extremely beautiful...

A pure and eternal love instantly consumed the young Cassandra's heart as she held her baby boy for the first time. *He was so small.* If there was any one thing Cassandra knew, she knew she loved this baby with every inch of her soul. A smile cracked across her face as she wondered what his future might hold. Kiko's future, on the other hand, had consisted of her running to the nearest toilet and throwing up in it rather violently. I guess this would rather mean that both of the Attetson women were getting something out of their bodies at Saint Moira's hospital today. Approximately an hour later, Kiko had found herself standing outside the hospital's nursery. And there he was, the newborn Vincent Attetson. Cooing away in amongst the many cribs that furnished this brightly painted room. Kiko stood there, for a second, staring in through the window. Digging deep to find the courage to go in. *(Or trying to block the images of the ordeal she had just witnessed.)* She quickly entered to spend time with her older brother. *(Who was technically now much younger than her...)* She stood staring over his little body in his crib.

"Hello, Vincent. I'm your sister, Kiko." She said with both a soft voice and a soft smile as she held her hand out to him.

Four chubby, yet still bafflingly small and tiny-winy, ickle fingers and a tinsky-winsky, dinky little thumb wrapped themselves around Kiko's index finger and gripped her ever so tightly. It had been a good, strong grip. The kind that would melt even the coldest of hearts. For a second Kiko thought that her heart might actually explode from how adorable this little treasure had been. *Vincent was so small.* He was so frail and so entirely precious that he had somehow managed to make it feel like time had stopped. Just for a single, pure moment. As he gripped his sister's finger he had made a sound that sat somewhere on the spectrum between a wet gurgle and the world's sweetest little laugh. The recent darkness of the world seemed to dissolve away as a pure and warm joy flooded Kiko's torso. His tubby, little cheeks lifted themselves into a wide and endearing smile as he kicked at the air with his itsy-bitsy toes on his teeny-weeny feet, scrunching the sheet beneath him as he did so. *He was so cuddly looking!* All Kiko wanted to do was scoop him up and hold him tight. Forever. He was the dearest bundle of innocent joy Kiko had ever witnessed in her entire life. He was amazing and he was pure. Wriggling away without a single care in the world. Like seriously, she had never seen anything in her life that had made her feel this way before. Vincent was the most beautiful thing she had ever seen in her entire life. *Screw any alien planet, magical creature or anything else she had ever witnessed.* She would trade it all in. Each and every last second, for just one more moment to be right here with her baby brother. Right here, right now. In this time and place; all she felt was love. But it was not necessarily a good feeling. *If truth be told, it was terrible and absolutely mortifying.*

Kiko thought over what potentially lay in store for the newborn baby. If it was true that a Changeling was on its way then there was nothing she would be able to do to stop it from killing her brother. She wasn't allowed to intervene. Changing the timeline would create a self depleting paradox. This realisation was awful. If she tried to intervene she would risk destroying all of time. *Hang on, what was she even doing here?* A deeply rooted doubt consumed here. Looking over this happy, bouncing little bundle of joy made everything feel so much worse. *Should she just leave?* She had no intentions of actually wanting to see anything horrible happen to him with her own eyes! *Could she even bring herself to just go and abandon him to his fate?* What kind of sister would do that? *How could she sacrifice him like that?* What kind of person could ever do something so cold and so awful? She had made a mistake coming here tonight, she realised that now. What the hell was she thinking? How would she ever be able to bring herself to let anything bad happen to him? She knew she was not allowed to interfere with the established timeline. If her brother was meant to die, then there was nothing she could do to stop it. If she tried to do so, then her actions would erase all life. Past, present and future. Vincent, herself and everyone else throughout the rest of the universe would just cease to exist! A little secret of the Arcane Intelligence Agency was that if any of their Temporal Bureau agents willingly disrupted or altered time then they would be executed. But as she looked at Vincent as he lay there, looking as helpless and sweet as any innocent baby should, it had almost seemed worth the risk. Almost, but not quite.

Kiko pulled herself away from Vincent's grip around her finger and turned away from him. As she did so she quickly found herself leaning over the edge of a nearby desk, rocking herself back and forth off of it as she tried to suppress the upcoming onslaught of tears that whelmed around her red-rimmed eyes, like the first warnings of a great approaching rainstorm. She knew that if she had started to cry then she would not be able to stop.

"*Come on! Come on!* Get a grip, Kiko!" She said to herself as she raised her head and let loose a tremendously deep sigh.

She violently shook her arms as if to try and 'reset' her emotions and fluttered her hands around her eyes, as if to try and dry them out. On account of the day she was currently having, do you know what? *It did not work.* Not that such a failure should have been in any way surprising. If anything was an undeniable truth, it was that you were allowed to show emotions if you thought someone was about to die. Yet for some reason, Kiko was still trying to get her emotions under wrap. Maybe it was to help her maintain her slipping sanity at this moment? Maybe it had been for Vincent's sake, as she didn't want to upset the little baby boy. Who knew? *Perhaps you have an idea as to why keeping her composure was so important to her?* Maybe it was because if it had been true that the brother she had known for her entire life wasn't actually her brother, that this would mean that this was the first and only time that Kiko had ever actually met her older brother. If that was true, then she wasn't about to ruin it by being a crying mess.

The inner relationships of the Attetson family were a little rocky right now, what with everything that was unfolding. So she had intended to make the most of this time with Vincent for as long as possible. I mean, she had just seen an angle of her mother that no child should ever have to see. It wasn't like she would be looking her mother in the eye anytime soon. So that relationship would need time to recover. And no doubt both of her real-time parents would be an absolute wreck at home right now. She couldn't even remember the last time she had seen her other brother. So even though it hurt like being kicked by a mule, she would stay with Vincent until the end. Kiko viewed it rather like staying with a family member as their life support ran out. The only difference was that the killer wasn't an illness, like cancer. It was another form of home-wrecking monster entirely. I mean, who knew? Maybe Kiko was right before and a Changeling might not have been inbound to consume Vincent.

Unfortunately, she was wrong.

About five minutes later there was a sudden crash from outside the newborn nursery, as the sounds of a clattering bedpan clashed against the hard floor. A terrible smell, almost like rotting pumpkins, filled the air. Kiko quickly turned herself invisible and held her breath. The door of the nursery suddenly bounded open as a brown, hairy Changeling scurried its way in. It was a lot smaller than the one Kara had beheaded years from now, but it smelled just as bad. This one was about the size of a Jack Russell Terrier. Its movements were feral and erratic. Long black fingernails dragged across the floor as it scuttled across the hospital floor on its lanky arms and legs, making a terrible series of tapping noises as it went. The creature filled the room with a deep groaning wheeze. Kiko felt her jaw tighten as she tried to overthrow the will to stop what she knew was about to happen. She looked towards the open door, but she was too powerless to move. Fear had drained her whole. With a single leap it effortlessly made its way on top of the desk Kiko had been standing by earlier. It sniffed at the air as six horrible little bug eyes shifted through the room, hunting for its prey.

The Changeling let loose a strange chirping noise as it locked onto its intended target. I have no interest in describing to you the nitty-gritty horror of teeth and claws which Kiko had witnessed next, you can figure it out for yourselves. I won't be telling you. All I will say is that what Kiko had witnessed this night had broken her. Well and truly. Emotionally and physically. Deep within her soul. I genuinely don't think she will ever look at the world the same way ever again. I mean, how could she? *Some horrors change a person forever, they're just too awful not to.* Kiko had been undone, utterly and completely. She barrelled out of the room and dashed around the corner.

In her arrogance she had refused to accept the world as it was, she thought she could either change it or disprove it. Tears burst forth from her devastated face. She had genuinely believed that she would have found something here to disprove what had happened all those years in the future. But this was not what she had found. In her hubris, she had set forth a series of actions that had led to her seeing the single worst thing a person could ever see. All the strength vacated her body as her trembling legs gave way. She fell to the ground with an awful thump of anguish and pain. If only she had listened to her father when he had told her what the monster was! Her whole body pulsated and heaved with tremendous sorrow. She shook and she bleated here for what felt like a life age, in a pile on the floor. Either trying to forget or come to terms with the nightmare of horrific fangs and teeth she had just seen. The nightmare that she had allowed to unfold. So here she stayed and here she wept.

The blackness was all around her, all-consuming and eternal. Kiko felt cold colder than she had ever been in her entire life as icy winds of pervasive sorrow lashed against her soul, like a storm against a seafaring vessel. Like life itself had been ripped out from her very existence. She felt a guilty rage burn within. Was she angry at herself? *Of course she was!* She could have saved Vincent. She should have! It was all too much. It was another opportunity in life that she had missed.

Miss?

...Miss?

"Miss, are you alright?" A nurses voice rang out through the darkness. Kiko snapped back to reality. Which quite frankly sucked.

"No. I'm not alright."

Rest in peace, Vincent Attetson. I'm sorry you had such a short life.

These rules for time travel; what was even the point of them? Why gift a person the ability to walk through history if they were not allowed to change anything? Why allow the passage to bygone events, if you were powerless to help those you loved? It was a cruel curse and a blight. A trick to cause further pain. *Fuck time travel and fuck the rules.* It was just another way for the universe to screw you over.

Chapter Sixteen

MUHREN ATTETSON

When introducing a family it was customary to present them all at once. To introduce such a key and important family member at such a late stage could come across as rude, crass and a tiny bit sloppy from a narrative's perspective. Some readers will have already come to their own conclusions about such things as the Attetson family dynamic, sibling squabbles and power hierarchies. To reveal a secret brother in the sixteenth chapter does rather throw a spanner in the works. Who, or what, does it mean to be Muhren Attetson? Where does he fit within the family tree? What was he like growing up? *Does he prefer pizza or a salad?* Muhren Attetson was the second born. He was one year younger than Vincent and a year older than Kiko. Being born so closely between his siblings meant that he had been given little to offer in the way of anything that could differentiate him from his peers. Like all of his peers, he preferred pizza over salad, stop lying to yourself. *Everyone does.* Like most middle born children, he was wasn't the leader of the pack. *(As the year age gap meant Vincent was bolder, smarter, faster and stronger.)* But he also only really had a year's worth of experience when it came to be the baby of the group. Being neither the assertive leader that a firstborn child usually finds themselves thrust into becoming, nor being the youngest child, a role that is usually the most pampered and protected in the household, had led Muhren down a path of constantly butting heads with his siblings; trying to find both his power and his place within his kin. Any middle born child will admit to having a hard time growing up. Being ostracised from both roles either as an heir to the throne or as a doted upon infant. Usually left to their own devices to carve their own path, as raising several children is not easy. Any mother, father or carer will tell you it's a full-time job in its own right. The firstborn succeeds due to their age and the benefit of the 'one-on-one' time spent with mommy and daddy before these other kids cluttered the house. The last born, however, will be stuck in an everlasting visage of being the youngest, li'll cutest baby in the whole wide world, which can cause its own issues. But what role is left for the child born in-between?

This occurrence was only further exasperated by the fact that Vincent was a prodigal virtuoso unlike the world had ever seen before before. This when combined with Kiko's tendency to seclude herself within her books which spurred her social ineptitude which in turn strengthened Collin and Cassandra's parental instinct to dote upon her growing up. Vincent being a *'prodigal virtuoso'* would now make sense, as he was only perceived as being a master of the arcane when compared to a human standard. Muhren found himself living a carefree lifestyle, deliberately unburdened with the weight of the Attetson name. When they zigged, he zagged. Either out of a desire to agitate and annoy his mother by being awkward, or by a desire to be free himself of the trap of feeling like he did not belong. This lifestyle choice led Muhren to cut himself free of the shackles of his family as soon as he could. Putting as many miles between him and them as was feasibly possible at the time. To walk the Earth as his own man, not as a carbon copy of the Attetson brand image. There was a concern that he disliked his family, but this was not the case. A point Collin had made several times to a distraught Cassandra, who in herself could not understand why her second born was always so dismissive of this life of luxury. Muhren had always been well fed, well kept, well educated, and most importantly, he was well loved. *All of these children were.* Each one was like a limb to Cassandra. Truth be told, she would rather lose a million limbs a thousand times over than have a single hair damaged upon the heads of any of her amazing children. So, all things considered, right now? *She was not okay.*

The sky had drawn black. The wind howled at the soul. The sun had hurtled down in all its might and crashed into the moon. The ground cracked underfoot. The world had sunken into the sea, drowning in a dark abyss. Flames blazed in the night. All creatures of all the heavens and all the Earths were burned to ash. Smoke gnawed at the throat. Blisters burned and popped the eyes. Minds were split, fractured and splintered into an overwhelming madness. Despair was king now, ruling supreme from its throne of grief. *All other emotions were lost to Cassandra.* An inconceivable, maddening loss had turned her life upside down. Her son had been taken from her. But not recently, no. Her firstborn son had been stolen, ripped away in the night all those years ago. She had failed to notice that Vincent's chubby baby cheeks and tiny fingers were not his own, but instead the claws and the face of a monster. No, not just a monster. The monster that had killed her baby. The monster she had fed, clothed, bathed, raised and had loved. *Loved with all of her heart.* She was unfit to call herself a mother. She had failed, in her mind at least. A cancerous symbiotic being had strolled right into her house and what was worse, she had held the door open for it. *She let in.* She had let it sit at the kitchen table. She had fed it. She had told it bedtime stories, tucked it in at night and watched it as it played with her other children. *How could she not have known?* She should have known! She wasn't a mother. She was a witless pretender, a fraud and a clueless imbecile. No proper mother would have allowed this to happen. *A real mother would have known.* Even without magic, they would have seen it. They would have sensed it. They would have avenged their child.

So when the decision had been made to tell Muhren about his brother, a secondary subconscious decision had been made that it should probably not be Cassandra to tell him. Even without anyone saying a word, everyone agreed. Wherever her mind was, it was definitely not in any fit state to be discussing such awful things. So by a process of elimination, Kiko had been chosen to be the bearer of this bad news. Again, this decision was made in stone-like silence. Collin had reverted to the basics of the only thing he could currently think of to do right now. He stayed with Cassandra, he held her tight and he listened. Kara, having just lopped the head off of the once would-be Vincent, decided to keep a low profile, sticking to the shadows as it were, keeping herself to herself. Operating a one-woman cleanup crew… as all this blood was probably not a calming influence on Cassandra. Yeah…. Nah… Plus, even though she would never admit it, Kara was terrified that all of the Attetsons would turn around in great unison, en masse, pointing the finger of blame at her. Naming her as Vincent's murderer and then casting her out for killing their heroic child. Every now and then a person is presented with a moment where it's best to just stay quiet. To shut up and say nothing. You never know when one of those moments will arise, but you always know when you're in one. And Kara knew this to be one of those moments.

It was approximately nine am on a rainy Seattle morning. The rain gently hammered upon the outside of a rustic wooden cabin, surrounded by a fluttering of Yoshino cherry trees and red cedars. The smell of nature clung to the air and calmed the mind. The not so distant sound of birdsong cradled the building. If not perfect, this house was at least peaceful. It was quiet. It was rural and Muhren loved it. Nothing was stirring, not even a mouse. The main reason why nothing was stirring in this house, not even a mouse, at nine o'clock in the morning, on a weekday no less, was due to the previous drunken night. A littering of cans and spirit bottles camouflaged and dampened the floor. The smell of questionable pizza peppered the air and almost drowned out the smell of all the drink that had been consumed. *(If such a thing were possible!)* Much like how all of that drink from last night was now drowning all of Muhren's senses into a drowsy stupor. The kind of stupor where a man might not notice a fire beginning to burn within his own home. Deep within the lands of the living room, which with a hangover might as well have been on a separate continent from the bedroom, somewhere amongst the far off lands between the island nation of the couch, some may call it a sofa, and the mountain range of the television, a selection of discarded beer cans began to rumble and rock into a jittering motion due to a series of small flames that jabbed at them. Then as these embers and flames underneath continued to be ignored, these abandoned empty cans began to leap and jump, almost as if they were worried about the fire. Which, yes would currently mean, beer cans one, Muhren zero. If anyone was keeping score… and not putting out the fire…

The beer cans were launched across the room in a whole multitude of directions. Any crevice, corner or hidey-hole of this room that in its history had somehow not been bathed in the amber droplets of alcoholic pointing, hugging, overzealous gesturing or a whole host of accidental beverage spillings events, had now succumbed to being awashed with beer. The epicentre for these cans, the fire, had risen and was now standing on four legs. Muhren did not live alone in this house, he had a pet. And as all pet owners know, pets decided when it is time to eat. '*Namonar*' comes from both the Elven words for fire, '*nar*,' and '*namo*,' which means wolf. By literal definition, Namonar means fire-wolf, or rather, the wolf that is fire. Hence why Muhren chose to name his pet this, as that is exactly what this pet was. A sentient wolf made entirely from fire.

Namonar burst through the bedroom door and bound onto the bed in a single leap and began pawing at his master and licking his face.

"Alright, alright! I'm up. I'm up!" One of Muhren's muscle-bound, tattooed, arms arose to pet his friend. Well, to both pet this pet and also to protect his face, neck and beard from any more fire like saliva. At this point, it would be idealistic to point out that despite being made from fire, Namonar doesn't actually burn you; *unless he wanted to.*

The existence of a wolf being made entirely from fire and flames is probably a shocking realisation. It definitely was for the twenty, or thirty, something year old Elven woman that was sleeping next to Muhren. She had met this missing Attetson link last night. Her name was… s… something. She definitely had a name and during that point of the conversation it was the most important name in existence. She had a job, probably, or maybe not… *It's so hard to tell these days.* She definitely had hobbies, these included doing stuff and things. Everyone has hobbies that include stuff and things. She liked to talk, she was definitely a talker. She could go on and on and on. She was good with her mouth. She was clearly a blonde. That much was obvious… *or maybe it was dyed?* The only real tangible fact was that she was screaming. Good god, she was loud. Both Muhren and Namonar thought so, and for the record, Namonar didn't much care for being shouted or screamed at within his own home. Also for the record, if you refer to anyone's pet as *'that thing'* and demand they *'get that thing out of here'* then the only thing vacating the premises is you. As was the case with old *'what's her name?'* who may or may not have any discernable qualities besides *'existing,'* but Muhren was not going to be the one to hang around to discover if this was the case.

It was mere seconds between the front door of the house closing and the fridge door opening. Namonar was presented with leftover pizza whilst Muhren tried to imagine what meals could be made from butter, leftover hot sauce, questionable smelling milk and a half-drunk bottle of white wine. He slammed the fridge door shut and almost died of a heart attack as there stood his sister. He went to make a joke, either about Kiko's appearance or her even being there at all *(As the role as the funny sibling it was his birthright.)* But every funnyman knows how to read a room, the need for this having spawned from several improper jokes at improper times creating awkward silences or ending friendships. Instead, Muhren ran on instinct, looking at the broken Kiko he knew something wasn't right. He walked towards his baby sister and held her as she burst like a damn of flooded tears, collapsing in his arms and falling to the floor. It was as if all the air had been knocked out of her as she wailed and wept at the passing of her eldest brother.

Some time had passed. No one was sure exactly how long, as Muhren listened to the story of how Kiko had bounded through time and space with Kara. How she had discovered the Revanspear and how this spear had revealed the truths about their brother. How a Changeling had killed Vincent and that awful, awful night she had spent at the hospital all those years ago and about how badly Cassandra was currently doing. Muhren's response to this was surprisingly *'British.'* He summoned as many cups of tea as were required to soothe the sorrows of both himself and his sister. Muhren never really knew this, but he was always useful. He had a keen eye when it came to both conjuration and restorative magic. This led him to a fairly stressful job at the Arcane Intelligence Agency as a Cleric on the Western Coast. This job role being similar to a high ranking medical profession in our world. This job meant he was used to speaking to people and families and delivering bad news. However, it was a wholly bizarre experience to be told bad news by a person who is in your family. He was used to being more of an active member and less of a bystander. The twang of guilt sparked away, maybe if he had been there he could have done something.

Kiko could feel exactly two things cut through the all-consuming numbness currently devouring her soul. These being that her eyes stung, redraw and exhausted from all the crying. She could also feel a gentle hum of heat from the tea she cradled in her hands. She wondered if Muhren minded her having her feet on his couch, but as he had made no comment about it she chose to remain sat in a fetal position. With her knees shielding her face from the nasty and mean world. It just felt right. Besides his place wasn't exactly tidy, so Muhren probably didn't even notice.

Muhren had always been her favourite brother, probably in no small part because he was the most relatable. They had shared a lot of the same sideways glances, jokes and sighs about Vincent when growing up. The same feelings of abandonment caused by being left in the wake of Vincent's greatness. It was perplexing to think that all of that was now over. That vile, disgusting thing that had pretended to be Vincent for all these years, was gone. *There was no going back.* The Vincent she knew had never really existed. He had died several years before she was ever even born. This trickster, this nightmarish ghoul, had robbed her of him her entire life. Every memory was a lie. Truly, and all too technically, she only ever knew one brother. This hulking, wild-haired man sat across the room from her now.

"Is that a new tattoo?" She found herself clumsily asking as something to break the newly set silence.

"Which one?" Muhren replied, with a cocky grin as he looked at his arms.

There was another pause.

"I'm… I'm sorry, this is all so…" Kiko gave an awkward involuntary smile before looking down towards her tea.

Muhren, seeing that his sister was struggling for words replied with the best 'yep' he could muster at the time. Vincent was always a pretentious dick, as far as he was concerned. Not enough to make Muhren wish for anything bad to happen or for him to be glad that Vincent was dead. But there was definitely enough resentment to create a confused resonance of emotions within him.

Namonar gently arose next to Kiko and rested his warm head on her lap. Kiko dropped her knees that were shielding her face and began stroking the fire-wolf.

"I can't believe how big he's gotten!" Kiko said as she tried balancing her tea on the arm of the couch. *(Or again, sofa if you're that way inclined.)* "I still remember the day you summoned him! You were so tiny then, yes you were." Kiko's voice broke into a playful tone, as do all voices when addressing a pet directly, as she gently poked him on the nose. Namonar didn't seem to mind being poked in the face. He knew Kiko was family and he could sense her pain, so he'd allow it. And if anything came through that door trying to cause more pain, they'd regret it. *Namonar would make sure of it.*

And so a conversation broke out about Namonar, how Muhren had conjured Namonar from a bonfire some ten years ago. How both Cassandra and Collin were so proud and impressed with their boy. Kiko could recall the night well, but it was interesting hearing events she had partaken in from another's perspective. It was a good distraction, in the way that a good distraction is great when all you can think about is the thing you're trying not to think about. Kiko remarked upon a time when she had managed to conjure a squirrel, with an effervescent, almost translucent, dark purple coat that resembled a clear starry night sky. If the room was bright enough, you could almost see straight through the squirrel. But she could neither recall his name nor where he had ended up.

"Vincent named him Marlaketh, remember?" Muhren replied, half-smiling behind his cup as he prepared for another sip.

And with that simple mention of Vincent's name, Kiko was back to crying again. Apparently, she still had tears left to cry.

Another allotted period of time had now passed as the sun began to lower and the conversation gradually turned into a discussion comparing what they both knew of the Changelings as a species.

Whilst Kiko knew considerably more than Muhren, neither exactly knew a lot. As this new debate raged on Muhren rose his hand and a book came hurtling in from another room. He began to examine this book thoroughly, as both Kiko and Namonar sat staring at him.

Staring at him.

Still staring at him.

Waiting… still… *still waiting…*

Kiko went to say something about how long she had been *'patiently'* waiting when Muhren exclaimed with glee, thrusting a finger into the air.

"I knew it!" He hurried his way excitedly to Kiko, towering over her as he gestured to a paragraph within the book.

'Changelings are not a creature prone slothful or lackadaisical behaviour.

> *Given the nature of how one feeds and grows its strength, it is never safe for one to be caught. No parent has ever been recorded as sitting down for a discussion with a changeling.*
>
> *These so-called 'nests' changelings make, whilst it both nurtures and feeds them, will breed a very dangerous place to stay for too long.*

It is a given fact that the families these changelings feed upon will always rise up, either as a family or as a local society, clan or neighbourhood. Given its very nature, a Changeling is always at risk of being challenged, it will know this. As the infant it consumes obviously dies, the Changeling will only have a short duration before the risk of being caught becomes an inevitable outcome. A changeling will only stay with a family for a short period of time. Up to three or four months maximum. The longest recorded changeling infestation comes from Paris, France, in the March of 1524, when a Changeling found an immense power source and managed to stay nearby for up to five years, before dying of old age.'

Muhren cast an inquisitive look at Kiko.

"So how did this one stick around for twenty-odd years then?"

Kiko gave a blank look through her glasses as her mind flooded with ideas. She opened her mouth and the ideas fell out.

"So we know a Changeling steals the identity of the child, we know that much." She rested her chin within her hand. "It's also kind of obvious that they would be at risk if they blew their cover or hung around too long. So why would something willingly draw attention to itself as Vincent's Changeling did?" She looked towards Namonar as if looking for answers. He had none. "Why risk having the whole world know your name? I… I… I don't think it can be as simple as an egotistical Changeling. As nice and easy of an answer as that would be." She thrust her hands in the air animatedly. "Twenty years far exceeds their natural lifespan as a species, I knew this! This book, it's a good book by the way, sorry!" Kiko shook her head, before continuing. Now was not a time to get distracted by books. "This book states that this French Changeling was drawn to a magical artefact of immense power. But what was the artefact?" She flicked through some more pages. "If we knew what that was, maybe we could understand how, or why, this Changeling stuck around for so long."

Muhren gave a dry, wiry smile towards his sister. "Looks like we're going to Paris then, doesn't it, Kiko."

…

This statement boggled her mind…

...

"Um… excuse me?" Kiko managed to stutter out from her state of confusion, this hardly felt like the time for a holiday. Although, the idea of running far, far away did not sound at all awful. "Why?"

"We know where a Changeling was and when it was." He nodded gleefully. "All we don't know is why he was there." Muhren shrugged his shoulders as if to say, that this was all of the problems they'd face.

He had clearly gone mad. *Maybe those drinks from last night were still in his system?!*

"Oh, I don't know, man. It's a whole year and, oh that's right, one of the busiest cities in the entire world!" Kiko answered back, slightly bewildered and dismayed, looking at her brother like he had just drooled on himself. The similarities of trying to find a needle in a haystack came to mind. That being the case if a needle had just killed your brother and had stolen his face. You'd probably not want to see a needle again for a long while.

"Well, apparently you can travel through time now." He gave his sister a cheeky nudge. "So we can go back and then we cast a divination spell and b-o-o-m." Muhren said mockingly. "We find it. We get ourselves some answers."

Kiko was shocked, partially because she should have been the one to think of using a divination spell to find something, but mainly because Muhren had actually come up with a solid plan. Yes, there were a few kinks, but what plan was ever perfect and without risk? Maybe he was crazy. *Maybe he was an idiot.* Or maybe it was just crazy and idiotic enough to work. Maybe again it was completely logical, she was too frazzled by the day's events to tell anymore.

There was only one way to find out for sure.

Chapter Seventeen
TRIALS AND TRIBULATIONS

Kara sat awkwardly across the bed in the Attetson manor's spare room. Trying her best to not make a sound. The woeful wailings and weepings from downstairs were borderline deafening. Cassandra's howls of bereavement were enough to make the ears bleed and the heart cry. The undeniable shrieks of sorrow were occasionally interrupted by a pause. This pause would only last as long as was required for Cassandra to find the emotional strength to begin crying all over again. The sound penetrated this well-presented guest room and only served to draw attention to its emptiness. The manilla walls matched the cream bedding which contrasted against the off-black, slate-grey wooden furniture. Whilst being fairly modern and picturesque, this room lacked the small bits-n-bobs that turn a room into '*your*' room. Sure, months had past and Kara had accumulated stuff in this time. But she was always mindful to not overstate her welcome. Every morning she expected to be told that this morning was the last, final morning. Despite several offerings of payment, she was always refused. Kara was not used to people not wanting to take her money. It was weird. But not as weird, she felt, as watching a muted television with the subtitles turned on. Subtitles being a thing televisions used to help deaf people so they knew what was being said. It was also useful, as it turned out, when you're terrified to make a noise that may draw attention to yourself. As if either Cassandra or Collin had the time or care or barge into the room with the night they had just had. Yet, the subtitles remained. Whatever this inane garbage was, it wasn't captivating. It wasn't the show's fault. After all, it had a lot to contend with tonight. I'm sure the show's producers, director, writers and cast would make the argument that Kara just had a lot on her mind right now and it was an unfair time to make any sort of rash judgement about the show's quality and she would be welcome to try watching again after all this had died down. Perhaps whoever made this argument would use slightly more appropriate terminology than 'to die down' when addressing a grieving BNI agent, or more likely would have asked, *'who the hell is Kara?'*

A similar question was about to be asked by the drained Half-Elf when something clacked against the guttering outside her room.

"What the hell was that?" She asked, just like I said she would, turning her head towards the closed curtains.

There was a faint blip of light as Kiko, Muhren and Namonar returned to the Attetson household. For Kiko, this time spent away had been several hours. For Muhren this was closer to several years. It felt weird to be back again. Strange. Oh god, the house looked the same. Maybe if he was really quiet, Kiko wouldn't notice if he just went.

"Bah!" Kiko hissed pointing at him with a frown scowled across her face. "I know that look!" She accused. "Don't you dare!" Her whispering was almost like that of a snake. "You're not going anywhere!"

Namonar stepped back from Kiko. He had no idea what the noises coming from her mouth were, but man was her body language intense! After insisting she'd be right back, Kiko shot off scouring the garden for small rocks. Given the fact that this was a garden, this took little time at all, despite the poor lighting that was available from it being ten o'clock at night.

'Clink!' The first rock bounced off of the outside wall and tumbled back to earth. *'Thwang!'* That one clattered against the metal guttering. The third landed painfully on the roof. This was not going well. Kiko raised her arm one final time. This one, this blessed rock, was the one. It would expertly, and oh so stealthily attract Kara's attention. Kiko, her best friend and her brother would then very quickly make their way to ye' olde Paris, circa 1524, and they would manage all this without alerting Kiko's parents. This important and simple act of silent compassion would alleviate any further stresses potentially caused by learning your last two children were hunting the very thing that had killed your first one. Hunting the very thing that was the reason why you were crying now. It was of the utmost importance that these grieving parents were not interrupted. By this time tomorrow

morning, or five hundred or so years after the would-be night in Paris, they would all sit down for a nice family breakfast and discuss the future. But discussing the future required a quick visit to the past. But for all of this to happen it is important for you to know I can actually see you, you know, Kiko.

"I can actually see you, you know, Kiko. You realise that right?" Collin's voice washed over Kiko and locked her in a panic-stricken pose. Either a second, or an eternity, passed when the blessed rock that was totally going to be the chosen rock, fell to the ground like its other failed comrades. Kiko's wide eyes slowly drifted over and locked upon her father, who for the first time in many years was smoking a cigarette under the back canopy that overlooked the garden. For the record, yeah. Kiko was still stuck in the awkward pose.

"I'm not interested in whatever '*this*' is." This cold demeanour was something rarely seen from the usually smiley Collin. His open arms were closed, crossed tightly across his chest. "But you owe your mother more respect than to be running around in the middle of the night, hiding." He had the wrong gist of what was occurring in his back garden. "How dare you try and…" This new rant was cut short by the soft glow of a fire, as both Namonar and Muhren walked around the corner.

Collin, having completely forgotten about being mad at Kiko, was now awestruck by the son he had not seen for far too long. The two men embraced in the stereotypical two pat hug. Anyone who has ever seen two men attempt a hug knows exactly the one I mean.

Knowing exactly what to do or what to think or say was something entirely beyond what Kiko was currently capable of right now. Having never had her father raise his voice or get angry at her in any way during her entire twenty-three years of life meant that she had no grid of reference to compare this newly found darkness to. It served both to turn her entire body into a state of lockdown and distract her from the upcoming goal. She lost the will to attempt any more rock throws tonight. Her arms lacked the strength, not that they had much to start with. As she stared at the open door that led into the house, it felt a lifetime away and only seemed to draw further away from her the more she looked at it. For a door she had both seen and walked through on countless occasions, it was now sickeningly daunting, completely horrific and it felt as if the concept of stepping over that threshold again was just about the hardest thing to do in the entire world. *This was because everything in that house was real.* Returning meant everything had really happened. It almost felt worth the risk of creating a paradox, even if undoing all this hurt could result in the complete loss of all time and life in the universe. That must have been better than this, *right?*

There was a soft rapping of knuckles against the guest room door. Kara stared uneasily at it. *Perhaps if she was quiet whoever it was would think she was asleep!* The voices of doubt began burning away at her mind once more.

"Kara!" Kiko whispered through the door. "Psst, oi! Lemme in!" Kiko hissed, having somehow found her courage to traverse the house once more. "I swear, you better not be asleep in there!" She knocked again.

"Nah, I'm totally sleeping!" Kara whispered back in a hiss. "Totally going to get a full night sleep tonight, mate!"

And with that, Kiko over exaggeratedly barrelled into the room. Any preprepared words of comfort Kara had readied herself with were ill-prepared when being confronted with the idea of Paris. Travelling to a time where any woman who was viewed as powerful was burned at the stake, the fact she was a witch rarely had anything to do with it. The thought of two *'female wizards'* parading around olden day France, using magic and fighting fairy monsters wreaked of a bad idea. The idea that they would also most likely be referred to as witches only served to cause further insult. It was a well-established fact that all men who cast magic were smart, kind and loveable wizards with rosy cheeks, endearing beards and goofy hats. If they were cool enough they could be a sorcerer and have a sweet looking set of robes. All women who cast magic were witches. For some reason, this meant being a hag with a hideously crooked nose, a hideously crooked spine and a hideously crooked broom. They all had green skin and were portrayed as spinsters who ate children fresh out of a cauldron. A shared hatred for this lacklustre cliché was one of the founding things a young Kiko and Kara had bonded over. Choosing all those years ago that the title of a *'female wizard'* was better, so long as the beard was non-compulsory.

So to now choose to vacate to the heart of Europe, in a time when witches were at their least popular was a recipe for disaster. Being called a green-skinned, child-eating spinster-hag, with a hooked nose was a lot better than being called a green-skinned, child-eating spinster-hag, with a hooked nose whilst half of France cheered and laughed at you as you were unable to do anything about the fire flaying the skin from your bones and boiling your blood. Being called names you disliked didn't seem so bad when compared to the idea of people cheering as your muscles melted and your organs popped. This was to say very little of what would happen if the Changeling was not willing to just accept them asking it questions. What if it fancied a fight?

"I mean, what if it was the same one?" Kara asked, being entirely unaware that the life span of a changeling was approximately one-hundredth of the time required for this French dwelling changeling to be the same as the decapitated one she had clumsily disposed of earlier that evening.

"I'm sorry Kara, but I really need answers for all this." Kiko looked directly into Kara's eyes as they sat at the foot of the bed. "And I would really like my best friend to be there with me. I honestly don't know what I'd do without her..." Kiko smiled softly and tears began to dampen her face.

"Ugh!" Kara groaned as she rose to her feet. "I hate it when you look at me like that!" She snapped back with a faint glare. *"Fine!* Let's go die in France!" Her body language having gesticulations of a sarcastic excitement. "This is a great idea by the way!" She grabbed one of her signature axes and held it tight. "But I swear to God if any French dude tries to tie me to a stake, I'll kill him!"

Kara pulled a face that seemed to mimic the facial expression this would be Frenchman would have as she held her axe blade to her throat. If this expression was anything to go by, one eye would be shut and his tongue sticking out. This was generally a poor face to pull when dying. This was down to the question, *'what would happen next if you didn't die, but survived?'* Your tongue protruding in such a manner was guaranteed to be bitten off by the force of your fall locking your jaw shut. If this loss of blood wasn't what was going to kill you now, then good luck ever speaking again.

The girls met up with Muhren and Kiko cast her spell of temporal displacement. Upon this spell realising where they were going a holographic-like message appeared.

'Please be aware that you have chosen a dangerous time period.

The Arcane Intelligence Agency and all of its subsidiaries are not responsible for any negative or harmful events you engage in or witness.

By accepting below you agree that the responsibilities of any potential outcome are your own. You also agree that you are doing so of your own free will. The Arcane Intelligence Agency, including all personnel and offices, are not liable for loss of limb, life or anything else that may or may not happen to you.

If you should engage in any acts deemed dangerous to the timeline you also agree to be dealt with in whichever manner the Temporal Bureau of Investigations deems fit.'

The year was 1524. This had been a rather boring year for France as a whole and this was no different for Paris. If this had been a movie there would have been some sort of establishing shot, some iconic French landmark to let you know that this was France. Some oversized title card would have told you the year. But as the Eiffel Tower was some three-hundred-and-sixty-three years away, Hollywood would have had to find some other building to show you how French things were about to become.

What was supposed to happen upon the arrival to this long-forgotten time was, on the surface, what seemed to be a very simple and straightforward series of objectives.

'Objective A: Find clothes.'

Nothing ranked quite as high as finding native clothing. There wasn't much else that could make a time traveller more conspicuous than not looking the part. Every era was defined by its own style. If man had evolved from a single-celled amoeba into what we recognised today, fashion had also had a similar evolution all of its own. A person wandering down the street now in nothing but leather pelts or a loincloth would, by its very nature, draw attention to themselves. The same was true of the opposite. The main issue right now was Kiko's bright coat. As dye was expensive, rare and hard to produce. Likewise, Kara and her finely trimmed leather jacket would be too well cut for the times. Muhren's tank top would probably have distracted the local women for a different reason. Sixteenth-century men rarely looked this ripped, toned or rugged. Namonar had no use for clothes.

Unfortunately for this fashionable lot, they had entered the time of beige. Beige robes and beige dresses being the height of normality at the time. I will humour the locals and call the bonnets and aprons white; as for the time they were thought to be so. But when compared to what we had readily available today, it was a little more than a vile muddied cream. Later, when washing machines and varieties of detergents would become a thing, whites would find their true calling in life.

'Objective B: Find somewhere secluded.'

The divination spell, while simple enough to cast, required a safe place to do so. Some private location away from beady eyes. Their disguises would be meaningless without the act of secrecy. Skipping straight to this stage, or having their cover blown midway, would result in their execution. Given that the rather painless option of a guillotine would not become a choice for almost another two hundred years, all witches had either the option of a long drop with a sudden stop or being burned at the stake. *Which would you choose?*

It's worth mentioning that the choice was never actually yours to make. Only once in history was a witch asked how she wanted to die. When asked the rather dumb question 'what do you want to happen next?' She chose none of the options presented to her, instead choosing to leave. As the peasants were all plebeians, they had not planned that she may not want to be drowned, hanged or roasted like a proverbial marshmallow on a campfire. Somehow this had resulted in them letting her go. When asked later as to why she was allowed to leave uncontested, it was too embarrassing to admit that they might be stupid and instead decided that this was further evidence of witchcraft. Bethan Jones of Cardiff, was not a witch. Admittedly, the fact she spoke and understood the Welsh language might have at least been a tiny bit proof of a Demonic possession, if not counting as proof of full-blown witchcraft in its own right. Any visitors to the Isle of Dragons can be forgiven for not knowing what this *'anodd ei ddeall'* language was saying.

After the stupidity shown by Bethan's captors, it was also generally decided it was a bad idea to just release prisoners because they asked you to. So the next time you've been kidnapped and your abductor refuses to let you go, you know who to thank. *Cheers, Bethan!* You'll probably need to cancel your dinner plans and hunker down for the long haul of however many days, week, months or years it took for Stockholm Syndrome to kick in. *At such a point, why would you even want to leave?*

Leave is an interesting word. Mainly being interesting and an entirely flabbergasting occurrence to witness for James Barker, who was currently watching as all of his patrons and guests were leaving his new hotel he'd just recently bought. His only mistake was pouring his entire life's worth of savings into a hotel in Stockholm city the same week that the idea of Stockholm Syndrome was unveiled to the world. Following this reveal, Sweden had its worst ever recorded year in all tourist-related industries. The rest of the world had clearly had a private conversation about Sweden and they had come to the unanimous decision that it was probably for the best to avoid Stockholm for a while, as some shady shit was clearly occurring. And no one was willing to be kidnapped.

The fear of being kidnapped played a huge part in the reasoning as to why sixteenth-century witches were so unpopular. These ungodly women were seen as tricksters and as bad omens. You would either be stolen away in the night, lose all your crops, or be turned into something unnatural. It never hurt to keep an eye out for the unnatural.

'Objective C: Keeping an eye out for the unnatural.'

Somewhere in this city, there was a Changeling. Well, that was if the book was correct. Upon finding it they needed to be able to differentiate it from any ordinary child. If they were successful in this, a problem would arise. This being that everyone in the local vicinity wouldn't deal well with the visage of this Parisian terror. There would be one of two results. One of these being that the people of Paris would do their best wild buffalo impersonations and stampede down the streets, retreating, yelling and screaming. Or they would do their best impression of a sixteenth-century's mob of angry villagers and grab every pitchfork, torch, club, axe, sword, dagger and cross and chase them. This choice felt more likely, seeing how they were already sixteenth-century commoners.

So as Kiko, Kara, Muhren and Namonar arrived in 1524 they knew they had to be careful. It was at this moment they realised that they had overlooked a highly important and utterly crucial detail.

No one could speak French.

So when a French commoner began screaming 'Sorcière! Sorcière!' as he pointed at Namonar. A hellhound made of pure fire that had just walked around the corner, all these plans went out the window. Good going guys. *Nice one!*

As Kara was still fairly new to the whole time travel malarkey, sixteenth-century Paris was a big deal. To walk where these people had once walked and now did so again. To breathe the air of her world hundreds of years before her birth. To smell the scents and see the sights of a world that should never have been available to her. It all looked so similar, just more rustic and with less finesse. Surprisingly a lot of the city was made of wood, or was supported by wood as stone walls would slowly be built up around them. The hustle and bustle of the city heard all around them sounded the same as if she had just walked into a modern city centre, but her eyes told a very different story. She saw some Parisian Orc take a slip and land on his knees in the mud. This randomly insignificant moment, meaningless to all of existence had been allowed to repeat itself and live more. It was like time was rewatching an old movie it had not seen for years. *Hang on!* Does that mean this was the second time he had fallen over? Had Kara and her friends forced this guy to relive the fall all over again? Had he already fallen, once in 1524 and forced to repeat himself again in 1524-2.0 because of their random appearance?

"Sorcière! Sorcière!" The falling Orc's voice called out as he began pointing at them. *Shit!*

There was no satisfaction for Kara having been proven right about her predictions about them being caught sneaking through time. They had only been there a matter of seconds, not that any length of time would have made this any better. Panic gripped under her ribs and her breath froze in her lungs as she turned to Kiko, wide-eyed and looking for help.

"Run!" Kiko yelped as she shoved her friend down an adjacent side alley.

The gang had made a run for it! In terms of the greatest ideas of all time, this was not one of them. As they stood hunched behind a series of discarded barrels and crates Kiko decided it was time to say something.

"What the hell, Muhren!" She gestured towards him as she snapped. "What part of the plan made you think that not dismissing Namonar was a good idea?"

To be fair Muhren had tried to redeem himself, suggesting they cast a translation spell so they could actually speak French, so that helped with his redemption arc. Despite this not being exactly true, the part where they would now be speaking French. They'd keep speaking normally, just the people around them would hear something they could understand. When they were spoken to a person would hear a language they were comfortable with. It was a *'translation spell'* not an *'I now speak French spell!'*

At some point during the cross- Paris-sprint Muhren had dispelled Namonar. He had done this with a facial expression reminiscent of a man hiding contraband whilst on the run from the police. Muhren currently made no effort in the way of a reply to his sister. Maybe he was embarrassed or maybe he just hadn't thought of a good enough of a come back yet. And for anyone concerned, dispelling or dismissing Namonar did not hurt him in any way. Being dismissed from our dimension was the closest thing he had to sleep.

All three sank further in behind their barrels and watched in unison as a family of Halflings walked on by. From what they could tell they had not been followed. There was no doubt that this Orc had informed others of what he had seen, the only concern was did they believe him? This city was so noisy it was hard to tell the good sounds from the bad. Kiko fully expected a hand to grab her from behind at any moment and to be clapped in irons. To be dragged away and never be seen again. The fact she had not foreseen Namonar being an issue worried her.

"Oh god, what am I doing?" Her words broke softly against the uproar of the city as she dipped her head, resting it against her barrel.

Their newfound hidey-hole was in what appeared to be an abandoned courtyard. From this vantage point, a trader could be seen selling clothes off the back of a wagon. *'Objective A'* was back in action! Kiko threw her coat over Kara and shot off from behind her barrel with intent. This boldness shook Muhren and Kara-the-coat-rack who were both speechless at her movement and offered support in the way of a terrified gaze. Watching attentively as their red-haired companion awkwardly tiptoed and strided towards the trader. These two shared a moment where they locked eyes and mouthed concern at each other.

"What the hell!" Muhren asked with a wide-eyed fear.

"What's she doing?" Kara asked back in a whisper almost snake-like.

"I don't know! Where is she going?"

"What do we do?"

"What is she playing at?"

"We are going home right now!" Kara demanded.

"What?"

"WE ARE GOING HOME RIGHT NOW!" Kara repeated again, slightly louder.

"What...?"

"WE... ARE..."

Kara got annoyed and stopped trying to talk instead opting to glare at Muhren. If he couldn't understand her miming, *he'd damn well understand her glare!*

Kiko was close. She was so close. *She could almost touch it!* As she sat hunched behind the cart, her heart raced. The blood pumped through her veins. Her brain was on maximum alert. The adrenaline was like a drug. Right now she felt like she could run faster, jump higher and fight harder than ever before. She was aware of all of her surroundings. At this moment it felt like she was alone with every single item in the universe simultaneously. That man was afraid he had bad breath. She was upset by something off in the distance. That kid was at risk of losing his ball if he kept kicking it so hard. Another man was complaining about money. Some women were commenting on another's clothes. An old couple complained about how modern everything was. Two guards were off in the distance. A man pretended not to notice what his dog had just done.

A shaky hand slowly made its way up the side of the cart.

A lady was complaining about the price of bread. Adriane had caught leprosy. Some man had made a fool of himself the night before and was trying to explain. Some woman was fed up with being married to a fool. But no one was talking about Kiko.

No one had noticed her hand slip up the back of the cart. No one had seen how her watch had gotten stuck on the wooden backing and how she had shaken herself free. She snatched up a handful of clothes and waddled back stressfully to her onlookers and threw the brown ball of smelly clothing at their feet.

Muhren made quick work of getting changed, the fabric itched.

"I am not wearing that!" Kara held at arm's length a coffee-coloured robe that smelled of cheese and regret. "That's vile. That's..." She tried not to be sick from disdain. "No, no I'm not..." She looked back and forth between her friends hoping one would share her haughty derision. This look would have been spurred on if only she knew of the leper who had donned it prior.

"Would you rather die?" Kiko had a dark brown gown. The fabric also itched. "I'll happily get a guard!" Kiko's sarcastic counter-argument was supported by the araignée that crawled up the side of her neck. Being French, it only felt right to call the spider, the araignée, by a name it would recognise. *This respect for spiders was not shared by Kara.*

"SPIDER!"

It was either Kara's shouting or her slapping Kiko in the neck that drew everyone's attention to them. It was also either her shouting or her slapping Kiko in the neck that made a female Elf approach. Perhaps this Elf was hideous by our modern standards and an absolute babe by theirs. Time had a strange way to alter the perception of beauty. It mattered not, like the dead spider on a wheezing Kiko's neck, this Elf had seen something she liked and wanted to trap it in her web. No man this Elf had ever seen had ever had muscles like Muhren. *The butterflies in her stomach wanted to see more.*

"Hey, you aw'ite luv." She said, leaning into Muhren. "Fancy a good time?" She smiled at him. This Elf smelled not too dissimilar to an onion that had farted in a garlic and skunk soup whilst being given the run around by a wet dog on a warm summers day next to a sewage plant. *But again this was 1524, everyone smelled like that.*

"Not to be a critic, but -uh- no thanks. I'm taken!" Muhren replied with a fake smile as he ran away like a terrified school child and put his arm around Kara. Kara looked confused at the arm that was now wrapping around her neck like a muscular snake.

"Ay, now. I dunno who you callin' a cricket, but I ain't one of what that is!" The Elf was enraged. She knew not how to criticise this as the word critic was lost on her, in her confusion she had thought Muhren had just called her an insect.

Kiko ran up to her brother and stamped hard on his foot. The pain from Muhren's crushed toes found itself traversing up his leg and through his abs. It punched through his diaphragm and used the lungs to hasten its retreat out of his mouth through the sound of a sustained groan that eluded from his wincing red face. Not being a member of the TBI himself, he knew not of the mistake he had just made. Translation spells only work if they can be translated into something the other person would be able to understand at the time. *A caveman wouldn't care for a phone.* William Shakespeare would not coin the term '*critic*' until the big day of Love's Labour Lost in 1598. Being unaware that this word had not been made up yet did not improve Muhren's lacklustre mood. Likewise, being the great wordsmith he was, Shakespeare had also not gotten around to creating the words unaware and lacklustre, on account of being born in 1564. So that sentence would also have caused unwanted concern. Lacklustre and unwanted weren't available to shake a spear at.

As a tip to any would-be traveller of the fourth dimension, I strongly recommend avoiding unnecessary words if you were unaware of where they came from. Uneducated time travellers wanting to avoid unsolicited attention should undoubtedly avoid all words undone by beginning with the prefix '*un.*' Undeniably, unintentionally undoing your attempt at keeping a low profile would result in a problem, usually the loss of life. As a test, see how many of these '*un*' words you can count in this paragraph. Consider this your first test to see if you would be eligible to be a time traveller.

Kiko pulled her best counter-commoner face she could muster.

"There was no harm meant. My brother has had a case of the old typhoid fever. He is not feeling well so we are on our way to a church."

This lie seemed to work. When speaking to an idiot, it was always best to speak slowly and without abbreviation. If you were still worried, you could try simplifying the words to help them understand. This dark-haired Elf seemed to understand and she wanted nothing to do with a fever.

So off she popped with her onion scent and her sweaty uni-brow.

"Muhren?" Kara turned to him. "Get off me."

CHAPTER SEVENTEEN PART TWO

RUNNING AWAY FROM THE ONION WOMAN

A blurred darkness. Earth was a dangerous place, a planet where a group of strangers would willingly gather to cheer at an individual's execution. How a numberless, seemingly random lot of strangers could unite in unison to witness pain was not unusual on this world at this time. To flourish and thrive at the passing of someone's life. To consume the atmosphere and to be lost in the thrilling moment. Dark friendships were forged here as they watched death unfold together, applauding as the life left a person's eyes leaving a dead-eyed stare. To feel joy as the last gasp of the soul frantically called out searching for a person to help. *Just one.* They only needed one person to care. But there is no one. In the maddening crowd of bloodlust, there was no helping hand. Only boos and hisses from people with their hands outstretched to rip the flesh clean off your bones if they could. To dig their fingernails through muscle. To have you become completely undone. *Vultures of man's demise.*

This was what Kiko saw here now. That blurry darkness of the potato sack that had once obscured her senses had now been lifted. Under these grey clouds, from this wooden platform, she saw only a sea of malcontents set ablaze with harrowing glee. From up high she saw how happily the workers threw more firewood to the pile and grinned broadly at what was to come.

She remembered being led up the heavy wooden stairs by her executioner to be, just as well as she'd remembered the rest of the events that led her here. She remembered it all.

Her arms were manacled around an old ship's mast behind her back. Try as hard as she might, she could not break free. The clicking and cracking of burning kindle started smoking beneath her feet. A cloud of black smoke began to bellow and feed the cheers. Kiko choked on the damp rag bundled around her mouth.

She desperately looked for help. If she looked left she'd have seen Kara. If she looked right she'd have seen Muhren. They could not save her. Time had run out. In the crowd, she saw a child hiding behind their mother. If for a second she could have thought this child might have done something to save her, it spat at her and skulked in behind her parents.

There was no mistake as the crowds applauded. *They were all there to see the face of the witches that die today.*

I will admit that it is uncommon to split a chapter into two parts. *I appreciate that.* But likewise, these events in 1524 would have been too long for a single chapter. Unfortunately, this still counts as the seventeenth chapter. So for anyone who prides themselves on speed reading a chapter at a time, you'd best get reading. Large bodies of text usually needed to be split into several parts. Fantasy readers may already know of the style that I'm '*Tolkien*' about, so it's not unheard of. Likewise, writing a chapter about time travel is difficult. When time is no longer a constraint, then who is to say you can't begin the chapter at the end? We could have just as easily begun with the jokes of the hilarious Kara, who had found great glee in Muhren's discomfort with the lady now only known as the Onion Woman. This name, Onion Woman, being of Kara's design. She took great delight in teasing Muhren about the events that had unfolded. The look on his face was apparently something he should have seen for himself. It was something to behold. She took wild jabs at what their future might have been like together. About the number of onion babies that could have lived in their big onion house on Cheesy Lane. When was the wedding? Would her uni-brow be the best man? And whether or not you had to register to buy soap and perfume as wedding gifts. This comedy gold was entirely lost on Muhren. Kara's musing, whilst either hilarious or cruel (*This usually depends on your own subjective opinion of insult based comedy.*) seemed only to agitate him and was not appreciated. Kiko was currently trying her best not to get involved. The joking jibes and teasing taunts served nothing more than a distraction. Although this had been the exact kind of distraction that Kara had needed to take her mind off wearing the robes that she had previously refused to accept. On the surface, she looked no different to the rest of the bygone era that walked around them.

Kiko was on fire, metaphorically speaking. That moment of pure adrenaline-fuelled focus when she had 'accommodated' these clothes had still not faded. *'Objective A'* was complete! Now it was time to haunt the child-snatching bogeyman, or rather bogeyfairy. This being said, the idea of a bogeyman conjured up images of a nightmarish minion of fear. Something to prowl the nights and torment the young. Beware, beware, the bogeyman comes.

A shadow in the night.

Creeping. Crawling. Hiding. Waiting. Always waiting. Always watching. Lying there under your bed. You can't ever let your leg slip as you sleep. Otherwise, be damned by a demented demon, determined on dragging you down to darkness. Seen within the emptiness of a wardrobe door slowly creaking open. Heard within the scrapes of a tree against a window. He is everywhere.

However, a bogeyfairy sounds utterly ridiculous. This pertaining to the fact that the word *'bogey'* is in no way scary. A wererat, werecat or werebat all lead to the same image of a beast-like humanoid. We as a species know exactly what the *'were'* of *'werewolf'* ascertains to because we know the story of the wolf-man so well. The term *'bogey'* conjures images of some snot ridden, sneezing, overly-sized-nosed-having drip of a fairy with a lisp reminiscent of a man with a blocked nose, and such an idea was not where I thought this chapter would take me when I first began writing it. Life always had a way to turn out differently than you expected. Bogey also sounded too similar to boogie. Thanks to the 1980s, boogie was not scary. *You can boogie all you want.* Dance your heart out. Nobody cares. Except for your children. *'For the love of God, why are you dancing? Please stop!'* Your children are about to be the worlds first case of a person dying from embarrassment. *Good going.*

Also, if the idea of a dancing fairy is scary to you, then I'm not watching a horror movie with you. This thought process was lifted, almost verbatim from Kiko's mind as she made her way through Paris. However, it was probably in her best interest to focus on what was currently happening around her at the moment.

This was in this way not too different to what was unfolding on the other side of the great French capital. As an eager Onion Woman, who was thinking about her own best interest, frantically sold out a dark-haired man with a case of typhoid fever and his two female associates. The Orc had told on our trio and he had been believed and now the city guards were on the hunt. These two guards, with their well-kept metal armours, looked a tiny bit bizarre. So little time had passed between being told of this creature of fire and now looking for it, they had not had the time to construct a good wanted poster. What they had was… it was… it was probably a better idea to have had no poster at all. Three stick men and a stick dog had been all they could muster. Namonar having been made of fire wasn't even properly displayed. Instead of drawing fire on or around the stick dog, they merely wrote '*dog but fire*' and even had an arrow pointing towards the dog, in case you couldn't tell what had been drawn. This fat Dwarf and Orc guard combo were failing art class if nothing else.

The allure of the gold they had offered was enough to entice the Onion Woman. She was at least getting something out of today, even if it wasn't a shower. The guards now knew to look for a gingery girl, a blonde Half-Elf and the man of their dreams. *Neither guard really felt comfortable with that last part of the description.*

There was a splitter and a splatter as rain began to fall. Seeing how no one had invented waterproof clothing yet, the crowds quickly disappeared. This allowed Kiko to gauge which buildings would be best suited to cast their divination spell in. *Wherever the dampening crowds didn't retreat to would be their goal.* As luck would have it, there was one such door. This door, like most doors, was a part of a building. This building was grey and wooden just like the rest. As the three peered through the widows of it, they could see no one inside. *Perfect!* Finally, things were looking up! The building had the appearance of a theatre or a hippodrome. Rows of benches faced a pair of oversized curtains that hid a rustic, or technically state of the art, staging area. Muhren saw fit to bar the door they had entered through with a nearby metal candlestick holder.

This room was cold, I mean seriously come on what did you expect? There was no central heating. Light poured in from the windows, giving a quaint but creepy feeling to the dust that floated in the air. Kara was the first to peer in behind the curtain. As her floating head poked on through there was not a soul to be seen. *This would do very nicely!* A divination spell was easy to cast. All you needed was a chain and a black opal crystal. Sorry, all you really needed was a chain, a black opal crystal, a clear image in your mind of what you wanted to find and the ability to cast magic. As Kiko held the chain in a way that allowed the crystal to hang freely she spoke the magic words. She knew what she wanted. *She wanted answers.* An amber coloured light blasted all around her as a giant translucent compass emerged at her feet. *There was a rush of light as the stage curtains flew open!* Kiko turned her head frantically merely to see the rear end of a hilt as it struck her face. *'Crack!'* This force being enough to knock her out. Two axes appeared from purple smoke as Kara watched the theatre flood with guards. Muhren summoned a shield as if from nowhere. On it could be seen the emblem of a wolf howling at a mechanical moon. With it he summoned his greatsword and rested it atop of the shield as it rose, ready to stab anyone who got close.

The pair turned to see Kiko fall.

"Aye! See here, now! Drop it or the lassy gets it!" The Dwarf that had struck Kiko now held a dagger to her unconscious throat. "Ah am deadly serious, lad!"

Try imagining what a Scottish/French Dwarf would sound like if you're too worried about Kiko and the gang's prospect of seeing another day. *Or just keep reading.*

Have you ever been a part of a moment that was so awful that time seemed to almost stand still? To witness something so horrific that you were powerless to stop it? If you are one of the select few unfortunate enough to say yes, then you could begin to imagine what Kiko felt as her hooded bringer of death walked ever closer. Kiko's fingers fumbled awkwardly behind her, obstructed by the weight of the ever so clunky manacles that trapped her to her post. She watched, panic-stricken, as he lit his torch. Her heart was beating so fast that it hurt as she struggled like a snared beast trying to free herself. Under his mask, Mister Executioner was having the best kind of day imaginable. As he approached he knew each stride brought him closer to fulfilling God's righteous will. *Tonight there would be one less heathen and the world would be ever grateful for it.*

These *'heathens'* being my three main protagonists puts me in an awkward position. But a writer does what he must. If a hero must die, then die a hero will. I cannot stop it, I am only the narrator. I too share the inability to alter the outcome. Time is set in stone and cannot be undone when the dice are cast. Maybe it's not too late to change this books name to *'Mister Executioner?'* I'm sure at least one person out there would be interested in the tales of a French, witch-killing extraordinaire. This faceless harbinger of God's will walked up to them and paraded his torch around like a great prize. The crowds cheered and roared with the screams of anticipation. Kara, who was some half a dozen feet away from Kiko swore and writhed as she tried to break free. Her body crashing like a wave against the rocks that was her own stake. Frantically stirring, hoping the chains would loosen. Muhren had retired into a final moment of solitude and reflection as he waited for the end.

The executioner raised his torch one final time and eagerly thrust it into the debris of wood that lay at the gang's feet! *The clicking and cracking of the burning kindle caused smoke to rise.* The joyous catcalling reached a fever pitch. *But then it just stopped.* One could say it stopped almost as if by some sort of curious magic. The disappointed executioner raised his fallen torch with confusion. *'What was wrong with it?'* To his dismay, the flames were still intact. It almost looked alive. It almost looked like a wolf…

Namonar turned in a heated blaze, as an inferno of glowing teeth seared this bad man's face with an all-engulfing bite. The guard dropped the wolf-faced-torch as he yelped and pleaded, holding his melted face. Doing so freed Namonar's body from the torch as it landed with a metallic *'thunk.'* This stunning spectacle of a canine bounded forth in a three-pointed motion and melted each of the chains restraining his friends as he landed. From across the boardwalk a gathering of guards ran forth. They were met by a growling Namonar, who summoned a great wall of fire from his shoulders. Crossbow bolts turned to ash as they flew through the air and it was as if spears had no effect on this burning pup. It was within this commotion that had arisen from several hundred people witnessing a canine of ignited indignation turning on the local militia that Kara, Kiko and Muhren had made their escape. Hidden in amongst a few hundred terrified souls who were more worried about their own self-preservation than whoever was in front of them. Self-interest and self-preservation were two of the key personality traits that had always defined the inhabitants of Earth. These definitive traits often led to moments of blindness. Wherein these self-serving, terrified egomaniacs couldn't see the forest for the trees or the witch that ran beside them as they fled in a maddened crowd.

See, this is why a dog is man's best friend! A cat would not care if you were about to be burned alive. A cat would wait until the fires settled into a lukewarm state and roll in the heat. Then be mad that you got your ashen remains all over its clean coat. Namonar was a good boy, even though the people of Paris thought otherwise. *Beauty was often recorded in the eye of the beholder.* In this way, the same person can be thought of as either a hero and villain, depending on who named them. Or in this case, Namonar was our trio's saviour but also the terrified talk of the entire city. Word had spread fast from the mouths of these people whose eyes had witnessed such fresh horrors. This wasn't the first time a canine had been used to rain fire down upon its enemies. The first being in the far off reaches of the second world war. This war was either nearly eighty years before any of the gang's usual day-to-day affairs or over four hundred years on from this time of witch burning. *I guess this was depending on how you looked at it.* This perplexing temporal tongue twister for the mind was the exact reason most people avoided time travel. It took a certain kind of person to keep up with the times and to realise '*it could be both.*' In this war, the Soviet Union had a uniquely bizarre, amazingly fantastical and horrifically horrendous idea. Some pre-Russia Russian decided that the best way in fighting off the German army was to strap literal bombs onto literal dogs. The idea being that these bomber dogs would run under enemy tanks. *Boom!* No more tank; which was great. Unless you actually like dogs more than humans. Then this was a terrible outcome. But not nearly as bad, as it turned out as their training technique. These kamikaze canines were trained using Soviet tanks. As it turned out on the big day, Soviet dogs can't speak German. When these dogs saw a German tank for the first time they had no idea what it was. These Soviets had joined together in unison in greatly overestimating the brains of their hounds of war. These dogs did however recognise the tanks they were trained to blow up. So no more Soviet Union tank. But more importantly, no more Soviet Union dog.

In terms of the greatest failed plans of all time, the gang's '*Objective B*' was definitely one of them. You could say it was right up there with the bomber dogs. Having a whole city perpetrating a literal witch hunt for you was considered the polar opposite of keeping a low profile. If you were to imagine this *'Objective B'* as a glass dish, then imagine if you will, climbing up a really tall ladder. *Have you done that?* Are you okay with heights? Alright, now throw this dish as hard and as high as you can. Imagine the point of impact when that dish hits the Earth. How many tiny shards there would be? *That's what this plan had become.*

It was exactly twenty-seven streets over from the site of the would-be execution where we found a breathless Kara, Kiko and Muhren. This tangled Web of a path that had led them here had consisted of the grand total of seventeen left turns, eleven rights, four U-turns, fifty or so terrified screamers and three magic users who desired nothing more than to leave France and never come back.

"Psssssst!" A voice called out from a door that was ajar. This being entirely different to how a *'jar'* is a *'jar.'* From behind this door, which wasn't anything like a jar, a young girl beckoned them to enter.

Even at this range, she had a visible facial scar, no hair and a single white eye. Usually, if a creepy porcelain child asks you to enter their house, you'd say no. But options were thin when an entire city wanted you dead. For some weird reason, this little bald thing knew Kiko's name.

"Mademoiselle Kiko, I bring a message from your future." The would-be fortune teller declared brazenly. Kara entered the home, eyeballing this girl furiously as she did so. "Oh fantastic, I see Kara still lives…" The girl sighed.

"Who the flying *truck* are you?" Kara enquired aggressively as she towered over the child.

It's important to note Kara had not intended to use the word truck. Kiko, in her wisdom, had chosen to use a *'parental lock'* on Kara when casting the translation spell. Altering any offensive words she may end up using with the closest approximate alternative. Kara did not trust this *'trucking shady looking bunt'* and she wasn't afraid to say so.

"Mademoiselle Kara, I am Charity." The pale girl gave a near toothless grin as she bowed sarcastically, spitting on Kara's shoes.

"MUHREN-NEVER-SUMMONED-THAT-WOLF-THING-BACK-THEN-YOU-SHOULD-HAVE-ALL-DIED!" Charity proclaimed as a single terrified word, shielding herself as Kiko and Muhren grabbed at an extremely vexated Kara that had gone to punch a child in her stupid spitting face.

Kiko looked at her brother with concern.

"Oh yeah!" Muhren said dumbly into a room of angry-eyed stares.

"What does that have to do with anything?" Kara inquired as she grimaced at Charity. "We're going trucking home!"

"Gawd, you're so stu-u-upid!" Charity sneered back as Kiko grabbed at her Half-Elven friend's collar. "You can't." Charity stuck her tongue out at Kara. "The red'un with glasses said you couldn't." She pointed towards Kiko. "That'un said I had to stop you to save yourselves."

"Hold up, we aren't actually listening to this little pre-pubescent brat, are we?" Kara looked over her friends with a face of scornful contempt. This child ripped straight from a horror movie had just spat on her like an animal!

"You said I should say Kara was actin' like her ma' if she disagreed too m..." The look on Charity's face seemed to indicate she knew she had gone too far.

The look on Kara's face seemed to indicate she was considering giving a charitable donation of a black eye or a slit throat to the girl who just compared her to her mother. *No one was ever brave enough to make that comparison for a good reason.* Kara didn't care if she was just a little girl, one more insult like that and she'd have no more teeth. Besides, Charity's teeth were rotten and yellow anyway. So Kara reckoned she'd be doing her a favour.

As it would appear, they weren't listening to Charity at all. From what Kiko could gather by putting together all of the information, it seemed that an alternate version of them existed. If Muhren hadn't re-summoned Namonar, then how did the fire-wolf save the day? How did Charity know their names and how to trigger Kara with the perfect comparison? The odds of a complete stranger knowing the names of everyone was about three-hundred-and-fifty-thousand to one. The odds of Namonar being summoned when his owner was unable to do so were zero. A child they had never met before knowing all this was impossible, unless she had already been told.

There must have been another set of Kiko, Kara and Muhren here that day. This meant no one was going home just yet. *The trio still had three lives yet to save.*

Chapter Seventeen part three

WHY ARE WE STILL IN FRANCE?

It is a commonly accepted rule that any large body of text can be split up into three parts. The people of Earth saw the number three as being a somewhat magical number; and who was I to break tradition? This is a book about magic after all. There was once three wise men, three musketeers and three blind mice. Likewise, it was common for stories to revolve around three central figures. This being deemed the perfect ratio in which to divide a reader's attention. Too many characters *'spoiled the pot'* and diluted the attention of the spotlight. This resulted in characters being underdeveloped. Too few characters in the mix and the hero would run the risk of seeming overpowered or this might end with the world around them feeling underdeveloped. This of course wasn't the case with romance based materials, where three was the loneliest number.

Again my apologies to any speedrunners trying to reach the end of the seventeenth chapter in a single sitting. *Likewise, sorry to anyone who hated the idea of being in France for so long.* But to be fair, Kiko, Muhren and Kara hated it more. All they wanted was to go home!

Trying to explain to Kara and Muhren how they had only survived because they had helped themselves to do so in their future had been painful. The concept of a self sustaining paradox was, in its entirety, lost on her friend and brother. They were in no mood for hypothetical temporal terminology. Not with the day they'd just had. Hearing how their only option (*If they wanted to stay alive!*) was to go back in time again was infuriating. It was time travel that had gotten them into this mess, therefore time travel would only cause more trouble, Kara had adamantly decided. Kara's unshakeable determinism to return to her own time was getting under Kiko's skin and beginning to annoy her. The continual explanation of how simply 'choosing to leave' would directly *'guarantee all of their collective deaths'* was becoming exhausting. Everyone was wound up and they all just wanted to go to sleep. But ideally not in the way that was for all of eternity in a wooden box.

But there was nothing for it, they would all have to go back to the scene of their failed execution once more. Kara now found herself looking over the scene of her attempted death from the sanctuary of some scaffolding that lay at the back of the giant courtyard where she had almost been executed less than an hour before. It still felt weird seeing it unfold again now. The execution was happening either for the second or first time, depending on how you chose to look at it. It was like the falling Orc all over again. Upon this construction site, she could see a pulley system that held some stonework up high on a rope. If this mechanism was hit at the right time and at the right angle, she assumed it would cause the entire series of rudimentary scaffolding around her to collapse like a house of cards. From under her robed hood, she could see a similarly dressed Kiko as she discretely planted little jars of frozen fire not too far from the jubilating crowds. It felt somewhat bizarre for Kiko to see her past self about to be burned alive. *Also, that peasant gown did nothing for her figure!* The jars she was currently placing would explode at their chosen locations. These locations had been chosen to be in places where they would do the least amount of damage to a person, but would still be dangerous enough to guarantee that the fleeing, frantic crowd would be herded in a direction that lent their past selves the best degree of cover as they escaped within the maddening crowds. As she placed one of these jars she caught a glimpse of a disguised Muhren as he handed the unsuspecting executioner a secretly wolf-ridden torch. Mister Executioner had no idea of what he was walking into or the fire-wolf currently lying in wait within the depths of the flame from his torch. He was too distracted by the idea of dealing with the heretic heathens and killing witches.

Speaking of dealing, a deal had all too recently been made with a ghastly looking Charity. But not the version of Charity they had already met, but Charity's past self. This little vagabond girl, despite being named after one, was not all too charitable. The idea of being the gang's mysterious messenger on how to save their lives had not been as enticing as one would have hoped. Charity had much preferred the idea of being the gang's mysterious messenger, who got had been bribed with a gold necklace. Kiko was pulling out all the stops into making sure that their past selves would be saved, to be fair, her life depended on it. The gold necklace that was used to bribe charity had until right now, belonged to Kara. Having had her jewellery *'stolen'* by the creepy little bald girl had made Kara's childish feud with Charity worsen. But the loss of this necklace was vital in assuring that the future version of Charity would come to the gang's rescue when the time came for it. Even if Kara couldn't quite wrap her head around the idea, as to her Charity had already helped them. *It was rather like a down payment to assure their survival.* If it helps anyone confused, it was their *'present'* selves in their past, talking to a previous version of Charity (*that had never met them before*) assuring that their now *'past'* selves were not about to die in what was now the near future of them escaping their execution. Even though the execution was technically in their past from their current perspective, they had gone back to before it had happened. Confusing time loops like this is why people often avoided writing about time travel.

Kara swore by any god that was listening; even if she had to get a shovel and exhume every single last peasant's grave in Paris, she was getting this necklace back the second she got back home to her own time.

Namonar sunk his teeth into Mister Executioner's face, both for the first time and like he had done before. This was the first time Kara had smiled since the teasing of the Onion Woman. A sinister, revengeful grin broke across her face as she broke the mechanism that held the pulley in place. All of that rock slammed down as if it wanted to prove Sir Isaac Newton's theory of gravity one-hundred-and-sixty-three years before he had first theorised it. *Although if a crate of concrete had landed on his head, instead of an apple, it would have simply been a theory on how a big pile of rocks will kill you on the spot.* The scaffolding shattered sending chunks and pillars of wood tumbling and flying in numerous directions. This sudden flurry of ligneous debris fell with a mighty din. Falling buildings of any variety always inspired nearby onlookers to put as much distance as possible between themselves and the possibility of an accidental close encounter with death. After all who didn't have a fear of being buried alive under a pile of debris?

The uproar from Kiko's explosions turned the fleeing crowd back in on itself. These people unwittingly found themselves being herded, or rather redirected, like running water gushing through a freshly dug out trench. Being caught between a hound from hell, the spontaneous bouts of fire that was now erupting as if from nowhere across the courtyard and all the sudden semi-constructed building that had randomly started collapsing, the guards were too distracted to see their would-be prizes escape. Technically, Kiko, Kara and Muhren were now escaping twice. Had these guards been aware of how they had allowed them to escape twice in the same day, they probably have all spontaneously collapsed from shock or embarrassment on the spot. To fail killing someone twice within the exact same moment was a rare opportunity, and not one anyone was looking to repeat.

Kiko had made a repeated point that none of them were allowed to be seen by their former selves. The magical feedback loop created when an entity saw its future self apparently deleted that time duplicate. This is to say that if *'future'* Kiko, Kara or Muhren had been spotted by the *'past'* Kiko, Kara or Muhren they would have simply have been wiped from time. No one knew what happened when a person was wiped from time, as no one who had ever been wiped had ever just spontaneously popped back. The fear of this unknown led people to be resistant to try. With the day they'd all had, no one was willing to be a lab-rat for what would happen if their past selves did unwittingly blow their cover. So as the past gang retreated to the west, the future gang went east. Discretely skulking and sneaking as they went. *However, as they ran Kiko felt the pulling draw deep in her gut of another magical artefact, not too far away in the city!* Much to Kara's disdain, Kiko insisted they all had to go see.

"We have to go see what it is! We simply can't just leave it here!" Kiko demanded.

"Are you crazy?" Kara snapped back. "We have to go home!"

Unfortunately Muhren had agreed with his sister, so the trio of frantically fleeing wizards quickly found themselves on the outskirts of the grand Parisian city. This sinking feeling of magical power had led them to what appeared to be an old abandoned church. Now, I'm no detective, but the fact that it was a church felt fairly evident from the big ornate cross that stuck out from the roof above the front door. *Let's just call it a hunch.* It was also a hunch that this building was abandoned. This felt like a safe assumption due to all the vines of creeping ivy that had wrapped around the side of the building and ensnared it in its grasp. Again, I'm not a detective, but all of the smashed in windows and the missing *(and potentially stolen)* door of this bedraggled building felt like other key giveaways. I mean, I might be wrong. I have been so before. Perhaps this church belonged to the patron saint of missing doors, broken glass, messy floors and untamed gardening. But that felt like a reach.

The sinking feeling had hit a crescendoed fever pitch. The tingling sensation that had gripped their guts had led them by the hand to this exact point. The magical artefact was definitely inside this church and it had brought them like moths to a flame. Two of these moths were fairly happy to be here, these being the Attetson children. All the third moth, Kara, had wanted to do was go home and have a long, hot bath. To soak away with a face mask on in a tub full of thick bubbles, relaxing suds and cleansing oils to wash away her stresses from almost being burned alive. After all, water was the exact opposite of fire, so there was some logic there. She had also fully intended upon twirling a dagger several times into the ceiling as a petty act of revenge against Kiko and Muhren for making her stay here, as she knew Kiko would be deeply annoyed by the property damage done to her house. Actually, no. With Cassandra and Kiko having had so recently lost Vincent, such an act of petty vandalism would be in terribly bad taste. *But there would also be wine.* Lots of red wine to help her forget how awful her day had been. But this awful day was still continuing! *Why?* Because no one was listening to her! Who cared if there was some dumb magical item lost somewhere in medieval Paris? *Let it remain lost!* Whatever it was, it was not worth dying over. Kara thought over Vincent's death, both as a Changeling and as a baby. If traipsing over olden day France was Kiko's way of dealing with the bereavement of her brother, then maybe Kara should humour her. She would play along. Well, she would try. She was still a stubborn mule and she was having an awful day. But she'd try biting her tongue, metaphorically speaking of course. Kara would do it for Kiko's sake. If the hot-tempered Half-Elf being at least willing to try and keep her composure *(especially after the day she was having!)* wasn't a testament towards how much she cared for her friend, then nothing was. Kara wouldn't be keeping quiet for just any old run of the mill person. But if her pseudo-sister needed to do this, then that's what they'd do.

The inside of the church was as barren and as utterly crap as the outside was. A desolate and deserted denomination dedicated to some long-forgotten decrepit and crumbling dainty deity. A plethora of cracked and broken pews lay across a floor of mossy stone. A giant and cracked stone altar stood at the back of the room. It looked like something had been carved into the stone, but whatever it was had been consumed by the ravages of time. It was now almost completely indiscernible. Faded away, relegated to nothing more than a distant memory. But the metal chair that sat behind it? *Now that was something special!*

A magnificent throne of towering authority. A splendid structure that stood defiant to the passing of time. Unchanged and unmoving. Unyielding and powerful. It stood in a sharp juxtaposition to the rest of the dilapidation suffocating the rest of the church. Whereas time and nature had invaded and conquered the rest of the room, it was as if both mother nature and father time had been too scared to encroach upon this holy chair. Not a single speck of dirt or rust dared to touch upon it. A hallowed and consecrated ground of holy respect. The kind of thing that no man, woman, child, beast, creature or insect would dare desecrate. Either out of fear or respect. Moss and ferns refused to grow in a perfect four-inch diameter across the floor around it. Spider webs and rat droppings wouldn't dare deface it, but the rest of this room was fair game. *So mind your step!* The rafters crawled with wildlife. These beams fluttered with the sounds of tiny unseen wings and squeaked with a sweet chirping. Happy-go-lucky mice played in the field of broken benches and ferns. None of these creatures seemed too concerned about their new visitors and paid them no second thought. Perhaps these critters were too busy paying their undying and holy respects to the patron saint of missing doors, broken glass, messy floors and untamed gardening.

"No? It can't be!" Muhren proclaimed as he dashed towards the mysterious chair. He knew exactly what this metallic seat of ebony steel and golden highlights was and what it was for, even if he couldn't believe he was seeing on in person. "It's an Åethínaríum!" He said with about as much eager excitement as a hyper child opening his gifts on a jolly Christmas morning. The term Åethínaríum was lost on the two girls, who just stood staring at him blankly.

"It's said that if a person sits in any of these things then they would apparently be able to talk directly with the gods! *Crazy right?* I think the Elves made them. See that blue rock in the eye, that's a crystal from the god's home planet, I think. Yeah, oh and see those handcuff looking slabs? They would strap you in, in case you went crazy from seeing the deity or from what they said to you. Oh and those spikes by the shoulders? If you upset the god or angel? *WHACK!* Different Åethínaríums - I think they're supposed to be like, what, nine of them? - were said to grant you an audience with your chosen ethereal or celestial entity. Say you found an Åethínaríum for Thor. Boom, you're talking to Thor. Or maybe some lackey of his, I dunno. Find one for Chronos? *Boom, audience with the time god!* I believe olden day wise men had been gifted a direct audience with different ethereal and celestial entities. Like you had to be worthy of the audience, or something? These wise men, priests, vicars, whatever, would use these chairs to learn and spread the word of whatever god the chair was made to commune with. *But this chair shouldn't exist!* All of the Åethínaríums were said to have been destroyed like ten thousand years ago! Either by the followers of some rival god, yeah, or by the gods themselves. These things are supposed to be a myth!"

I'm sorry, no. *No.* I'm going to have to stop Muhren there. His overly simplistic bastardisation and trivialised debasement of the true history, nature and actual purpose of the Åethínaríum hurt to listen to. Any self-respecting history teacher would have graded this attempt as a C- at best. He was correct in his observation that the Åethínaríum was impossibly old. It had dated back to approximately 4,000 BC. Muhren was right, there was an eye of hard cast metal that sat on top of the Åethínaríum. The eye itself was very ornately and delicately carved. And yes a blue stone did sit in the centre of it. However, this special sapphire did not come from Eden, the home of the gods. This should have been obvious, as this chair was made on planet Earth, so naturally, all the rocks and minerals had also come from Earth. The ancient Elves and Dwarves had called the stone '*Zűll-yuill-ënhéllem-ŕomianeske.*' Not a single historian could agree on how to pronounce this word. The only real mention of Zűll-yuill-ënhéllem-ŕomianeske (*pronounced 'zule yule en-hellim romian esck' for anyone struggling!*) comes from the '*Dwarven book of Rocks,*' otherwise known as '*Thaemekillö.*' Thaemekillö is the oldest books ever discovered. It dates back to 3,500 BC. Written by the Dwarves of the mountain Thren, Thaemekillö was a Dwarven documentation of mineral deposits and rock formations. Its words were a series of runes carved into sheets of pure stone, these sheets were clasped together by a hundred or so metal rings that ran down the spine. A rough translation of the god stone follows below.

> *'Velles Day. Deep deeds of devoted digging divulged the secrets*
> *of the Earthen crust. Many sleeps reported being required.*
> *Deep, deep dark beneath the foot of mountain soil.*
>
> *Drara-vyn (*Dwarven*) Hyemmers and Packs (*hammers and pickaxes*)*
> *cracked pious stone of Earth. We dig deep. We dig well. Praise stone*
> *and resolve for bountiful harvest. Mines were tall and mines big.*
>
> *Words speak of shimmering beauty. Bright beauty. Eyes weep and*
> *hearts gallop at sight. Was said worthless now are ruby, diamond and*
> *emerald. Such words fill heart with Murruil. (*The blasphemous treason
> and heresy of disliking rocks, mining and things of the Earth.*)*
>
> *A summer's blue sky trapped in a stone.*
> *Zűll-yuill-ënhéllem-rómianeske.*
>
> *Drara-vyn and Xuin~Alves (*Elves*) bow alike*
> *before the bountiful stone of god."*

A second recording came from the Elven document, *'The Book of Heretics.'* This book was approximately a hundred years older than Thaemekillö. It was apparently a complete and thorough documentation of the partnership between the Elves and Dwarves but has since faded into dust. A rough translation of this overly long name, Zűll-yuill-ënhéllem-rómianeske, is *'blue rock that brings God.'* Although I much prefer Professor Llanam's (*an Elven historian from 1872*) translation, who wrote that the name could have been a translation of *'a summer's blue sky trapped in stone.'*

This blue rock had powered the whole Åethínaríum, by granting the person that sat in this contraption the ability to transmit their consciousness straight into the heavens. To directly beam their conscience right into the arcane dimension of Eden. However the Åethínaríum chair wasn't crafted by the Elves, so Muhren got that bit wrong. Elves lacked the physical prowess and skills with metalwork to craft anything as intricate as the eye, or the chair as a whole. Especially back then. They didn't have the means or the tools. No, the chair was crafted by the hands and tools of the Dwarves. However, the concept behind the Åethínaríum, and the actual science behind these chairs' simplistic design, was far beyond anything the limited brains of the Dwarves could conceive or even begin to comprehend. The idea behind the Åethínaríum, all of the plans and blueprints, had been of Elven design.

The nine Åethínaríums stood as a testament to what the Elves and Dwarves could achieve if they put down their bows and axes and worked together for once. The unison of these great species had created the ability to transcend the mortal coil and seek celestial counsel from transdimensional deities. *Not bad going.* This was rarely a 'direct line' through to a god though, and it was unclear whether or not if these seraphic entities and old gods, which had been beseeched for divine guidance, had been okay with the idea of being called upon and summoned in this manner. Using an Åethínaríum was also extremely difficult. Straps and shackles were laced into the arms of the Åethínaríum because of the apparent risks. *After all, people are frail.* Please bear in mind how fragile the human mind is. Epileptic seizures can be caused by a person witnessing a flashing light in the wrong way, and a person could be driven insane by schoolyard bullying. So just exactly how do you think a person would cope with seeing an angel or a god, or any other creature that would defy their concept of reality? Some people would go instantly blind from witnessing a celestial's true form. Their eyes would pop and flame in their heads. Some would be driven into a spontaneously deranged state of senseless, mind-boggling insanity with a single word. This was to say nothing of the inherent risk of metaphorically packing up your consciousness into a tiny little box and punching it through a dimensional barrier and shipping it into another dimension that defied the laws of physics. *Yes, there were casualties.* Yes, there had been more than one. Also, the spikes were there above the shoulder-line of the chair were installed to satisfy the gods. If the entity you spoke to didn't like you, you were getting impaled!

"But the million-dollar question is; whose Åethínaríum is it?" Muhren continued as he ran in behind the metal chair towards a faded plaque that was built directly into the wall.

This metal sign was rusted and worn down into nothing more than an almost smoothed, featureless stubby slab. With a simple wave of Muhren's hand, this bronzed plate sprung back to life as the specks of dust and crumbs of a forgotten life-age crept back into existence around the metallic picture. Dragging with them the stylised shapes and substance of the engraved image that had long since been lost to the passing of time. This intricately etched regal decoration that was restoring itself through the fading dirt was an image split into four parts. *Of four men.* As a great many details crept their way back into existence around the ornate carving, a deeper understanding returned along with them. This engraved slab of four parts told the story of four men. These four men had great wings that protruded from their backs. So they were Angels. One winged man was jamming a great spear through the neck of a dragon. Under his image was the name '*Michael*.' To the right of him was another winged man. He was stood in a forest, and in his right hand he held a long spindly flower. Under his image lay the name '*Gabriel*.' The bottom left image told the story of a third winged man. He was wielding a long ornate sword that he used to defend a small child in a burned-out city. Under his image was the name '*Raphael*.' The final image showed a winged man hovering above the ground. In his hands he held a highly detailed book that he seemed to be gripping tightly. The name '*Uriel*' was carved under his image. Above them read the words '*Deliver Us From Evil*' and beneath the four could be seen '*Oh almighty Archangels. Protect us from the Devil.*'

Muhren gasped. *Archangels were just about the most powerful creatures in existence.* The greatest of Demon slayers. The first who went to war with the Demons, long before Earth was even a thing. These four were the first angels and they were said to be great warriors, leaders and ornate oracles of the old gods' will. *They were the alphas of celestial society.* The top of rung of the ladder of a divine hierarchy. Seraphic, saintly spirits. *The power of the sun in an almost human form.* Pious and stout. Iron willed and iron skinned. So powerful in fact that it was said that no person from Earth had ever even seen one. But if this chair, this supposed Åethínarĺum, granted you an audience with them...? *Who knew what was possible?*

Muhren looked towards Kiko and Kara with a determined stare. An important part of the Arcane Intelligence Agency was their conversing with the Angelic realm. If these three had found something to make that task any easier, then they would be rewarded greatly by the Agency. Even if you ignored selfish gain, such an item couldn't just be allowed to sit here unguarded. Who knows what might try and seek an audience with the Angels and what they might do or learn.

"No!" Kara snapped. "We're not staying here any longer."

"But don't you see, Kara? What we have here is an opportunity to learn! And a chance to bring it back to the Agency. Just think of how well received that would be... Kiko we'd be free from the shadow of Vincent! We would finally be treated as our own people and not his afterthought! Okay, to be fair Kara, I know very little about you, and I'm sorry about that by the way, but there must be something you want? – And don't say to go home, you're smarter than that! – *Your family!* This chair will buy you enough power that you would never need to see them ever again. But also, can you imagine how annoyed they'd be if you brought back an actual Åethínarium? *They'd be so pissed at you!* You'd be the most successful De'Carusso ever!"

A faint smile cracked across Kara's lips as she thought over just how annoyed her father would be at Kara achieving something so grand.

"And Kiko? You want answers about Changelings, right? Angels have watched this planet for centuries! Think of all the knowledge you'd be gifted, first-hand!"

Kiko nodded in agreement. Muhren was right. They couldn't just leave the Åethínarium here. The risk was too great. Also, such a reward would almost make up for nearly being executed and would turn this whole day around from the greatest failure to a bountiful success. She could seek counsel on Changelings. To find some modicum of peace for Vincent's death. The real one, not that baby-killing monster. But she could also ask the Angels what they knew of the non consenting spirits disappearance and where they had gone!

Muhren set about preparing the Åethínarium. Kara took this opportunity to grab some fresh air. *(Fresh air being a secret code to go and smoke a cigarette!)* Kiko went with her to the outside of the church. Kiko grabbed Kara's hand a she was about to light her cigarette and pointed cautiously towards the horizon. Icy winds swept over the hillsides and through a small clearing of trees of a nearby forest. Within this small opening, the trees began to billow and move. The two girls saw a pair of cave trolls lurching and lumbering their way through the treeline.

I don't know if any of you have ever had the displeasure of actually meeting a cave troll before. *Perhaps you're related to one?* Or perhaps you married into a family where someone looks like one? Anyone who has seen a cave troll before would know that these horrendous creatures stand at a usual height of approximately eight-foot. A lifetime of unhealthy dieting (*Usually consisting of unwilling Goblins, fish, wild animals and trash.*) had resulted in most trolls being horrifically bloated around the waist and bulging at their putrid seems. *They were particularly fond of leftover cans of beer.* They are usually thick-skinned with broad double chins. They were slimy and usually quite gross. Their skin was pale and blotchy, due to a deep dislike of the sun. Often smelling like old cheese. They are also fairly unintelligent creatures. Based on this description alone, no doubt a lot of readers are beginning to question if their in-laws were actually troll people or not. If it helped you to gain a better understanding for comparison, trolls also lacked the mental prowess to understand either numbers or the concept of mathematics as a whole. They drooled when they spoke and disliked words longer than two syllables long. They were rather fond of wild acts of violence and barbarity.

However, trolls aren't actually people. They have never been and they never will be *'people.'* There was a common misconception of them being human-related. Some people even believed trolls were a form of reptile. *But technically they were a subspecies of big-cat.* Like a tiger or a lion, but just super fat and ugly and shaped in a giant humanoid form. The lesser spotted cave troll originated from eastern Europe and liked to spend their time in caves or in the shelter of large forests. They were by far the largest species of big-cat to be found on Earth. But they had no tail, no whiskers and they had flat ears. Given their nefarious scavenging lifestyle and diet structure, perhaps they were more comparable to giant bald, humanesque foxes. They were also the only species of cat that stood upright on two legs. Hence why people mistook them for humanoids. Cave trolls were also rather resilient and tough. *They were physically strong as well.* There were tales of whole groups of people being required to bring a single one down. Some people claimed that this was because trolls were too stupid to feel pain. Some said it was due to an ingrained feral brutality. But everyone agreed that these colossal brutes were rarely worth the risk or effort it took in fighting them. Due to how stupid the species was sometimes the best course of action was to ignore them entirely. Like a wasp or a hornet or an annoying drunkard, if left alone they would probably just leave. The best course of action was to avoid them and hope they hadn't noticed you. You could even pray if you believed such an act might help, but I'd probably do it quietly if I were you! *It would draw less attention.* If a fight should break out, keep a distance between you and the troll or trolls. You need to hit them hard and hit them fast with anything that could cause damage at long range. Unless you want to be pancaked.

So as Kiko and Kara watched these lumbering terrors from afar, wide-eyed and scared like a pair of deer on a busy road, an agreement was made to slowly retreat without drawing any attention to themselves. This decision to fall back inside the abandoned church was never actually vocalised. Perhaps their lack of words was a testament to how strong their friendship was; that they were so in-tune with each other's emotional frequency that they both knew what the other was thinking without the use of words. *Or perhaps nothing needed to be said because the risk of death or injury was so apparent that only a fool would feel the need to say it out loud.* The pair of terrified witches fled quickly back into the ruined church, wishing there had still been a door there for them to slam shut. Kiko fled to Muhren and prodded him in the side as she whispered.

"There are two cave trolls outside!"

Muhren didn't have long to think about what this would entail as a sudden roar from outside erupted as the cracked body of an uplifted tree smashed and splintered into a thousand pieces against the now crumbling doorway. *Kara was washed in a myriad of wooden remains and old stone as she ducked for cover!* A bountifully bounding troll of fatty flubber and fetid flabs stroppily stomped towards Kiko and Muhren, impolitely ignoring Kara as he ran. As he heftily headed in their direction he brandished a makeshift pitchfork aggressively overhead. Before this dumb old troll could do anything an amazing beam of pure light slammed into its pale torso. *A blazing beautiful ray of purely concentrated radiance lit up the entire room as it burned straight through the troll's now ashen torso.* Turning him into nothing more than glimmering dust and stinking smoke on the wind.

This beam had not come from Kiko. Nor had it been cast by Kara or Muhren. *It had originated from the eye sat on top of the Åethínarium!* And as a side note, perhaps trolls were right to not like the light. As it turns out it was painful, it hurt and it was deadly. Deadly enough that the second troll, having seen what happened, turned around and ran away. Like a terrified toddler who had just drawn on the walls. Or like a giant ogre-like creature that had just seen her mating partner explode into fire. Trolls mated for life, this troll had just seen her one true love disintegrate into nothing. She had not long given birth to a baby troll and without the support of her masculine counterpart, she would later become extremely desperate to find food to eat. In this animalistic desperation, she would become more and more careless. *She was hunting both for herself and her baby.* This desire to not die from starvation would drive her to be increasingly more and more reckless in her scavenging from the French city. This wild and injudicious approach to hunting would mean that in less than two months time, the same villagers that had cheered at the trios attempted execution today, would find themselves cheering once more as they tore both mother and child apart limb from limb. Avenging the children this troll had killed and tried to eat.

However, not long after Kiko, Kara and Muhren had seen this male troll burn up, they had all flopped to the floor like dead salmon. The Åethínaríum had ripped their minds clean out of their bodies and hurtled their inner-selfs across dimensions. Through entire Solar Systems, burning Nebulas, great star fields, medium star clusters, lesser star constellations, space battles and magnificent cosmic voids. Directly through giant weirdly coloured space clouds, through solar flares, black holes, hurtling past asteroids and comets and over ornate supernovas. Through it all until they now faced nothing but an endless void of black.

Kara couldn't help but think about how crap and rather dull this new found black looked. Eden wasn't all that and apparently neither was the Angels. Kiko grabbed Kara by the shoulder and span her on the spot to face the same way as the ginger witch, - sorry, *'female wizard'* - and her brother. Kara had been looking the wrong way! Kara now shared seeing the most amazing spectacle of the universe. A tall pale-skinned man. His skin was so white that it was like a piece of paper in a snowstorm. Four ornate brown wings protruded from his back and spread impressively across the void, they flapped gently around him as he hovered. Great golden chains were dangled from around his wrists and wrapped up high around his bare arms. A red cloth was wrapped around his right hand. This cloth was also wrapped around his waist and hung far towards the ground. In his right hand, he carried a long silver spear engraved with unknown designs. He wore golden boots and a golden belt. *He wore a silver armour that words couldn't even begin to describe.* This armour also covered his legs. His long brown hair hung freely from underneath a large golden helmet that completely sealed his face and all facial features underneath it. An immaculate sheet of shiny metal, entirely free of any dents or marks of either craftsmanship or battle. The only marking on it at all was a large '*M*' engraved into the front. Radiant light leaked from every pore of this impressive incandescent being, en-blazing the darkness around him.

"I am the Archangel Michael. And I've been waiting for you...."

Chapter Eighteen

THE WHITE QUEEN'S GAMBIT

I'd like to start off by apologising when I said that Archangel Michael's armour was indescribable. This was of course not true; there is nothing that cannot be explained so long as you're willing to take the time to explain it. But his armour was a very difficult thing to try and explain without either writing a two hundred-thousand word essay about the backstory behind its creation or without failing to do the armour the justice it rightfully deserved. The gold chains around his wrists were used by Michael and his three Archangel brothers to drag and pull all the stars of this thirteenth universe's reality into position across the cosmos. Preparing these celestial bodies and heaving gas giants into the most idyllic locations for the Divines (*like the one Kiko and Kara saw on the HMS Edinheim*.) to later find them and eventually grow into the planets that they would later become. Readying all the pieces of the maiden universe like a cosmic game of astronomical chess spanning all of existence. The totality of creation was strategically placed like the pieces of a giant engine. Every planet and star was powering something, somewhere. But the old gods always refused to say exactly what it was or where this infinitude of power was going. *Hopefully, all of creation wasn't part of something embarrassing, like the cogs of a great cosmic washing machine or running power to some benevolent deity's hairdryer.* The Archangel's chains were fused into his skin, this was probably because an average star burns at approximately ten-thousand Kelvin. Stars are also one of the heaviest things in existence. I would try and explain how just how heavy these luminary spheres were to you, but you're a species that still struggles to carry a couple of bags of grocery shopping from your car (*or bus*) to your home. I don't think your brain could quite comprehend just how heavy the weight would be of lugging a literal star across space. *Some numbers and stats were just never meant to be known.* Even seeing the numbers written as clear as day would mean almost nothing, like a secret code, to a person who hadn't spent an entire life trying to crack them. One of the secret riddles of the universe. *(If you must know, it would be like carrying $7,338,998,009^2$ ($5.3860892e+19$) bag of shopping $245,768,913,334^9$ ($3.27146700E+102$) miles. Are you happy now?)*

The illustrious silvered metals of Michael's cuirass were said to have been forged in the fires of the First Forge of Elysium and hammered into shape by Thor on top of his mighty anvil. *A cosmic call to war for Michael and his three brothers to avenge.* After the great and harrowing deeds of treason suffered by the gods at the very dawn of time from his fifth brother, the Great Betrayer, that had sought to undo the simplistic beauty of creation upon the very seed and foundation of its inception. To intercept and corrupt the universe at ground zero. This corruption ultimately led to the birth of the Demons, so in turn, the four Archangels set about creating lesser Angels to watch over the universe and keep these Demons in check. The spear of Michael was the first spear ever forged, much like how the sword of Raphael was the first sword. His spear was everything that a spear needed to be. No more. No less. It was pure metal, wreathed in ebonies, golds and whites. His helmet was featureless and hid his face for two reasons. The first was to conceal his true form from the physical mortal realm., his true image would pop your brain into a mushy, runny soup that would pour out of your ears like a squeezed tomato. Your eyes would be consumed with a bright white light as they turned to stone. This newfound pressure in your skull would make your teeth shoot out of your face. '*Pip-pap-pop*' and a '*racka-crack-clack*' as your teeth abandoned you and scattered across the floor. And here you would stand, a toothless, tomato-puree-brained, rock-eyed simpleton with a '*hurt-dee-durr*' unintelligible prattling of nonsensical words falling out from your mouth as you rocked back and forth with a literally brainless look upon your drooling face. The second reason he wore this golden helmet was out of shame for not being able to stop his fifth brother's betrayal.

So, that was Michael.

That is who was now stood in front of Kiko, Kara and Muhren inside this endless cosmic veil of ebony ink. It's hard to describe the exact feeling of standing in the dimension of Eden. It was somewhat similar to the sensation of taking a sudden plunge into a crisp, cold river as the waters wash over your face. The way your lungs would stiffen and you felt it hard to breathe. That way your senses and your nerve endings came to life and began to tingle all around you as your brain woke up. *Except Eden wasn't wet.* Also, it wasn't cold. But it wasn't hot either. It felt like nothing, but also everything. It was a shock to the system and it was alarming. Yet peaceful and tranquil, like sunbathing by a pool on a holiday. But again, it wasn't hot. If you're able to imagine such a thing, there was no temperature. There was no light, but it wasn't dark. It felt like you had just bitten into ice cream and like you were eating your favourite warm meal. It was somehow both euphoric and harrowing. Michael slowly landed, as he did so a small cosy room rippled into existence from his feet and around the astonished and bemused trio of startled wizards. This room of quaint, quality furnishings wrapped around them and sealed high above their heads. Three white chairs grew out of the floor. Originally as blossoming seedlings, growing into stubby little trees, then seamlessly transitioning into the chairs themselves. The whole spanning timeline of this colourless seat panned out and condensed into the blink of an eye.

"Please sit..." Michael voiced as he gestured to the seats.

His voice carried a reserved and subdued power behind every word he spoke. Like the roar of a lion, the rush of a waterfall or the tremble of an earthquake. A refined microscopic fleck of what majestic boundless elemental strength which potentially lay beneath the surface.

"Your helmet looks like a dustbin." Kara interrupted in a cold defiance as Kiko and Muhren glared at her with an all consumed bafflement.

The two Attetson siblings stared at her with wild bewilderment burning in their eyes, they looked at Kara as a deep penetrative dread burned their hearts and their minds. *The history books were filled to the brim with examples of why one should always be polite and courteous to any ornate oracles of divine retribution they should happen across.* All divine deities, and their underlings who represent them, were imbued with a grandiose sense of importance. With an unrestrained sense of unquestionable totalitarianistic superiority that granted them an absolute and unfaltering immunity to both any form of questioning or mockery. Especially mockery. How would you respond if an ant crawled up your leg and said you had a crappy haircut? *(A slow sarcastic round of applause for everyone who made the prototypical joke of 'I'd sell the talking ant and become super-rich!' Very droll and very original. Please take some time off to pat yourself on the back...)*

"This isn't going to work for me..." Michael responded after a moment's pause.

With a simple click of his fingers the trio was split up as the room they were in disappeared from around them. Kiko now found herself standing in a tall impressive forest of pine trees. A landscape of emerald peaks standing out like a barrage of spears brandishing against a cool indigo sky. The air was chilled, but in a calm and relaxing way. A gentle mist rolled over the fresh ground of thick, springy green grass. Not once in her entire life had Kiko ever seen a hummingbird before, despite always having a deep desire and wanting to do so. A secret need that was etched onto her metaphorical bucket-list. The opportunity to see one of these frantically happy birds with her own two eyes had simply never arisen. *But now she could see two!* Playing together in a great flappy game across the sky of interwoven trees. They zipped and they dashed, bountifully through the pale blue sky. Kiko watched with a contentedly cheerful, child-like sense of peaceful joy as they danced together overhead. *A moment in time that was forged in her heart to be remembered for eternity.* A mulberry plumbed peacock called out from under a nearby table. This splendidly lavish bird was as resplendent as he was monarchical. The purple regal king of all birds. He had an ornate display of tail feathers, a majestic kaleidoscope of deep greens and admirable blues. Like a crazy headdress that belonged to some mad-hat neon-coloured psychedelic chieftain who was also a fabulous fashionista with a point to prove on the catwalk in an hour's time. This table he was currently idling under was a structure of deeply interwoven and twisted narrow trunks whose roots reach far beneath. The branches were as flat as possibly imaginable across the top of the surface, whilst still nobbly and bubbly underneath. Across this surface of the tree-table was a series of black and white squares. A chessboard with all of the pieces ready and prepared. The white pieces were carved into the shape of different angels and good guys. The black was carved into a series of Demons and monsters. On either side of the board lay a chair.

'Wait!'

As Kiko examined more closely... *No! It couldn't be...* The white queen piece was impeccably carved into the delicately detailed shape of a woman with long and wild hair. She wore a coat identical in design to Kiko's and had a pair of glasses upon her white marble face as she looked downwards, studiously reading a book she held in her right hand. *Was this supposed to be Kiko?* No, wait! *Yes!* The rooks (*the tower pieces*) were of a pointy-eared woman with two axes! She was frozen mid-run and mid snarl. Ready to charge headfirst in a straight line, directly into danger at a moment's notice. *That was clearly supposed to be Kara!* And there was Muhren! He was the Bishop pieces. He stood behind his howling-wolf shield and seemed to be watching over the board with a troubled look upon his bearded face! *Oh and of course!* The knights were Namonar! Frozen mid pounce, detailed in chalky stone. Upon closer inspection, the king piece was a white stone figure carved into the shapely design of the Archangel Michael. It even had the little '*M*' that was carved into his helmet and a miniature version of his spear! The pawns were carved into tombstones.

As Kiko looked over the black pieces, she found she recognised some of them as well. The king and queen pieces she did not recognise, however the Bishop was a cut to look like a Pesadilla-niño glaring away with his metal insignia over his head as his robes billowed, and the rook was a Nekrith soldier, brandishing a big gun! The knight piece struck an uncanny resemblance to the Changeling that she had seen kill Vincent. *She hated that piece the most!* The pawns were cut into the musing of classic horn-headed Demons with pitchforks.

"I'm sorry for all the mystery and subterfuge. I know you to be logical and smart, my dearest Kiko." Michael re-emerged as he sat in one of the chairs smiling at Kiko as he stooped. "I know you're the smart one of the group and will pay attention to my words when I speak. I come to you now with tidings of utmost importance. A mission of unprecedented significance. The fate of all life hangs in the balance. I sent the other two away, don't worry somewhere safe, so that we may take a minute to talk like adults. To discuss with logic and reason. *Just you and me.* After all, you are the obvious leader of your ragtag lot. You are the only one who would understand the gravitas of the situation. But whilst we talk, perhaps you would humour me with a game?" He gestured towards the board. "I shan't belittle you, or condescend by disguising that this board is a metaphorical parable for the situation you find yourself in now. It's an analogy for what has happened and what may happen next, depending upon the choices you make now and will forever continue to make. You have been blind thus far, but you have been a key. You have unlocked a great many doors, both intentionally and by accident, in this endless game of war between me and the Devil's Demonic children. I shall play the side of the Demons in this game, even though it disgusts me, in the hope that you play your pieces well. With logic and purpose. Never waste a move, or else you shall be destroyed. Both in the game and in whatever will happen after it. You have been chosen as the first Human to play 'chess' alongside an Angel in the great game of wit. The quills of history are writing this day. How the ink dries, now that's entirely up to you, Kiko Attetson. The child of time who bends it to her will."

Michael gestured towards the second chair.

"Please sit."

Muhren had been surprised to find himself now standing in a small tavern. He was surprised, but this was not in an unhappy way. After all, no one is ever really truly unhappy when they're in a tavern? It was almost like there was a law against it. Maybe stemming from the fact that these merry inns are where alcohol lived and flowed freely. However, he was surprised to see photographs of himself and the times he had shared with family and friends mounted upon the walls. About thirty of them. Frozen images of bygone moments long since relegated to memory and the passage of time. All of these photos were slightly blurry and grey-scaled. However, regardless of how vague some of these memories were in Muhren's head, he could distinctly recall there not being a single camera taking a single photo at any of these times.

This room he was currently in was old and rustic. Like an old family cottage. The walls were of a bulky thick stone, yet the interior was fairly modern. A crimson red carpet ran underfoot. On top of this carpet, in the centre of the room, was a glass table with two black metal chairs. Across the room from it stood a fireplace with a warm fire crackling away within. A black wooden bar ran near the rear wall. Behind this bar was a series of shelves, upon them lay every conceivable drink you could imagine. Each drink had a single row. The drinks also continued through into a series of chillers spanning the underside of the interior of the bar itself. It had every imaginable brand of brandy and fruity flavoured sip of cider on display. Every wantable whiskey and available ale. An endless parade of beautiful beers, tasty tequilas and generous gins. Wonderful wines that wavered effortlessly through every hue and verifiably voguish vodkas were up for grabs at an arm's-reach. Apprehensive absinthes and madcap moonshines were also available for anyone who felt brave enough to face the risk.

But, perhaps for the first time in his life, Muhren wasn't feeling in the mood for a drink. He was too focused on why these pictures of his life were scattered around him. *His life was like an intrusive scrap-booked collage from the camera of some uninvited stalker.* One such photo was from the first time he had successfully resuscitated a man in his line of work. He remembered it well, that feeling of halting death dead in its tracks. That delayed disbelief and sense of satisfaction. The realisation of positive change he'd had on the world. A man was alive here and now because of him. It was such a great feeling and one he had actually forgotten. But he remembered it now. The force of his hands pressing repeatedly down and the power of his chest compressions around the old dude's chest. That controlled sense of determination that took control of him upon that day. The stress and panic in the room as everyone else ran around him. The metaphorical deep breath before the plunge. He remembered now that feeling of iron will. To be the change in the tides of the universe that had refused to accept that today was supposed to be that man's last. *He also distinctly remembered no one running around taking pictures.*

As he looked over this picture he couldn't help but think over how far he had come. The fact that he had forgotten saving this man *(And even what his name was!)* was because Muhren had changed so many people's lives for the better at this point that they almost blended into one. *A faceless crowd of good deeds.* If being a doctor was comparable to a person working in a shop, he couldn't remember the first person he had served in his first transaction upon his first day at the shop because he had served so many by now. As Muhren stood here contemplating just how many people he had saved with his magics he realised something else. *He was his own man all along.* Sure he was no Vincent Attetson, but as it turned out neither was Vincent. A pang of shame stabbed at him as he recalled his sister telling him about her time at Saint Moira's hospital and what Kiko had seen. *He should have been there for her, but he was too busy hiding away.*

Another picture grabbed his attention. Before Muhren had worked as a medic for the Arcane Intelligence Agency he was originally working for them as a member of the Bureau of Necrological Investigations. He had worked for his father and this photo was of his old Death Squad. And there they all were, the people who he had trusted with his life and had killed monsters with, all sat around and on top of an old jeep. There was Ogler, the Orc who prided himself on punching anything that hit him back twice as hard. He was mid-toke of a cigar he had found whilst in Cuba. Muhren laughed as he remembered how Ogler would (*not too much*) later go on to cough up his lungs and bite the cigar with rage, thus burning his tongue. There was Veriel Morgenstern, a hard-cut and mysterious man with long black hair. He was the best scout Muhren had ever seen. Veriel could track a needle in a haystack the size of New York, or so Veriel claimed. There was the little Halfling man who no one knew the name of. Everyone just called him Tea-Leaf. But if you ever wanted anything at all, Tea-Leaf knew the perfect black market for it. There was also Yip. Yip was Muhren's best friend. *(Still is despite Muhren never really getting the chance to see him.)* Yip was rather special. He was a happy go lucky scallywag who liked to rock the status quo. He found everything funny and you couldn't help but be caught up in the humour with him. His love for being an impish rapscallion had resulted in him being cursed by a witch, who was an ex of his, into becoming a humanoid fox. Apparently that was the appearance that had best suited his personality. Muhren remembered being told by his fox-faced friend, how he had swapped out Ogler's cigar with a joke toy one that would taste like old pickled eggs, cheesy feet and spicy chilli powders.

Muhren realised now how he had cut off and run away from his friends after the accident that broke his heart some two years ago. He felt ashamed as he realised how many loved ones he had cut off from. Both his friends and his family. The loss that shattered his world and ripped it with the thunder of sorrowed sunder. The day the love of his life died.

And there she was now.

Elmin Bravewater.

Her beautiful radiant smile beaming away in the middle of the group with Muhren's arm wrapped around her. This smile lighting up the land without a care in the world, like the sun on a summer's day. She was dazzlingly beautiful and utterly brilliant. She was a Venetian Elf who Muhren had met three years before the events of this picture. She was entirely captivating with her long black hair and olive skin. Every moment of every day he had ever spent in her company was pure gold. She was so kind, warm, forthright and smart. *It was actually Elmin that had nicknamed their death squad the*

Argentavis Squad. Everyone had loved it so much that they all got matching tattoos of the name. Truth be told he never knew what an argentavis was, apparently it was some sort of bird. According to Elmin this group would never fall and would always rise up. Rise away from defeat and race towards victory. *Up, up and away on the hefty wings of fortune, like the argentavis of old.* However, this plucky attitude didn't save her from dying. About six months after this frozen moment with the jeep. Muhren felt a great sense of fear, hoping that there was no image here of their time together as she died. He could see their first dance, their first night together and several other moments of their time shared. But none of the night he had panically held her shoulder together as he tried to seal the wounds of that fucking werewolf's bite. He remembered how Tea-Leaf and Ogler tried lifting the fallen scaffolding off of her broken legs. *He remembered her tears.* He remembered the sounds of Veriel and Yip chasing down the wolf-man in the rain. He remembered her lifeless dead eyes and he remembered why he chose to run away. Why he had packed in this life of the sword and hunting monsters and had decided to use his hands to help people in another way. *A better way.* He remembered his vow to honour Elmin's memory. That despite not being able to save her, he would save as many as he could in her name. No man alive would have to suffer losing his '*Elmin*,' not whilst Muhren was still around.

He then saw a photograph of himself, Kiko and Kara as they walked the streets of Paris before the failed execution. Of when Kara was teasing him about the Onion Lady. As he looked across the picture, he realised something he wasn't all too entirely comfortable with. He felt a warm glow from within as he looked at the teasing Half-Elf... a warm smile broke across his face. *Wait! Did he have feelings for Kara...?*

"Hey man." Michael's voice called out as the Archangel poured himself a drink of gin into a glass. "What are you having?"

The Archangel gestured to the wall of endless drinks.

"I'm sorry what? What's going on?"

"I came here in the hopes that we could have a heart to heart. To talk, man to man."

"And parading my life like a gallery aids that how?" Muhren asked with a stern look.

"Look, I like you. Muhren, you're a good man and I respect that about you. Whilst most are too busy fighting you're busy trying to drag people out of the dirt and chaos. Busy trying to fix this broken world. I respect all clerics and doctors. That desire to fix the world by healing it, instead of killing. That takes true effort and resolve. You have an ingrained humility and kindness, even if you've forgotten it. You're reasonable and you push people onto the right path. You take the time to try and make the world better, and that's why I've chosen to speak to you. You're clearly the glue that holds your ragtag lot together. *You're the backbone and obvious leader.* So I come to you now in the hope that we may have a civilised conversation about a troubling matter. I've sent the girls away to somewhere safe. They're rash and impulsive and I rather worry they'll get in the way. I had hoped that by approaching you as a friend you'd be more willing to 'break bread' with me. So we can talk calmly over a couple of drinks about how I need someone to help me end this war against the Demon-kind. *I need someone who understands the importance of healing a broken universe.* But who also knows how to pack a punch, or rather swing a sword. Muhren, you are both sides of the coin of war. Healer and fighter. The universe needs you; so what do you say?"

"I think I'll have a whiskey..." Muhren replied as he took a seat.

Kara had found herself stood in what appeared to be a large training room or sparring hall. A series of impressively sharp looking weapons hung on all the walls upon several mounts. A multitude of practice and training dummies were was also scattered through the room. There was also a great deal of padded mats that lay strewn across the floor. The room she was in looked like a dojo, a place for great warriors and fighters to hone their skills and train for the gruelling challenges of battle. The walls and the ceiling were painted white. This white was broken up by a great number of wooden streaks of dark brown oak that ran up the walls and supported the ceiling above. Across the rear wall was a series of armours. From left to right there was a Samurai with an impressive helmet, an imposing noble knight of the crusades, a scarily iron-clad Viking, a robust Dwarven armour made from stone, a classic regal European Elven armour with big fancy shoulders, a shiny suit of Maximilian plate armour, the feral Orcish bone armour of

Greenland, a Germanic Gothic plate armour and the Bren-kakinà armour of the Amazonian Woodland Elves.

As Kara looked across them all she couldn't decide which was her favourite. *She loved them all.* They were pristine and they were immaculate. Each suit embodied a different aspect of the history of war. Pieces of a puzzle of war's past, a history Kara respected. To her armours were beautiful. Noble clothes of metal designed to protect and defend. A luscious safe haven that held you tight. A man-made cocoon of forged perfection.

Weirdly these armours in front of her were all of her favourite designs. She had often drawn them in books and looked them up on the Internet. As she looked upon these suits, seemingly ripped from history upon the eve of battle, she realised that they were actually arranged in order of her preference. Only now seeing them all together did Kara even realise that she had even had a favourite. Truth be told, the only one of these armours she had ever actually seen with her own eyes before was that of the Samurai. This was when she had fought a zombie-Samurai in Japan with Kiko, upon her first day with the Bureau of Necrological Investigations. *'God, that felt like so long ago!'* Only now with this reflection did she realise how out of sorts she had been feeling lately. A wave of embarrassment washed over her as she recalled starting a fight at the Drunken Dutchess and how she had shoved Kiko when they were in London. Even though she would never admit it, her time spent with the Revantide woman had cut her deeply. *Deeper than she could ever admit.* She was emotionally wounded. Snared by grief. Lashing out at the world because she didn't know how to stop it. As she looked across this room of war she wondered how long she could keep lashing out before she lost all of her friends for good. She was surprised that the idea of being hated by Muhren would upset her almost as much as the idea of Kiko hating her would. But she knew, even though the idea of a lonely future terrified her, she would always lack the ability to speak what was on her mind. *It was just the way she was programmed.*

This sorrow was short-lived as Kara noticed a series of ornate shields upon the wall. She ran to them like a child in a sweet shop. She held a rounded shield from the lost Elven city of Ellenaùrr tight in her hands and examined intently the bronzed falcon carved into it. These shields were said to have all been destroyed by the great fires of Surtr!

"I know all about you." Michael called out as the loud sound of the falcon shield of Ellenaùrr clattered and clashed upon the floor.

Kara gave a wide-eyed stare reminiscent of a child who had been caught raiding the cookie jar, as she quickly looked down to the shield at her feet before locking back onto Michael.

"I'm sorry about th-"

"You're a woman of action. *And I respect that about you.* As such, I won't waste your time with honeyed words. I know you well enough to know I'd just be wasting both of our time. You're too smart for it, but you don't stop to think about what you do or say. I think that's because your head is so full of grief. Your pain makes you unpredictable. You lash out in bouts of unkempt fury like a savage because you cannot fathom another manner in which to express yourself. You rely on sarcasm and brash violence to insincerely voice your opinions because your upbringing told you that you had no value. And you chose to believe it. *You jest with jokes like a clown because you don't believe your words are worthy of an audience.* You rush towards the finishing line of every conversation because you're terrified you'll be ignored. I get that. But you're not a woman of words. Words are for libraries and milk-willed philosophers. That is why I have chosen to speak to you, Kara. *You are clearly the leader of your ragtag lot.* I need a person of action. A person who can rise up and deliver a much needed and desperately required result whilst everyone else around you is still too busy discussing the ramifications of their actions or trying to heal something already broken. I need a leader. A person who isn't afraid to make the hard calls and get their hands dirty in a fight. Someone who knows that to stop an enemy, you rip out their heart. Not someone who will waste time with words of *'reason and logic.'* I see such a leader in you. That's why I'm choosing to speak with you, alone here and now. I have sent your friends away. They're safe for now, chatting away with each other. I stand before you now to test your mettle. I know you're a fighter. *I know you will never truly trust or respect me until I prove myself to you in the ring.* So I want you to hit me."

"You want me to do what?" Kara replied in a state of shock at the strange request.

"I said that I want you to hit me. I wish to test your skills in battle, as this is the only way we soldiers know how to talk. The armies of the Demon move against us. Your fury is clouding your mind. So I offer myself as a proverbial 'punching bag' for you to vent your frustrations upon in the hope you refocus and reforge yourself."

"Yeah, I'm sorry? What? Chill out dude, I don't want to hurt you. I just-"

"I'm not sure you can conceive how insulting of a notion it is, that something like you could even begin to hurt something like me. I stand tall, far beyond your limited grasp, child. This would be the second time you've insulted me now. Be warned, there is no third. When the Archangel Lord of All tells you to do something, you do not stop to question why. You just do it; you do as you are told. And you do it now."

The Archangel stood in front of Kara once more.

"Now hit me."

Kiko moved her last remaining Bishop to G5 in the hopes that this piece would be able to intercept Michael's rook before he took her knight. Both of her own rooks and this knight she sought to defend were holding Michael's queen from locking her king into checking. *This game was not going well.* She had spent almost the entire game on the defensive. Michael was an amazing opponent, the likes of which Kiko had never really had the privilege of playing against before. She both loved and hated it in equal measure. It had been about two years since her last game of chess, because people hated playing her. She always won. Every time. Even when it looked like she was losing, it was a trap to mask her approaching victory. On the board she was as ruthless as Jack the Ripper was as he combed the Victorian streets of old London. Kiko hadn't actually lost a game of chess since she was six. She had cried for an hour after it and swore it would never happen again. Yet here she was, less than twenty years later, losing again. Every masterful plan and carefully adapted strategy collapsed in on itself with a surgical degree of precision from Michael's counter-attacks. He was so good that Kiko jokingly toyed with the idea he might be cheating. It helped her feel better about facing defeat and her not being the first human to both play and beat an Angel in a game of chess all at the same time. If anyone had the skill to overcome Michael at this old game of wit and logic, it wasn't going to be Kiko.

However the conversation was going well, and it was riveting.

"You see this is because the Revanspear spear is a part of a set." Michael explained. "Two parts of the one whole. The true purpose of these two parts far exceeds the limited potential either one has by itself. I need both to stop Lilith and it's why I sent you to go acquire the spear of Revantide."

"Why '*you*' sent me?" Kiko asked as her knight fell to Michael's rook. She had assumed her arrival at Revantide was a part of the fake Vincent's plan to cover his tracks.

"Yes. For you see I was unable to interact with it myself, not directly anyway. Cosmic rules and all of that. I also apologise for the secrecy and subterfuge. But I also sent you away, through time and space, to keep you safe. The ever-watching eyes of the Demon Queen is watching over you. If I ever came to you directly I would have forced her hand. This would have put you at risk and forced her to speed up her plans against me. Plans I'm still not ready to halt. I would have sacrificed my best piece on the board and left myself exposed to defeat, all in a single move. I knew a Changeling was nearby and would run the risk of outing any interaction – oh, it's your move by the way - we might have had. Which leads us to the question I know you want to ask..." Michael gestured towards Kiko.

"Oh... um... yeah, right. Do you know why the Changeling was there and what had led to it living so long?"

"No one knows why the Changelings do anything at all. They're a wild and reckless lot. Unfortunately, you and I simply have nothing at all besides wild unsubstantiated guesses. Not unless you were to storm and raid the Convergence of Ckaàragor and interrogate the Changeling King Kraàtha yourself." Michael faked a laugh with a repressed smile. "Or unless you had a huge amount of power at your disposal, that meant that you could punch through their ancient transdimensional barrier and snatch the Fairy king away with some sort of teleportation spell."

"Oh. Okay." Kiko replied crestfallen, as she tried to hide her disappointment and used her rook to take Michael's queen.

'*ZAP!*' Kiko's eyes shot open as a huge light emitted from Michael's hand and a fat, strange, dumpy creature emerged; choking and struggling in the Angel's tight grasp. This creature was short and round and rather slimy. It had six big bug-like wings sticking out from it; flapping frantically from his shoulders and a huge hooked nose that dripped as he struggled against Michael. There were two glazed yellow eyes under a bulging forehead. These eyes seemed terrified at Michael's presence. To be fair, the Fairy king had just been chowing down on (*and choking upon*) a roasted hog, in his empire of Ckaàragor, which he had been ripping at with his bare hands. Lumps of burned pig were still stuck between his jagged teeth. A crown of bone sat on top of a receding hairline of thickly matted dreadlocks. These putrid dreads were filled with twigs and egg shell, as well as other unknowns. He smelled like a six-month-old Chinese takeaway that had been left out in the sun. To be fair, he probably tasted this way too. He wore sandals with socks, which was potentially the worst thing about him, as well as a thick red robe laced with golden threads.

"Kraàtha. I know that you know who I am. I think you know exactly what will happen next if you dare to lie to me. This here is Kiko Attetson. Daughter of Cassandra and Collin Attetson. One of your own was in their company. Tell me why and do so before I lose my patience."

"Crrrakkthck." Kraàtha chocked. "Please - oh mighty one." His voice cracked as he spoke. "Please show this one mercy! Lilith made us - Lilith made us! She made us! We know no choice. She - know - who - you - is, Kiko! Great prophecy of old speak of you - it say Attetson daugh-ter stop Lilith with - with weapon. You, child of time - bring weapon to stop great war - in your future! Lilith want war. Lilith needs - I sent my son, Xxyll, to watch - over you - and drain you of power. Ready and waiting, long before - your birth. To drain you of your magic. Keep - you weak. Keep you safe. Lilith's orders. Not mine! Might Kraàtha say - how beautiful you look! Too much beautiful - Kiko- to allow poor - defenceless Kraàtha to die! Lilith - she must have - war. She must kill all Angels and -"

And with that Kraàtha burned. He burst into a thousand angry, righteous flames as Michael allowed his charred body to flop to the ground.

The concept of a clandestine prophecy raced through Kiko's mind. Maybe this weapon was whatever Michael had wanted for her to acquire for him?! *Equally, maybe not.* But she couldn't help but feel both heartbroken and angry about the idea of it all. She felt deep sorrow that Vincent had been destined for the chopping block because of her, whilst also furious that her brother had died, in a manner not too different to being sacrificed, because of some cosmic game of chess between Lilith and Michael. If Michael had been more forthcoming about his desires, maybe her parents could have kept everyone safe. Maybe, if these two had just fought it out, and not used everyone else to fight their battles for them, perhaps Kiko's family would remain intact.

"I'm sorry Kiko, I apologise for the theatrics. I admit I have always known of the prophecy that says that you will stop Lilith. I suspected that the truth would have been more conceivable if heard directly from the source. *It is said that you will stop the Arcanium war.* And I need the Eye of Obsidius. To end the war before it can start. Combining it with the Revanspear will create a key that will lock the doors to the Demonscapes forevermore. Trapping all of the Demons within and freeing your universe forevermore. But to get it, I need you to return to the Nekrith. I am sorry for that. As they have the Eye. I need you to get it for me."

She was angry at Michael. *But the idea of sealing away the Demons forever?* Now that was an idea she could get behind. Full heartedly. She might not have been able to save Vincent, but she could get some revenge. And maybe even save anyone else from feeling this pain of having your family toyed with by Angels and Demons.

Muhren and Michael laughed full-heartedly at their little table. Undoubtedly there may be some readers who are ultimately confused by how Michael was seemingly playing chess, drinking and fighting with Kara all at the same time. Michael was a being that transcended our very understanding of time and space. Being in two or even three places at once was as easy for him as being in a single place at a single time was for us. Also, don't forget the trio's bodies are still in Paris, flopped at the feet of the Åethínarium. So things like the *'laws of physics,'* or *'time'* and *'rational logic'* are slightly more fluid.

"So yeah, no. Basically, Muhren, what I need is for someone to help me acquire something. I want to lock the doors that lead to the Demon worlds. I want to trap them there forever. Simply, no more Demons. To do this, I need a key. The first half your sister already has. *But she's young and reckless.* I fear her successes have been birthed from luck and not skill. Despite her being skilled, I want you to make sure her and Kara don't fly off the rails and damn us all."

"Oh, okay then. So nothing big then!" Muhren said sarcastically as he took another sip of his drink and Michael laughed.

"Yeah, just another day at the office I'm afraid. I need you to go into space, as the key I mentioned before was split in two. Kept on two separate planets to keep them apart. Now is the time to reunite them. Don't you agree?" Muhren nodded when Michael paused. "The Demon Queen is hot on your heels, she sent the Changeling to drain you of your magic. But because you were smart enough to leave when you did, you're at full strength. Kiko is still healing. I can't afford the failure of half measures. I need the Eye of Obsidius."

"If it can close the gates to hell, then you'll have it." Muhren replied as he downed his drink and stoop up.

Kara cracked her knuckles across Michael's face and it did nothing.

"Again." He demanded.

So she hit him in the stomach and again it did nothing.

"Again!" He instructed again and again. Quite literally.

Kara threw everything thing she had at him until she collapsed in a ball of breathless sweaty exhaustion. As she landed she didn't quite feel better for it. Not in a traditional sense, but she did feel satisfied. For anyone who wasn't an angry little Half-Elf, this sensation she now felt wasn't all too dissimilar to the feeling of getting something unstuck, that's been bothering you for a while, from beneath your teeth or using a cotton bud in your ear. Like finally finishing a race, or finally repairing something in your house that you've been putting off for a while. *It felt therapeutic.*

"There you are." Michael said as he sat down next to her, offering her a bottle of cool water. "Now here's what I need of you. An enemy of mine has a weapon that will severely hurt the Demons. I want you and your friends to get it for me. Through me, all of our enemies shall be vanquished. I will see them all burn at the end of my spear. In return, every single thing in this room shall be yours. Except for me, of course. But you will have something more. I know that there's some out there who call you the *'Ragnarök Child.'* The supposed ender of all things good. I know of how you were raised, in that tower, and the deal your parents made without your consent. *I propose another way to view their words.* Another way to look at your curse. *What if Ragnarök wasn't the end of us and our universe, but the end of all things Demon?* You could be the Ragnarök for all Demon-kind. The ender of evil and the purveyor of light. Use the name they taunt you with and use it against them."

"I thought you weren't going to waste my time with words?" Kara coldly lashed out, pretending that Michael's words didn't shake her at her core. But of course they did. This is the same Kara who had once spent a whole morning nervous about why Collin had wanted to speak with her, if you can remember that far back, when she first got her new job.

"Quite. Go to the Nekrith ship, the Scarrabellum and acquire for me the Eye of Obsidius."

"Oh, um... the Nekrith?" Kara replied as she bolted back upright. "See, ummm, thing is... I had a bad run-in with this woman when I last saw the Nekri-"

"I thought you were above the need for words." Michael interrupted. "A rule for one is a rule for all."

Michael stood up and disappeared.

Chapter Nineteen

THE SCARRABELLUM HEART

The Scarrabellum was the crown jewel of the Nekrith warships. It was currently hung in the outer reaches of the Sculptor Galaxy in the year 5036. Here it sat within the empty void of space. To call the Scarrabellum a spaceship felt like an injustice. Spaceships rarely came in this size. She was an impressive sight to behold. With a width over two thousand miles long, this construct was more like a small planet or moon, based on the size of it. It was a horrendous purple, cybernetic hornet's nest encircled by a thousand smaller Nekrithian warships. For context on how bad this could be, it had only been six of these smaller warships that had decimated Revantide and all of its people under their metalled heel of damnation earlier on. Each one of these ships had close to a thousand angry metal soldiers on board. That was approximately ten million Nekrith on the nearby ships alone. With potentially another million actually on board the Scarrabellum herself. *And nothing had changed.* Zebras were still striped, a cheetah hadn't changed its spots and the Nekrith were still hatred incarnate. Death personified in a metal shell. *All they wanted was to kill.* The Scarrabellum was just about the most dangerous place in existence. As such, no person in their right mind would willingly choose to visit there. Not in a billion years; so I guess that would either mean that Kiko and the gang were either crazy or had a severe death wish. To enter this Nekrithian domain would be like speedrunning an act of suicide through a minefield.

Some said that had said that the Scarrabellum had resembled the appearance of a planet-sized, mechanized spider. Her back was a curved web of rusted bronzes, silvers, blacks and shiny purples, descending into two points on either side. A series of great, steely orbs stuck out at equidistant intervals all across her entire top half. Each one of these orbs had a half-mile diameter and gave her the texture of the universe's scariest pine cone. Each of these orbs could open up, if given the need to do so, revealing a great series of guns and missiles hidden within each one. From underneath this oversized ship, a great number of landing gears protruded and hung. A plurality of impressive, ornate legs, tendrils and claws, designed for a wide range of nefarious goals of villainy. They dangled off of her belly like the tentacles and oral arms of a jellyfish.

The Nekrith had recently been swarming the colonies of the nearby planets and stealing away their residents. The fate of these intergalactic colonists had been an undesirable one. They had all been coerced into joining the Nekrith cause by the means of an all too literal gut-wrenching, metallic pain of saws and probes. The variety of Nekrith on display here was vastly greater than what Kiko and Kara had witnessed on Revantide as well. The standard infantry, with their tall frames, long necks and spindly limbs were here. Most of these soldiers had two arms. But this was far from a universally defining state shared by all. Some Nekrith had managed to acquire as many as six arms! Some had none. Some Nekrith were short, at approximately five foot tall. These shorter ones didn't share the Nekrith's trademark long necks. They didn't even any have legs. They managed to get around on a great metal ball that rolled around beneath them. They were attached to this ball by a small connecting pipe. Some looked like gigantic robotic crabs whilst some looked like robotic-humanoid sharks with legs. Some had smooth domed heads whilst some had pyramid-shaped ones. All the Nekrith shared the same red lights in their electronic eyes, as well as the skull of their former race on display within in the hard plastic casings they all called heads.

All of these cybernetic monstrosities patrolled the Scarrabellum through a series of metal tunnels, rooms and cold platforms from within the awful ship of untold despair, death and destruction. A malevolent empire of steely blues and artificial design. The room in which the trio of Kiko, Kara and Muhren had arrived in was cold, ghostly and emotionless. It was immense and it was formidable. If one so wished they could swing a whole mammoth in here by its feet with ease. *(Even though this was an extremely unlikely purpose for this room! The Nekrith were not in the habit of transporting intergalactic mammoths, but it was nice to know that they had the space for it if the desire to do so should ever arise.)* Tall sleek pipes of a non-terrestrial design fed directly into the ceiling of this vast metallic meadow of cybernetic constructs. A low thick fog hung around their thighs and enshrouded the actions of their feet, which *'clacked'* briskly against the hard surface of the floor as they walked.

A heated and discontented Kara felt a weighty frustration crushing down upon her. If it had not been obvious by the number of times she had clearly and plainly stated so, she was less than delighted at the idea (*and much less the reality*) of returning to the Nekrith, or to the vacuum of space in general so soon after her last encounter with these mechanical foes. To be quite frank, she would have been more than happy to have lived out the rest of her entire life without ever seeing one of those horrible space-age monstrosities again. As her eyes gazed over her futuristic and enigmatic surroundings a deep and primal sensation of regret and dejection raked through her soul. *So what?* She had survived being executed in olden day Paris for what exactly? Just to die on an alien spacecraft? *How was that in any way better?* At least being burned to a cinder by witch fearing commoners was actually a form of death. The trepidations of spending the rest of eternity as a mindless Nekrith, ambling mercilessly through the cosmos felt so much worse!

Kiko wasn't handling the idea of their shared return to the Nekrith much better than Kara was, although she was being a lot more reserved in how she portrayed her unease and apprehension of their current location in the universe. Maybe this was because of the white queen's chess piece she had stashed in her pocket to remember her celestial chess game by. To the untrained eye she would have appeared completely normal and calm. Kiko kept a self-controlled stiff upper lip, despite the odds. It had been difficult to remain equanimous in the face of such imminent peril, but yet (*at least on the surface*) she seemed undisturbed by her current reality. The importance of their shared goal had imbued her with a vigorous resolve. The fact that this objective had been given to them by a literal Archangel had made her determination all the more prevalent. If it was true that this artefact that they sought could wipe all Demons from the face of the Earth, then this quite simply meant that they had to have it. *Regardless of the cost.* If the Demons were so scared of Kiko acquiring the Eye of Obsidius that they had felt the need to plant a Changeling to rob her of her strength, this probably meant that there was a good chance that she would succeed. *After all, why would they go to so much effort to stop her if this task was a fool's errand?* If the Demons had believed that there was a chance that Kiko could succeed then this was good enough for Kiko and meant it meant that she would believe it too. If Kiko had been destined to die here then the Demons would have just left her to it and not felt the need to cheat the odds. This (*somewhat overly simple*) deduction had been enough to bestow Kiko with the courage to at least try and attempt her mission, despite the seemingly insurmountable odds.

But regardless, as Kiko looked across the dark, soulless room of this dangerous space station she couldn't help but feel a newfound appreciation for her safe little office back at the Arcane Intelligence Agency. *That little safe space that she had taken for granted.* Her own little world behind that desk, where aliens robots didn't shoot at her, where evil fairies didn't kidnap her family members, where ghost-houses didn't try to squash her and where medieval Pilgrims didn't try to burn the flesh off her bones. Somewhat ironically, she used to wish for a more exciting life. Now she had one, she couldn't help but feel the *'exciting life'* wasn't all it was cracked up to be. After she acquired the Eye of Obsidius for Michael, she would never set foot out from behind that desk again. In that chair was where she would remain behind a protective wall of paperwork and a lifetime supply of hot chocolates and marshmallows.

For Muhren, this had been his first time in space and he didn't quite know what to make of it all. He felt weirdly out of place and like he didn't belong here, rather like a fart let loose in an uncomfortable astronaut's airtight spacesuit. He prodded inquisitively at one of the nearby pipes and wondered what they might have been used for. In a loose manner of speaking, the room beneath them was a *'kitchen.'* Okay, technically it was an *'Organics Separations Facility.'* But the idea of a kitchen sounded nicer! If you must know, it was a room where organic creatures (*like the missing colonists and other alien abductees*) were torn apart and sifted, strained, pulped, lacerated, mashed, smashed, bashed, crashed and scraped by a whole menagerie of malicious machinery, which prepared them all into a thick pulpy *'soup'* to be ingested by the Nekrith later on. *(As, if you can recall, a Nekrith soldier still had a fairly large amount of their original organics intact under their armours. It was useful in keeping some systems running. This 'goo' from the 'kitchen' kept all of their more squishy parts alive and functioning.)* And the room above the trio was a 'Decontamination Room,' this being a room where the liquidated meats of these pulverised people were injected and sprayed with chemicals, which was another step in readying them to be fed into the Nekrithian creatures. The pipe Muhren was currently curiously touching was filled with the bulging liquefied pulp of this biological and bodily broth, as it was being transported from one room into the other. If he had known what was inside, he probably wouldn't be poking it with his bare hand! *(And yeah, the Nekrith were both unethical and gross!)*

The trio stood for a silent moment as they tried to see if they could sense the presence of the artefact they were hunting for. It had been a lot harder to detect the location of the Eye of Obsidius than it had been for the Revanspear. Perhaps this was because all of the metal constructs and humming machinery had been managed to conceal the masked item behind their thick metal walls and distracting noises, or perhaps it was because the Amaranth wasn't leading them directly to the artefact this time? But after a short while Kiko felt herself attune with the Eye's magical frequency! It was approximately two miles away to her left. Muhren had felt it too and Kara pretended she felt it as well, it was never nice to feel like the odd one out. The trio of inter-chronological time wizards slowly crept their way into the long adjacent hallway of overbearing space-age architecture. To their surprise, there was not a single Nekrith to be seen. *Not a single evil robot insight.* No guards, no patrols and no aimless wanderers. *Where were they all?* A vessel this size should have been swarming with their cybernetic nemeses, but the long hall was empty. This was a stroke of good luck! Maybe all the Nekrith were all on one giant shared lunch-break, or perhaps they had all simultaneously decided to go on holiday together at the same time? Wherever they were they were not here. *Which definitely made things a whole lot easier.*

The cold lens of an all-seeing camera gazed down upon them from afar. A slow blinking red light flashed with imperilled glee as it silently tracked everything they did from the shadows. Not so far away, in a lavishly decorated cyber-room, the putrescent hand of a shadowy figure gently caressed the screen of a nearby monitor as it showed the movements of a certain Kiko and co.

"Yes, good. The Time-Witch has arrived." A shrill male voice proclaimed as his cold lifeless eyes watched the unfolding developments on the flickering screen.

"To permit the safe passage of stowaways is illogical. Analysis indicates it is negligent. Explication is required, Lord Controller." A nearby Nekrith

soldier barked as he turned to face the indistinguishably hidden figure that watched the screens with a might metallic thud.

The '*person*' watching the screen was entirely enveloped in a deep shadow cast by his dim surroundings and none of his characteristics could be discerned from the clouded darkness that concealed his appearance.

"Yet you forget, soldier, I do not answer to you!" Enraged words fled from behind a legion of rusted metal teeth. "Do not overstep your rank. My intent is beyond your limited programming. The child of time is a mouse and I am the cat." He let loose a maniacal laugh that sounded like scraping, screeching metal. "I know why she has come here, it was foretold. Three dullards pale in comparison against the might of the Nekrith race, yet still, you cower like a shrieking, weeping child." The hidden figure turned his concealed head as he turned in the shadows of the great room. "Why do they scare you so? *Tell me, do you also fear ants?* You were built for more than this. Fear is a defect! An impurity! Perhaps I should have you scrapped? Let me have my fun, unless you desire my attention to befall on you..."

The Nekrithian soldier backed away from the Nekrith Controller with a silent unease.

"How predictable. Our 'guests' are to remain unaccosted and unharmed until I give the order! For the glory of the Nekrith!" A shrill laugh emitted from the shadows where the Controller remained concealed as the hundred or so nearby Nekrithians all chanted 'for the glory of the Nekrith' back at him in a terrifying unison of husky robotic voices. *"Ready the beast, my children!"*

Kiko and Muhren pried at a large metal door. Given the fact Kara didn't actually want to be here, she thought it was only fair that she didn't actually give a helping hand with the manual labour. Eventually the door popped open to reveal the vast metallic exterior of an artificial cityscape of tall daunting slate monoliths and neon green accented sci-fi tombstone-like buildings. This mechanical metropolis of cybernetic creation sat beneath the surface of a thick sheet of metal that spanned as far as the eye could see. A hard silvery cloud of sooty greys and rusted purples that was peppered with harsh halogen lights that illuminated the city beneath with a jaded green light. In the distance a large series of cylinder-shaped buildings hummed and flashed with a green light. Tall buildings rose out in all directions like Earthly skyscrapers. Each of these grey buildings had a strange sigil of green light carved near to the top of it. Directly in front of the misplaced magicians was a long and imposing bridge (*which was of course made from metal and illuminated with a green light.*) which ran directly into an ebony pyramid-shaped monolith that lay straight ahead. As the three crossed the bridge they were suddenly startled by a loud crashing noise from behind them. *As they all dramatically turned in a display of overtly outstanding distress, they witnessed the building they had recently been in rising up on a series of impressive and vast crab-like legs.* A singular bright green eye lit up on the side of it. They watched with horror as this stumpy, pyramid-shaped building stood up with a thunderous din and simply began to walk away, scurrying over the other buildings like a spider in the night!

"What the hell was that?" Kara shouted as she pointed towards the retreating structure. This question got no reply from her friends. "Do you guys not think it's weird we haven't seen a single Nekrith soldier? Don't you think that's far too suspicious? It's clearly a trap!"

"Of course it's a trap!" Muhren replied back to her as he laughed at how obvious Kara was being.

"Then why are you laughing?" Kara snapped back. *"Oh, right!* Because you don't actually know what we're up against!"

"I've fought stuff before!" Muhren replied with an arrogant smile.

"Guys, that's enough!" Kiko interrupted. "We can't allow ourselves to become distracted by in-house fighting."

"Oh right, yeah, of course. My bad!" Kara turned to face Kiko. "I forgot, we all gotta focus on dying on the whims of some flappy-winged Angel!"

"You know what, Kara? It's fine if you don't want to help. But please don't slow us down with your incessant complaining. We've been given orders." Kiko remarked as she went to continue down the bridge.

"Excuse me?" Kara glared towards the Time-Witch. "This is clearly a suicide mission. I get you're hurting about Vincent and whatnot, but if Michael had told you to jump off a bridge, would you?"

But Kara's words fell on deaf ears as Kiko just kept on walking towards the monolith and away from the stroppy Half-Elf. *To be fair, Kara was right, but Kiko wasn't willing to listen.* It was a fairly common occurrence for people to be unable to listen to a person when they were right about something. But she wasn't the only one who was listening though. Deep within the cyber-room, a cackling Nekrith Controller laughed hysterically to himself as he watched the seeds of both mistrust and distrust as they began to take root between the hearts of the invasive hitchers. He threw his metallic head back in a fit of impetuous delight, a trickle of light illuminated across the side of his face; revealing a slither of a cracked porcelain skull and bronzed metals from the darkness.

Upon entering the ebony looking monolith, Kiko Kara and Muhren were confronted with a wide-open area littered with several holographic projections of the same small alien. This alien had the top half of a snake and the bottom half of a squid. His long tentacles hung off the edge of a large floating hoverchair. All of these holograms were singing a deep, ghostly lamenting chant that almost sounded like a prayer. Sat on top of each head was an ornate crown, that rose into two points and somewhat resembled an inverted Egyptian Pharaoh's headdress.

"What do you suppose they're singing about?" Muhren asked as he peered at one nearby projection.

"No idea, probably something horrific." Kiko replied scathingly as she looked down on one of the other holographic projections. The semi-glitching projected creature's head was wide and flat, given the long neck, it rather looked like an arm-and-legless torso of a scorpion or like the head of a wide space-aged cobra. Kiko's face grimaced with disgust before she ducked down next to the metal platform of the other-worldly projection, lifted off a part of its metal casing and started examining and stickybeaking at the wires inside.

"Um, what are you doing?" Kara enquired with an angered bemusement.

"I'm trying to… *ow…!* isolate the… *ow…!* audio… *ow…!* feed… *ow…!*" The repeated interruptions during Kiko's attempt to explain what she was doing was caused by her flinching from a small repeated electrical shock that she was receiving from the wires as she held them. With each jittering jolt her red hair had become more unkept, bushier and thicker.

A happy smile broke out across her face as she cast a translation spell upon the right wire.

*"We who burn planets to dust.
We who are stripped of flesh.
We who never decay and never age.*

The age of steel and the age of metal.

*Perfection for the glory of the Nekrith Empire.
For the glory of our noble Controller.
Whatever he desires.*

*The ground trembles wherever we go.
All who oppose us rejoice.
They hear the sound of approaching enlightenment.*

*Take us to them.
We will purify the unclean with our inferno.
The true power is here.
We who reap the waste of mortals.
The seed of life is perverted.
An affront to all.*

*We who swear that no seed of life will remain.
Conversion is the only true answer.
We who are the Nekrith's will made manifest.
We who are endless divine perfection.*

*The whole universe shall be converted.
By our will, it shall be so.*

*By the light of the seven moons,
We who flay the flesh and break the bone,
Strip the man and-"*

"That's enough of that!" Kiko said with a wave of her hand as the song faded back to the unrecognisable chanting from before. "I didn't expect anything nice, yet I'm still disgusted!"

Another blinking camera observed their actions.

"It is time, oh faithful soldiers. Release the beast!" The Controller's metal teeth broke into a twisted smile. "Let us see how my latest design pans out."

Kiko quickly stood upright as the sound of a distant roar ripped through the wailing song. Suddenly a nearby door was ripped off of its hinges and crashed through several of the holograms as a giant cybernetic troll burst through it and crashed a mighty mace on the ground where Kara had just been. *The metal ground cracked under its heavyweight and splintered!* Thank god she moved out of the way! What remained of the troll's skin was as pale as ice. However, there wasn't a great deal of skin left. The majority of this creature was cold metals and chilling machinery. Only one of his great limbs remained, this being the creature's right arm and even that arm had a robotic hand! Parts of its belly and its skull were organic as well, the rest had been converted into artificial Nekrithian perfection. Ruby red eyes shone on its face as another red light emitted from its chest. The feral cybernetic monstrosity bellowed once more. As it lifted its great head a series of wires could be seen, feeding under its jaw and the front of its neck. As it moved its joints released small jets of steam from around its hinges. These hinges squeaked and groaned under its great weight.

The trap had been set, and now it was sprung.

The creature took another mighty swing, this time at Kiko.

"Oh, shit!"

The Eye of Obsidius had better be worth it.

Chapter Twenty

THE RAGE OF THE SPACE-VIKING

With all of the agility of a terrified cat, Kiko leapt out of the way of the troll's rusted hammer as it tore through her summoned shield as if it had been made from egg shells and she landed in a messy heap as her glasses fell from her face and clattered across the metal floor. The world became a blurry mire of indistinguishable shapes and hazed actions. Which is less than ideal when a lumbering troll wants to snap you in twain like a twig and tear you asunder.

"They've got a robotic troll!" Kara yelled.

"Yeah, I can see that! Muhren replied with an irritated tone as he watched Kiko clambering around on her hands and knees as she tried to find her missing glasses and narrowly avoided being stepped on by giant metal feet.

Seeing his sister crawling so precariously close to a squishy death, Muhren launched Namonar at their mechanical aggressor from his chest as if he was a cannon and the fire-wolf was a cannonball. *An orange glow erupted from Muhren's torso as Namonar cascaded against the Nekrith's troll with fiery retribution.* This impact of wolf-on-troll violence barely even caused the troll to flinch, but it had been enough to save Kiko from her pancaked destiny. With a flick of Muhren's left hand, a lasso of light pulled his young sister to safety as his right yeeted her glasses to him as he made his way for the door with Kara as the trio ran for safety. Namonar, who was scared of the metal lunging monstrosity, launched himself into Muhren's back and was absorbed into his master. The trio ran down an impressive hallway and turned around a large corner. *Only to be met with a thick wall of Nekrith soldiers and their numerous guns.* A countless sea of metal bodies and evil faces. The three ducked to safety from a steady flurry of laser bolts that sparked and fizzed against the wall behind them as they were pushed back, retreating towards the troll once more. As they turned back they saw the heavy-footed troll angrily marching towards them.

Rock, meet hard Place...

Kara grabbed Muhren's arm as she kicked in a door and dragged her friends to a temporarily safe space. Upon entering this room Kiko and Kara instantly began casting and summoning several luminous sigil markings (*circular looking magical traps*) that lit up the ground with a series of oranges and blues, all gathered within the narrow opening of the door. Kiko sprinted down to the rear wall of the long room, removing her stethoscope from her coat pocket as she ran. Upon reaching the wall, she began listening to it intently, trying to find any form of structural weakness. Any poorly fused seam or any natural flaws or faults in the metalwork. After a few seconds she pointed to such an exact point.

"Muhren, absorb Namonar directly into this point and have him heat it up, now!"

So that's what Muhren did. Namonar dashed into the wall and disappeared. The wall began to glow with orange light as the troll entered through the front door and triggered all the sigil traps. The floor burst with angry fire pillars and sparked with dancing bolts of electricity, yet the troll remained unscathed and unfazed by the bombardment of the arcane onslaught he was being assaulted with. The metal wall popped behind the trio like a volcano on its day of the month. Kiko looked down across the long steeply sloped exterior wall that ran down to the ground outside. She suddenly realised how high up they currently were. *Oh boy, it looked like a long way down!* But the world's most dangerous slip and slide was a better thing to endure than being torn apart limb by limb or being shot at!

"Jump!"

The three slid down the side of the ebony pyramid with tremendous speed. The back of Kiko's coat lifted as it dragged behind her, as it lifted it also pulled at her shirt and exposed the skin on her back, which rubbed against the black metal. The heat of this friction caused a metal-burn rash to break out, *which hurt like a bitch!* The three spell-casters landed in the street bellow amongst a crowd of red-tinted Nekrith who carried long bronzed spears. *(Their sudden arrival into the street had made some of the smaller Nekrith flee.)* A small (*and rather short*) skirmish broke out amongst them. The fight was over rather quickly, with our trio being the victors. Any relief that this victory may have brought was short-lived, as the deafening and booming sound of the solid troll impacting against the thick ground rang out in all directions and washed over them as they cowered in this Nekrithian street of futuristic design. A blue light flickered over Kiko as she summoned twenty or so illusionary copies of herself, Kara and Muhren. These copies and clones ran off and scattered in a multitude of directions. The goal was for Kiko and her friends to escape under this camouflage caused by her myriad of identical doppelgänger in relative safety. As previously stated, all variants of troll are incredibly dumb and as such, they are easily confused. So hopefully the trio would be able to escape whilst the troll wasted its time with the fake copies. *Smart right?* But also as previously stated back in Paris, trolls also don't like numbers. They never really understood what they were or how they worked. They could never really grasp how things such as quantities and groups worked, what they were and how two was bigger than one.

As such it is pretty difficult to explain the exact range of emotions that went through this cybernetic troll's brain when he had witnessed his small numbered prey suddenly explode into a much larger quantity, but I'll do best. Just remember, trolls don't have thoughts per se, they only feel emotions. And even these emotions weren't all that complex or in-depth. *This troll definitely didn't like the sudden increase of people, that much should be obvious.* The unexpected influx of new people was confusing. It was perplexing and it was a tiny bit ghastly. This confusion had made him panic. It felt intimidating and scary. *It had made him feel bad.* The sudden spike of hysteria and terror that washed over him was similar to one that a pet owner might recognise from their animals; when your pet gets stuck somewhere or on something and the absolute terror this confusion causes in them. How a dog freaks out when it gets its head stuck in a tight place or when a cat gets its claw stuck in fabric and can't pull itself free. That knee-jerk reaction and sudden abandonment of rational response. They don't understand what's happening so they become lost to an all-consuming inability to maintain their composure. *They freak out in a big way.* That total collapse into primal bewilderment and need to escape the confusing threat of danger is exactly what had caused the troll's next action. The troll reacted instinctively as he gasped deeply and his mouth and eyes widened with a childlike fear, and a sudden minigun unfolded out from his shoulder and frantically fired through the fake crowd of imaginary Kikos, Karas and Muhrens as he screamed a scream of unyielding terror. The real Kiko, Kara and Muhren fell to the ground flat on their stomachs and cowered in the dirt with bated breath as an inferno of dangerous lights ricocheted over their heads. They did their best to avoid the sudden bombardment of deadly lights as the myriad of their ill-fated illusionary clones and doppelgänger shattered and broke down around them like glass.

See, overreactions like this was why people hated fighting trolls. Also, trolls have guns now, so that's good to know.

A sudden defiant arrow of light launched mercilessly through the air as Kara shot it from her bow. This arrow raced through the oncoming laser beams like a singular radiant beam of iron-willed determination and slammed straight into the troll's chest as Kara stood out in the open, obstinate and unshaken amongst the corpses of the fallen red Nekrithian soldiers and the destroyed rubble of the city walls. The troll snarled and Kara snarled back. *If some dumb space-troll wanted to kill her then it was certainly welcome to come and try.* If he wanted a fight, then that's what he would get. Kara had no intention of making it easy for him, and she had no intention of running away anymore. So here she would stand. It was time to take a stand and regain control of her own life. Sure the robo-troll was a daunting adversary, but y'know what? *So was she.* If a battle to the death was to unfold, pitting her unwavering resolve and uncompromising will against the wrath and fury of some fat techno slob, she bet to herself that he would come up short. Every other tough-looking bastard that had ever drawn a sword against her had died. This troll was welcome to add himself to the long list of forgotten masses. Besides, technically speaking, only one of them had survived punching an Angel in the face today.

Within the blink of an eye, her bow had transformed into a circular crimson shield. This round shield was framed by an ebony metal. It had the design of three angry dragon heads imbued on it in black paint stemming from the centre most point. All three of these dragons were frozen mid snarl and had a Celtic or Norse aesthetic to their design. These screaming mythical beasts were surrounded by a series of inky runes that were also painted onto the shield; which she gripped tightly in her hands with an iron-clad determination. Her contemporary leather jacket and jeans had fizzled away into a thick leather armour that enveloped her. This armour was multilayered and coarse. The top layer was that of two wolves carved into a rich black leather, facing each other across either side of a chest plate of ornate Celtic knots and tribal designs. The layer of leather hidden directly under this fancy design of Norse canines and twisted knots was a deep red that shone out in places from beneath the gaps in the top layers knots. It also decorated the wolves' bloodshot eyes and detailed the raised gums around their exposed teeth. Upon a closer inspection, this crimson leather was embossed with the fine print of small elegant roses, this being her family insignia after all. This leather-work also ran down doth of Kara's arm. The armour also laced up the back, with a ruby-red ribbon. The armour's iron pauldrons (*the bits on the shoulders*) consisted of a metal maze of thick studs that encircled a delicately interwoven metal rose's head on either side. Her dark leather wrist guards had a series of knotted ravens carved in them as they fought off another pair of tribal looking wolves.

Kara held her shield tightly in front of her face as a predictable second wave of deadly neon lights fired directly down upon her. She felt a surprisingly clear sense of focus sink in around her as her shield trembled violently in her taut grip, under the relentless force of the troll's heavy bombardment of lasers. Yet despite certain death, she did not panic. *She listened.* She listened eagerly and waited. Waiting patiently like a hunter watching its prey. Ready to pounce. *Ready to kill.*

Only one of them was going to die today and it wasn't going to be her.

The simple-minded troll had become furious that the '*not-dead*' Kara wasn't '*dead*' despite him shooting at her until she was supposed to be '*dead.*' So he decided '*little girl go squish-squish now!*' He ran towards the obstinate Viking-wannabe Half-Elf with his rusted hammer raised high above him. Maybe Kara was secretly insane, because for some reason this had been exactly what she had wanted. Most girls had normally wanted flowers and chocolates. Or ponies and clothes, at least this was according to what people had told Kara her entire life. The troll furiously rushed towards Kara, his heavy drumbeat of footsteps resounded with an impassioned rage. At the last conceivable second Kara quickly darted between his robotic legs, mid-step, and hacked at his ankle as she went through with her eager axe. The force of her blade combined with his speed made him topple over like a really scary domino, face first. This had left his back dangerously exposed to a second cleave of Kara's cantankerous cleaver. Her blade bit through his metal skin with a single astonishingly agonising act of swiftly pinpointed savagery. She used this buried hatchet to swing herself further up his unsuspecting back, where she landed with the full force of her second axe burrowing down upon him. *Rather impressively, her shield had transformed into her second axe whilst she was mid-jump!* From this new vantage point, somewhere near the creature's shoulder-blade, she began mercilessly wailing on the gun that protruded from it. *Never underestimate the agility of an Elf, and never underestimate the skill of a certain Kara De'Carusso.* She hung on for dear life with an impassioned fury as the troll tried to shake free. But Kara had no intention of going anywhere. No, she was here to stay. She had been pushed around far too much for far too long. And it was this troll that was going to be made to pay the price for every flutter of rage she felt. Some people felt butterflies in their stomach, Kara had dragons. They scorched at her with the flames of a palpitating fury. Their fires fed her soul and steadied her mind. Like any good weapon, Kara wasn't wild and random. She wasn't some untempered simpleton waving wildly at the world with reckless abandonment. No. *She was meticulous and she was accurate.* She was an unbridled fury with a plan. She didn't need Michael's approval or his Janus-faced comradery. All of those people who were afraid of the wrath of trolls should have been afraid of her. Or at least that was her take on it. Oh, and for the record, she was also winning.

As Kara loomed down on the gun, she had no idea what any of the parts were for. *So if it looked important, it got a hearty whack.* If it looked valuable, it got an en-crazed wallop. If it looked like it did anything at all, it got a ferocious thump. Her axe maniacally hacked and slashed as it dug its way through the flashing gun and its sparking metal support. Her beady little eyes locked onto her struggling target with an awoken intensity, like a shark sensing blood in the water for the very first time.

Sensing he was in danger, the troll tried to flee. It did this through a series of thrusters in his feet. A sudden boom ripped as the cyber troll began to take flight, like a terrifyingly gruesome airline carrier with a single passenger, Kara. *To be fair this fat airliner would have had the worst safety rating in the history of safety ratings.* Zero stars, there was no seat belts or chairs, there wasn't even a safety demonstration of what to do in the sudden event of imminent engine failure. *Also, there were no peanuts.* This was the worst flight ever, and as such Kara wanted to ground her bulky metal pilot as soon as possible. But she didn't want to just jump off as she felt like that would fall too closely as to being a '*victory*' for the hovering troll. *She was still out for blood.* Failing that, if this creature was bloodless, she'd settle for its head. Muhren threw his summoned lasso of light towards Kara, it was intended as a safety line or a lifebelt to tether her to them and stop her from being carried away upon the shoulders of the troll. Kara had misunderstood Muhren's intention as this isn't what she used it for. She quickly flipped around an exposed piece of piping that stuck out from a nearby Nekrithian wall and wrapped the rope around it as she span. This had been directly after she had tightened it around the troll's neck, like a noose. Within a second the line was pulled taut, snapping and locking in around the troll's metal neck. Thanks to the force of the thrusters, which the troll had not been smart enough to turn off or disengage, the rope remained taut and it was only getting tighter. Tighter. *Tighter.* Metal creaked and metal crumpled. The sensation of crushing pain snapping at his neck spurred the troll to pull away harder and faster, with even more power being given to his thrusters, which in turn made the '*spicy light noodle*' wrapped around his neck hurt even more. Ironically, all he had wanted to do was escape and get away from the light constricting around his neck. *But this over-eagerness to retreat was being his demise.* A vicious cycle with only one possible result, with a singularly determined Kara stood on the exposed piping making sure the lasso didn't surrender or slacken. She looked over the choking troll and felt a dark sense of satisfaction as she watched the rope take its toll. Like a fisherman with a fish or an executioner standing at the hangman's gallows, which was ironic given her own brush with death earlier. She had pinned the rope down by trapping it under the handles of both of her axes, which had been buried deep into the pipeline. She held the end of the line tightly in her hands as she pulled with all of her weight, pushing up her with her left leg as the right leg remained planted like a rooted tree. She yelled with frustration as the fat metal boy still speedily tried to pull himself free in a frozen struggling standstill, waiting for something to give.

'Pop!'

A jet of black oils ejected from the troll's neck as he was beheaded and washed over Kara. It wasn't blood, but it'd do. As Kara jumped back down, with her emerald eyes shining through her covering of viscous black oils, she noticed Muhren was staring at her blankly. He felt a strange sensation in his stomach, one that he had not felt for a long time. For so long, he almost forgot what the feeling was.

"What are you looking at?" She asked with a slightly confused and passive-aggressive tone.

"Uh-um, nothing. What are you looking at?" He replied back like an awkward twelve-year-old, as he went red and quickly looked away riddled with guilt as he recalled Elmin's radiant smile.

Shit! Maybe Muhren did like Kara after all...

Of course, it goes without saying that Kara's victory over the Nekrithian troll, regardless of how awe-struck it had made Muhren, was short-lived. The Nekrith Controller was only interested in seeing how well his newest cybernetic monstrosity would operate against his unwelcomed intruders. Now the troll was defeated, the need for games was coming to an end. As such our time travelling trio were running out of good will. *They didn't need to be kept alive.* A downpour of metal soldiers swarmed towards the three. An indiscernible wave of metal arms, legs and faces, like a ruptured ant's nest. They frantically clambered over the walls and quickly sprinted down the streets, all carrying big and scary looking guns. It was only a moment later that the wizards were entirely surrounded. See, it was stuff like this that was why magic users rarely ever went into space.

The cold emotionless Nekrith army led them through the streets, parading them at a maintained gunpoint. This was the second time this week that Kiko and Kara had had guns pointed at them. Some things weren't made better with a second experience, and funnily enough, being held at gunpoint was one such thing. Kiko, Kara and Muhren held their hands high as they walked the Nekrithian streets eagerly trying to spot a way out. There was none, the crowd of Nekrith was too thick to see through. Weirdly both times that the girls had been held up at gunpoint was in space. Maybe this meant Kara was right for not wanting to return into the expansive vacuum of the universe. Maybe space was the problem after all! Maybe there had been some correlation between intergalactic travelling and guns. *Or maybe it was because the girls kept crossing paths with the Nekrith and other military-based organisations.* Intergalactic hippy communes filled with cosmic vagabonds rarely had this sort of gun-related problem, so maybe space wasn't the issue here. Maybe it was the company the girls were keeping. This had actually been the sixteenth time a gun had been pointed at Muhren. The Argentavis Squad had been prone to reckless exploits back in the day. However this was by far the longest period of time he had had a gun pointed at him for, and he didn't like it. Currently, he estimated them to be outnumbered by approximately nine-thousand-to-one.

He didn't much care for those odds.

Weirdly, for some unknown reason, Kiko couldn't help but think over how much the Nekrithian aesthetic reminded her of the ancient Egyptians back on Earth. Like robotic, snake-necked ancient Egyptians. Both shared an abnormal monomania and unhealthy fascination with death. Building monuments, structures and their whole societies around it. Both had a penchant for overbearing designs and ornate lavish buildings. They both liked statues of strange-looking creatures. The only real difference was that one was an ancient society of sand whilst the other was a futuristic one of green neon lights. Oh and the fact that the Nekrith were robotic, killing machines and had big guns. And they resurrected the dead. *(To be fair, ancient Egyptians also raised the dead, but nothing on this scale!)*

Before long the trio was ushered into a building. The tingling sensation caused by the artefact they sought intensified. Wherever they were being led, it was actually in the right direction for where they needed to be heading, so at least that was a possibly positive outlook for what was about to happen next. Ultimately Kiko, Kara and Muhren were led into a great dark room. This room was tall and imposing. A crypt of immortalised technology. A computerised Gothic catacomb. The nightmarish idea of a cybernetic future wrapped in an exaggerated tenebrosity. Dirty, rusted pipes and wires hung high overhead. Towering impressive walls of slated metal rose dauntingly high over their heads and were covered in carvings of weird alien skulls, creatures and deformed bodies. These carvings of horrifically mutilated figures were interlaced with a series of pipes and wires as well as other unrecognisable and unsightly things. These etchings stretched as far as the eye could see, before fading into the shadows. This room was poorly lit and overbearing. Any feelings of dread were not eased by the cracks of green lightning that leapt up off of coils and crashed as they ran through the machinery around them. Green and orange blinking lights were scattered through the room from a multitude of places, screens and gizmos. Like everything that was Nekrith related, it was ornate, cold and horrible. It was soulless, but it was worse than that. It was intentionally designed to be horrifying and frightfully ghastly. It was ghoulish, but in a futuristic way. *Like a nightmarish cathedral to the metallic damned.* A long series of wires and thin plastic pipes fed directly into a small structure near the centre of this room. This centre was upon a raised, three-tiered platform of rusted black metals surrounded by four black metal pillars, one upon each side. These pillars had green lights that ran down the side of them. These green and orange neons would pulsate whenever the green lightning struck any of these pillars. Another four, much smaller pillars stood on top of the uppermost layer of the platform, one in each corner. There was also a rather crude looking squarish altar with a long and nasty looking spike sticking out of the top of it. The sides of this circular altar also had a series of green neon lights running down the side, flickering and jolting erratically. To everyone's surprise, the structure that was in the centre of the room started to move around on top of the platform. These pipes and wires weren't feeding into a structure at all. *It was a man!*

Kiko, Kara and Muhren had been granted an audience with the Nekrith Controller.

I worry that the term '*man*' may be incorrect as this would only serve to humanise the undead metallic monstrosity before them. Even the Nekrith Controller would resent such a title, as he considered himself to be high above it. A god of artificial perfection. Any comparison or insinuation of mortality would be nothing less than an all-encompassing insult. He had spent a lot of time purging all of the impurities from himself and the world around him. Things such as flesh and skin were obscene and disgusting to him. A failed impurity in need of removing. Bones were weak and could be easily broken and snapped. *So he had none.* What he had inside him was metal, that was much harder to break. Mortal eyes were weak and inattentive, with a pitiful clarity that translated into a mere five-hundred-and-seventy-six megapixels. What he had was a series of camera lenses, each one with a resolution approximately two-thousand times clearer than an eye. These eyes transmitted directly into an endless cloud storage, where endless reams of memories had been stored for all eternity. He even had a two-million terabyte hard-rive in his head in case of emergencies. Everything he had ever done or said in his life could be recalled at a single moment's notice. He had a series of processors that were attached to his brain that ran complex logical and mathematical equations almost instantaneously. His stomach was a series of insulated tubes carrying biological nutrients to his lungs and his brain. Other tubes carried fuel and oils to mechanical places. He even had a literal filter to process out any bacteria or pathogens that may be in the food or impurities in these oils. He didn't have teeth, again what he had was metal as teeth decayed. A series of small pistons ran across his back and his shoulders. When they lifted they discharged tiny electrical shocks of green energy. These pistons also ran across the surface of his head. Inside all of his joints were a series of tiny gears that turned and span for maximum flexibility. In some ways, the Nekrith Controller was a hybrid. *He was both Doctor Frankenstein and Frankenstein's monster*, a horrific nightmare of his own creation. He was also the embodiment of a *'man-made machine.'* Not in the sense that he was made by humans, god no, but he was literally a man made into a machine. A nightmarish potential destiny of cybernetics that could be in store for the human race.

According to the *'The Universal Guide to the Universe and Everything In It,'* the Nekrith controller was listed as the sixteenth most dangerous creature in the universe. Number one was the first crisp (*chip*) in a packet, because no one could ever fight the temptation and just have one. Apparently, once you popped, you couldn't stop. This was a lie, the number one most dangerous thing in the universe was the fire breathing, six-headed Grim Reaper of Drakollis, but of course, everyone knew that. The Nekrith Controller couldn't breathe fire, he couldn't fly and he only had the one head. But what he lacked in the ability to breathe fire he made up for in being cruel and heartless. *A mad scientist without limitation.* What he lacked in extra heads he made up for by having an endless army. And despite not having wings, he could still fly around in a spaceship. Which was actually cooler and less tiring than flying around on wings. Also, being ranked in the top twenty for anything in the universe is impressive. Just bear in mind how many people live there. *(The answer is 'all of them.' Everyone lived in the universe. Well, except the Demons and their worshippers. Oh, and the Angels, but none of them count.)*

The Nekrith Controller was plugged directly into the Scarrabellum. A series of wires and thin pipes connected this hulking monstrosity to the ceiling directly through his back. It was impossible to see exactly where these pipes had connected into the ceiling, but it seemed to be at a movable location, as he didn't seem limited in his manoeuvrability. He stood menacingly proud upon a series of eight sharp spider-like legs. His face was carved into the shape of a platinum humanoid skull and red neon eyes shone from it. His body was ebony, grey and slated rusty metals with gold highlights.

And there it was; the reason why they were all here, about to die on an alien spacecraft the size of a planet. *The Eye of Obsidius.* As the name suggests, it was an eye of obsidian metal and it was wrapped around the Nekrith Controller's neck on a thick chain. It was a metal ouroboros (*a circular self-eating snake*) wreathed around a black, soulless eye, set onto a sheet of dark metal reminiscent of a spearhead.

"I know why you have come. *You have not been the first and you won't be the last.* " The Controller gesticulated with palpable glee. A series of twenty or so green holographic skulls emerged, floating in mid-air around them all in a vast circle. These skulls quickly grew into a series of twenty or so different heads with cold ghostly frozen green faces. Like a monument from a museum of nightmares, chronicling those who had come to fail against impossible odds before them. "You time travellers are indeed an insidious lot. Impish purveyors and plunderers of what is rightfully mine. You have no concept of propriety and the rightful order. Charlatans and poachers the lot of you! I know what you seek and I know you will not have it." The Controller pointed at the Eye of Obsidius tied around his neck. "But tell me, who are you this time? Tell me, timer traveller, who has come raiding my home from the past only to die this day?"

A Nekrith soldier shoved Kiko after a moment's silence. The hit was painful as it made contact with her shoulder. The idea of not being the first Michael had sent to retrieve the artefact filled her with dread as she looked at the green images of her failed predecessors.

"You shall speak!" The Nekrithian demanded with a metallically angered voice of cold contempt. The Nekrith in this room broke out into a similar barking of '*speak*' and '*talk*.' A thousand angry voices. Kiko gulped as her throat went dry. A great fear had stolen her words and her previous strength. As she stood looking out over an endless horde of lifeless and artificial faces, she couldn't help but question how stupid, full hardy and reckless the plan had been.

"My... my name is... is Kiko." She said uncertainly. "Kiko Attetson."

The Nekrith Controller hissed and snarled in disgust at the mentioning of the Attetson family name.

"He dares! The great defender of Earth, a curse on him and his name! He dares to insult me and everything that I am by sending an inferior in his place! *How dare he?* He besmirches me and sullies my life's work. *Who*

does he think he is? He who insults and belittles the Nekrithian supremacy with this affronted insult! To send a terrified, cowering and nervous little girl in his place! Tell me, where is your brother, the great Vincent Attetson? Does he dare send the forgotten wall-flower of the Attetson name in place of where the fabled champion of light should be standing? He dare send a lifeform as insignificant as you to steal from me? *How insulting!* I am a god! I deserve respect! He sends you, a mewling quim? I will make Vincent pay for parading his mediocre minion in front of me. I shall reap unprecedented and unparalleled vengeance against that sarcastic criticiser who thinks a weak-willed, trivial and shrinking violet could ever challenge me! That such an insignificant worm deserves to walk the halls of my design! *A nothing nobody!* A trifling commoner and spineless nonentity. I shall rip the head clean of your shoulders, pathetic minion girl! Then we will see if Vincent deems me important enough to deal with me in person!"

So that was rude. Kiko was frozen in shock and deeply hurt by the Controller's outburst. Such a reaction to her name had completely caught her off guard. It was traumatising and distressing. So, it was actually quite befitting of the rest of the day she was currently having. To realise Michael had sent them off to die as pawns in chess was heartbreaking and soul-destroying. She wondered how many other people had played chess with him and how many others he had lied to? *What a truly terrible and awful day she was having.* For once in her life she had thought herself special. Hand chosen by some arcane cosmic force for a higher purpose. *She was finally her own person.* But even here, even thousands of miles and years from her time, she still couldn't escape Vincent's shadow. Even in her final moments, she couldn't break free of his name and his legend. *How did the Nekrith Controller even know about Vincent?* What had he done that was so special that some sanctimonious, robotic dickhead from the future knew so much about him? Even after his death and learning the secret of who he really was and everything he had done, here Kiko was still trapped under the weight of being Vincent's sister. Sorry no, that was a force of habit. *She wasn't actually his sister.* A realisation kicked in, she wasn't *'that'* Vincent's sister at all. She never had been. The *'Vincent'* that had killed the real Vincent (*the baby one*) was the same Vincent that everyone praised and doted upon. And it didn't feel right. But she didn't have to accept it. Her brother Vincent and the Changeling Vincent were two different 'people.' *(Also I think that this paragraph might be the most amount of times that the name Vincent has been written in such quick succession.)*

I'm going to be honest with you, writing about traumatic events like this and how it really feels is hard. It's hard to convey any true emotions that Kiko felt and generate an understanding that's both accurate and doesn't trivialise the pain. *I suppose that is why trauma is such a horrible thing to have to deal with.* You're always alone, even when in a crowd of people. You'll never understand how something truly feels by just writing about it. You'll also never understand how it feels by just reading words on a page. You will only truly understand what something feels like by having it happen directly to you. *For you to be the victim.* It feels unfair, but it's true. This was the curse of reality. This is why trauma is such a hard thing to understand and why it's so hard to talk about. You have to suffer pain to really understand it. It was a confusing concept. This is how Kiko felt when dealing with the loss of her brother and her reluctance when it came to dealing with the reality of the Changeling. Both had shared the same name, Vincent. One had been her brother by birth, but the other one was the one she had actually known and had grown up with. The second one was the villainous monster. Every time she thought of one *'brother'* it would cause a tidal wave of thought and confusion. *Of pain and hurt.* If you do understand what I'm talking about now, and if you have ever felt anything similar yourself, then you have my condolences. If you will, Kiko's emotions hung overhead like thick and heavy clouds. Her sorrow washed down upon her like rain. *(Have you ever tried persevering and continuing to do something whilst it rained?)* All Kiko wanted to do was to focus on the inevitable death that waited for her. *(It was probably a wise course of action.)* She wanted to find an escape. But all of these thoughts of Vincent, or rather the Changeling, kept raining down upon her. Causing distraction and getting in the way. These thoughts metaphorically soaked her clothes and reduced her visibility. Her inability to maintain focus was making her frustrated, as all she wanted to do was to keep going. She didn't want to stop just because it was raining. She wished she could lift her head up and scream directly into the negative thought clouds that were making it rain all around her. Scream with such a force that her throat would be red-raw and bleeding. That it would physically hurt and feel like her throat was ripping apart. *Until these clouds would ultimately tear apart and dissipate from around her.*

It felt like every time she tried to do anything, and I do mean anything at all, that there was always a person around every corner, waiting eagerly to run up to her and shout *'Vincent did it better'* before punching her in the stomach and knocking the wind out of her with a swift uppercut. It was as if the entire world had existed just to remind her that she could never quite live up to his legacy. That no matter what she did, or how hard she tried, she would never quite be *'Vincent'* enough, despite never wanting to be. Even when in the far reaches of space, her life was little more than an endless line of people who apparently only existed to remind her that her best would always be bested. *That whatever good she did was not good enough.* The shadow of Vincent was a well and every time Kiko tried to crawl out from it, to have agency or autonomy in her own individuality, life was always waiting at the top with a hammer. Ready to strike at her climbing hands and send her back down. She was sick of it.

"Vincent's dead. But I don't thi-"

"Good." The Nekrith interrupted with zero care. "The simple idea of such a..."

"I'm not finished speaking!" Kiko interrupted back. "Who the hell do you think you're speaking to?" The Nekrith Controller gave Kiko a curious look. *"Who do you think you are?* Looking down your nose at me! At least I have a nose! You sanctimonious prick! I don't care if you're about to shoot me, what gives you the right to judge me or my life? *Wow, okay.* Sure, I'm no Vincent Attetson. *Boohoo!!* But I'm not a nothing nobody, and I'm not a shrinking violet!"

The Nekrith Controller laughed.

"You misunderstand. I speak not with the words of self-righteous opinion. I speak the words of truth. Take her!"

With his final words, a Nekrith soldier ruthlessly grabbed Kiko by the hand and dragged her towards the altar with the needle-like spike on top of it. The spike was thin and approximately eight inches long. Kiko looked on with horror as she tried to pull herself away and tried to break free. *Whatever this thing was it looked horrible and painful.* She dreaded to think what it might be for. Whatever she did, she couldn't quite squirm her way free of the soldier's tight and painful grip around her wrist. As it would turn out, a metal hand was much stronger than a human one. A shooting hot pain stabbed through her hand as the soldier slammed it down upon the spike. It broke through her skin and pierced her hand like a needle stabbing through fabric. Like a knife through butter or a nail being hammered into a wall. The machine seemed to come alive the second it sensed her blood. Like a computer for Vampires. Gears quickly creaked as they span and lights sparked into life with a hearty groan and meaty whir. Kiko was surprised that she didn't scream from the pain. But her tears did whelm in her eyes from the pain and she did make was some weird noise that was almost like a gasp mixed with a groan.

"Allow me to show you the person you truly are, little Kiko Attetson." A thunderous series of green and orange orbs projected into the room and began flying around in a mad rush, spinning around her like a tornado of memories.

"You are weak-willed, non-miraculous and forgettable." These orbs span and shook as images began to emerge from within them as they dashed frantically around her. These images were ripped directly from Kiko's life; a cruel collection of past moments of failures and regret. Unwanted highlights from her history. Times of inadequacy and shortfalls. Moments of personal defeat and forced silences. A myriad of mundane and normal decisions of when Kiko turned their back on a life of importance. A lifetime of stupid things said at stupid times. A life of embarrassment and shame. Times spent crying, hiding in her locked room. A highlight reel of regret revisiting times spent alone with no one else around. Of arguments and fights she had walked away from despite the fact she still had stuff left unsaid because she felt like she couldn't win.

"Non-threatening and unable to commit and dedicate yourself to anything long enough to see it through. Always coming up short." The orbs showed still moments of preferably forgotten times from her life. *A gallery of her past.* A collection of her worst moments and personal failures that she had tried to forget. Of times were peers pretended to look the other way or deliberately ignored her. Times where she was spoken over and looked down upon. This altar was seemingly able to feed off of a person's blood and see their past. To view memories and restore them. Zipping and parading them around like little balls of torment. Times such as when she had broken her leg in a race or when she had been dumped by her ex. Of times where people would be confused as to why Kiko was even there at all. *Of several nights spent crying.*

"You are lacklustre and benign." These orbs showed moments of Kiko's life where people gave her judgemental looks of derision and laughed at her as she walked by, of times life had passed her by. Kara and Muhren watched helplessly as Kiko's past was paraded around them, still trapped under a Nekrithian grasp. "No man, woman or child can hide from their true selves; and that is what the Pilantir of Life shows. Look at it all, Kiko, take it all in. Watch the reflections of remembrance. Let me show you your true self. Understand why it is hard to take acts of violence or indignation seriously from one such as you. A little girl who leaves words unspoken and deeds unfinished."

The orbs of reflected remembrance began to take shape into events you would recognise.

"Allow me to show you all of the people you betray with your acts of cowardice and indecisive will. Of the people you have left to die and suffer as you always do what you do best. Run away."

These reflections began to show the faces of people you've already met. Of Lieutenant Amirah Miller and Captain Orellan of the HMS Edinheim, of the Amaranth and the other residents of Revantide as they died against the Nekrith. Of the young and terrified boy Kiko and Kara had abandoned to the Pesadilla-niño. The people Kiko had left to their fates. Of the baby Vincent and his death as she stood there and did nothing about it.

"You are no hero!" The Nekrith Controller said whilst laughing to himself. "Yet you get angry when anyone reminds you of it. You take ordinary people and you betray them. It matters not their fate, so long as you survive. The desire for preservation is something I understand, trust me I really do. But why? Why are you so eager to continue your life of undercut victories and benign existence? Why does everyone else have to die just so you can live one more day of a shallowed complacency? Interesting... how much thought did you give into betraying your Earth for fanciful stories of grandeur? *How goes the investigation of those missing war ghosts?* You were expressly told to only work on that by your superiors. *Did you ever find even a single ghost?* Did you ever capture a single perpetrator? Why are you here? How much time did you actually spend doing as you were told? A week, a day, a few hours or even a matter of minutes? How long did it take for you to get distracted? *Or was it too hard?* How long did it take before you betrayed your orders and were off gallivanting across the universe seeking fanciful stories of personal betrayal and prophecies? No, I am not impressed by you. A woman who would let her own flesh and blood die because some *'rule'* said so. A true hero always finds a way. A true legend always finds a way. *You always find a way to be second best.* To be passive and complacent. Unable to settle, finish or close any chapter of your life's book, always racing off in the face of hardship."

The Nekrith Controller laughed once more. *"Kiko the underachiever."*

I mean, he's not wrong... I would make an argument that any summary of a life spent was open to bias and prejudice depending upon your perspective, your outlook and how you chose to view things. *Any act can be viewed in any way.* People said history was written by the victor, this was just a fancy way of saying that whoever was the last man standing would have the final say about something. No one is truly a bad guy, not to themselves. So if they're the last person left speaking, then they're the only person left telling the story. They decide upon the narrative and how their deeds are viewed. *Life was also complex.* You could take any series of frozen moments from anyone's life and tell any story you wanted. *Like you.* You're a bad person because you once walked past a homeless beggar without giving them any money. You lost your temper and either shouted at or hurt someone. You once lied to a friend or a loved one to get out of something. You also once ignored a person because you weren't in the mood to talk to them, which was rude. *Of course, this is complete rubbish.* We've never met and I don't know you. *I merely listed off generic occurrences that we've all done and been guilty of.* I could have just as easily told a story of how these acts unite us all, and how it actually makes you a good person. How it was fine that you chose to ignore the beggar because you don't actually owe anyone anything. That you have helped other people and you can't save everyone. If you helped everyone who asked for it, you would be run dry. So it's fine to pick your battles and charitable deeds. That we have all lost our temper and to do so is only human. You lied to a close friend or family member because it was a better alternative than hurting them, so you were actually helping them. Oh and you're not a machine, so you don't have to speak on command to everyone in your life. *These are basically the same actions.* How you choose to view them is how they are remembered. *You give it strength, you either validate or invalidate the world around you.* Clearly, the Nekrith Controller had never been taught the etiquette of not passing comment on other people's life. A principle that was portrayed well in the 2002 film *'8 Mile.'* The words immortalised by a certain Eminem, the B-Rabbit, mister Marshall Mathers or the Real Slim Shady. *'Don't ever try to judge me, dude. You don't know what the fuck I've been* through.' I couldn't have portrayed Kiko's current emotions better myself. So thank you to the real Slim Shady, you can sit down now. But to be fair, the Nekrith Controller did make a good argument against Kiko. It was persuasive, well structured and right enough to not be inherently wrong. It was right enough to be triggering.

Kiko froze as a red hot rage flashed over her. Anger spat at her and fury prickled in her bones.

"What did you just call me?" She replied with a frown.

"*Underachiever?*" She repeated. "*UNDERACHIEVER?*"

There was a sudden terrible flash as the Nekrith that was pinning Kiko to the spike from Pilantir of Life exploded into ice. No one had been watching Kiko's other hand and in their hubris they had given her an out. Kiko ripped her hand free and ran into the centre of the room. Kara and Muhren looked on in shock.

"Well, we'll just see about that!" She shouted as she disappeared into a green swirling time vortex.

But where was she going?

Chapter Twenty-one

THE UNDERACHIEVER

As it turns out there was precisely one thing you should never, ever call a time traveller. One thing you should never, ever say if you placed any value in having any integrity and you didn't want your statement to blow up in your face. If you were smart and never liked to be proven wrong then you should avoid ever uttering this one sentence at any cost. You should never call a time traveller an underachiever. *You should never imply that their life's work was underwhelming and their accomplishments lacking.* It was probably not wise to belittle them. To insinuate that they had failed to make a lasting impact on the universe or that they underutilised their time spent. To imply that they had no value and would die as a nothing-nobody. The reason for this was simple. If a time traveller has all of time to play with - and if they're also either arrogant or stubborn enough!- then labelling them as an underachiever can be viewed as something of a challenge. *Like a red flag to a bull.* An open door to a dare. Some invitational taunt to do more. To be better. To rise. To be legendary. To achieve a multitude of accomplishments just so that they can say that they could. All for the purpose so that they may be able to rub it in your face, or the face of a certain judgemental Nekrith Controller who implied they were lacking, lackadaisical or lame. In short, it's never a good idea to challenge a time traveller, especially when they feel like they have something to prove. When time isn't a restraint then there isn't really anything you can to stop them from doing whatever it is that they want. *They literally have all of the time in the universe to ready themselves for revenge.* So off Kiko went with a determined sense of indignation burning in her heart. According to the Controller, she had some loose ends to tie up. It was nice of him to let her know. In return, Kiko would teach him humility and about the correct way in which to speak to a person. The Nekrith Controller was about to receive a crash course in manners. It was said that it was nice to be important. However, it was also a common occurrence for these '*important people*' to forget that it was also important to be nice. A mother will always teach you to never play with your food and a good hunter knows to show respect to his kill. To this end, the Nekrith should not have taunted Kiko in front of her friends. They should have killed them before Kiko had a chance to escape. Kiko the underachiever, the uninteresting, the non-miraculous and insipid. Well, now she felt capricious, indignant and affronted. So off she went running through time. Her goal was simple. It was time to stop hiding in the shadows, and there was one certain Nekrithian commander to put back in his place.

The planet was Revantide, the year was 5036.

You might, hopefully, remember a somewhat stubborn lieutenant by the name of Amirah Miller. The last time we had seen her she had been facing certain death. Currently, she had found herself lost, alone and outgunned by an ever-approaching Nekrith platoon deep within the heart of the planet Revantide. Readers who were paying attention may remember her. Chunks of rock from the pillars and statues of this vast room collapsed around her as an endless bombardment of laser beams danced on every side. As she knelt, staring at her gun, her heart burst with thoughts of all the loved ones she was about to be reunited with. Her brother, her parents and all of those friends that had died at the hands of the Nekrith. All that death and all that loss weighing down upon her. *The endless rivers of bodies flowed through her mind.* A tally of those who would never grow old or weary. It was time. She was ready for her last hurrah. You can only dance with death for so long before the turmoil becomes monotonous and soul-destroying. *What more could she possibly have to lose?* This was the final curtain call. The war had taken everything she had to offer. She was tired of it all, and it was time to accept her fate.

She let lose a final sigh of relief as a cocky smile broke across her face. So this was how it all was to end? With a final heave, she dragged herself from the dirt of this dying planet. To depart this life in a blaze of glory, on her own terms. As she rose she screamed a roar reminiscent of the war cries of the Valkyries of old. *(It was also a war cry not too dissimilar to Kara's when she popped the head off of that space troll!)* Tammy, Brian, Captain Orellan, mamma, pappa. Your girl was coming home with open arms. You best be ready to welcome her home after all this time. Her final symbolic gesture would be to take as many of these corrupted lifeforms with her as she went. The deed would be entirely meaningless, but at least one more Nekrith would be dead because of her.

But the horde of Nekrithian soldiers lay abandoned and broken across the ground. A figure stood defiantly in the wreckage. An all too familiar tangle of rose-red hair and a blue bohemian coat blew courageously in the wind.

"Heya!" Kiko's chirpy voice echoed through the Revantider's deteriorating church with a curious sense of both confidence and ebullience, as she slid her glasses up her nose. *"Can I borrow you for a sec?"* A cocky smile of her own broke across her face.

There may be some out there who assumed that Amirah had now been saved. However the act of *'being saved'* required for you to be removed from a dangerous time or location and moved, well, to somewhere *'safe.'* There always needs to be a notable difference in the level of threat from one location to the other. So, let's say if the first location was a war zone on a dying planet, almost anywhere else would have been a better alternative, right? Kiko grabbed the trembling hand of a questioning Amirah. Having had the Nekrith belittle her was actually a blessing. Admittedly maybe not for them. For them, it was a final jab at an enemy near death which they had grossly underestimated. For Kiko, it had created a laundry list of objectives and goals. A series of unfinished events that awaited completion. Any gamer (*this being a person who plays video-games*) would be aware of this process. The clearing of one's *'Quest Log'* before you can say that a game has been truly completed. Kiko knew in her heart what she had to do. To travel through time and solve as many issues as she could without altering the pre-existing timeline too much.

Truth be told the previous resolution of the Nekrith invasion of Revantide had never sat quite right with her. It always pulled at her heart and weighed on her soul. It never felt like an actual ending. *It felt unresolved.* The few nights where she had been able to go to bed had resulted in her laying there until three am, as her mind raced through the *'whats, ifs and buts'* of Revantide's demise. Anyone who has experienced a similar sense of sleep deprivation is aware of how this feels. To lie there powerlessly two hours before your alarm sounds for work, as your brain is deciding that now is the time to remind you of some embarrassing or wasted time in your life. However, letting a whole planet die as you did nothing wasn't quite comparable to a time you said something embarrassing to that person you had a crush on ten years ago. Also, even if you're a time traveller, you can still be swept off your feet by time and lost to it. This is to say that so much had happened between now and then (*when Kiko had visited Revantide for the first time.*) that Kiko hadn't been able to find the time to do anything about the part that she had played on the day this planet had originally fallen. (*Anyone needing a refresher on all that has happened to Kiko during this time can re-read from that part of the book onwards, I'm not repeating myself!*)

This invasion sat as the ideal starting point for what Kiko knew she had to do. Not only was it still very recent for her, but it was also a good place to start for where the Nekrith were concerned. The plan was twofold. Saving the planet that she had found so endearing was of course of utmost importance. But if done right, this return through time would also spell a defeat to the Nekrith. *And what better way was there to teach them a lesson?*

The dying sacred grounds of the underground Revantide church were swapped for a war-torn starcruiser that was falling out of orbit. A spaceship that was about to hurtle down and nosedive into the side of a planet was not a better place to be when compared to the planet below. *But hey, at least Amirah got to be back on the HMS Edinheim one last time.* Machinery sparked and screens flickered all around Kiko and Amirah as they had returned to the ill-fated warship. Amirah's head reeled as she tried to wrap her head around how she could possibly be on the same ship that she had just seen destroyed only a few hours earlier. She had seen it with her own eyes. Broken across the mountainsides of Revantide. However, the floor felt the same underfoot and all the rooms looked the same. She recognised this room, it was the cockpit! She had been here many times before. She also recognised all the dead and deceased that lay strewn and discarded around her. She had spoken to them all on many occasions. One face, in particular, shone out from the cold crowded cadavers. It was Captain Orellan. A good captain always went down with his ship. *But how could she be back here?* She knew she had seen it all destroyed. Shipwrecked and marooned. She had seen it with her own eyes. However, she didn't have long to stand around. There was no time to adjust to the fourth dimension. None at all as Kiko shot off towards the back of the ship.

"Where are you going?" She called after her ginger saviour.

"I'm going to the back of the ship!" Kiko called out with a hint of indignation as she clamoured through the blistered wreckage.

Steel pipes hissed and creaked as the HMS Edinheim did its best not to disintegrate from the pressures ripping her apart.

"Why...?"

"We're falling out of orbit, Amirah. We're about to nosedive directly into the planet below." Kiko stuck her head back from around the edge of the doorway at frowned at the clueless lieutenant. A pang of annoyance washed over her face and furrowed her brow. *"Use your brain!* The front of the ship is going to crash first!" She shook her head in disbelief. "So we're going to the back! I have no intention of being here when the crash happens, now come along. I'm not saving you for a third time."

A third time?

"No, why are we here?" Amirah called out after Kiko as she disappeared again. But there was no reply.

The HMS Edinheim was in a state, and I don't mean Texas. This vessel had been one of the crown jewels of the New Andromeda Republic. A defiant warrior against a menacing horde. They called her unsinkable. *(However, we all know what happens when you call a ship that! When life gave you lemons, you'd make lemonade. But when life gave you an iceberg, you couldn't just add ice to the lemonade. This wouldn't fix anything. Occasionally when life gave you lemons, you just had to accept your sinking fate in cold, dark seas.)* The reason they called this ship unsinkable was due to its secret weapon. Its all-powerful passenger. *The Divine cargo.* This baby Divine was also why Kiko had returned here through time, even though saving Amirah felt unquestionably like the right thing to do. She knew in her heart that to keep such a magnificent creature enslaved was barbaric. But to allow it to die was an even worse act of treason against all that was good in this life. A Divine's singular purpose was to create. *To birth life.* As the great engine room doors jolted open, she saw the giant god-fetus once more. She knew what had to be done next.

"I do have a plan, Amirah." Kiko said as she glanced over the engine room. "I'm not crazy... *Well, no plan is crazy if it works right?*" Her words broke into a fake laugh as she thrust a spacesuit into the lieutenant's arms. "Put these on. I just don't have the time to explain what it is." She smiled as reassuringly as she could muster. "I need you to trust me. Can you do that?" There was a pause as the two girls made direct eye contact. *"Do you trust me?"*

Lieutenant Miller gave the most assertive nod she could muster. It was hard given the circumstances. Kiko spun on the spot and turned her attention to the Divine, as Amirah got changed. *'Now what to do with you?'* Kiko knew Divines thrived off cosmic radiation and solar energy. Any peaks of solar activity drew their attention like moths to a flame. She also knew that simply freeing this Divine here would only result in one of two disastrous outcomes, the first being the most obvious. The Nekrith would just steal it away and use it for much more nefarious means. The second was that Kiko was unsure as to what would happen if a Divine was let loose this close to a pre-existing planet. Would the Divine try and consume the planet? *Maybe?* There were no records to substantiate this either way. Was this planet also built around another Divine? *Probably?* How would the two Divines react to each other? There were simply too many unknown variables to risk discovering the answers for herself. So Kiko knew it had to go somewhere. *But where?* Hang on! No. Not somewhere. *Somewhen?* Where in time could this baby demigod be sent? It needed to be somewhere where it wouldn't cause a paradox or cause instant death or genocide. *But when?* There must have been some unexplained phenomenon in time that was caused by the sudden appearance of a Divine... Sure Kiko couldn't rewrite time, but herein lay a loophole. *What if she had already done so?* Like how she had saved herself in Paris. If some event had always been undone by this Divine, then she wasn't changing anything. She was simply making sure the sands of time flowed correctly. Like they always had and needed to do so.

Bingo! She knew what to do.

Perfect!

There was a flash of green light that filled the room the second Amirah put on her helmet. The surroundings of the doomed ship had been replaced by the vacuum of space. *Amirah panicked at the sight of the empty void.* But maybe not for the reason you were initially thinking. She had been in space her entire life, so seeing it wasn't as surprising as it would be for the likes of me and you, similar to how a lion tamer wouldn't be bothered by the sight of a lion. The reason she was alarmed at the sight of space was that she hadn't quite gotten around to engaging the oxygen pump. As soon as the flow of oxygen was restored, she sighed a sigh of relief. To her surprise, Kiko wasn't wearing a suit. However, it looked like there was some sort of a bubble around her head. To Amirah's surprise, an old starship blasted off next to her, seemingly retreating from a star. This ship wasn't old as in elderly. No, it was old as in it was antiquated and relic-like. From Amirah's perspective spaceships like this one hadn't existed for hundreds or thousands of years. They only lived in museums, as fossils and buckets of rust. This one was in near-mint condition. Due to its speed and trajectory, it seemed to be running from something. And, oh boy! It definitely was. There was a muffled boom as something far off in the vacuum of space drew her attention. What she turned to witness was just about the worst thing a person could ever see. Unbeknownst to her, she was neither in the year 5036 or in the Andromeda galaxy. She currently floated in the space of Alpha Centauri. This being the closest neighbouring constellation to our own. This constellation had three stars, and in the year 4112, a band of oil tycoons decided it would be a grand idea to mine one of them! *Because that was apparently a smart thing to do.* They had chosen the star Proxima Centauri. Proxima Centauri, however, had decided it didn't like the idea of having people strip it of its resources or touch it in any way. As it turned out Proxima Centauri was a bit of a diva. And like all divas, it knew how to send a message. This being a message of *'do not ever touch my stuff or I'll burn your face off.'* This message consisted of pure, unadulterated solar radiation and fire. This shock wave of pure rage and fiery cosmic energy was about to slam into the adjacent facing side of the four planets that orbited it. Sucks being those guys, they had a good life! But Kiko had long read about the disastrous folly of man that had befallen upon this day. - History books work in both directions, depending on when you read them. - Something had happened that had stopped the unprecedented death toll in its tracks… but no one knew what….

Kiko watched the far off, but quickly, approaching radiation spike. With all the strength she could muster she catapulted this baby Divine, hurtling through the void of space towards the dying star. There was no record as to what the relationship was like between the demigod-like Divines and the celestial bodies that we call stars. Divines had never directly come into contact with a star before. But Kiko knew how they liked to feed off of the solar energy and other miscellaneous radiations. She knew Divines bestowed the power to create and to give life. Stress and anticipation ate at her bones and she hoped and prayed from afar. Staring out into the nothingness of space. Hopefully, the clouded shock-wave of radiation had served as a smorgasbord of delectable appetizers for the Divine as it flew through. *'Come on.'* She watched the far off star and waited. *'Come on!'* The Divine had to be able to figure it out. *'To do something!'* She knew in her heart that this creature was amazing. *'Come on!'* It could figure it out. *'Come on, please.'* Please figure it out. There had to have been enough radiation here to awaken it. *'Come on. Please be strong.'* Every future part of her plan hung in the balance. All the lives on all the four planets hung in the balance too. Divines fed on radiation to give life. *'Come on.'* Just this one time, defy the odds. Be that one spark in a million. Be brilliant. *'Come on!'* Be the Divine that didn't just settle for creating life. Be the Divine that saves it. *'Come on, you clever little demigod, figure it out.'* Figure out a way.

Yet the waves of radiated retribution still approached.

"Come on…" Kiko muttered out loud. "Come on…!"

Her mind flooded with the faces of her loved ones. Of Kara, Muhren, Cassandra and Collin. Of Ozzy, Bailey and even bitchy Penelope and Marvin the octopus. The message from the Angel burned at her soul. *'The child of time who bends it to her will.'* This plan had to work. It simply had to. If she had acted in time, or if she was correct in her musings, there should be enough power here to save both. To fix the dying star and the broken demigod by merging them together. A single entity. If a Divine had the ability to bestow life unto the universe then what was to stop it from being able to give that power to this fallen star? To heal it. To seal the wounds. In return for its generosity, this Divine would be fuelled forever by all the solar energy it could ever need. It felt like a fair trade. If only it could figure out what to do next.

By now Kiko had uttered the phrase *'come on'* so many times it had become one singular endless word as she stared out into space.

"Comoncomoncomoncomoncomoncomon."

Panic gnawed at her. Yet still, she watched. Still, she waited.

A secondary shock wave emerged. But this one was hopefully one of success. Suddenly, and almost instantaneously, all the encroaching radiation had snapped back in on itself. Back into the star. There was a sudden seemingly endless moment where the star, Proxima Centauri, went dark. This darkness was short-lived where a light shone anew. Brighter than ever.

It had worked. An entire constellation had been saved.

But there was no time for celebration. Revantide still needed saving. This part of the plan was going to be simpler. These four planets that orbited Proxima Centauri had been at war with one another for the longest time. Millenniums of war had left them with very little to agree on. So, much to the shock of everyone involved, all four leaders of all four planets now found themselves sat around a table. They had all been summoned by the same singular red-headed woman. This woman had given them an ultimatum and an invitation to war. Some thousand years from now a planet in the Andromeda galaxy was about to fall. The armies of these four planets had to be ready to help. The price for failure was surprisingly simple. Any one of these warlords could say no. But the cost of even one refusal meant she'd *'take her Divine back.'* These warring warlords were welcome to refuse her and she would simply find others. They could choose to unite against a new common enemy, the Nekrith, or they could unite in the death of star-fall. In poker, it is sometimes a good idea to call someone's bluff. However, it is always best to do so if you can either afford the loss or have good enough cards of your own to play. These warlords found they had neither. So reluctantly they had agreed to these terms.

A barrage of missiles bombarded against the surface of Revantide. The Nekrith's conquering of this planet was nearing completion. Or so they thought. What this outright victory against Revantide had actually been was the first day of a decade of defeat. As some ten-thousand ships had befallen upon them. These ships had seemingly come out of nowhere. Worse, they somehow knew of every weakness that they had had. Almost as if they had been given secrets far beyond their years. In reality, these mysterious saviours of Revantide had been gifted almost a millennia to study, learn and master the Nekrith. The fear of absolute death had spurred them at first, but over the passing of generations, these four planets had both developed and flourished under Kiko's cultivated times of peace. They had also eventually begun a new religion where they worshipped the Sun God and praised his fire-haired oracle, Kenshua. A woman whose head was said to be on fire with flaming red hair and with a coat crafted from blue space clouds. This oracle had told them of the Sun God's will, a goal to vanquish an absolute evil. This divined agenda had given them purpose. The defeat of the Nekrith in the Revantide skies had marked a turning point for Andromeda. The greatest defeat ever recorded for the Nekrithian armies that spanned a decade.

Some ten years later there were no traces of the Nekrith to be found anywhere within the Andromeda galaxy. This victory for the New Andromeda Republic had been entirely because of Kiko's fast thinking. As had their new cultivated relationship with the four new planets. Which wasn't bad going for the forgotten daughter of the Attetson name. It's amazing what you can achieve with a little time and a demigod on your side. It was somewhat ironic that all Kiko had to remember this great victory by was a single photograph Amirah had taken of her as she had sat arguing with the warlords of old, some thousand years prior.

But this does not mean Kiko was finished yet. *Not by a long shot.* She despised the Nekrith with all of her heart. And she was nowhere near done teaching them a lesson. She had never really had much in the way of a purpose to her life before all this. But now she knew. She knew who she was and what her purpose was in life. There was good and there was evil out there. She had witnessed both with her own two eyes. She had seen evil and she knew that she hated it and that she wanted to help stop it whenever she could. She wanted to be decent and help those who couldn't help themselves. To show mercy to a crippled universe. She wanted to be the antithesis to everything Nekrithian. *She wanted to be kind.*

On the fourth of July, 1776, a certain John Hancock had found himself shy of exactly one quill. This was a rather embarrassing turn of events, as the Earth was sat patiently awaiting him to sign perhaps the most important document of Earth's history. But don't worry, Kiko let him borrow hers. In the year 1066 armies now spoke of a crimson witch that had heralded the victories of their king to be, William the First. This wise-woman's words had even donned him a new title, '*William the Conqueror.*' In the 1970s a certain Richard Nixon swore blindly that a red-headed spokeswoman had not given him counsel that had ended the Vietnamese war. In 1973 a band of people spoke of how a Pesadilla-niño had been slain by a scrawny little girl and how she had saved a nameless child. Legend spoke of a witch that sixteenth-century Parisians believed in, this '*Femme Rouge*' bestowed bountiful crops and had even sought to teach them better farming and societal techniques. She had even taught them how to scare away trolls without the need of hurting them.

There was a flash of light as Kiko returned to the Scarrabellum, back to Kara and Muhren.

"How's this for underachieving?" She shouted as she slammed her hand back onto the spikey dial of the Pilantir of Life.

'*Ow!*'

The orbs became flooded with images of her new accomplishments. Of this child of time and everything she had recently done. Of the legendary oracle, Kenshua, and of the Femme Rouge. All those lives saved or improved for the better. The Nekrithian controller looked out in horror as he saw now who it was that had been responsible for his armies greatest defeats.

"But that's not my only question." A devious smile broke across her face as she grabbed hold of her friends. "Who's going to ask me what I did with all those bombs?"

Before anyone had had a chance to ask about what bombs she referring to, there was a sudden ripping sensation as the Eye of Obsidius was wrestled from around the Controller's metal neck. Kara grabbed it as it flew towards her and Kiko quickly teleported the three away, within the blink of an eye. They were far away, both in space and time, from the Scarrabellum as a wave of fiery retribution engulfed it and all of the metal dominions within. It had required exactly twelve thousand bombs to dispose of this once great ship. It was a payment that the Andromeda Republic had been happy to cover. It had just taken them three years of continuous manufacturing to ready them for Kiko. *For Kiko, it had taken as long as it was required for her to buy and finish a coffee.* But there was an important lesson learned by all this day.

Never call a time traveller an underachiever, it never ends well.

Chapter Twenty-two

THE END OF TIMES

So here we all find ourselves. *At the end.* In the final chapter; the swan song at the end of time. Both for this book and for the Demons. Our time together is coming to an end in the last moments of victory before the final curtain call. The last round and final stretch before the finish line. A time of celebration for a job well done and a proverbial pat-on-the-back. The trio of unlikely heroes had achieved the seemingly impossible and acquired the peculiar-looking Eye of Obsidius despite the overwhelming odds. Admittedly this had been down to Kiko, but the others played their parts. I wish that I could say that Kiko's heroic deeds had been inspired by benevolent or valiant reasons. But this wasn't entirely true. Her final push, as we all know, was caused by her inability to face her insecurities. Her craving to be noticed and observed and not for the paramount reason of acquiring the Eye of Obsidius for the right reason. This is to say that her victory had not been inspired by noble agendas. She hadn't claimed the Eye of Obsidius to seal away the Demons for all eternity; she had defeated the Nekrith because of what basically amounted to being a tantrum. Quintessentially, they had called her a name that she didn't appreciate and she had lashed out. The fact that she had obtained the eye was secondary to proving she was special. The fact she had wrestled the key that will lock all the Demon doors wasn't as much of a key factor to her as it should have been. *But since when were heroes perfect?* The point still stands that she had still won, and that's the important part. She would always be remembered as the woman who defeated the Demons, in contrast to that any nuances of intention or reasoning behind her victory would be trivial and inconsequential. All that this proved was that heroes and legends are still just flawed people underneath. The purpose behind a hero isn't the person of flesh and blood. It's an idea. That's all. No more no less. This is why you should never meet your heroes. Childhood was a time to think that adults were gods and fountains of knowledge. Growing up and becoming one was a time of realising otherwise. No one was perfect, so who cares why Kiko won. *All that matters was that she did.* Besides, she wasn't the only one who was acting from selfish angles. Bear in mind that Michael had told each and everyone one of the three that he viewed them as the leader and he was only speaking to them. That their goal had beneath the other two and all three wizards ate it up like starved orphans. They all arrogantly believed they were protagonists of their own story. - *Yes I know Kiko is technically the protagonist, shut up. I'm being hyperbolic and exaggerative to prove a point!*- Not one stopped to think that maybe the Archangel was playing them against each other. Well, Kara almost did. *Perhaps you didn't notice it either?* But why would an Angel want to divide and conquer? That doesn't seem very benevolent, compassionate or any of the other words we associate with angelic people. Subterfuge and trickery, lies and deception feels immoral and wrong. All three worked for the Arcane Intelligence Agency. They all shared a vested interest in stopping Demon attacks. It's not like any of the three would refuse the chance to cripple the Demon-kind. It was literally a part of their job. Now I think of it, isn't it weird that Michael didn't reach out to them via the Agency? Oh, that's right... he had cosmic reasonings for secrecy. *How silly of me.*

Upon success, the trio of time-hoppers were instructed to meet Michael in a grand graveyard deep in the heart of Berlin. A great city with a long history. But a cemetery was a strange place for such an important and ceremonial handoff. A hidden world of corpses secreted under a coating of dirt didn't feel like a place an Archangel would willingly choose to receive such an important artefact. I mean there were plenty of churches to choose from... Yet here Kiko was. In a morbidly beautiful maze of tall tombstones, commemorative monuments and overhanging trees that surrounded her. She was stood on a crossroads with a long line of spine-chilling graves in all directions and strong trees dashed throughout. The air was brisk and a tiny bit wet. But it was still a beautiful sunny day with a proud sun working hard in a clear sky. It was also quiet with the only sounds coming from the Germanic comings-and-goings upon the horizon. Kara and Muhren were currently back in Liarath acquiring the Revanspear to bring it back here to this quaint and eerily beautiful cemetery. The place where the power of the Demons would be undone once and for all.

Kiko watched as a blue cloud rippled about six feet above the ground and Michael emerged from it. He walked toward her, but something didn't feel right. Kiko doubted herself which in turn was spoiling her feelings about the great deed about to be done. Souring the victory ahead.

"You seem troubled my friend." Michael said down unto her as she handed him the Eye. It felt strange how the Eye of Obsidius had been so bulky that Kiko had required both hands to hold it, but Michael only needed one due to his impressive stature.

"Something just doesn't feel right. Something feels wrong." Kiko muttered as she rolled a rock under her foot with a subdued body language.

"It is a strange creature indeed that feels trepidation in the face of such a victory." Michael replied to her, as if such a vague use of words would've made things in any way better. A bird dropped from the sky as he continued.

"Where is the Revanspear?" He asked as he monitored and watched the horizon of the endless dead.

"Oh, Kara and Muhren are grabbing it now. They'll be teleporting here any..." Kiko paused as she felt the tickling of leaves fall upon her from the branches above her, she then noticed a decaying flower upon the ground, quickly withering away. "...any... second now."

She looked towards the Archangel.

"It is a mighty feat that you three have accomplished. An achievement that required great courage, skill and strength. A testimonial to the power of friendship and of love. How Kiko the wise-"

"Do you always tell people what they want to hear?" Kiko asked with an annoyed tone as she fiddled with the chess piece in her pocket. "I'm curious, Michael. *Why?* What is achieved with honeyed words? You played to our strengths are relied on our weaknesses." Kiko was finally thinking tactfully. The real game of chess had been exposed. "It's obvious that you also spoke to Muhren and Kara. To be honest, I'm an idiot for not noticing it sooner. You played upon my inherent desire to appear smart and played upon my love of fanciful stories and grandiose concept and ideas. You literally

distracted me with a game and beautiful sceneries and creatures you knew I loved. Was any of it true? The prophecy and the Fairy king? *Why did my brother actually die?* I wonder what did you say to the others? No doubt you played on Muhren's humanity and relied on Kara's strength and determination to prove herself. What did you do? Did you summon Elmin back from the grave? Did you toy with his heart? What games did you play with Kara? I don't understand. *Why?* Why toy with us? We would have helped you regardless."

"Well done. *Because you're a Human.* Or half Elf half, Human in certain cases. You cannot be trusted with things of such importance. You were the latest in a long line of potential *'yous.'* But you are the only one who succeeded. And yes, the prophecy was real. Lilith hates you and knows you want to stop her war. She wants to keep you as far away from that moment as Demonically possible. But here you are, succeeding. You're about to beat her before the war even starts. Dividing and conquering you three as individuals was essential to achieve this victory. But you're not angry at me, or the methods I use. You're angry at yourself. You're angry because despite everything you've achieved, you can't force into fruition the one thing you actually want. *You cannot undo the death of Vincent.* You can't reunite your family and quick-fix the pain that lies ahead and you're angry because you know I can't undo it either." Kiko quickly looked away as he continued. "But let's not ruin this joyous moment with name-calling and finger-pointing."

There was a sudden crack as Kara reappeared carrying the Revanspear and with Muhren directly behind her off in the distance. Namonar had also decided to come, he was happily chewing an old bone he had found. Kara and Muhren seemed to be jokingly arguing about something.

"All I'm saying, Muhren, is that you won't be able to out-drink me."

"Ha, I so could! It would be easy." He replied in a laugh.

"Fine, we get this spear dropped off and I'll drink you under the table." Kara replied laughing, but wondering why all the trees were dead. What a creepy graveyard. The weather was shit too.

"We'll see about that!" Muhren replied once more as he looked up at the thick black clouds. "But we're not drinking here."

This place was morbid and depressing.

"Agreed. It's a date." Kara said with a slight blush as she tested the waters.

"It's a date." Muhren confirmed with a crimsoned blush of his own.

Wait! Do they like each other?

Upon entering the vicinity of the Archangel the Revanspear locked into place and began shaking. This vibration broke out into a horrific terrified screech. Like a cat having its tail stepped on. Like a clunky old car with engine failure. Like the noise of nails scratching on a chalkboard or two sheets of metal scraping against each other. This proved it. Kiko's hunch was right. The Revanspear was clever and knew a lie when it saw one. *Something was wrong!*

"You really love her, don't you?" The Archangel asked as he looked over at Kara who was off in the distance trying to pull at the spear.

"Yeah, I do." Kiko said after a confused long pause as she looked back at the angel with a troubled look.

"You saw her standing on the brink and thought it a kindness to allow her pain to endure." A horrible smile broke across Michael's face. "You fancied yourself her rescuer from perdition, but only served to keep her under boot like a trophy dog." Kiko turned in a cold fit of confusion to face the Angel. "To fancy yourself 'good' for allowing her suffering to continue." The angel began to smile. *"You are nothing but blight!"*

With a flick of his wrist this great angel struck Kiko across her face sending her to her knees, Muhren ran towards his sister as Kara froze on the spot.

"The great child of time. The blind herald of her own destruction." Michael laughed. "I thought you were supposed to be formidable, child..."

Kiko leapt defiantly through the air as the spear was ripped from Kara's grasp. She tried to stop the Revanspear as Michael summoned it and it pulled it in towards him. But she wasn't quick enough. As Michael grabbed the Revanspear a shock-wave emitted from him, knocking everyone back. This dark pulse made them all feel as if they could all either pass out or throw up at a moment's notice. His illusionary appearance faded into that of a woman-like creature. What Kiko looked at now was not the great archaic Archangel of old. No, this was something so much worse.

This was Lilith. The Queen of all the Demons.

Some said that the Devil's greatest trick was pretending he had never existed. Lilith's greatest trick had been pretending she was one of the Angels. The Archangel. But there may be some of you out there asking *'who exactly was Lilith?'* Lilith was the firstborn child of the Prince of Darkness. The Four-Winged Angel. The Great Deceiver. According to legend, this angelic trickster had been the reason behind the fire giant, Surtr, and the ice queen, Shiva, going to war. These mighty gods had unwittingly raged war upon the false foundations of poisoned counsel. When these two titans of old had found themselves evenly matched, this twister of lies, the king of all unholy, took from them the power that he sought. From Surtr he ripped the secrets of the Fire Crown. From Shiva? He reached deep within her chest and scooped out her icy, cold heart. These arcane elements were always meant to be in balance. In the falling of one, the other would rise, until the time came for the other to rise once more. A self-sustaining balance. Now that this four-winged angel had the power of both, the balance of life was knocked askew. This prince had even found a new way to utilise this arcane magic like never before. The Old Gods had created life bringers. They called these children the Divines, you've met one already. This prince sneaked onto their home dimension, Eden, the night before the Divines were to be ushered across the cosmos. He used the fires of Surtr to fan the flames of rage in their pure and innocent hearts. He then used the secrets of the ice to freeze other good emotions. The grand plan of the gods was the desire to bring life to the virginal universe. Unfortunately, this plan was doomed before it had even begun. Before anyone had realised the corruption that had been bestowed upon these Divines, it was too late. They'd already set off on their voyages to birth the planets we would all call home. Within them, the four-winged Angel had planted the seeds of malice and hatred across all of existence. This evil would seep into the soil of every planet, tarnishing all life for all time to come. *His great victory.* By the time Thor and Hercules had learned of their servant's betrayal, it was too late.

This prince went by many names. Some called him the Old Evil, some referred to him as the Blackmouth, others knew him as the Fallen One. Some people called him Satan, Lucifer, the Prince of Darkness, the Great

Betrayer, the Trickster, the Hound-Master, the King of Serpents, the Devil and the King of Hell. This last title wasn't exactly true though. If Satan was the king of all evil, then why would he rule a domain that existed purely to punish all the wrongdoers and all the wicked? Think about it. It doesn't make sense. What the devil had created was an entirely different realm, although the principle ideal remained the same. The Halls of the Howling Hordes. This realm existed entirely out of the jurisdiction of the gods. And here was where the four-winged betrayer had created a new form of life, the Demons. A life that served as a twisted reflection of the lifeforms to come and as an insult to the Old Gods.

Not long after creating the Demons, Satan proceeded to kill himself. This suicide wasn't an act birthed out of fear or self-doubt, but one of prepared sacrilege to cause further insult to the Old Gods after everything he had done to them. By taking his own life he had robbed these gods of any primordial justice that they may have claimed in ending his life by their own hands. But now there was nothing they could do about his elaborate treason. Instead, this heinous betrayal would remain unpunished for all eternity. The ornate scales of divine retribution would remain unbalanced; forever tipped askew and never truly avenged. His evil would endure. This was the final thorn in the Old Gods' side. *His final insult.* Not only had he made an utter fool of them and betrayed them so, they now couldn't do anything about it. And acts of rapturous retribution were a big deal to the gods. This affront to the natural order of things also fuelled the Devil's reputation. By Lucifer not allowing himself to be punished by the gods, he had become a phenomenon that had transcended the physical plane of existence. As a living creature, he was little more than flesh and blood. He could be stopped. He could be killed and destroyed. He could have been marched down the streets in front of jeering crowds and made an example out of for all of the universe to see. To live on as a warning of what happens when you anger the gods. But now no god, man, woman or child could touch him. He would live on forever as an ideal. *He would live on forever in the darkest hearts of man as a symbol.* An unpunished deed, that you could do whatever you want and get away with it. As a feared thought, the man who outsmarted the gods. A fabled myth, the Angel who had proved that the Old Gods were fallible and flawed.

The first of his Demons was Lilith. Lilith was the mother of all demons. A statement that especially rang true if you were unlucky enough to perceive her appearance. Her legs were animal-like with cloven hooves, similar to that of Centaur. Her skin was a blackish purple with the texture of a melted candle that dripped down her back. From this back, the jagged spine of a lizard-man poked through holes in her rotten, zombie-like flesh. Her hair was a riddle of dead snakes, like the Gorgon. Unlike the Gorgons, she also had four goat-like horns, similar to those of the great demon lord, Baphomet. Two small wing-like flaps covered her mouth that looked reminiscent of the wings of a tiny succubus. This mouth was redolent of a shark's mouth, with rows of endless teeth that lined the inside of her mouth. In here lay the teeth of a werewolf, the fangs of a vampire and a whole host of other horror monster's gnashers. Her fingers were long like those of the Lamashtu. On the tip of each lingering finger was a long, sharp and pointy nail like those of a Ghoul. *So Lilith was definitely a blighted eyesore to behold.* She was also holding the Revanspear and the Eye of Obsidius. Both relics bestowed upon her by our unsuspecting trio.

Whatever was about to happen next, definitely wouldn't be good.

The first to act had been Muhren who swung his sword at Lilith. There was a loud crack as he shot off into the sky at a tremendous speed! Namonar faded away into dust and the girls were alone with the Demon Queen that had fooled them both so easily with angelic words. *Muhren's broken body fell and collapsed through a shed roof on a farm approximately three miles away.* He felt the taste of blood fill his mouth as his ribs stuck out from his chest and his arm was splintered. The room began to fade away as he drowned upon his own blood. *I guess Muhren and Kara would never get to have that drink after all...*

Lilith hissed as she stabbed the Earth with the underside of the Eye of Obsidius. Its black eye trembled as a ripple of green light emitted outwards from it. Unbeknownst to the girls, this rippled emerald ring of evil light lashed out over the entire planet from this point of origin. They did however notice that the residents of this cemetery's graves began to stir. A myriad of rotten putrid hands ripped through the soil and clawed at the air. Bony mushed faces emerged groaning from the shadows as they breathlessly choked down mud and worms.

Every subsidiary of the Arcane Intelligence Agency had a single red bell. On the last Sunday of every month, Cataeno Albrecht (*who was one of the Agency's many janitors*) would clean these bells. Truth be told, he didn't actually know why he had to. This was because he wasn't quite sure what these bells were for. Truth be told, no one knew. These bells were thick and they were the colour of a faded red. They were all wired directly into the wall, even if no one knew exactly where any of these wires led to. But today was the day that everyone was going to find out what these ancient bells were here. The uproar and confusion that all five of these mysterious bells ringing out at once had caused was hilarious to behold. *Well, this would be the case if you found the idea of the end of the world and all life to be in any way funny.* Everything and everyone that had ever died was currently being resurrected by the Eye of Obsidius all over the surface of the Earth. All of these freshly risen horrors were under the control of Lilith. And yes, that is not good news. But unfortunately, it was only the tip of the iceberg.

It was common knowledge that bad things came in sets of three. This was also true of the end of the world. Strike number one, Lilith had returned and used the disguise of an Angel to get what she wanted. This being the death of all things. She had lied, cheated and outmanoeuvred her enemy. She fancied herself as the greatest secret weapon of all time. (*The number one most deadly secret weapon of all time was actually the Toblerone. This due to the fact it was impossible to eat the Toblerone without hurting yourself. No one was quite sure what cruel maliciousness went into creating such an evil Swiss chocolate bar. But whatever it was that drove these ill-natured chocolate-makers to inflict pain upon the mouths of so many unexpected innocent consumers with their pointy triangle shaped pieces, was a stroke of pure sadistic destructive genius. Perhaps they were driven mad by the insistent chirping of the cuckoo-clock on the wall. Almost everyone who had ever eaten one of these chocolates had done so wrongly on their first try. These aggressive triangles of chocolate ripping a hole in the top off the mouths of anyone brave enough to eat more than one mountain shaped piece at a time. They say that the appearance of the chocolate bar was based on the Alps; but since when did the Alps look like a giant brown saw?*)

Strike number two was that the Eye of Obsidius was currently returning all of the planet's dead back to life, ripping them from their graves. It was unclear how large this number of zombies was, but it was known that the number of the dead greatly outweighed the number of the living. But what was strike number three? *What was the Revanspear currently doing?*

The Arcane Intelligence Agency had also been home to a great number of maps. These were no ordinary maps, each one had been approximately five foot in height and made from glass. Whenever the Angels felt great evil, red dots would shine on the maps to indicate the source of the issue.

All five hundred of these maps were glowing under an all-consuming red, as if they had been on fire, due to the huge influx of dangers that had been detected. Under Lilith's command, the Revanspear sent a ball of purple light straight up into the sky. The Revanspear had sensed the greatest illusionary spell ever cast, and it had latched onto it like the teeth of a hunting dog dragging its prey down to Earth. As previously stated, the spear could not differentiate between spells that hid things for good or for bad reasons. As such it was currently eating away at the ancient barrier that hid the realm of the Angels from the world of man. *Eden.* It was cracking heaven like an egg, the last ingredient of the 'Apocalypse Omelet.' It was dragging the Angels out from hiding. Quite literally.

Despite the undead rising all around her and Lilith stood nearby, Kiko could not help but find herself raise a watchful eye to the skies as an endless barrage of infinite, thunderous explosions lit up all across it from behind a screen of ashen clouds. Little did Kiko know that this horrific light show encased the entire planet. The clouds of Earth were suddenly torn to pieces as hundreds of thousands of meteor-like objects lit up the once blue sky and fell through the air, down towards the planet below. The problem was that this meteor shower was engulfing the entire planet and was about to crash down all across it. Oh, and these objects were not meteors or asteroids.

"What's happening?" Kara asked as she looked ever upwards.

The Angels had been ripped out of Heaven and they were now falling to Earth; and they were about to rain down like hellfire on the poor, unsuspecting people below.

A cornerstone for the foundation of the entire cosmos had been the barrier that allowed the ancient Angels of old to govern and watch down upon all life across every planet in the universe. As it turns out, the effect of having the Revanspear destroy one barrier had caused them all to fail all across the universe. Across every planet. Like one great big game of Jenga, every planet in the entire universe was currently being bombarded by falling Angel bodies. These falling Arcane entities crashed and collided with the worlds below. On Earth they peppered into the sides of buildings, they collided with travelling cars, they smashed aeroplanes out of the sky and laid waste to battered cities and rural districts alike under their plummeting descent. Several fell around the shocked Kiko and Kara. One completely obliterated a gravestone near them as he fell. *It was like an endless carpet bombing for the entire planet.* People tried to run away from the onslaught of falling winged creatures. They ducked, dipped and dived out of the way as best as they could. But not everyone was lucky enough to avoid the terrible assault from on high. Hundreds of millions of people had been caught off guard and were now dead, in a literal instant. This was to say nothing of the vast number that was about to die in the next five seconds alone. Think of every plane or car crash you have ever seen or heard of in your entire life, and now imagine they were all happening at once. In one single awful moment of unparalleled destruction. Combine that level of death with the hundred or so tsunamis that had been caused by the vast number of Angels falling into the oceans of the world causing the tides to rise. Now imagine all of that death being spread across the entire planet and occurring over ten seconds. *Can you even begin to imagine that level of destruction?* Whole cities, which seconds before had been fine, were now on fire. As if washed over by an atom bomb. Entire buildings had collapsed in on themselves. Hundreds of thousands of Angels crashed into the Earth like a hundred thousand shooting stars. Whole stretches of land had been instantaneously flattened and transformed into fields of countless craters. It mattered not what they had been before this moment of unbridled all-consuming death. Great forests and bustling cities fell alike. Some of these vast crater sights had once been home to vast amounts of populations from different cities and countries. They had all died in the time it would take for you to sneeze.

This was only half of it all though. Don't forget that the Eye of Obsidius had also set about resurrecting everything that had ever died. Rotting dead arms and faces erupted through fresh soils across the entire planet. *Every graveyard across every continent was now alive once more.* And they were all under the control of Lilith. But the undead was not alone, the Demons had also arrived in a great number. This was the end of the world after all, there was no way that these Demons were about to sit on the sidelines and just watch. An endless tidal wave of decaying flesh and gnashing teeth ripped through scores of defenceless people as a baragement of Angels fell from the skies around them. These fallen Angels, the ones who had survived the fall, quickly found themselves drawing swords against their ancient Demonic enemies.

A series of flashes fluttered around Kiko and Kara as seemingly all of the wizards from the Arcane Intelligence Agency rushed to the source of the conflict, ready to fight. Numerous fireballs, thunderbolts and lights flashed through the air colliding against undead and Demon-kind alike, as these AIA agents joined forces alongside the confused fallen Angels.

The Arcanium Wars had begun, and this had just been the beginning.

And it wasn't just on Earth. On almost every planet the scene was the same. An endless score of Demon on Angel and alien violence. The incessant clashing from the steel of swords, axes and spears colliding across the entirety of existence. A quadrillion lives had just been snuffed out across the entire universe in the last three seconds. Rather awkwardly, it had looked like it was all Kiko's fault. *Oops!* Well, Kara and Muhren also shared some of the blame, but Muhren might be dead so I doubt he can feel shame right now. They had been the unwitting harbingers of ubiquitous destruction. The great Angel had been nothing more than a clever lie to trick our unaware heroes into kick-starting the entire Apocalypse and end of days. The great Demon Queen was back. Bigger and stronger than ever before. *All hail Lilith.*

Kiko and Kara looked upon this cacophony of Demonic hybridisation in woman form. This twisted Queen of perfected evil and harrowing malcontent. *Lilith the victorious.*

Little did Kiko or Kara know that this wasn't the entirety of Lilith's evil agenda. She still had a purpose for her kidnapped non consenting spirits. Deep within the scorched lands of the Howling Halls (*the lands of the Demons*) these stolen spirits screamed and cried, trapped within a great series of giant green glass orbs. These ghosts were still endowed with their mortal souls; these souls were exactly what Lilith's army had wanted and needed for their weapon that was to splinter time and bend it to their evil wills. A myriad of pipes was attached to these ghost-filled orbs that fed directly into a series of tall, intimidating machines. These towers were as tall as houses. They were made from a terrible ebony metal that was as cold and as dark as night. These towers were Paradox Converters, because apparently such a thing had been possible. It was supposed to be that time would break when a person changed or altered it. But Demons were smart. This machine would stop that from happening. These machines would allow the Demon Queen to re-write history in any way she saw fit. Because you see, none of this was supposed to have ever happened. The Arcane Intelligence Agency and the Temporal Bureau of Investigations would have never have allowed an Apocalypse of endless genocide to begin. They would have seen it coming. None of this was supposed to have happened. But thanks to these machines fuelled by the souls of ghosts, it had was happening right now. This unprecedented level of death made Lilith fancy herself as the embodiment of the Goddess of Death and the God of War all rolled into one.

The pain of an unimaginably devastating horror gripped deep within Kiko's heart as she looked across this horizon of destruction and death. *What had they done?* The great hero, Vincent Attetson, wouldn't have let this happen... The screams of war pierced her eardrums. This was worse than any nightmare she could have ever imagined. She watched helplessly at all of the death that encircled her. An endless sea of warring Demons, Angels, zombies and friends from the Arcane Intelligence Agency. Kiko and Kara shared one final determined look. They knew there was nothing they could do, but if they were going to die then they would die fighting. They sprinted at Lilith as fast as they could. They watched as Lilith's hideous face jolted into a cracked smile of crooked teeth as both girls disappeared from existence in a green light brought forth by the Paradox Converters. The girls were scattered into time.

Welcome to the beginning of the end. The end of the world and the universe. The end of time and all life.

To be continued...

Epilogue: Kara

Kara slammed down hard against a dense rocky ground. The force of which knocked the air clean out of her as her body broke against the unforgiving surface. The foul smell of sulphur invaded her nose as an icy cold blanket of air wrapped around her. As the defiant Half-Elf rose she quickly realised that the world of falling Angels and restless dead was nowhere to be seen! In their place was the surroundings of an endless darkness. A lightless void of nothing. A harrowing inky vacuum of desolate nothingness.

"Crap! Am I dead?" She asked herself as she peered through the endless sea of black.

Don't worry. *No.* No, she wasn't dead! Not yet anyway… It's just that a person's eyes can take a while to adjust to any sudden differences in the level of available light. As such the wall of rock of this chamber she found herself in slowly became visible around her. A crunchy floor of twigs became visible under her feet. She felt a great and troubling confusion as the world of a grim canvas of red stone came into focus, the details of which were seemingly being painted in around her. The last thing Kara had remembered was seeing Lilith and charging at her. For the record, Kara felt no satisfaction in her being right about not trusting the supposed arcane Angel. Being right was worthless when it had meant the absolute destruction of so many innocent lives. Like that which she had just witnessed. As Kara looked out across the chamber she couldn't help but wonder where she might be? *Wherever Lilith had sent her could not have been good.*

As Kara came to terms with her current location in the universe, she noticed something. Those twigs under her feet. They weren't sticks. They were bones. Hundreds of thousands, if not potentially millions, of brittle white remnants of splintered bone. A bedding of chalky dead heads, shoulders, knees and toes that stretched as far as the eye could see. The sudden realisation that she was standing on top of a thick skeletal flooring hadn't actually shocked Kara in the slightest. In fact, rather worryingly, the realisation had stirred no emotion in her at all. She didn't flinch and barely cared about how horrible her current surroundings were. The only thing that had concerned her was not knowing what creature had done this killing of the things that lay beneath her. Kara slowly crept through the piles of the discarded bones towards an entranceway.

Okay... Now she cared! *Now she cared a great deal.*

To her utter dismay, she saw what lay beyond her current rocky chamber. A vast canyon of ebony rock that seemed to stretch on for miles. This cesspit of gravelled inequity was filled to the brim with the frantic toings and froings of an endless stream of Demonic soldiers. An endless diabolic parade of marching devilry and eternal damnation that broke loose across the pit in all directions. An omnipresent display of unending horns, tails, claws and fangs. Shit. Even though Kara didn't want to believe it (*and even though she couldn't believe her eyes!*) she knew exactly where she was. *She was in the Howling Halls.* The home of the Demons.

Amongst the sea of Demons, she could make out a large glass structure. From within this structure, the Half-Elf could see what appeared to be thousands of ghosts trapped inside. Screaming silently for an escape. Even though she didn't know what it was, a Paradox Converter was here.

"How long I have waited for you." A familiar voice called out from the darkness. It couldn't be! Kara knew that voice. She had heard it for as long as she could remember. *In every dark moment of her life.* In every moment of her endless hell. The voice that was always in her head.

The voice that spoke to her now, once more.

As she turned, white as a sheet and wide-eyed with a childlike innocence of a panicked and all-consuming terror that entirely stripped her of her faculties, she had seen the one thing she feared the most in all of the cosmos.

"No, no, no, no, no, no, no, no, no, no, no, no, no, no! Not him! Anyone but him!"

The voice of her endless torment given physical form arose from the shadows. Her deepest fears and darkest doubts and thoughts seemingly ripped from her mind and given substance. The endless whispering voice of malcontent that had always torn her down and told her she was never good enough, was made sentient and manifested into reality for all to see before her very eyes. He slowly walked towards her, fully aware she was too afraid to move. Her inner darkness in human form. A tall, muscular humanoid with cracked chalky white skin, that hated Kara with an utmost contempt. A myriad of red, bleeding runes were carved directly into his arms and across his chest. His hands, forearms, back and legs were stained with the residue of a thick dark ink of dried blood. So was his neck. This tribalesque pagan of nightmares made incarnate also wore a series of bone necklaces and bracelets. Kara wanted to cry but she was too scared to even do that. *All of her strength and all of her iron-clad will had abandoned her to her fate.* His words were deep and heavy and dripped with utter evil. His head was that of a great white skull. But not that of a human, but of a giant deer. From within the eye sockets of this demonic-looking stag dripped a black goo. Of all the evils Kara had ever faced, she had never had to witness something that broke her so utterly and truly before.

His thick hand grabbed at her throat and slammed her against the wall.

"You shouldn't have run from me."

Kara yelped as a sudden burning sensation stabbed at her gut as this demonic deer-skulled horror ran a crude, rusty blade through her stomach. A downpour of crimson escaped her as she bled out like a stuck pig ready for slaughter. She clamoured and grasped desperately at her bleeding wound. Blood gushed through her fingers like a broken dam and flooded the bones beneath her feet.

Here she was. Dying alone, lost to her overpowering darkness. *Fatally wounded and bleeding in the homeworld of the Demons.* Surrounded by Lilith's endless army. Face to face with her worst nightmare. The voice that had wrecked her brain ever since she was a young child.

Will Kara survive this?
Tune in next time to find out...

Epilogue: Kiko

The hallowed screams of war instantly fell silent as a bright green light faded away from around Kiko and she found herself in a dauntingly quiet street. Where was Lilith? Where was Kara? The intense brutality of the end of time had come to a shockingly abrupt end. A thousand questioning knives of doubt and confusion stabbed at her mind. *Where was she?* Nothing felt right. A sharp wind carried the wasted remains of a discarded newspaper and an assortment of leaves as Kiko span on the spot in a long street of red-bricked buildings. A grey sky of sad-looking clouds hung above her. Wherever she was, it wasn't where she needed to be. An indignant blue light absorbed her as she returned to the fight. The fight she had been responsible for. *How had she been so stupid?* Kiko might have felt a great deal of responsibility for the end of the world, but that didn't mean that she had to accept that it was over. Lilith had tricked her, this much was true. It was also a bit embarrassing that Kiko had been hoodwinked so easily. But she chose not to focus too much on that. *The fight was far from over.* Kiko had been knocked down to the mat several times now and every time she had found the strength to get back up. *There was no way she was backing down now.* Lilith had made a serious mistake. There was a great big flaw in Lilith's plan. One painfully obvious thing the Demon Queen had overlooked. *She had underestimated Kiko.* And like the Nekrith controller before her, Lilith was about to learn what happens when you vex a traveller of the fourth dimension. Lies had been Lilith's weapon of choice. So Kiko would fight that sneaky Demonic bitch with the full power of time at her side. Time; that was the greatest weapon of all. Whoever controlled it controlled the final outcome of the entire universe. Kiko knew how to make Lilith pay for everything she had done. And she was going to make that ugly bitch pay for every life lost.

All Kiko needed was to return to the end of the world. The blue lights of her teleportation flashed green as her spell was ripped apart and her arms pushed themselves aside.

What?

What the hell was that?

That was the power of a nearby Paradox Converter stopping Kiko's escape. It was like Kiko had said to herself, whoever controlled time controlled the final outcome of the entire universe. *And this timeline was under Lilith's control.* Kiko tried teleporting away for a second time, but a second green light painfully stopped her once more. *What had Lilith done to her?* Wherever Kiko was, she was staying here until she found another way out! She cast another temporal coordinates spell. She was in London in the year 1983... *But why?* Why was she here? *Why here?* Lilith could have sent her anywhere. Why London? Kiko walked down to the end of the quiet street to see if she could try and find herself some answers to her current predicament. When she came to the end of this avenue she saw a sight that she had instantly recognised, but it brought her no peace. None at all.

She had seen the calm floating waters of the River Thames and the instantly recognisable Houses of Parliament standing proudly on the other side of the great British river. But as she looked at the brown regal building, something was wrong. A terrible sight both so utterly appalling and horrendously harrowing that it would have united every historian across time and space in a singular pained hysteria. An image so wrong that it would shatter the very fabric of the soul. Every history book would tremble at the idea of it. Something so utterly wrong that it would have instantly broken the heart of every soldier, humanitarian and time travelling-witch that might set eyes upon it. Across the side of Elizabeth Tower (*the clock tower famously misnamed Big Ben.*) was draped a long red flag. This crimson horror of instantly recognisable fame had a single white circle upon the centre of it. At the heart of the colourless void lay the marking of Britain's most notorious adversary. *A swastika!*

Here Kiko now stood. In the heart of London. Forty years after the end of the Second World War. The symbol of Britain's most prominent enemy hung proudly over its most famous landmark. *Something was wrong!* Terribly, terribly wrong. There was no way that a British government would hang

Nazi colours. Not now, not ever. Even suggesting such an idea would be met with fury, rage and utter contempt from the British. To even think it, was an act of heresy to the natural order of everything Britain claimed to stand for. So this could only mean one thing.

The reality of Kiko's situation sank in around her. Literally. As she stood here lost to the shock numbing her heart, the rest of her surroundings came into focus. Statues of Adolf Hitler and saluting Nazis were scattered down the street and posters of tyrannical propaganda donned the walls.

This was not possible! What was going on? Britain had never been invaded by the Nazis. So why were they here now? The Allied forces had won! They were always supposed to win! If Nazi propaganda was alive and well in the 1980s, then this could only mean that the Nazis had won the war. But that would also mean something was screwing with time and whatever it was needed to be stopped! *Whatever event that had changed history needed to be undone!*

A green light snapped around Kiko once more as she tried teleporting back in an attempt to discover what had changed the result of the old war. Whatever had altered time needed to be undone! The damage such a change would do to the established timeline was unimaginable. *The entire universe might be at risk!* The green light locked her in place and refused her passage. But Kiko was used to being told what to do and refused to accept the emerald light's refusal. She pushed and she strained against the power of the Paradox Converter with all of her strength. It felt like her arms would pop out of their sockets at any moment and that her ears might explode from the pressure. Her throat also burned from the rising tide of vomit from forgotten food that had chosen now to try and return unto the world. But even if her own body would fight against her, she couldn't give in! The fate of everything that ever was and ever should be hung in the balance. *She wouldn't give up.* Her name was Kiko Attetson and she was going to save everyone. *She was going to set everything right.* This alternate timeline, the Demon war with the Angels. *Everything.* She just needed time to think and time to act. And no stupid green light was going to stop her! Not now, not ever. Not in a million years. Not in a trillion. She would find what was altering time and she would put a stop to it, for the sake of the universe. Then she would rip Lilith's head clean off of her shoulders, for the sake of her friends and family. God, she hoped they were all still okay!

The unnatural green magics of the Paradox Converter exploded against Kiko's sustained attempt at teleportation, sending her flying some sixty foot straight up in the air. *'Woosh!'* She felt a great fear as she found herself falling. *'Splosh!'* She fell straight into the Thames, near a place where two Nazi soldiers were holding a woman at gunpoint. The sudden splash of disturbed waters had alarmed them as they turned to face a newly saturated Kiko for a moment before turning their attention back at towards woman. Kiko's once wild hair was now tamed, in a gross way, and draped over her wet face as she pulled herself from the icy depths with a cough and a groan. As if today wasn't already bad enough, now her clothes were ruined. *'Great!'*

But she didn't have long to focus on feeling sorry for newly dampened herself. As she looked towards the imposing ebonised Nazi soldiers (*who wore scary full-faced gas masks and intimidating trench coats adorned with swastikas and metal eagles.*) she saw them pointing their nasty little guns at a frightened woman as she tightly clutched a child that was cowering in front of her.

The fate of the universe and the end of the world would have to wait a minute. There was no way Kiko was about to ignore a frightened family facing a firing squad all alone with no one to defend them.

Kiko Attetson will return...

A Note from the Author

A thank you to all of you. For those who picked up this book and read it, but also a thank you to my friends. My family. I would not be where I am today without you. I am who I am because of you. Thank you. For those of you who continue to read, I will reveal a sneak peek behind the curtain of the creation of this book. A breakdown of how Kiko came into existence and the world that was formed around her.

But before continuing, I wanted to thank you for reading. Genuinely and sincerely from the bottom of my heart. Yes, you. Dear reader. I hope you enjoyed reading what I've written and shared with the world. (If you've had a genuinely awful time, then... *I'm sorry...?* I guess... but I owe you extra thanks for continuing to read and persevering to the end. You have my respect, if nothing else.) I hope you like Kiko and Kara. I hope you're fond of Muhren and Namonar. I hope you enjoyed the beginning of the Apocalypse. But I'm speaking to you now, breaking that fourth wall, to say hello. To ask how you are and hope that you're doing well. Life can be hard and so can the things in it. I would like to take this opportunity to share my thanks to my friends for helping me find the courage to publish a book. Writing this first instalment was a fairly intense couple of months. So thank you for your words of support. But back to you, dear reader, aren't words amazing? Words of support helped me create a world and the people in it. Words allowed you to see through this world and its events that unfolded. So, if anyone needs to hear the power of words, if someone out there is struggling and needs to hear words of encouragement.

"Hello there. I'm sorry life hasn't quite turned out the way you wanted. I'm sorry life has been hard. But it can get better. You are stronger than you know and I have faith in you. Rise like a phoenix and spread your wings. Be the change you want to see in the world. Everyone deserves to feel love and happiness and you are no exception."

There is no shame in asking for help if you need it. Kara did from Kiko. Oh, I know that she's a fictional character and so it doesn't count. But that doesn't change the fact that we are stronger united. People who love you don't want you to suffer alone. The fear of them turning on you is just the voices of doubt in your head. So don't give in. Don't give up. If that voice telling you that you can't succeed is so right, then what about this voice right here, right now? Asking for help is scary. Asking for help is hard. Admitting that you are running short isn't a weakness. Asking for help is sometimes the hardest thing to do in the entire universe. Yet, I'm going to do it anyway.

There is a great secret power buried deep within the foundations of the human race. A great weapon that can topple tyrannical empires into dust, a great strength that can forge lowly men into gods. A great endless force that can unite us all. A great unifying source of power that I have no qualms in potentially harnessing because I think I need your help. I need to harness the power of you. Or rather, the power of words and community.

I merely ask that if you have enjoyed your time this far reading The Curious Magics Saga (*Again apologies to those of you who did not!*) that you share your opinions of it. Share this book with your friends. Share it with your family. Discuss it with your neighbours over your fence. Tell the world but only if you enjoyed it and if you want to. Share it with your cats and your dogs. You can read it to your goldfish if you want. (Although being an arachnophobic myself, I'd appreciate it if you didn't let your spiders read my book! I mean how would a spider even read a book? Would they dangle above it, hung high on a thread, and gently turn the pages in their long, spindly legs? Or would they curl up in a ball on their backs and jovially peruse through the words, holstering the book up upon six of their legs, whilst the seventh turned the pages and their eighth sipped from a milkshake of minced flies? Or would they simply scamper across the pages at a great crazed speed, reading one line at a time as they ran? Who knows?)

These magical lands and mystical earths that we all know so well aren't really a thing without you. Middle Earth was just the idea of a single, admittedly great, man. What Middle Earth has become now is because of all of you. A million shared thoughts and ideas that brought it to life far beyond Tolkien's wildest dreams. The curious magics of Hogwarts is just a handful of words on a page. *(It was also filmed at Alnwick Castle during the movies, but shut up. I'm trying to make a point over here.)* The tall halls, numerous classes and long corridors were brought to life by you. *(Also by J.K. Rowling, but all of you gave it a soul!)*

The cost of publishing books, whilst not inherently high, is daunting enough to delay any potential sequel; whilst I frantically squirrel together funds. But I have no interest in gifting or conning you out of your coin. I won't utilise a pyramid-schemed Kick-Starter or flaunt myself on Only-Fans. (I'll spare the world from the horrors of that.) All I want to see is if my work has resounded with you. If you've enjoyed it. This will inspire me to continue faster. If you're creative and you want to use the adventures of Kiko to express yourself, then show me! Let me be a part of your story. I would love to see it. Any daring cosplayer who wants to dress up, please do so. Go crazy with it. See if you can dress up as a cybernetic cave troll. Any budding artists who are skilled with a pen or with a brush, and who want to paint, sketch or doodle anything from these pages, I would consider it an absolute honour. My heart would probably explode. I'd also be honoured if you can't draw and show me what you've made anyway. I might even respect you for it. Post your work on Instagram and let me see it. Use #CuriousMagic, #CuriousMagics or #TheCuriousMagicsSaga and let me share in your work. You could even lookup the preliminary artwork and cover designs I myself have posted there. You can even follow me *(Not in a creepy I'm outside your house kind of way... please...!)* over on Instagram at robfromthenorth_. *(The underscore at the end is important. Another robfromthenorth beat me to it.)* I will also announce the release of the second book on there and on this page's Facebook page. Search for '*Curious Magics Saga*' on Facebook if you want to see it for yourself.

And now as promised, a sneak peek behind the curtain. Consider this the optional DVD extras. Starting with the most obvious juicy morsel. I originally started writing this story a decade ago. However, Vincent was my original protagonist. I created a great many number of potential story arcs. The god in the heart of the spaceship Edinheim was one such story. But my eyes were bigger than my belly. Writing a single book is usually hard, and I'd put myself in the position of having to write like six! So I got scared and I ran away from the daunting task. But Vincent as his adventures never left my side. Vincent's original name was Vincent Arkanstone. He would use magic to travel time and space. He had a big hat and a long flowing scarf. I never quite sunk my teeth into Vincent. He never felt quite right. He always felt like a cheap rip-off of Doctor Who. (This was probably due to the scarf!) But he always felt too close to the idea of 'Doctor Who plus Harry Potter magic.' I was never quite sold. Not until the day Kiko was born. Her existence was literally by happenstance almost seven years later. The hands of fate and destiny intertwining around me.

She was literally created by a dice roll.

After many years of persuasion from a close friend, I started playing Dungeons and Dragons. My character was Muhren Attetson. A life domain cleric, if such a class means anything to you. But I apparently needed a backstory for him, and I didn't have one. I decided to roll a dice, using some D&D chart to decide for me. The dice decided Muhren had two siblings, one of which had to be female. I had no idea for a name, so I rolled the dice once more. Seeking randomised guidance from the powers of fate. The dice rolled whatever number which had resulted in the name Kiko. Boom. I had never even heard of such a name before in my life. However, this Kiko was a pious muscle bounded military leader of an army called the Iron Legion. She was the Legion Mother. My second character was the hot-headed Kara De'Carusso. She was a Half-Elf bard, but unlike your usual bard, she rarely played music. She was a performer in her spare time, her instrument of choice being a pair of axes and the occasional violin solo. She was also a noble-born Half-Elf of Viking descent. So she had a passion for hacking people up with axes. Her main 'personality trait' was that she wanted to fit in with the everyday crowd, but due to her elitist birth, didn't quite know how to. She sailed the seas in an ebony Viking longboat with her friends. This ship had a secret fire compartment hidden in the dragons head that would shoot fire as the party raided nearby settlements. The two coolest things that this game-Kara ever did was to shoot at a rival pirate ship with a cannon filled with tiny ball bearings. The entire rival crew turned into a red mist of sinew and torn flesh. The second was when she turned a high levelled Cyclops into a goldfish and threw it over the side of a cliff. It died on the rocks far below.

The third character was a chronomamcer wizard. A time traveller. So I was initially going to use Vincent. My book character from aeons ago would finally live. But a higher voice called to me. "Use Kiko." This version was a complete contrast to the military leader from before. This Kiko was weak and mild, so she had to use her intelligence to survive. She was squishy and would die too easily in a direct conflict. Her world was beset by Giants and a plucky group of adventurers would have to rise up to stop them. Kiko wasn't a soldier, she was a student travelling the land for her final exam. She was writing a thesis on the conflict between good and evil. How evil was so much stronger than the forces that fought for good. So how could good survive? By any logical evaluation, evil should always win. Being good wasn't a viable strategy if you wanted to live long enough to see tomorrow. Acts of love and compassion should be a weakness, something to leave you vulnerable and exposed. It takes courage and loyalty. Good required empathy and hard work. So why does good prevail? Evil by its very nature was both larger in number and had more extensive capabilities for acts of war. So what was maintaining the balance? Why was good still not losing the fight? Kiko would travel the world seeking answers to these questions. She questioned and interrogated bandits about their lifestyle choices and what had led them to this point. She wrote their answers down in a great series of journals. Why were they like this? Why did they choose to hurt people? Kiko had also once picked a verbal fight with a dragon about the morality of good and evil. She was loving and caring, but with a temper. She was also smart and could defuse fights with her words and make wrathful people see a reasonable alternative to violence. She would always utilise the logic of brains over the brawn of muscle. *(Because she knew if she hit you, she'd get hit back twice as hard.)*

At level one she already had the maximum level of intelligence that the game would allow me to have. She could speak seven different languages and was eager to travel. Eager to live. She was designed to defend the weak, to be bookish and smart and to never be cruel or cowardly. She believed that knowledge was power and that it was nice to be important, but it was more important to be nice. She would protect those less intelligent than herself from people who sought to take advantage of their naivety, and teach them a new better way when she could.

She ended up being everything I had wanted Vincent to be all those years ago. However this book only really came around thanks to two colleagues, that I view as friends. In the early part of 2021, one of these coworkers was discussing with me how he was writing a book of his own. This started a conversation about how I had once tried to do the same. I let him read a concept I had written all those years ago. With a few minor tweaks, this was the first chapter of this book. He shared it with another colleague who filled me with words of praise. It was the second colleague who had insisted that I "had to get this published." That I was good and that I had skill. So, you know who you are and I thank you for it. I would have probably never have written this without your words of kindness. Kiko and Kara live because of you. I'm only the man who put words on paper.

I discussed with the other writer (*a talented artist you should follow on Instagram, search for skinny_gud and tell him I sent you!*) the idea I had of making Kiko my protagonist. Not because the world needed a strong female protagonist to tick some box, but because I genuinely loved her character and wanted to write about her. - *And hopefully do her justice!* - To me, there was just something about her that clicked in a way that Vincent never had. Maybe it was because I was in love with the idea of how the universe had created her upon the whims of a dice. And I felt, deep in my heart, that a friendship between her and Kara would have been amazing. It is something I would have wanted to read myself. My angry Viking warrior and my kindly wizard. *(Kiko's disdain for the term witch actually comes from playing D&D, how she drunkenly argued with someone how any man who partakes in magic is always a kindly loving wizard. So why was every woman who practised magic a hunchbacked evil witch with a long nose?)* Although, given the fact Kiko could travel through time, I felt the need to modernise them both to suit the times. Doing so was surprisingly easy. I also discussed the original idea of making Vincent the antagonist. (He was literally dressed like an overbearing superhero and even had a cape at the time! I hated this idea too...) But the story of a woman trapped under the power of a man, realising that she had the power all along, felt clichéd. It felt like a story I'd heard or seen a thousand times before. I felt that this idea would trap me into some political stance that would betray Kiko. And my co-worker agreed.

In this story, Vincent wasn't the bad guy. To me, Vincent was just as much a victim as his sister was. *(He was supposed to be the starring role after all. But his sister crept up behind him and took the glory all for herself. What a bitch!)* However, the big bad monster that killed him definitely was a bad guy. This monster, the Changeling, had hurt them both equally. They were both victims of its evil. Vincent and Kiko are united by this common ground they both shared. A thing that transcends genders. *A monster in the night.* The Changeling had been draining Kiko of her magic since her birth. But it had also killed Vincent as a baby.

Marvin the octopus was inspired by true-life events. An octopus had escaped his tank in an aquarium and eaten the nearby fish and an octopus

was used to predict football results in Australia. And I find the idea of that amazing! However, I had discovered these stories about the intellect of octopuses after seeing a pack of sliced octopus meat in a local shop. Buying it out of a curious sense of wondering what it would taste like. I then read these stories about what such a creature was capable of. It had humanised the sliced squid in my fridge and now I had no intention of eating it.
I couldn't bring myself to do so. I hope that the hollow gesture of me dedicating a character in my book undoes some of the horrors you faced, my eight-limbed friend. I'm also sorry if you actually wanted to be eaten and if throwing you out in the trash two weeks later was an even bigger insult. *(I'm sorry, but I also won't be dedicating a character to every animal I've ever eaten. I wouldn't know where to start.)*

I must also apologise for leaving this book on a cliffhanger. I want you to know that I didn't choose to do so easily or without many hours of thought and reflection. I often toyed with the idea of stalling the release and publishing the book as one single story. But I had always intended to write this first book in such a way that it felt like an old cheesy sci-fi show. A, hopefully, easy read. An interlocking series of short stories linked by the protagonists and via you reading about them. Each couple of chapters being like a smaller, episodic arc of a television show's larger seasonal theme. And what TV show would be complete without a cliffhanger to make you want to return next year?

So I do hope that I get to see you all next time. If not, I'd like to thank you once more for reading this far. Any kind words you wish to share about the time we have spent together would mean a lot. Ever since I was a child I dreamed of writing for the world and here I am, doing exactly that.

But know this, if I can find the courage to follow my dreams, so can you.

I believe in you.

R. B. Fraser

Printed in Great Britain
by Amazon